A SISTER'S SHAME

Carol Rivers, whose family comes from the Isle of Dogs, East London, now lives in Dorset.

CAROL RIVERS
A SISTER'S SHAME

**SIMON &
SCHUSTER**

London · New York · Sydney · Toronto · New Delhi

A CBS COMPANY

First published in Great Britain by Simon & Schuster, 2012
An imprint of Simon & Schuster UK
A CBS company

1 3 5 7 9 10 8 6 4 2

Simon & Schuster UK Ltd
1st Floor
222 Gray's Inn Road
London WC1X 8HB

www.simonandschuster.co.uk

Simon & Schuster Australia, Sydney
Simon & Schuster India, New Delhi

A CIP catalogue record for this book is available from the British Library

Hardback ISBN: 978-0-85720-829-3
Paperback ISBN: 978-1-47113-878-2
Ebook ISBN: 978-0-85720-831-6

Typeset by Hewer Text UK Ltd, Edinburgh
Printed and bound in Great Britain by CPI Group (UK) Ltd, Croydon, CR0 4YY

This book is for you, Vic and Jess.

Acknowledgements

My thanks go to Anne and Norman for all your support, to Margaret and Jim, a long way away but always in my thoughts, and to Island History Trust and its wonderful work in preserving memories of a past and precious time – and from where the idea for this book first came. As always, many thanks go to my agent, Dorothy Lumley, to Emma, my editor, and to Maxine and the entire team at Simon & Schuster for such a creative and artistic production of the Rivers novels.

Chapter 1

Marie woke in a cold sweat. The dream was always the same. She was staring up at a stranger, who was standing in the middle of a room. There were beads of sweat on his heavily jowled face and his small eyes flicked suspiciously around. Beneath his large hooked nose was a thin, cruel mouth, which suddenly released an animal cry of fury. His concentration was focused on his victim: a small, cowering woman, her arms folded protectively across the swell of her belly. Her pleas for mercy were ignored as she stumbled away from his outstretched hands.

Marie cried out, but always her scream was silent. She was terrified, yet she knew the man could not see or hear her, that she was invisible. And then Marie saw what she dreaded most. The sobbing woman was grabbed and shaken with unbearable force.

How those powerful giant's hands shook and squeezed. How they whipped across the delicate skin of her face.

And when at last it was over and she lay still on the bare
floorboards, again Marie tried to scream, to bring someone to her rescue. But, as always in the dream, she was a
powerless witness, trapped in a haunting silence until she
woke and returned to reality.

'Marie? Marie, wake up.'

Marie heard her twin sister's voice and found the strength
to lift her head. In the dream she had been unable to move
and it was with relief that she wiped the sticky wetness from
her eyes. Her breathing was short and sharp as Vesta's face,
surrounded by a cloud of blonde curls, appeared in the faint
light of the moon shining through the window.

'Vesta, is that you?'

'Course it is.'

Marie tried to sit up. 'I was . . . dreaming . . .'

'I should say you were,' complained Vesta sleepily as
she snuggled back down beside Marie. 'You were shouting out loud.'

'In the dream I can't make any noise. I try to make
someone hear me, but no one can.'

Vesta yawned, propping herself on the thin pillow. 'So
it was the same dream again?'

'Yes.' Marie pushed back her damp hair matted to her
face. 'This young woman is having a baby. A man beats
her and she falls to the floor. If only I could scream and
bring help.'

'But it's a dream, Marie. Not real life.'

Marie sat shivering in her flimsy nightdress. It was
August and very warm, but she felt cold inside, and the

sweat on her skin was pure fear. 'Why do I keep dreaming the same dream?'

'I don't know. I never have dreams like that.'

'You're lucky.'

'Well, it's over now. Go back to sleep.'

Marie pushed away the bedclothes, trying not to make a disturbance. Their double bed always creaked when either one of them moved. 'I'll have to change me nightdress first. It's wet through.'

'Hurry up, then, or else we'll be awake all night.'

Getting out of bed, Marie put on the light. The furniture in their bedroom was solid good quality, though none of it belonged to her family. It was all Elsie Goldberg's, their landlady's. Beside the wardrobe was a solid oak chest of drawers, on which stood their treasured Victor phonograph with its great brass horn and soft, velvety turntable. The heavy records they loved to collect were all in a box beside it and were nearly worn out as the twins played them endlessly.

After exchanging her damp nightdress for a dry one, Marie was reluctant to climb back into bed. If she were to lie awake in the dark, the dream might haunt her. Had Vesta gone back to sleep?

She stared into the long bevelled mirror on the wardrobe door reflecting her slender five foot seven inches, hidden under the thin cotton nightdress. Though she and Vesta were not identical twins, their mother had always dressed them the same. They both had tumbling, shoulder-length wavy blonde hair and blue eyes.

Marie smiled at the memory of the tricks they used to play on people. Only their mother, Ada, and Elsie had been able to tell them apart. But last June they had turned eighteen, and now they had their own taste in fashion; if one pinned up her hair, the other would wear hers down. If one wore a dress, the other would choose a skirt.

The one thing they both still shared was a love of singing and dancing to the latest tunes. They'd made up a double act, and often talked about one day going on the stage. Their mother had made them promise to wait. She wanted to see them have a trade and they knew she wanted them to get married and settle down. She hoped their theatrical dream would fade.

As Marie sat on the edge of the bed, avoiding the most creaky bit, she gave a deep sigh. Her mother pulled them one way and their father the other. Hector had left his Kent home at fourteen to join a travelling theatre group. With his strong, clear voice he'd become a good singer and performer, taking many famous parts as the group toured the length and breadth of Britain. But after he'd met and married Ada, a Stepney girl, things had to change. With a wife and family to support, he only earned a few pennies busking on the streets of London.

'Girls!' he'd boom, using his powerful stage voice. 'You can achieve anything with talent like yours. You'll knock 'em dead!'

Ada would shake her head and purse her lips, and Hector would subside.

Marie frowned. She'd always known there was some-thing – some pact between her parents – which meant that it was Ada's word that counted, not Hector's. But what was this secret? They never talked about it. And she knew she could never ask.

'What are you doing now?' asked Vesta impatiently. She wasn't asleep!

'Sitting with a straight back and improving my posture, like Dad taught us.'

Vesta pulled the bedclothes over her head.

Marie gazed again in the mirror. Her damp and tangled waves fell around her ears to her shoulders. She shook them back, stiffening her spine and lifting her chin. What would it be like to sing and dance on a real stage? She would give anything to become a performer! All she ever thought of was singing and dancing. She practised all the time, making her own the steps she'd learned in dancing class at school. She looked at pictures of ballet dancers in books in the library, trying to copy their elegance and poise. In her head, she saw herself and Vesta performing the popular songs of the day to the delight of a vast audience. There was never a moment when she didn't think about a career on the stage. And yet she wasn't unhappy at the factory. It was dusty and dirty work sometimes, but she liked most of the girls and enjoyed their company. Even so, how wonderful it would be to achieve the dream the sisters shared. Marie imagined herself staring out at the audience, the spotlights dazzling as they stood breathless and excited. She did a little twirl, followed by a curtsy, imagining the applause.

'There's an elephant in the bedroom!' bellowed Vesta, throwing back the covers.

Marie came sharply back to the present. 'I'm as quiet as a mouse!'

'Mice don't do curtsies in the middle of the night.'

Marie giggled. 'They might.'

They both fell about laughing, until Marie switched off the light and climbed into bed.

'Thank goodness for that,' sighed Vesta as Marie lay beside her. 'Now I can get me beauty sleep.'

'Once, you would have got up and practised with me.'

'Not in the night, I wouldn't.'

'You poor old lazy bones,' smiled Marie, closing her eyes.

The minutes ticked by and Marie was still awake, thoughts whirling in her mind, one minute to the stage, the next to her nightmare. Who was the woman in it? Could it be herself? She'd read somewhere that people could have dreams that foretold the future. But she wasn't anywhere near being married or even falling in love! Did she want to get married if that was the fate that awaited her?

She turned and flopped on her back.

Vesta did the same. In the darkness, they began to laugh again.

'I'm wide awake now, thanks to the elephant,' giggled Vesta.

Marie gave a yawn but it was Vesta who now kept her awake.

'I can't wait to hear Teddy sing,' she breathed excitedly. 'I hope he can see me from the stage. It's going to be wonderful going to the Queen's tomorrow!'

Marie, too, was excited. As a birthday treat from their landlady, Elsie Goldberg, who was more like a grandmother to them as they'd known her since they were very young, she and Vesta and Ada were being taken to see handsome singer and fellow-lodger, Teddy Turner. And though Teddy had been living at Sphinx Street for only six months, it was no secret that Vesta had a crush on him. As for Marie, he was too full of charm and not her type at all. Which was good, as they weren't going to fight over him!

'What shall we wear?' asked Marie, knowing this was going through Vesta's mind too.

'I haven't got a thing.'

'Only half a whole wardrobe!'

'But nothing to catch Teddy's eye,' Vesta sulked.

'Perhaps we could go to Cox Street market after work?'

'I'm fed up with second-hand clothes.'

'Oh, pardon me for speaking,' chuckled Marie, 'but beggars can't be choosers.'

'We aren't beggars,' argued Vesta indignantly. 'We take after Dad and are performers!' Adding quickly, 'Well, I do anyway!'

Marie spluttered. 'Not if you don't practise.'

'I have to be in the mood for that.'

'You'll have to remember our routines if you want everyone to know who we are,' Marie said determinedly.

'We won't see our names up in lights at the Queen's unless we're really good.'

'Course we will,' protested Vesta. 'We're natural performers, silly.'

Marie admired Vesta for her confidence, though when it came to practising their act it was a different matter. Vesta believed it all came naturally, without much effort. And in a way, it was true for Vesta, who was a bit of a show-off, like Hector. But Marie made her sister practise in any spare half-hour they had, even when walking home from the shoe factory where they worked. In their long hours spent at Ellisdon's, they didn't have much time for themselves.

As Vesta's breathing deepened, showing she had fallen asleep, Marie wondered if they would ever have their spot in the limelight. But when sleep finally overcame her, her last thoughts were of the woman in her dream. Who was she and why was that horrible brute attacking her? It was only she who had this nightmare. Never her twin, Vesta.

Chapter 2

'I can't wait for tonight!' Vesta linked her arm through Marie's as they made their way home from the factory the next day. 'I hope we sit in the front row.'

'Elsie knows one of the usherettes, so we're bound to get good seats.' Marie hurried their steps a little. It was almost one o'clock and the market would be well underway.

'Elsie knows everyone from her years at the Cubby Hole,' Vesta agreed. 'Being the landlady of such a popular pub must have been very exciting.'

'Yes, but hard work and long hours.'

'I wish we'd known her husband,' Vesta sighed. 'She says they made a success of the pub together. Joe was the love of her life.'

'She must have been very upset when he died.'

'Elsie isn't the type to show it,' Vesta pointed out. 'Perhaps we turned up at the right time and made up for her loss. She says we are like family to her. Don't forget we were only seven when Mum and Dad first came to the island and she gave us two rooms over the pub.'

'Until she retired,' Marie added thoughtfully, 'and moved us all to Sphinx Street along with her.'

'Do you think Elsie is rich?' Vesta glanced quickly at Marie.

'Don't know. She told Mum that Sphinx Street was left to Joe by his parents. They were wealthy Jewish people, who owned a theatre up north.'

Vesta nodded. 'Elsie does wear all that gold jewellery.'

Marie smiled. 'Elsie is our fairy godmother. She took the Haskinses under her wing, lucky for us.'

But for Elsie's kindness ten years ago, Marie reflected, when she had taken pity on the poor and homeless Haskins family, newly arrived on the Isle of Dogs, they might have lived a very different existence from the comfortable one they now enjoyed.

Not that Elsie ever acknowledged her role as their benefactor. All she ever said was that if her late husband, Joe, wasn't around to enjoy the fruits of their labour as hard-working publicans, then she was glad her best friends could.

'I believe she's got a soft spot for Dad,' Vesta confided. 'Being in the entertainment business, like her Joe, who was once an actor.'

Marie smiled at this. 'Dad isn't really a performer now.'

'Well, he was once,' Vesta reminded her. 'He was very famous in his time and had a lovely voice.'

Marie didn't really believe he'd been *that* famous. But it was true that he had a lovely deep voice and knew lots of songs, and he could also recite many passages from literature. Sadly for her father, however, the modern audiences were going to the pictures to enjoy the talkies now. They didn't bother so much about the music halls or travelling groups that had been popular a generation ago.

'Talking of nice voices . . .' Vesta continued eagerly, 'sometimes I can't believe we're living in the same house as Teddy Turner. Just imagine, he's only one ceiling above us.'

Marie laughed. 'You'd think he was royalty, the way you go on.'

'He might not be royalty but he's gorgeous,' Vesta insisted. 'And he has a lovely voice.'

'You haven't heard him sing yet.'

'I have!'

'When?'

'The other morning,' Vesta replied. 'He was coming downstairs and sang a line from "If I Had A Talking Picture Of You". Then he gave me a smile that made me knees knock.'

'He doesn't make *my* knees knock.'

'He doesn't sing to you.'

'I'd laugh if he did.'

'You're so unromantic, Marie. Anyway, what would he be doing at the Queen's tonight, if he couldn't sing?'

'Any hopeful can sing on amateur night.'

'Not if they don't want to risk people throwing rotten veg at them.'

'That's true.'

'Do you know he's got a job at that new club, the Duke's, near the Queen's?'

'Doing what?' Marie asked.

'Singing, of course.' Vesta stopped abruptly. 'Why are you so against him?'

'I'm not against him. I don't know him. He's only lived at Elsie's since February. Where did he come from? What does he do, other than sing? Even Elsie don't know his background.'

'He's a man of mystery,' said Vesta, going misty-eyed.

Marie giggled. 'You've got it bad.'

As they walked on, Marie gazed up at the beautiful summer sky and felt excited. Work was over for the weekend. The noise and clatter of the factory was behind them. Tonight they were going out for a special treat.

A shaft of sunlight caught the top of an old ship's mainsail overhanging a cluttered back yard. Marie wondered where, in all the rest of England, you could see such a picturesque sight. It was not unusual to spot a ship's rigging poking above the roofs of the houses or hear dozens of hoots and toots from the river mixed in with the street vendors' calls. The ice-cream man and his three-wheeled cart, the muffin man and his tray of muffins, the shrimp and winkle seller and the stalls of hot chestnuts all vied for space and attention in the busy streets of the East End. But what Marie loved most was the history of this part of Docklands.

They had learned at school that the Isle of Dogs, a horseshoe of land jutting out into the great River Thames, harked back to the Roman occupation. Then, London was called Londinium. Even that long ago, the island traded goods, such as wood, wine, silks and spices and made the port one of the most important in the world. She always marvelled that even today those same trades continued. In fact, every conceivable type of ship, tug, barge and skip was moored in Docklands. How lucky she and Vesta were that their parents had come to live here.

Just then they heard the shouts and cries of the stall-holders at Cox Street. Marie felt another shiver of excitement. As much as the river and docks held a mystery, so did the busy markets of the East End. 'Come on, we're nearly there,' she encouraged her sister.

But Vesta pulled back. Raising her eyebrows, just like their father often did when reciting from Shakespeare, she shrugged. 'I think we should look somewhere else for our clothes.'

'Such as?'

'Oxford Street, perhaps.'

'The West End?' Marie was astonished.

'We need new costumes, don't forget.'

'They would cost a fortune there.'

Vesta tossed her head. 'When we're famous, we'll have plenty to spend wherever we like.'

Marie laughed. 'You've got high hopes.'

'Better than none,' said Vesta, wagging a finger.

Just then a loud cockney voice called out. Marie saw two familiar figures emerge from the dock gates. The men wore the uniform of the dockyards; shirtsleeves rolled up to the elbows, dirty corduroy trousers and rough working boots, their soles studded with Blakey's. But no dockyard dirt could disguise the spiky golden mop of Bobby Brown. Better known as 'Bing', he played the piano at the Cubby Hole pub. He was always whistling or singing Bing Crosby's popular songs. Vesta had no time for him but Marie liked his friendly manner.

'Just our luck, it's that mouthy Bing Brown and daft Charlie Wiggins,' Vesta hissed, pulling Marie's arm to go in the other direction. 'Let's cross the road before they see us.'

'Vesta, they *have* seen us.'

'Well, I'm not stopping to gas,' Vesta decided impatiently.

'Good afternoon, ladies,' called Bing in his rough accent. 'Charlie, ain't we the lucky ones, bumping into such a concoction of beauty?'

Marie went crimson and smiled.

'Me repertoire must be doing the trick,' said Bing from the side of his mouth, 'for there's a twinkle in these lovely ladies' eyes.'

'I wouldn't touch you with a barge pole, Robert Brown,' huffed Vesta, much to Marie's embarrassment. 'Just look at the state of you.'

'Oh, like that, is it?' Bing answered mischievously. 'Well, just wait a tick, milady. I'll call for me servant to polish me boots and find a plum to stick in me gob.'

Marie burst out laughing but Vesta looked furious.

'May we be so bold as to offer you an escort home?' Bing's brown eyes were full of teasing.

'We don't need one,' Vesta snapped. 'And even if we did, you'd be the last person we'd ask.'

Charlie Wiggins roared with laughter whilst Marie went red trying to smother her amusement.

'I'll try to bear the disappointment,' sighed Bing, giving Marie a conspiratorial wink. 'Anyway, perhaps me broken heart will be mended by the time we see you girls at the Queen's tonight.'

'You're never going to the Queen's?' Vesta gasped, looking horrified.

'We've got our suits and shirts pressed ready, ain't we, Charlie?' Bing nudged his friend's arm. 'Up in the gods, we'll be, communing with the greats.'

'Well, we're bound to be in the front row,' said Vesta coolly. 'So don't bother shouting at us, as we won't hear you.'

Marie decided it was time to leave before Vesta said something really rude. 'We'd better go now,' Marie said sweetly, glancing under her lashes at Bing.

'Not goodbye, but haw-rev-you-are, as the French say,' chuckled Bing, watching them walk away, his eyes twinkling.

'The cheek!' Vesta exploded, hurrying Marie on. 'Do you really think they'll turn up at the Queen's?'

Marie shrugged. 'Don't know.'

'How did he find out we're going?'

'It was Dad, I suppose. He goes to the Cubby Hole where Bing plays, doesn't he?'

Vesta groaned miserably. 'I forgot. If only Dad would keep better company.'

'Oh, Vesta, Bing's all right.'

'He's common and loud.'

'He might be, but he's been a good friend to Dad. Don't you remember when Mum sent me to fetch Dad back from the pub one Sunday? Bing was the one who helped me to persuade Dad to leave his pals and come home.'

Vesta gave this some thought. 'Well, he may have a few good points,' she agreed reluctantly, 'but he's certainly no gentleman like Teddy is.'

Marie sighed. Vesta was completely under Teddy's charm. With his thick, black hair combed glamorously in a wave over his head, and his flawless suits with fashionable double-breasted jackets, Teddy Turner was enough to turn any girl's head. But he was also conceited and arrogant. He did have a nice smile, but in Marie's opinion it never reached his eyes.

She decided not to say as much. Vesta wouldn't like that at all.

'How are yer, me darlings?' Fat Freda ran the fruit and veg stall at Cox Street market and beckoned them over. 'Let you out from that stinking prison, 'ave they?'

Marie laughed. 'It's not so bad at the factory, Freda.'

'Girls like you should be out in the fresh air, not 'ammerin' leather all day.'

'We don't hammer,' Vesta corrected primly. 'We trim the leather. And our jobs there are only temporary before we find something more suited to our taste.'

Fat Freda smiled. 'Yeah, course, ducks. You're the next Ginger Rogers, ain't you? I forgot. Now, how's your mum?'

'She's very well, thanks, Freda,' Marie replied, as Vesta gazed uninterestedly around at the well-stocked market stall.

'Now, what can I flog yer?' Freda asked. 'A pound of apples or pears? Or do you fancy a nice white cauli?'

'No, thank you,' declined Vesta, raising her chin. 'We're looking for something to wear. We're going to the Queen's tonight.'

'Lucky devils. Who's on?'

'Teddy Turner, of course,' answered Vesta, with a toss of her head. 'Perhaps you've heard of him?'

'Can't say as I have. What's he do, darlin'?'

'He's a singer.'

Fat Freda laughed coarsely. 'Isn't everyone these days? Even my old man sings like a linnet after a night up the boozer.'

As the costermonger turned to serve a customer, Vesta pulled Marie away. 'She wouldn't know a good voice if she heard one,' she whispered angrily. 'Mark my words, one day Teddy will make everyone wish they *did* know him.'

Marie began to wonder if Vesta's recent airs and graces had begun when Teddy had arrived on the scene. It wasn't just Fat Freda or the market stall-holders that she didn't care for, but the girls at work had begun to notice a change in her. She only wanted to speak about herself and couldn't be bothered with other people's interests. Working in a factory meant you had to get along with everyone. Marie was worried that soon the girls would give Vesta the cold shoulder.

'What do you think of this?' Vesta was rummaging on the second-hand clothes stall. She turned over a crumpled black frock with shiny beads sewn over the bodice. 'It's very Greta Garbo, don't you think?' Vesta pondered.

Marie laughed. 'We're only going to the Queen's.'

'I would be noticed in this, though.'

'You could wear a big hat and a feather boa, too,' Marie teased, thinking Vesta was joking.

Vesta dropped the dress immediately. 'Now you're making fun of me, just like that horrid Bing and his mate.'

'No one is making fun of you.'

'I wish Teddy was here to give me advice. He says with my looks, I could easily go on the stage.'

Marie stared at her sister. 'When did he say that?'

Vesta looked guilty. 'Oh, just when he talks to me. Why shouldn't he tell me nice things if they're true?'

'Vesta, try to keep a level head.'

'There was a time you believed in our dreams,' Vesta protested. 'But now you seem happy at the factory.'

'It pays our wages. And the girls are all right.'

'Is the factory all there is to our lives?' Vesta asked dramatically.

Marie couldn't help but giggle. 'You sound like Dad when he has one of his moments. Remember, you're not on the stage yet.'

'I will be!' Vesta exclaimed fiercely. 'And no one is going to stop me.'

'We don't know what the future holds,' Marie warned.

'You sound like Mum now,' Vesta flung back. 'Always going on about meeting the right man and settling down.' She took in a sharp, tearful breath. 'Well, I don't want to settle down! I want a glamorous life and people around me who appreciate me. Like Teddy.'

'Mum wants us to be practical,' Marie argued in defence of their mother. 'As Dad don't earn much money busking, it's her who has kept us going. She don't want us to end up poor.'

Vesta shrugged sullenly. 'She didn't mind us singing and dancing when we were kids.'

'Yes, but we're grown-up now. We have to support ourselves.'

'Oh, don't you go on too!'

'I want to sing and dance as much as you,' Marie insisted, 'but without Mum we could be like some of the girls at work who never have a penny to their names. Because they are so poor, they have to give everything to their mothers and it makes life very difficult for them.'

Vesta hung her head and mumbled, 'I know.'

'Is the dress really that important to you?'

Vesta looked up. 'The old girl is asking three bob for it.'

'Knock her down to two and I'll go halves.'

Vesta's blue eyes flew wide open. 'Would you?' She threw her arms around Marie. 'You're the best sister in the world.'

Ten minutes later they were on their way home and Vesta had the dress over her arm. Marie knew she was imagining what she would look like when Teddy saw her that evening.

'Thank you. Tonight means so much to me,' Vesta sighed.

Marie thought about their quarrel as they walked home. They never used to disagree. She hoped that they weren't growing apart.

Chapter 3

From the front room, Marie looked along the narrow passage to their bedroom. She could hear Vesta humming as she made the last adjustments to her black dress. Her parents were talking in the scullery, a small room to the left, where Hector was helping Ada to make the supper.

'You look lovely, dear,' Ada said as she came out, untying her apron and draping it over a chair.

Hector followed, a tall, portly figure wearing a big smile on his face under his walrus moustache. 'A real bobby-dazzler,' he agreed, nodding approvingly at his daughter.

Tonight Marie had chosen to wear a tailored belted navy-blue dress, black strapped shoes and a thin blue band in her hair with a sparkling slide to hold it. Glancing at her reflection in the mirror over the mantel, she was pleased with the way she looked. The soft pink lipstick suited her and the dab of powder disguised the freckles over her nose.

'Thanks, Dad.'

'Well, we'd better sit down and eat our meal,' said Hector, patting his generous stomach. 'I've set the table. So call your sister.'

Marie did so, and when Vesta joined them the talk was all about the coming evening.

'I haven't dressed up in a long while,' Ada said as she dished out the carrots and peas with a good helping of tender braised mutton. 'It'll be a real pleasure to sit in the theatre with all those smart types. I hope I do you girls justice.'

'You look lovely, Mum,' Marie said as she tucked into her meal. It wasn't often their mother took such care over her appearance. As a school cleaner, she had little time or money for herself. She spent it all on her family. But tonight was an exception. Going to the Queen's was a big event in any girl's book. Her fair hair was carefully arranged in a coil at the nape of her neck. Her pale blue eyes were shining, and her pressed grey suit moulded her still slender figure. The pearl brooch slipped through the collar of her jacket had been a wedding gift from their father.

'You should wear that suit more often, Mum,' Marie said encouragingly.

'Don't mind for a special occasion,' said Ada shyly. 'Anyway, this is your and Vesta's treat, not mine.'

'I'm glad we can share it,' Vesta said as she only picked at her food. Marie knew she was thinking of Teddy. 'But I wish Dad was coming.' She looked at her father. 'Couldn't you take a night off from busking?'

Hector quickly swallowed the large mouthful of meat and veg on the end of his fork and waved his hand. 'You girls won't miss me,' he declared. 'You'll be too busy watching the show. And anyway, I'll see you outside. It'll be a very good night for custom.'

'Yes, but you should be singing on the stage, Dad, not out in the street,' replied Vesta, pushing her plate away.

'Now, now, dear,' Ada interrupted. 'Your father is quite used to playing to the crowds outside. And missing a night's money won't help the larder.'

Marie saw Vesta give a slight frown of annoyance. She knew that Vesta didn't care for their father's profession of busking. It was a big comedown, Vesta felt, from his days with the travelling theatre and music halls.

'I still think . . .' began Vesta, but then got a look of warning from her mother as she cleared away the empty plates.

'There's custard and jelly for afters,' interrupted Ada sternly. 'But we'd better hurry up as time is getting on.'

Hector smiled and winked at his daughters. 'Custard and jelly!' Once more he pushed out his stomach and patted it. 'Your mother certainly knows the way to this man's heart!'

Though they both loved their father dearly, Marie knew that he still lived in the secret hope of becoming a famous performer one day. This upset their mother, who had always urged him to find a normal job. But Hector had managed to keep on with his busking and keep Ada happy with the little he did bring in. Marie knew he was happy doing what he did, and when he appeared outside the Queen's tonight, as they were waiting to go in, their applause would be louder than anyone else's.

After their meal and the washing-up was done, and Vesta had gone to change, Marie watched her father stand in front of the mirror wearing his best suit, black cape and silk cravat. As usual before going out, he twirled his moustache in a theatrical way. After clearing his throat loudly, and reciting a few verses to himself, he gave her a big grin.

'What d'you think of that?' he asked Marie, returning to his normal voice. 'Will I knock 'em dead?'

'Course you will, Dad.'

He looked very pleased, kissed her on the cheek and then marched out, calling over his shoulder, 'Cheerio, girls! See you later!'

'I'll just get me bag, then we'll call for Elsie,' Ada said as she came out of the kitchen in a fluster, patting her hair. 'Where's your sister? Oh, silly me,' she grinned, looking along the passage, 'I don't need to ask. I'll go along and give her a shout.'

Whilst waiting, Marie gazed around her at the room she had grown up in. It was elegant in its own way, with its high ceilings and Victorian embellishments. The view over Sphinx Street from the big bay window was what she loved most; you could always see what was going on, even quite a long way down the road. If you ignored the peeling wallpaper, damp patches and threadbare carpet, and looked only at Elsie's lovely furniture, like the big leather couch and sturdy dining table and four chairs, the room was quite a delight.

The fire in the grate was unlit and the room was cool, owing to the thick brick walls and heavy drapes. On the mantel was a photograph of the twins as children, just after they had moved here. Two smiling little blonde girls in ballet dresses that Ada had made, posing under an umbrella. Next to this was one of Ada and Hector. It had been taken long ago, just after they were married. Hector's walrus moustache and sleeked-back hair made him look very distinguished. Ada stood beside him in a long frock that hung down to her ankles. She looked young and innocent. They were such a handsome couple!

Suddenly Vesta appeared, followed by Ada. 'How do I look?' she asked, her blue eyes wide and sparkling.

'Perfect,' Marie told her, admiring the way Vesta had clipped up her hair to show off her long neck in the black dress. Her slim figure, an inch shorter than Marie's, looked dainty, but the black beads, Marie thought, were a bit gaudy for a young girl, though she smiled appreciatively nevertheless. She knew Vesta only wanted approval.

'I remember the time neither of you would go out wearing different dresses,' said Ada, sliding her small bag over her arm. 'Now look at you both.' She frowned. 'Vesta, that neck is rather low.'

'It's fashionable, Mum. I won't get cold.'

'It wasn't the cold I was thinking of,' remarked Ada, raising her eyebrows.

Vesta threw a dark glance at Marie, who quickly smiled.

'Elsie will be waiting,' Marie said hurriedly, and was relieved when Ada nodded.

'Come along then,' she smiled. 'We mustn't be late.'

When they walked into the hall, Elsie was already there. She was staring up at the first-floor half-landing and to the heavy oak banister where a little brown monkey with owl-like eyes and a white chin was perched. Between his sharp teeth was a cigarette.

'That bloody Kaiser,' Elsie swore loudly. 'He's pinched me fags again. And this time he's flamin' lit one. The smoke is coming out of his ears. Look!'

Everyone stared upwards. To Marie's amusement, the monkey chattered loudly and swung from one banister to the other. His long spidery legs and tail latched onto whatever hold he could find.

'Don't you drop that fag on me carpet, you little devil,' cried Elsie, 'or I'll skin you alive. And that's a promise!'

By now, everyone had begun to laugh, even Elsie, who was familiar with Kaiser's tricks. After a small accident when a lighted cigarette he'd dropped on the carpet had almost caused catastrophe, she kept a vigilant eye on his antics.

'Where are you, Wippet?' Elsie shouted up the stairs to the top-floor resident. 'Come and get your sodding animal and lock him away!'

There was a light shuffling sound and a small man appeared, no taller than a child, with a round smiling face. He was accompanied by a pretty blonde girl, another lodger, Nina Brass. Marie smiled at Wippet and Nina. She liked both of Elsie's top-floor residents and Kaiser was a favourite with everyone, despite inciting the landlady to bad language.

'Sorry, Mrs G,' apologized the little man, climbing on the banister and sliding down it to the last stair. 'Come here at once, Kaiser!'

The monkey, who was hanging from the cobweb-covered chandelier, made a defiant screeching. Everyone laughed again. Wippet and Kaiser had formerly been a sideshow at a fair and never failed to amuse. Marie knew Wippet was very brave. His acts at the fairground had included being tied with chains underwater and being shot from a cannon. His dark hair was short at the back and sides and had little patches in it, where for some reason the hair wouldn't grow.

Nina, who had come downstairs the conventional way, held out her arms and the monkey jumped into them. 'Naughty boy, Kaiser,' she whispered affectionately.

'Sorry, Mrs G,' apologized Wippet once more.

'He's dropped a fag end somewhere,' said Elsie sharply. 'We're going out so you'd better find it, Wippet, before I come home to find me place on fire.'

'Don't worry. It's here.' Wippet picked the cigarette butt from the stair and crunched the lit end with his stubby fingers. 'This won't happen again.' The monkey chattered and pushed his furry knuckles around his eyes. 'He's sorry, Mrs G. See, he's crying.'

Everyone laughed again, and Elsie relented. 'Poor little bugger. He shouldn't be cooped up all day in that cage of yours. He should be free, swinging from trees in Africa or wherever he comes from.'

'Oh, he was born in a circus,' Nina said as she held the little monkey close, 'and wouldn't leave Wippet even if he could.'

Marie knew that Nina worked as a cloakroom attendant in one of the West End clubs. She was rather glamorous, dressed this evening in a cream-coloured pleated skirt and top, and her blonde hair was long and smooth. It always amazed Marie that she didn't appear to have a boyfriend. She seemed more Teddy Turner's type, though Marie had noticed that she rarely spoke to him if they happened to pass on the stairs.

'You all look very smart,' Nina said in her quiet voice. 'Are you going somewhere special?'

'Yes,' said Vesta at once. 'To the Queen's, to see Teddy.'

Nina didn't reply. Marie felt sorry for her. She never seemed to have any friends other than Wippet. Elsie must have felt the same, she decided, as Elsie said quickly, 'You're welcome to join us, ducks, but you'll have to pay for yourself.'

'That's very nice of you, but no thanks.' Nina turned and ran up the two flights of stairs with the little monkey safe in her arms.

'Well, we ain't asking you, love,' chuckled Elsie to Wippet as he lingered. 'This is a girls' night out.'

Wippet laughed as he moved his small body almost painfully up the stairs. 'I wouldn't be able to see over the heads anyway, Mrs G,' he joked, and then, turning slowly, he added, 'but next week Kaiser and I are to return to the travelling fairground at Blackheath for a few days and perform a special trick. So if you all want to come and see us, you're welcome.'

'What's the trick?' asked Elsie curiously.

'I hope to escape my chains underwater.'

Marie gasped. 'Ain't that dangerous?'

'Only if I can't undo the locks. Then that will be the last you will ever see of poor Wippet!'

A gasp went round all the women before, finally, he grinned and went upstairs.

'Why did you ask Nina to come with us?' Marie heard Vesta ask Elsie as they trooped outside.

'She ain't a bad kid,' Elsie said kindly. 'Thought I'd make the offer as she looked a bit lonely.'

'Didn't fancy her tagging along,' Vesta said as she fell into step with Marie, behind Elsie and Ada. 'She's a strange sort. So is that Wippet. They make an odd couple, don't you think?'

'I like them,' Marie shrugged. 'Wippet's always very friendly and so is Nina, though she doesn't say much.'

'Wippet worked at a fairground before he came here a couple of years ago,' Elsie said, over her shoulder. 'He rescued Kaiser from a circus and taught him tricks to use in their act. Wippet and Nina might look a bit strange, but I ain't ever heard a bad word come from either of them.'

Marie noticed that, at Elsie's tactful rebuke, Vesta lost interest in the subject. Soon she began to talk about Teddy again. Marie smiled to herself. The characters in this house were what she loved most about living in Sphinx Street. Even Elsie was eccentric, this being apparent tonight as she led the way, dressed in all her finery. She had a love of gold, and was flaunting it: gold rings on her fingers, and a gold and black turban-shaped hat with a feather stuck in the folds. Her chocolate-coloured suit had little gold flecks in the fabric, which sparkled on her small, round figure. Her greying hair, which she died with henna, was twisted into kiss curls under her hat. For a woman in her seventies, she looked rather admirable. Marie had once heard her father remark that, thanks to Joe's parents, Elsie wasn't short of a bob or two.

'I've never been so excited,' breathed Vesta, as the theatre came into sight. 'My heart is pounding so loud I can hear it in me ears.'

Marie felt excited too. It wasn't often they had this kind of treat. She wondered if Bing really would be there, or had he been joking? If they did bump into him, she hoped that this time Vesta would mind her manners.

Chapter 4

Marie closed her eyes at the pain of her crushed toe whilst Vesta tried to distance herself from a small man with crooked brown teeth. In his arms he held a newspaper on top of which was an assortment of foul-smelling vegetables.

'Keep away from me!' Vesta exclaimed, trying to distance herself. 'You won't be allowed in the theatre with that.'

'Who's gonna stop me?' demanded the man.

'Take no notice,' Marie whispered. 'He won't get very far before the manager sees him.'

'I just hope he doesn't sit next to us.' Vesta moved up as far as she could.

The queue outside the theatre was supposed to be lining up in order, but as it was not a famous revue being performed and the seats were very cheap, it was first come first served. Everyone wanted to sit at the front. Marie had just been knocked by a large woman smelling of beer and perspiration, whilst Elsie and Ada, having got closer to the doors, were determined to hold their positions. Elsie's feather was waving this way and that and her loud voice could be heard as she spoke to the busker who held out his battered hat.

'Clear off, unless you want to deafen me!' she ordered, her feather shivering indignantly. 'We're waiting for Hector Haskins, I'll have you know. This is his pitch and he's got a voice that knocks socks off yours.'

Marie had hardly been able to hear the young man's rendition of Al Bowlly's 'I'll String Along With You'. He had soon lost heart at Elsie's rejection and made a swift retreat as one or two fists were shaken. Marie hoped her father would make a better impression on the crowd.

Everyone was out to enjoy themselves, whether by praise or ridicule. Amateur night was a favourite, where both street and stage performers were judged, sometimes unfairly, according to the public's mood.

Marie glanced at the posters hanging on the Queen's dirty walls. They announced the forthcoming shows, though she didn't recognize any names. The famous old theatre used to have many well-known acts appearing on its stage, from the twins' namesakes, Vesta Tilley and Marie Lloyd, to the famous Charlie Chaplin. But as cinemas had become more popular than theatres and music halls, the big stars rarely appeared at the Queen's any more. Marie thought that was a great pity, though she also liked to go to the pictures. There were any number of cinemas in the East End now: the Grand Palace Picture Theatre opposite the Blackwall Tunnel, the Grand in Tunnel Avenue and the Pavilion in the East India Dock Road. The Pavilion had been the first to offer talking pictures and the others had quickly followed. Luckily for her father, though, the Queen's had managed to attract a big audience tonight.

'I really don't think people should carry on like this,' said Vesta, trying to steady herself and clutching her bag against her chest. 'Throwing rotten veg and yelling must put the performers off.'

Marie stepped back sharply as the big woman yelled at the top of her voice, 'When are you going to open them doors?'

'If it's Teddy you're worried about, I don't think any of the girls who've come to see him would throw anything,' Marie replied with a smile.

'He's too talented by far to get boos,' nodded Vesta, though Marie had really meant that Teddy had all the confidence and charm of a man who knew his looks could speak for him. As for his voice, well, that remained to be heard. And even if Teddy was a looker, the East End crowds were notoriously hard to please.

Just then, a deep, rumbling voice boomed out and Vesta clutched Marie's arm, exclaiming, 'It's our dad!'

Sure enough, Hector sauntered along the road. When he saw his family and Elsie, he swept off his hat to reveal his thick dark hair.

Marie was filled with pride. He began by singing 'Oh! Susanna', and performing many flourishes, like the singer who originally sang the song, Carson Robison. But everyone was eager to get inside the theatre and Hector was being ignored.

'This is our dad!' shouted Marie to anyone who would listen, her cheeks pink with excitement.

'I shouldn't broadcast the fact, love,' warned the lady behind her. 'Not until you're out of range of this tomato.'

Vesta pulled Marie back as the crowd began to shout insults at Hector.

'Where did you appear from?' shouted a woman behind Elsie. 'The cemetery?'

Elsie turned and glared at her. She shoved the woman back with some force. 'Take that, you silly cow, and shut up or else you'll have Elsie Goldberg to deal with.' Elsie grabbed a soggy vegetable from the woman's bag. 'How would you like a bit of your own medicine, eh? Strikes me that pasty mug of yours could do with a bit of colour.'

The laughter changed to a great cheer and, knowing the crowd loved a fight, Elsie did a little bow as the woman backed away.

Marie knew that Elsie had learned to handle rough-necks from her years running the Cubby Hole. She turned triumphantly to Hector and shouted, 'Go on, ducks, give 'em all you've got.'

Undaunted, Hector took up his position again and began to sing, 'On Mother Kelly's Doorstep'.

Elsie moved close to Marie and Vesta. 'Flamin' 'ooli-gans,' she growled. 'Never mind, we'll be in them doors soon. Now, give your dad a big clap and the others will join in!'

When Hector had finished, Marie, Vesta, Ada and

Elsie all cheered. But as the theatre doors opened and the masses rushed in, Hector was soon forgotten. Marie saw him hurriedly run to catch a halfpenny that rolled his way.

Her heart ached to see her father ignored and unappreciated. How did a man of such talent end up trying to win the crowd's approval by performing silly songs in the street? She knew Vesta was thinking that too.

Once inside the theatre, with the tickets bought, they all followed Elsie down to the front stalls. Their seats were only six back from the first row, an excellent spot and directly in front of the stage. The orchestra, consisting of a pianist, a violinist and bass player, was tuning up. Marie's glance went straight up to the gallery, but there were too many people coming and going for her to be able to pick out Bing and Charlie.

Elsie made herself comfortable next to Ada and ushered the girls past. As Marie settled in the comfortable seat, she gazed round. The theatre's exterior was plain and shabby, with no wide carpeted steps, and marble and glass foyers, as some of the West End theatres had. But inside, the red, green and gold colours of the beautiful Victorian upholstery and ornate architecture gave the place a rich and dramatic feel. Even the cubby hole at the side of the stage from where the manager kept a watchful eye and the ladies' cloakrooms were all old-style elegance.

When the lights dimmed, there was a sudden silence. The musicians began to play and for the next hour, Marie was transported to another world. The one that she and Vesta had always dreamed of joining.

They watched in awe as the acts performed. Some, like the comedian who wasn't very funny and bored the audience, were booed off. The ventriloquist whose lips could be seen moving soon disappeared under a hail of tomatoes. But all the singers had strong voices. The men and women knew how to entertain the audience and got them to join in the well-known songs. Marie knew Vesta was imagining herself on the stage, dancing along with the pretty, slender dancers of the chorus line.

When the break for half-time came, Marie and Vesta hurried to the cloakroom. All the women were discussing the acts, and a young girl in front of them in the queue said she'd heard a handsome singer, who worked at the new club called the Duke's, was up next.

Vesta's cheeks went bright red. 'She means Teddy,' she whispered to Marie. 'Just think, we know someone who works at a posh club like the Duke's.'

'We don't really know if it's posh,' Marie said unwisely, drawing a look of horror from Vesta.

'Of course we do,' she spluttered. 'Teddy told me that it's a cabaret club and the owners will only hire the best acts.'

'You seem to know a lot.'

'That's because I show an interest – unlike some,' Vesta answered sharply and, Marie thought, rather off-handedly. 'Come on, there's a lav empty!'

By the time they returned to their seats, the lights were just going down. Elsie and Ada had brought sweets and noisily opened the bag of wine gums. In the exciting tension of the moment, Marie forgot all about the Duke's, which so far had occupied her thoughts. Teddy had said the club was the smartest and classiest in the East End. But sitting here, in this historic old theatre, Marie felt that this atmosphere was going to be hard to beat.

The curtains drew apart to reveal the presenter. He was an elderly man who had worn a gaudy checked suit for the first half but had now changed into a dress suit with a frilled white shirt and cuffs. He asked the audience to give a big welcome to the popular singing artiste Teddy Turner.

The audience held its breath as Teddy strode onto the stage. There were squeals of delight from the women, and Marie heard Vesta gasp, 'Isn't he handsome?'

Marie nodded. Tall, dark and dramatically handsome in his black evening suit, he gave a wide smile and touched the red rose in his buttonhole. He straightened his sleeves, while his dark eyes roamed the audience in a slow, enticing manner. His hair was slicked back even higher than usual in a glossy wave, and his eyes were framed by two distinctive black eyebrows. Marie wondered if he had drawn them in with pencil, they looked so perfect. She turned to Vesta, who seemed about to faint. She was sitting on the edge of her seat, and her mouth had fallen open as she took halting breaths.

Drawing himself up, Teddy put his smooth lips close to the microphone. He began to sing, 'I'm Through

With Love', a song made popular by Bing Crosby. Marie
noticed he started off in a low, drawling voice that didn't
quite match the tune the musicians were playing. As hard
as he tried, he just couldn't keep the rhythm. Eventually
he resorted to humming and ad-libbing some lines. To
Marie's surprise, two girls in the front row let out screams.
The manager rushed out to try to control them. But
undaunted, Teddy sang on, causing an even greater stir in
the audience.

'Oh my God,' gasped Vesta as he ended his first song.
'Didn't I tell you he was a wonderful singer?'

Marie stared at her sister. Was Vesta really listening to
the same person as she was?

Marie glanced at Elsie, who raised her eyebrows. 'All
the young girls seem to like him, and why not?'
commented Elsie. 'He's a charmer, without doubt. But a
singing voice that boy has not got.'

'Oh, Elsie!' exclaimed Vesta, astonished. 'He sings like
an angel!'

An older woman in the seat in front of them turned
round. 'He ain't my cup of tea either. But he can certainly
put on the style.'

'What about you, Mum?' Marie asked.

Ada frowned and gave a bewildered shrug. 'Perhaps
this is the modern thing,' she said diplomatically, 'and we
older women are a bit behind the times.'

When Teddy ended the number, it was long before
the musicians had finished. He didn't seem bothered and
smiled at the young women who applauded him.

Teddy took several curtain calls. On the last one, Vesta suddenly screamed out his name. She waved her hands and jumped up and down. On seeing her, Teddy took the rose from his buttonhole and threw it down.

Vesta caught it and clutched it close. Marie saw Teddy blow her a kiss. Once again, Marie thought Vesta was about to faint.

'He blew me a kiss,' gasped Vesta breathlessly as Teddy swaggered from the stage. 'And threw me his rose. I knew this dress would catch his eye!'

'It might have had something to do with the three feet you jumped in the air,' giggled Marie.

'You're just jealous cos you didn't get a rose.'

Marie wondered how Vesta could be taken in. Teddy was hopeless but won the young women's attention and revelled in it. She thought of Bing and looked up to the gods, the rows of seats high above the back of the theatre. Had he just been joking about coming tonight?

'Teddy was amazing,' repeated Vesta, her eyes lingering on the empty stage. 'And he only had eyes for me.'

Marie thought Teddy's attention had strayed far and wide; he was handsome and an artful performer. But he had made an awful hash of the song. She was glad when the next act came on, a young woman who wore a long, sparkling evening gown and had a good voice. She sang 'Ave Maria' and, although looking nervous, ended without fault. After Teddy's act, it was a pleasure to sit and listen to someone with talent.

★　　★　　★

Dusk had fallen by the time they left the theatre. Marie waited with Elsie and Ada, whilst Vesta spoke to a group of young girls who were still in raptures over Teddy. They were all asking her about how she knew him and Marie could see Vesta was loving every minute, basking in their attention.

'You'd never believe it, would you?' said Elsie in an amused voice. 'Whatever that Teddy Turner has got, he should bottle it.'

'He is very good-looking,' said Ada, frowning over at the group. 'I hope Vesta can keep a level head.'

'She seems to be doing all right,' Elsie mused, pulling her jacket around her. 'I wouldn't be surprised if someone asks for her autograph.'

Marie giggled. 'And Vesta would give it, I expect.'

Elsie laughed but Ada looked concerned. 'She wants to be famous so much.'

Elsie nodded. 'You never know, she might be one day.' She looked at Marie. 'How about you, love, did you enjoy it?'

'Yes, thanks, Elsie, the evening was wonderful.'

'You and Vesta are as good as any of them acts we saw tonight,' said Elsie kindly. 'You should have a go up there one day.'

'Thanks, Elsie. But we need to practise more to be better than the rest. Those other singers, especially the girl who sang "Ave Maria", were very good.'

As Ada and Elsie discussed the performances, Marie noticed they didn't say anything more about Teddy. Had she imagined how out of tune he was? Or were Ada and Elsie just being polite for Vesta's sake?

'Well, we'd better get cracking,' said Elsie. 'Got a long walk home.'

'I was hoping Hector might be here to meet us,' Ada said wistfully. 'But he's probably dropped in to the Cubby Hole.'

Marie saw Elsie's glance of pity. They all hoped Hector didn't spend any of his earnings on beer.

Marie slid her arm through her mother's. Over the last couple of years, their father had taken to spending a lot of time at the tavern. Ada never complained when he said he wasn't drinking, but mixing with the arty types at the Cubby Hole. He maintained it was all part of the business.

But Marie knew that Hector was well past his prime. He was unlikely to become popular again, as he still lived in the old world. That had been made perfectly clear tonight. For even some of the shrewd East End audience had approved of the talentless Teddy.

Chapter 5

As they strolled along in the warm evening, the street was lit softly by lamplight. The sky above was filled with stars, and music played faintly from a barrel organ, adding to the thrill and excitement of a summer's night. A small, ruby-coloured car with a black top and two shining headlights pulled up beside them. Out jumped the driver and strode to the pavement. To Marie's surprise, it was Bing.

He looked very different tonight. Dressed in a dark jacket and white flannels, he wore a striped tie that looked very smart against his white shirt. 'Evening, one and all.' He smiled as usual from ear to ear. 'Enjoy yourselves, did you?'

'Teddy threw me this rose,' said Vesta before anyone could reply. 'We sat at the front in the best seats. Didn't see you there, though.'

'No such luck for us,' Bing shrugged. 'Up in the gods, we was, with the rabble.'

'Where's Charlie?' Marie asked, and blushed as Bing looked at her.

'Gone off with his young lady.'

'Didn't know you had a car,' she said quietly, bending down to peer in the window.

'This is Ruby,' he introduced, sounding proud. 'She's a nice little runner. How would you ladies like a ride home?'

'I'd rather walk,' said Vesta rudely. 'I'd ruin me dress trying to squeeze up in that small space!' And she walked away, head held high, everyone staring after her.

'Come back here, my girl,' called Elsie. 'Walking's a doddle for you young ones, perhaps, but my bunions are killing me.'

Ada voiced her opinion: 'Vesta, we've been kindly offered a lift and in a very nice motor car, too.'

Marie saw Vesta turn round, a big scowl on her face.

Elsie stepped forward to give Bing's cheek a peck. 'You're looking grand, son. Found yourself a missus yet?'

'No, Elsie, 'fraid not. I was waiting for you.'

Elsie cackled loudly. 'Go on with you, I'm old enough to be your grandmother. Still playing at the Cubby Hole?'

'Yes, been there for two years now.'

'I must pay you a visit one day,' Elsie promised. 'See how things are going without me.'

'No one is as good as you, Elsie,' Bing assured her. 'Me dad still remembers when you and Joe ran the pub. How you was the life and soul of the party.'

Elsie turned to Ada and rolled her eyes. 'That shows me age. The boy saying his mum and dad remember me! And to be honest, I can remember them. They used to come in for a bevvy after their pie and mash at Gus's shop next door, leaving the youngster here to sit at the door outside. Poor little sod. Didn't know he'd grow up to be the good-looker he is now.' She pointed to the car. 'Tell your folks Elsie says hello when you see them next. Now, show me where to sit.'

'Royalty at the front,' said Bing, opening the door, and taking her arm, helped her in. 'Mrs H and your lovely daughters, you have the back seat all to yourselves.'

Marie found herself smiling as they climbed aboard. The leather seats smelled lovely. Vesta looked very squeezed up and uncomfortable, but to Marie's mind, this made a perfect end to the evening.

'Will you come in for a cuppa?' Ada invited when Bing stopped the car.

'No thanks, Mrs H. Another time, perhaps.'

'Well, thank you for the ride,' said Ada as they all trooped out onto the pavement. 'Goodnight, Bing.'

'You can buy me a sherry next time I'm up the pub,' Elsie bellowed as she followed Ada and Vesta up the steps.

'I'm counting the minutes,' shouted Bing. But as Marie was about to follow them, he caught her arm. 'Got a minute, Marie?' He gazed up at the sky. 'It's a lovely night, wouldn't you say?'

Marie smiled, waiting for the joke. 'Yes, why?'

'Do you remember that day two years ago when you walked into the pub, looking for your dad?'

'Yes, I do.'

'I'd just landed a job in the docks and was playing at the Cubby Hole, making a few bob for me old age. I thought life couldn't get much better. But it did. Cos I saw this vision standing at the pub door looking as though she'd found a tanner and lost a fiver.'

'And you came over and asked if I needed any help,' Marie added shyly. 'You were the only one who did.'

Bing gazed at her, stepping from one foot to the other. 'You were just a kid, then, but now that's all changed. You've grown up. And I've been trying to find the courage to ask you out.'

Marie blushed again. What would Vesta say if she went out with him? Her sister's opinion counted, but Bing wasn't asking Vesta. He was asking her.

'How about a walk to the park tomorrow?' he suggested, quickly filling the silence. 'Eleven o'clock, say?'

Marie hesitated.

'Just for an hour, that's all.'

She smiled. 'All right, then.'

He grinned, almost tripping over himself as he backed towards the car. After he'd driven off, Marie stood in the warm night, wondering if it was true that he'd had to find the courage to ask her out. She had liked him when she'd first met him at the Cubby Hole. But she had never thought about him in a romantic way. But now she was older – and she did find him amusing.

She breathed in deeply, closing her eyes. The smell of summer was everywhere: salt and tar from the river, the hot streets, cooked foods, the sewers and drains, and the smoking factory chimneys. It was one of those nights, she thought, that you wanted to last for ever.

'I thought you'd never stop talking to him,' complained Vesta, when Marie finally walked in the front room. Her sister flung herself on the couch, wearing her dressing gown and slippers. 'What did lover boy have to say for himself?'

Marie kicked off her shoes. 'Nothing much.'

'Are you seeing him again?'

Marie shrugged. 'Tomorrow – perhaps.'

'So he asked you out, then?'

'Only for a walk.' Marie decided to change the subject; she had the feeling that Vesta didn't want to think about anyone else but Teddy. 'Would you like a cup of cocoa?'

'No, I'm off to bed.' Vesta stood up, yawning. 'All that excitement at the theatre tired me out. I want to fall asleep and dream of Teddy.'

When Marie walked into the kitchen, the radio was playing music softly. Ada was sitting at the wooden table. 'You look happy, dear.'

'I am.'

'That boy is a nice lad.'

Marie went red. 'I don't really know him.'

'Your dad likes him. Has he asked you out?'

'For a walk tomorrow,' Marie admitted reluctantly. She didn't want her mother to get any ideas. 'I might not even go.'

Ada frowned. 'Then you'd be missing out, love.'

'Mum, just because he's got a job and a car, and Dad happens to like him—'

'I know, I know,' Ada said, putting up her hand. 'But you could do a lot worse.'

Marie put the kettle on with a bit of a clatter. 'I don't want to get married, Mum,' she said abruptly.

'You will, one day.'

Marie hoped that day was a long way off. She was about to say so when Ada gave a long yawn. 'Dearie me, I'm all in.'

'School cleaning must be very tiring.'

'I'm lucky to have a regular job.'

Marie never heard her mother complain. Their father didn't bring home much money, it was true. Even though she and Vesta put towards the housekeeping, it was hard for Ada to keep them afloat.

'Goodnight, love.' Her mother kissed her cheek.

''Night, Mum.'

'Leave the door unlocked for Dad, won't you?'

Marie nodded. When would their father come in? If he'd met up with a few of his friends, it could be a while. Marie thought again of Bing as the kettle boiled. She smiled. He was nice, but was he really her type?

Anyway, she didn't want to fall in love just yet. She wanted to sing and dance with Vesta, just as they had always dreamed of. But sometimes she thought this might be only that – a dream – as the sensible side of her knew from Ada's example that it was not dreams that filled the larder with food, or paid the rent, it was hard work. Life in the theatre was very appealing – the glamour and the bright lights – and though Marie was confident that she and Vesta could sing and dance, it wasn't everyone who made this a career. Unlike Vesta, she had her feet planted firmly on the ground. She knew their chances of finding fame and fortune were slim, whilst Ellisdon's provided regular work and a safe routine. Good jobs were not easy to find on the island. Life could be very hard for some.

Marie sighed. One part of her wanted adventure, the other was afraid to break out. With Vesta it was the other way round. But what counted was that they were together, and this, to Marie, was most important of all.

Chapter 6

Dressed in his vest and pants, Bing studied his freshly shaven jaw in the half-mirror hidden behind a leafy green aspidistra his mum had given him. The plant stood beside a kitchen of sorts: a large chipped china basin flanked by two old wooden draining boards and a neglected gas stove. He didn't bother to cook much because he was never here. He ate all he needed at the Cubby Hole or in the canteen at work. This place could hardly be called a palace, but he wasn't looking for luxury. He just wanted somewhere to lay his head, somewhere cheap, if not cheerful. His mum and dad had offered him lodgings, but their gaff was all the way up at Aldgate, too far from his work in the docks and his social life at the Cubby Hole.

Bing squashed his hair with the flat of his hand, but it only stood up again. The remains of the brilliantine that he'd slapped on last night for his visit to the Queen's made it look a mess. He didn't like the sticky stuff. Hair oil smelled a bit fancy for his liking. But it was time for him to improve his image. Merely saying hello to Marie every day and making a joke to cover up his true feelings was wearing a bit thin.

Quickly he bent and put his head under the tap. The cold water ran over his scalp. Using the bar of Sunlight soap, he managed to wash out the worst of the hair oil.

Pushing aside the piles of sheet music that were under the window, he leaned out. It was a wonderful summer's morning. The sea of grime-covered rooftops and tenement buildings was all around him. The smells from the factories weren't so strong on a Sunday. This morning he had a date with a beautiful girl who had been on his mind for so long.

Marie was the best-looking girl he'd ever seen. She had lovely tumbling blonde waves and big eyes that looked as blue as the sea. He had found the courage to ask her out at last but would she come out this morning? He'd feel a drip if she turned him away.

'Snap out of it,' he ordered himself. 'A bloke's not supposed to have nerves, don't you know that?' He turned round in the two feet of vacant space by his bed, a contraption made up of a solid steel frame that weighed a hundredweight. The new feather mattress was his own purchase. He liked a good night's sleep.

Bing drew back the curtain that hung across a recess and peered at his clothes. Ten minutes later, he was dressed, a spotted blue tie at his throat and white handkerchief in his top pocket.

Inspecting himself in the mirror, he tried to flatten his hair, but with no success.

By the time the mantel clock struck ten, he was ready. He was early, but he snatched up his key and let himself out. The dirty, smelly concrete passage stretched endlessly to his right and left. A rabbit warren of similar doors and passages ran four floors down. The tenement block echoed with the shouts of kids and arguments brewing. Averting his gaze from the shabby walls, he tried not to breathe in the smell of the blocked drains.

How would he ever be able to bring Marie back here, he wondered as he ran down the stone steps to the street. As he strode towards Sphinx Street, he thought of his plans to buy his own gaff, a piece of turf to call his own. Not somewhere the landlord called the tune and could kick him out at any minute. No, it was a chipper little terrace on the island he wanted. With a painted front door, a white step and a decent back garden. Well, a yard would do, but he wasn't going to share the lav with the rest of the street. On that fact, he would not be moved!

Bing knew he wanted to have something solid behind him. He'd saved hard since starting work in the docks and his Post Office account was healthy. One day he would be able to give his wife all she wanted. Would that wife be Marie?

He could think of no other. She was beautiful and bright and her smile always lit up his heart. She was also a really decent girl, a family girl who, like him, had grown up with values of home and hearth, as his mother would say. Still, he didn't even know if she really liked him.

Had she agreed on the spur of the moment to see him because he had been too pushy?

'Time you did some serious planning,' he told himself, straightening his shoulders. 'And don't blot your copy-book this morning.' If he messed this walk up, he wasn't likely to get another chance.

The thought scared him. He'd never felt this way before: all fingers and thumbs and hot around the collar. It was a unique experience. He just hoped it wouldn't be the *only* experience he had of taking out the girl of his dreams.

Marie rushed to the door. She had looked from the front window and seen Bing's tall figure coming down the street. Calling goodbye to her family, she hurried out. She was afraid Ada or Hector would invite him in, and they'd be there talking for hours.

Before that happened, she wanted to get to know a bit more about Bing. What did they have in common? Did he ever stop joking? What were his dreams in life? Up till now, it was just a few minutes of flirting on the way home from work.

At least if she was out this morning, she wouldn't have to listen to Vesta going on about Teddy. Her sister hadn't stopped singing his praises since the moment they'd woken up!

When she opened the front door, both Bing and Nina Brass stood on the step.

Nina smiled. 'Did you have a good time last night?'

'Yes, thank you. It was lovely.'

Nina looked very pretty, dressed in a long, belted summer frock and a small beret-type hat.

Nina stepped past Marie into the hall. 'Nice to meet you, Bing.'

'You too, Nina.'

'Bye, Marie.' Nina hurried up the stairs.

'It didn't take you long to introduce yourself to the neighbours,' Marie said as she closed the door behind her.

'Now, now,' he teased as they went down the steps. 'I don't want you getting jealous.'

'Don't flatter yourself.' Marie tossed her head. 'Why would I be jealous?' Though secretly she was annoyed to find herself wondering if he liked Nina.

'Right, shall we go?' Bing said quickly. 'Before you change your mind.'

'I thought about it,' she nodded, 'but decided to get seeing you over and done with.'

'Blimey, the girl don't mince her words,' Bing muttered, holding out his arm. 'Now, as we're racing along as if our lives depended on it, I'd suggest you put your hand over this and hold tight.'

Marie curled her hand over his arm. She took a slight breath. It felt very solid and strong.

'Am I allowed to say you look nice?' Bing asked as they went.

'If it's true.'

'In that case, I'll say it.'

Marie grinned, pleased she'd decided to look her best. Nina always looked lovely with her long blonde hair and smart clothes. But the dress Marie had chosen to wear was not particularly smart, as it was quite old. However, the colour was a soft dove grey, and it had a pretty white collar and white cuffs on the sleeves. The full skirt swirled around her legs and accentuated her small waist. Purchased cheaply at the market, it had ironed up well and seen at least three summers. She'd thought about wearing white gloves too, like Nina did, but for a walk that seemed a bit overdone.

Marie glanced at Bing. He was wearing a good suit and discreetly patterned tie. And unlike last night, when his golden mop of hair had been plastered down with hair oil, it now stood up on end, back to its old self.

For a moment, she felt a little dizzy.

He must have felt her looking at him and he turned to frown at her. She realized how brown his eyes were. They had a gentleness under the mischief. What kind of man was he really?

More to the point, Marie thought, with a little start, did she really want to find out?

Chapter 7

They reached the park and sat on a bench overlooking the pond. The sun had brought everyone out. Already the day was hot enough to cause a heat haze over the water. Children paddled and played whilst their parents looked on, taking the opportunity to talk and relax. The smells coming up from the river hung in the still air: a concoction of unseasoned wood and tar-paint, the oil and chemicals of the factories, the exotic perfumes brought in from the East and the spices and fruits from countries all over the world.

'So what do you and me dad talk about at the pub?' Marie asked as Bing stretched out his long legs.

'You and your sister, of course.'

She grinned. 'Oh?'

'He says nobody can sing and dance as good as his girls. And he should know. After all, he was a performer himself.'

'Yes, but that was a long time ago.'

'Don't matter,' Bing shrugged. 'He could be big again one day. It ain't your age that matters, it's what you've got inside you.'

Marie looked into Bing's big, kind eyes. 'Do you want to be famous one day?'

He stared at her in surprise, then laughed. 'Not on your nelly. I work in the pub so I can save for me nest egg. True, the pay's not good but the tips are. After a few ales and a good singsong, you'd be surprised what the blokes throw in my glass.'

Marie looked puzzled. 'What sort of nest egg? Do you want to travel and see the world?'

'Done that in the Navy,' he said easily.

'Then what?' Marie asked curiously.

'You'll be disappointed.' He looked at her as if he was thinking whether he should say. 'I'm ready to settle down,' he said at last. 'Get a place of my own. Somewhere I can knock about a few walls; do up the garden and grow me own vegetables, like my dad does.'

Marie was disappointed. She imagined there was a bit more glamour to his life; after all, he did play the piano and sing to an audience, even though it was only in the pub. 'I hope all your hard work will bring you what you deserve,' she answered, trying not to show her true feelings.

He gave a throaty chuckle. 'Blimey, you should be a politician.'

'Sorry,' she said, blushing.

After this, there was an awkward silence. Then Marie suggested they continue their walk. If Bing had another, more ambitious side to him, he wasn't admitting to it.

'How long have you been playing the piano?' she asked as they strolled.

'Since I was able to climb on the piano stool. Dad plays the ukulele and Mum the joanna. I suppose it was natural for me to have a musical bent.'

'You could play or sing professionally if you wanted,' she suggested, feeling a bit more interested.

But he shook his head. 'Not me. I'm happy as I am. I love the Marx Brothers and I crack their jokes, but I can't really tell 'em the way they do. I can copy the old crooner and get away with it, but only to the blokes in the boozer who don't know any better. It's all just a bit of fun to me. And if I can make some cash on the side, that's great. I ain't looking for fame and fortune as often it comes at a price.'

'What do you mean?'

'Well, it ain't a natural life, is it? You're away from home and don't see your family much. Just like your dad. Soon as he met your mum and they had kids, he couldn't live two lives. It's one or the other, ain't it? And, as I said, I ain't got the talent.'

As they walked into Island Gardens, past the entrance to the foot tunnel to Greenwich, Marie paused at the fence. She had decided to set Bing a challenge. 'Will you sing a song for me?'

'Why?' He looked startled.

'Last night I thought Teddy was dreadful. And he has the nerve to go on the stage. I'm sure you could do better.'

'I could be much worse.'

She smiled. 'Will you sing something?'

He thought about this, then laughed. 'What have I got to lose? But remember, I belt out songs at a pub, on an old joanna.'

'Can you sing the same song as Teddy did? It is one of Bing Crosby's.'

'"I'm Through With Love"?' He grinned. 'I'll give it a go.'

Marie nodded. 'This is your chance to impress me.'

For a few seconds there was a lot of throat clearing and patting of pockets. He pulled up his tie and looked around. Was he trying to think of an excuse not to do as she asked?

Marie had a sinking sensation. What if he was really awful? She liked him, but would she quickly go off him? Listening to Teddy last night had made her realize how quickly someone can fall in your estimation. The women had swooned over Teddy, but not because of his voice. It was his looks that had drawn the gasps. As for talent? He had none.

'Here we go, then,' Bing warned her.

Marie waited. When at last he began to sing, her mouth fell slowly open. Her heart thumped in her chest. She couldn't move and didn't want to. Bing's voice was like cream, a deep baritone, sliding into the quiet morning air. Perhaps he did sing in Bing Crosby's style but with a uniqueness all of his own. The words felt as though they were made for her. She didn't want him to stop.

When he did, she stood in silence. The magic of the moment lingered in the air, sending shivers down her spine.

He searched her gaze, then laughed awkwardly. 'I warned you it might be worse.'

'It wasn't.' Marie tried to catch her breath. 'It was beautiful.'

'You're trying not to hurt my feelings.'

'No, it's the truth. You have a wonderful voice.'

'I just copy, that's all.'

'You sounded like Bobby Brown to me.'

He looked embarrassed. 'Come on, time's getting on. Grab my arm and I'll walk you home.'

Marie was quiet most of the way. Her thoughts were spinning in her head. She could still hear his pitch-perfect notes as clear as any she'd ever heard on the radio. He just didn't seem to know how good he was.

'Can I see you again?' he asked as they came to Sphinx Street. 'Same walk, next Saturday afternoon?'

'Me and Vesta practise on Saturdays.' It was a white lie, as lately they hadn't done very much at all.

'Just for an hour?'

'You are persistent.'

'And good-looking!'

Marie laughed. 'All right.'

Would she regret it, she wondered, as they said goodbye. One half of her wanted to see him again, the other was against it. She realized now how much she liked him. Yet, if she did, wasn't that a good thing? It was if she wanted more than just friendship, something that might turn out to last. But only yesterday she had told Ada that settling down was definitely what she didn't want. Marie felt scared. She didn't want to fall in love, even though, just for a short while, Bing had turned all her ideas on their heads.

Chapter 8

'I warned you not to encourage him,' said Vesta the next day as they sat in the works canteen. 'He'll turn out to be one of those hangers-on you can't get rid of.'

'I tried to say no.'

'Obviously not hard enough.'

'He is a nice person.'

'Have it your way.' Vesta grimaced as she drank the weak tea from an enamel mug. 'This tastes like dishwater.'

It had been a busy Monday morning in the cutting-room. The sheets of leather were heavy and dusty and though the men were required to shape the big pieces, the women still had to work with the smaller ones. Now it was twelve thirty and they were having their break.

'He does have a good voice,' Marie added, returning to the subject of Bing.

Vesta sighed as she examined the dirt on her hands. Before Marie could continue, she pushed away the mug in disgust. 'I'm beginning to hate this place! Look at us all. We are just numbers to the bosses, and clock in and out as though we were nothing more than machines. You and I are expected to do the same work as the men for less pay. Marie, I promise you, I'd rather die young than spend my life working in a place like this.'

'Don't talk like that.'

'Why not? It's true. Just look at me hands, they're ruined!'

Marie felt the rough surface of her own hands. They were prone to blisters from the repetitive work of making the eyelets, toe puffs and stiffeners on the boots and shoes. Her skin would only be eased by spreading on Vaseline when she got home. Not only was it back-breaking work, but the dust went down your throat and often affected the lungs.

Marie listened to the noisy chatter of the people around her. The women weren't bad, but liked to gossip. She and Vesta said very little about their dream to any of the girls. They would be laughed at and told to get off their high horses. In the factory it was a case of head down and keep going. Vesta was right. They were treated like machines and had to dress identically in brown overalls, ugly hair-nets, and heavy boots that made their feet sweat and smell terrible. Everyone longed to take off the cumbersome leather aprons they were forced to wear in the cutting room. Mr Morton, the manager, was all right. He was a fair man and well respected, but no one ever saw him except at the works do at Christmas.

With only half an hour to eat in the stifling heat of the canteen, and ten minutes to go to the lavatory, the long afternoon lay ahead of them.

'So you've made up your mind to go out with him on Saturday?' Vesta asked. 'When we should be practising.'

'You usually say you're too tired,' Marie pointed out as she drank the last of her tea.

'I don't want to spend my life bashing leather.'

'Well then, we'll learn some new songs when we go home.'

'Mum's bound to say she wants something done.'

'We'll help her first and then do it.'

Vesta pushed the tips of her blonde hair under her cap as the loud ringing meant their break was over. 'Teddy said, if our act is good enough, he might be able to get us into the club where he works.'

'The Duke's, you mean?' Marie asked in surprise.

'Yesterday whilst you were out with lover boy, I met Teddy on the stairs. I thanked him for throwing me the rose. Then I told him about our act. I said how much we wanted to go on the stage.'

'What did he say?'

'That he'd see what he could do for us. He knows the bosses of the Duke's. The Scoresby brothers are always on the lookout for talent, though the acts must be of a very high standard, as we've heard.'

'So that's why you suddenly want to practise!' Marie grinned.

Vesta smiled. 'It might be our chance to get away from here.'

As they joined the queue filing out of the canteen, Marie wondered if Teddy had simply been trying to impress her sister and all his talk would come to nothing. Who were the Scoresby brothers? What was the Duke's like? Until there was something more to go on, Marie decided not to get her hopes up.

At least, not too much.

For the rest of the week they practised every spare moment they had. They chose two songs that Hector had taught them: 'Algy' by Vesta Tilley and 'When I Take My Morning Promenade' by Marie Lloyd. Both lent themselves to the type of cheeky routines that would show off the twins' dancing.

On Friday night, when they climbed into bed, Vesta snuggled close to Marie. 'I saw Teddy today on the stairs,' she whispered excitedly.

'Is it good news?'

'He says he's going to ask Mr Scoresby tomorrow.'

'Oh.' In spite of trying not to get excited, Marie was.

'He said one of the singers has left so there might be a slot. You never know, something wonderful might happen.'

'When will he tell us?'

'Teddy says we have to be patient. Wally and Leo Scoresby are important people and have business interests in the West End. Wally is the one we'll see if we're lucky enough to get an audition. Cabaret is really hard to get into.'

'What would they want with us, then?' Marie asked. 'We haven't had any experience at cabaret. I don't even really know what it is.'

'The acts sing and dance in front of a microphone, on a small stage.'

'Did Teddy tell you all this?'

'Yes, he made it sound wonderful.'

'Does he sing for the customers too?'

'Yes, of course. He's the lead act.'

Marie wondered what kind of people could like Teddy's voice. But if a lot of them were women, then Teddy could be popular.

'As it's our half-day tomorrow, we can practise all afternoon.'

'Don't forget I'm seeing Bing.'

'Oh,' sighed Vesta disappointedly.

'I won't be long.'

'Every minute counts now.'

Marie laughed. 'That's what I've always told you.'

'I'll ask Dad if we can borrow his top hat and cane, like we did as kids,' said Vesta dreamily.

'Will that be too old-fashioned?' asked Marie.

'Everyone liked it before.'

'Yes, but we've only sung and danced in front of a few people.'

'Doesn't matter. We'll do our best.' Vesta slipped beneath the covers and shivered. 'If we get a job at the club it will be because of Teddy. I shall be grateful to him for ever!'

Marie could hardly believe their names had been put forward to a real cabaret club. *Would* Teddy come up with an audition? They would have to wait and see. Only then would they be able to judge for themselves what the Duke's was like.

'You've got a big smile today,' Bing commented on Saturday afternoon when he called for Marie.

Again she noticed how well dressed he was. A blazer complemented his cream flannels and brown brogue shoes. With a little more attention to detail she was sure he could make something of himself and his talent.

'Yes, I have.'

He held out his arm and she took it. 'Has it got something to do with us?'

Marie laughed. 'No, why?'

'Just wondered,' he grinned as they turned into the main road. A big sun was high over the river, spreading its rays amongst the houses and factory buildings. The afternoon was very warm again and Marie had changed into a light summer frock, though she hadn't had time to wash her hair after work. She was worried it smelled of leather.

'Actually, I'm trying not to get too excited about something important,' she told him.

'Crikey, sounds a big deal.'

'It is.' She spoke in a rush, as she told him about Teddy putting in a good word with the Scoresbys and their hopes they might get an audition. 'Then we'll be able to see what sort of club it is,' she ended, glancing at him quickly.

'Are you sure it's on the up and up?' A doubtful frown creased his brow.

'Why shouldn't it be? Or do you think we're not good enough?'

'It's not that. But you are very young.'

'Mum always says that.' She felt like sulking as they entered Island Gardens. 'You could seem a bit more interested.'

'Oh, I am,' he said quietly and his gaze fell on her face. 'I'm interested in everything you do. It's just that . . .'

'What?'

'Nothing.'

'What aren't you telling me?' She pinched his arm. 'It's not like you to hold back.'

He gave her a long steady look. 'It's just that the two brothers who run it have got a mixed reputation. They opened a place up West that is said to be one of these gentlemen's clubs. Only it ain't very gentlemanly, if you see what I mean?'

Marie shook her head. 'No, I don't.'

Bing hesitated as he looked at her. 'The rumour is, it's for all these wealthy blokes who want a higher class of . . . well, women.'

Marie raised her eyebrows. 'So you're just adding to the rumour, is that right? Or do you know for sure?'

He took a long breath. 'No, I don't. And I'll admit, it's not up to me to put you off—'

'You won't,' Marie interrupted. 'My information is that this club is looking for quality acts, not hiring loose women. That is what you meant, isn't it?'

'I was only trying to help.'

'Well, you haven't. You've put the damper on it instead.'

'You did ask.'

'I wish I hadn't now.'

'Marie, I'm sorry. I spoke out of turn. But it's only because I care for you.'

Marie was upset. 'I think going out again with each other would be a mistake.'

He reached for her hand. 'Forget what I said. I won't mention it again. Let me drive you up West next Saturday.'

'No, thanks. We'll be busy practising.' She wanted to let him know she was serious about the Duke's.

'When can we meet, then?'

She heaved a deep breath. 'Bing, you are a very nice person. I'm sure you will find someone nice to settle down with. A girl who wants a home and a family and vegetables in the garden, just like you do.'

His eyebrows shot up. 'You mean you don't want vegetables in your garden?'

'Don't try to make me laugh. It won't work this time.'

'Tell you what, we'll toss for it. Heads we go up West, tails we call it a day and that's the last you'll ever see of Bobby Bing Brown. You have my word on it.'

'But that still gives you a chance.'

'Yes, a small one. Go on, live dangerously.'

She sighed and rolled her eyes. 'All right. But hurry as I've got to get back.'

He took a penny from his trouser pocket and flipped it. They both gazed at the coin on the back of his hand.

She groaned. 'Heads! That's not fair.'

'It's fate,' he said, grinning. 'All right, friends it is, but one day we'll drive up to Lyons and have a cream tea, then walk along the Embankment.'

'You don't give up easy, do you?'

'No.'

'I've got to go home,' she said, blushing. 'Vesta's waiting.'

'Righto. Hold on to this.' Again he gave her his arm. On the way, he began to talk about his parents, Ivy and Johnny Brown, who lived in Aldgate. He reminded her he'd done a little travelling in the Navy. He even said that he would like to go to America to see his idol, Bing Crosby.

'So you have got a dream,' she said in surprise.

'I don't expect I'll get round to it.'

'America . . .' she breathed, thinking of all the famous film stars she'd seen at the pictures. 'I'd like to visit, too.'

'You're on. With your looks and my money we could go a long way.'

She burst into laughter. As they walked, Marie knew she liked him – perhaps liked him too much. He always seemed to be able to win her round. But she had promised herself that romance wasn't yet for her. And she meant to keep that promise, even if Bing Brown had other ideas!

Chapter 9

'I'm not convinced we've got it right,' said Marie later that day after they had been practising to the records in their bedroom. They had the place to themselves as Ada and Hector had gone out. The Victor phonograph needed a new needle but that hadn't stopped them dressing up in their costumes; pale pink and silver dresses with full skirts and taffeta petticoats that bounced around them as they danced. They only just fitted now, Marie reflected as she tried to adjust the bodice. The dresses had seen many alterations since the day Ada had first found them hidden under piles of crumpled clothing on the market stall. But they still looked pretty.

'Why's that?' Vesta sank down on the bed, raising her feet to study the scuffs on her well-worn tap shoes. 'These songs are our signature tunes, made famous by our namesakes.'

'Yes, but it's all swing and jazz nowadays. Fanny Brice and Josephine Baker are more popular.'

'I still think our songs will do.'

Marie frowned thoughtfully as she played with the soft

silk bows on her dress. 'We know the words to "Falling In Love Again". We've sung it enough on the way home from work since we saw Marlene Dietrich looking so glamorous in *The Blue Angel*.'

'Yes, that's right, we do.'

'And what about "I Found A Million Dollar Baby"? We know the words to that too.'

Vesta giggled. 'It will make a change from all the old stuff.'

'Come on, we'll begin with Marlene's song.' Marie dragged Vesta up from the bed. 'Let's look in the mirror and practise.'

'Don't make me laugh.'

'I won't. This is serious.'

They practised for a good half an hour and finally got all the words right.

'We don't sound much like her,' said Marie afterwards.

'No, we're more like stray cats. But with a little more practice we'll be all right.' They were laughing when a loud knock came on the front door. When they rushed out to open it, they found Teddy standing in the hall.

'What are you dressed like that for?' His dark eyes gleamed as he stared at their costumes. Wearing a dark grey suit and a matching Homburg he looked very handsome. Marie could feel Vesta almost wilting beside her.

'We're rehearsing,' said Marie, feeling a little uncomfortable as Teddy's eyes strayed down to their bare legs and stayed there.

'Is there any news?' asked Vesta hopefully.

'Mr Scoresby has agreed to see you next Saturday.'

Vesta flew into his arms. 'Oh, Teddy, thank you!'

Marie was embarrassed as Teddy held her close. 'I told you I would try to fix you up.'

Vesta disentangled herself slowly. 'We're very grateful.'

Marie nodded. 'Thank you,' she said quietly.

'I'll drive you in my new car, if you like,' said Teddy casually, leaning a shoulder on the door jamb. 'But I'll be singing later that evening so you'll have to make your own way home.'

'Thank you,' said Vesta again, staring up at him with adoring eyes.

'Six thirty sharp, then.' He reached out and drew a finger down Vesta's cheek. 'Mr Scoresby will be impressed, I'm sure.'

Marie was suddenly aware again of their old dresses. In this last year the twins had both filled out and the buttons on the backs of their bodices were straining. She didn't like Teddy's expression, but Vesta seemed flattered.

'Better be going.' He raised himself slowly. 'Bye, girls.'

'Bye, Teddy.' Vesta watched him go up the stairs. Then she closed the door and fell back against it, sighing dreamily. 'Oh, he's simply wonderful. Fancy getting us an audition. And he said we would catch Mr Scoresby's eye.'

'Don't get your hopes up,' Marie warned her. 'We've got to tell Mum first.'

'She can't stop us. And anyway, why would she want to?'

But Marie knew they were dreading breaking the news to Ada.

'Why didn't you ask me first?' Ada stood stiffly in the kitchen after placing her bags of groceries on the table. 'I don't want you going off somewhere strange on your own.' Ada's face had gone white after Vesta had told her.

'But it's the Duke's, Mum,' pleaded Vesta. 'Everyone's talking about it and saying how posh it is. And anyway, Teddy will take us there in his car so we won't be on our own.' Red spots appeared on her cheeks and Marie waited for the full force of Vesta's disappointment to show itself.

'I should have been asked,' repeated Ada, beginning to unpack her groceries. 'Now take off those costumes. They're too small.'

'Teddy said we looked pretty in them.'

Ada glared at Vesta. 'You must tell him you can't go.'

'We can't do that,' Vesta gasped. 'He's gone out of his way to get us an audition. The Scoresby brothers are looking for quality acts. We're very lucky to get in.'

Ada turned to Marie. 'And what have you to say for yourself? Were you part of all this secret scheme?'

'It wasn't secret, Mum. It was just a vague offer from Teddy at first. Neither of us knew it would come to anything.'

'You were wearing those when he called?' Ada nodded to their dresses.

'It was just a coincidence,' Marie insisted. 'We were practising in our bedroom.'

'It was very underhand of you to go behind my back.'

'Only because we knew you'd object,' Vesta cried angrily. 'We're eighteen now and can do as we please.'

'Not in this house, you can't,' Ada said as Hector strode in.

'What's going on?' he asked, looking from one to the other as he heard the last of Ada's words.

'Your daughters will tell you.'

Marie knew that, as far as Hector was concerned, they could do no wrong. Vesta knew this too, and immediately turned on the tears. 'Mum's being horrible.'

'Now, now,' Hector soothed, threading an arm around Vesta's shoulders as she lifted a handkerchief to her eyes. 'What's this all about, Ada?'

'A storm in a teacup,' said Ada, waving her hand, 'but no doubt your presence will make it worse.'

Hector looked under his bushy eyebrows. 'Come along, Ada, this just needs a little discussion.'

'My answer is no,' Ada said firmly. 'They want to go off to this club that we don't know anything about. It could turn out to be a den of thieves, for all we know.'

Hector frowned at his wife. 'What club?'

Ada became flushed. 'Somewhere called the Duke's. Now don't go on about it as you'll only encourage them. They ain't old enough to go gallivanting round dives.'

Hector let out a long sigh. 'Ada, our girls have been singing and dancing since they were old enough to walk.'

'Not in clubs, they haven't.'

'This is our big chance, Dad,' Vesta told him eagerly, the tears shining in her eyes. 'We'll never get another one like it. Teddy's got an audition lined up for us at the Duke's. It's a real posh club and the owners will only audition good acts.'

'Is that so?' His eyebrows lifted and he nodded to the shopping. 'Well, give your mother a chance to think about it. I can see she's only just come in and could do with a nice cuppa.'

Marie knew her father was trying to smooth things over. With his walrus moustache and dark hair, only very slightly going grey, he looked very distinguished. He had an upright bearing and booming voice that could be dramatic one minute and quite normal the next, a legacy of the years he had spent touring the country.

'Tea won't make the slightest bit of difference,' said Ada, throwing him a stony look. 'I won't change my mind.'

'Ada, love—' Hector began, but quickly stopped as Ada's warning gaze landed on him. He turned to Vesta and said meekly, 'Your mother is the voice of reason here.'

Ada seemed satisfied and nodded. 'You already have a good job, Vesta. You don't want another one.'

'I hate the factory!' exclaimed Vesta angrily. 'Can't you see how unhappy I am there? Every moment I'm at

Ellisdon's, I long to be away from it. And now I could be. It's my one chance. Well, it's *our* chance,' Vesta corrected, looking at Marie. 'We have decent voices and can dance, and it would be no problem entertaining people. After all, that's what Dad is, an entertainer!'

Hector smiled at the compliment. He patted his daughter's shoulder. 'Yes, it does seem to run in the family, Ada. Just look at our daughters! They're beautiful and talented. They could have fine careers ahead of them if only we—'

'Hector!' Ada interrupted, her face now going red. 'Just tell me this. Who are these Scoresby brothers? Why should they be interested in two young girls who have never done anything professionally? Why don't they employ experienced people if they want new acts? Oh, it's no use – why can't you see the dangers?' She took in a sharp breath and placed her hands over her mouth. Her eyes went to the faces around her and then, turning sharply, she ran from the room. Everyone heard the bedroom door slam.

Hector gave a deep sigh. 'I'd better go after her.'

But Vesta caught his arm. 'Why can't Mum encourage us, Dad? What's wrong with wanting to better ourselves?'

'Nothing at all, love,' Hector said mildly. 'It's just that she don't want you to take risks or come to any harm.'

'We wouldn't, not with Teddy beside us,' Vesta insisted.

'He's a nice enough lad,' Hector agreed, rubbing his chin. 'But I'm not sure your mother would understand.'

'But we're turned eighteen and can look after ourselves,' Vesta cried as she, too, ran from the room.

When another door banged, Hector raised his eyes. 'What is happening to this household, Marie?'

Marie sat down on the chair. 'I don't know, Dad.'

'Do you want to go to this audition as much as your sister?'

Marie nodded. 'Yes, I do.'

Hector smiled and patted her arm. 'I'll see what I can do.'

As she sat alone, Marie couldn't help thinking that the answer to her father's question about what was happening to the family had something to do with Teddy. The trouble had started when Vesta had fallen under his spell. Perhaps their mother was frightened that Teddy would take Vesta away.

Elsie looked at Marie with fondness. She had come in to find the argument still in progress and Marie had told her what had happened.

'Well, Marie, what do you think about all this? Is that young whippersnapper Teddy to be trusted?'

Marie wanted to say he was, for Vesta's sake, but she held back. 'He did keep his word to Vesta and spoke up for us, even though I thought he might just be boasting.'

Elsie reflected on this. 'He seems nice enough, pays his rent and don't cause no trouble. But there's something I can't put me finger on. And when I have that feeling about someone, I'm usually right.'

As much as Marie wanted to go to the audition, she felt the same as Elsie about Teddy. At the back of Marie's mind was Bing's warning about the Duke's not being the right sort of club.

'When he came to this house earlier this year,' said Elsie, her face thoughtful, 'I took him at face value. Well, he's been no trouble and he looked clean and smart and had a fortnight's money up front. Not many like that these days. And you know I've got a soft spot for anyone connected with the boards. The room above was gathering dust, with no other enquiries to rent it, so I took him on. But that's as far as my knowledge stretches.'

Marie saw Elsie touch the many gold rings she had on her fingers. She was wearing a black dress, which made the gold look even brighter. In her ears were gold studs and her dark eyes were very piercing. 'Ah, well, it will all come out in the wash, as they say. Your mother will have the last say, even though you girls are nearly women now.'

'Elsie, why is Mum so against us performing?' Marie asked suddenly. 'It always causes a row between her and Dad.'

Elsie straightened up slowly, not meeting Marie's gaze. 'I told you, she's protective.'

'But is it only that?'

Elsie walked to the door quickly. 'Sorry, love, I've got to go. My friend from Bethnal Green is coming over and I've got to make tea. See you later.'

Marie noted Elsie hadn't answered her. Did she know more than she was saying? Elsie always gave a straight answer to any question.

Marie watched Elsie walk across the hall and take her key from her pocket. She always kept the key to her own rooms on her, rather than leaving it to hang on a string. She had too many precious things to risk losing.

Marie closed the door and wondered if her father had succeeded in changing her mother's mind. All was quiet, which usually meant the calm before the storm. But if Mum had her way and refused to let them go, who would be the one to tell Teddy?

Vesta refused to come out of the bedroom the next morning. After eating his breakfast, Hector decided to go out for a walk. 'Just to get a breath of air,' he told Ada. 'Would you like to come with me, dear?'

'No, I've got things to do.'

After he'd gone Ada sat at the kitchen table and dropped her head in her hands.

'What's the matter, Mum?' Marie sat beside her. 'Are you tired?'

'No more than usual.' Ada looked up at Marie. 'Your sister is being unreasonable. She makes me feel as though I'm a terrible mother. She hasn't spoken to me or eaten a thing.'

'She'll eat when she's hungry.'

'I want the best for you girls,' insisted Ada. 'But I'm afraid to let you go out into that world.'

'Why?'

'Sometimes the entertainment business can be dangerous.'

'But we have to learn.'

Ada looked hard at her. 'Your father sees only the good in everything.'

Marie smiled. 'That's why we love him. You can't shield us from life for ever, Mum.'

'You know so little about what life holds in store.'

'Do you want us to stay at Ellisdon's for ever?' Marie asked. 'Even though Vesta is unhappy there?'

'I didn't know she was. Are you unhappy too?'

Marie gave a brief shrug. 'I don't mind it, but I'd rather be singing and dancing.'

'But that's just a whim,' Ada said gently. 'One day you'll get married and have a family like all girls do.'

'Vesta and me want more in life.'

'Is that why you're not seeing Bing very often? I thought he was interested in you.'

Marie blushed. 'He's just a friend.'

'I see,' sighed Ada, looking dejected.

'Going on the stage is all me and Vesta ever think of.' Marie knew she had to tell the truth even if it was painful for Ada to accept. 'Since we were little girls, it's been our dream. You know that.'

'But you are still my two little girls,' Ada said heavily, 'and not grown-up.'

Marie gazed into her mother's sad face. 'But we are.'

Ada gave a little sob and wiped a tear from the corner of her eye with her handkerchief. 'What would happen if you went away? You might forget your dad and me.'

Marie's blue eyes filled with tenderness. 'Mum, we love you and would never do that.'

Ada sniffed and sighed deeply. 'I suppose I'll have to give in or risk losing you anyway. You had better tell Vesta I've changed my mind.' She added sharply, 'On the condition your father goes with you.'

'Oh, thanks, Mum.'

'I hope I won't regret this.'

'You won't.' Marie kissed her mother's cheek. 'Vesta will be very happy.'

Ada nodded. 'She always is when she gets her own way. What songs were you rehearsing?'

' "Algy" and "When I Take My Morning Promenade". It was you and Dad who gave us our names and set us off down the path to fame and fortune.' Marie laughed at her joke, but Ada only frowned.

'We had no idea you'd be following in those famous footsteps.'

'It's early days yet,' Marie pointed out. 'It could all come to nothing. If the Scoresby brothers don't like us, then you'll have nothing to fret about.'

Ada gave a sad smile. 'Who could not like such beautiful girls?'

They hugged and Marie felt Ada's small, wiry body tremble against her. She loved her mother very much and only wanted to make her proud, not add to all the worry in her life.

★　　★　　★

By the time Saturday came around, Marie was worried she would forget every word and Vesta was a bag of nerves. But from the moment Hector had agreed to go with them to the audition, Ada had shown interest. She had loosened the buttons on their costumes so the bodices weren't so tight and lengthened the hems half an inch.

'Wear your ordinary shoes and coats to the audition, girls,' Ada instructed them on the night they were to leave. 'And I'll pack your tap shoes in a bag. You may use a little lipstick, but no other make-up.'

'It's too warm for our coats,' complained Vesta. 'And anyway, they're old.'

'You've got nothing else,' replied Ada, bustling around them. 'Now stop complaining.'

She kissed them both goodbye, hugging them as though it was the last time she would ever see them.

'Please take care of them, Hector.'

'Course I will, Ada.' Hector was wearing his long black cape and big theatrical floppy hat. Marie knew he wanted to look the part in front of Mr Scoresby. 'They won't be out of my sight for a moment. Now just you enjoy your chat with Elsie. We won't be late home.'

At Teddy's knock they all rushed into the hall.

'Do you mind if Dad comes with us?' Vesta said quickly, blushing as she looked into Teddy's dark eyes.

'Well, no, but Mr Scoresby doesn't like—'

'Just to give them a bit of moral support,' interrupted Hector with a wink, pushing out his chest in a robust manner.

'I've allowed them to go this time,' Ada added sternly, 'but only because Hector is with them.'

Marie saw Teddy's surprised expression, but he said no more and led the way out to the car. Marie climbed in the back with Vesta whilst Hector sat at the front beside Teddy. Marie glanced over her shoulder through the wide glass window and they waved to Ada.

When they were out of sight, Vesta whispered, 'I was really embarrassed when Mum said Dad has to be with us.'

'She let us go and that's what counts.'

'I had to starve for a whole morning before she agreed.'

Marie smiled. 'You got your way in the end.'

'Of course,' whispered Vesta with a grin. 'I always do. Even so, it'd be nicer if we was on our own without Dad tagging along.'

Unlike Vesta, Marie was glad Hector was with them. What harm was there in his being at their sides? In fact, if this new world was full of dangers, as Ada feared, Hector would soon put them right.

Chapter 10

Teddy parked the car in Duke Street, Poplar, a road full of light, hustle and bustle with the evening traffic going by and the usual crowds making their way to the Queen's for the evening performance.

'The staff use the back entrance,' Teddy told them, walking past the two big green doors over which there was a sign saying 'The Duke's'. 'Follow me.'

He led them round to a dark alley filled with the stench of the dustbins from the café close by. Halfway down, just visible beyond all the rubbish strewn across their path, was a badly lit doorway. Teddy pushed the door open and one by one they filed down the flight of narrow steps. Marie heard the sound of a piano playing, together with the familiar tap of dancing feet.

As they entered the basement, they were met by a thick fog of cigarette smoke. Through this Marie could just about see a line of four girls dressed in shorts and blouses. They were dancing on a small wooden floor in front of a raised dais, which she took to be the stage. Here stood an upright piano, and the man seated in front of it with a cigarette dangling from his mouth was playing the popular melody 'My Baby Just Cares For Me'.

Marie gazed around at the big, noisy room with a low ceiling lit by dim lights. Chairs and tables were set out around the small dance floor. A long counter went round the bar in a banana shape. A row of mirrors hung behind the racks of optics. The ashtrays on the top of the counter were full of squashed butts. A young woman, wearing a turban and low-cut blouse, was trying to clear up the mess. A broom stood to one side, a pile of litter ready to be swept away. The air smelled of stale beer and tobacco, but Marie didn't find it unpleasant. In fact, it was all rather exciting.

'Wait here,' said Teddy sharply. 'I'll go and find Mr Scoresby.'

They stood still, watching the dancers, who did a few more steps, then one of them signalled an end to the pianist and they dispersed. A blonde girl with lots of make-up sat at the bar and smoked. The others went to sit at one of the tables. In no time at all, they were smoking too.

Hector placed his hands on their shoulders. 'Well, this is a little different from the Queen's, I have to say.'

'It's exciting,' breathed Vesta. 'I hope we'll be good enough.'

'You'll knock 'em dead,' Hector whispered under his breath.

They nodded obediently as they always did when being advised by their father, although he had long since given up taking any great interest in their routines. Marie smiled to herself. They had different ideas from his now, and he didn't appreciate modern music. But he still had faith in their talent.

'Do you think the piano player will know our numbers?' asked Marie.

'Just sing your songs as I taught you to,' Hector advised, 'and you won't go far wrong.'

But Marie was beginning to have doubts about their act. When they came in the girls had been rehearsing a popular song. Now the pianist started to play again, filling the air with a well-known current blues melody. What good would their old, dated songs be at a club like this?

'Remember,' said Hector, 'to sing the words clearly so everyone can hear them. Don't be put off by the bright lights.'

Just then a door opened behind the bar. A tall, heavily built man in a dark suit strode into the room. Teddy followed at his heels, pulling out a chair at one of the tables so that he could sit down. The man, who Marie thought must be Mr Scoresby, took a cigar from his pocket and waited for Teddy to bend down and light it. Despite Teddy pointing in their direction, Mr Scoresby ignored him and slowly crossed one leg over another.

The blonde dancer at the bar stood up and went over to him. She placed her hand on her hip and hesitated but he waved her away. A few minutes later she had joined the other girls and they all left the room. Even the piano player was dismissed with a casual flick of the hand.

When the room was empty, Teddy hurried over. 'Mr Scoresby will see you girls now. But, Mr Haskins, you—' he began, only to stop as Hector marched forward, propelling the girls with him.

'Mr Scoresby, these are my daughters, Vesta and Marie,' Hector announced as they drew near. 'Being an actor and performer myself, I—'

Wally Scoresby raised his huge hand again. This movement alone silenced Hector. A pair of narrowed eyes turned on them, slowly evaluating their presence.

Marie shuddered. Wally Scoresby was an extremely ugly man. He had a very large head covered in lank black hair thick with grease. His small eyes were close-set, and his long nose dominated a mean-looking mouth. His most unattractive feature was his skin. On one side, his face looked as though it had been burned, with the marks still red and raw. He had no smile or welcome, just a cold, critical stare and more puffs of smoke. Then he gave a sharp nod to Teddy, who almost ran over to Hector.

'Mr Scoresby would like you to wait outside.'

'Why?' Hector asked in an affronted voice.

'I did try to say before . . . but Mr Scoresby always auditions in private.'

'But I'm only going to watch,' Hector argued.

'This is a house rule,' said Teddy in a hurried voice. 'Just the act and Mr Scoresby.'

To Marie's surprise, Hector seemed lost for words. He mumbled to himself and twirled his moustache uncertainly.

'We'll be all right, Dad.' Marie clutched her father's arm. 'Rules are rules. Wait for us at the entrance in Duke Street. We won't be long.'

Eventually Hector nodded. 'Well, I suppose if that's the rule I'll have to go along with it.'

'Up you go on the stage,' whispered Teddy when Hector had reluctantly left. 'And you'd better be quick as Mr Scoresby is a busy man.'

'Where shall we leave our coats?' asked Marie.

'On one of the chairs.'

'Will the piano player come back?'

'No. He's gone off for a break now, before he starts playing again. Now, please, be quick.'

Marie was surprised at Teddy's nervousness. He had never seemed that way before. He was usually very self-composed, even arrogant. But his personality changed here, in the presence of Mr Scoresby.

They went close to the stage, took off their coats and put on their tap shoes. Vesta looked almost frightened as she stood there and Marie wasn't feeling much better herself.

'Well?' demanded a powerful voice suddenly. 'I ain't got all day. Get on with it.'

Marie clasped Vesta's hand and squeezed it as they shuffled into the middle of the small floor. Their voices came faintly as they began the first verse of 'Algy'. They couldn't see Mr Scoresby's reaction through the foggy atmosphere and Marie hurried the pace a little, feeling apprehensive as they went into their dancing routine. At least they both finished in time, she thought as they stood back to back, arms folded, with cheeky grins on their faces.

After a while, Marie's heart began to thud. Her smile was forced and her body was rigid with tension. What did Mr Scoresby think of them? Why didn't he say something? The seconds passed and still nothing.

'Let's go straight into "Promenade",' Marie whispered.

Vesta didn't reply. Marie gave her a little dig with her elbow and, to her relief, Vesta followed into their second song. But halfway through, a bone-chilling shout came from Mr Scoresby. 'What in the blazes are you singing? I ain't never heard such rubbish!'

Marie froze. Another long silence came. After what seemed like an eternity, Teddy came up to them. 'Mr Scoresby would like to speak to you.'

Marie's legs were shaking as they made their way over. As they stood in front of the club owner she tried not to breathe in the pungent smoke of his cigar.

'This a cabaret club, girls, ain't you sussed that yet?' barked Wally Scoresby. 'The Duke's is for grown-ups, not kids. Our audience looks for a bit of class on their evening out on the town. You can sing, I'll grant you. But those numbers would go down well at a Sally Army Christmas dinner! Now, I'll give you one more chance. Sing something I can recognize.'

Marie felt sick as they turned back and stood in the centre of the wooden floor. They'd only had time to practise their new songs for a week. And they hadn't brought Hector's top hat or cane.

'I can't do it,' whispered Vesta, shaking beside her. 'I've forgotten all the words.'

'No you haven't. Let's sing "Falling In Love Again" first.'

'You've got two minutes,' warned Wally Scoresby. 'And then you're out on your ear, the pair of you.'

Marie was nervous but now she also felt angry. Wally Scoresby was a very rude man, speaking to them in such a way. He had sent their father away without so much as a thank-you and hadn't even asked them their names.

'Come on, let's show him what we're made of,' she whispered to Vesta, who stood rooted to the spot.

Marie drew back her shoulders. He'd admitted they had good voices; now they must prove they could sing.

Chapter 11

'What happened?' Hector drew them against his big chest as they met in the dark, unpleasant-smelling alley.

'You should have waited out the front, Dad,' Marie scolded him gently.

'I was ready to rush in if you called.'

'I'm glad you didn't,' said Vesta in a shaky voice. 'We showed him we could sing, didn't we, Marie?'

'Yes.' Marie could hardly get her breath. After their performance, Mr Scoresby had said very little. She could still feel the adrenalin rushing through her blood. 'It wasn't quite what we expected.'

'He didn't like our songs,' blurted Vesta. 'They weren't modern enough.'

'What!' Hector exclaimed. 'Vesta Tilley and Marie Lloyd had great success with those music-hall classics. That's why I taught you to sing them.'

'Yes, but it was a long time ago,' said Marie gently. She didn't want to offend her father. 'He wanted to hear something more modern.'

'Modern? Such as?' asked Hector, frowning.

'Come along, we'll tell you everything on the way home.'

Soon, arm in arm, they were stepping out from the alley and into the bright lights of Duke Street. Marie listened to Vesta describing Wally Scoresby's reaction when they had sung 'Falling In Love Again'.

'He really liked us, Dad,' Vesta said excitedly, 'and when we did our second number, "You Must Have Been A Beautiful Baby", he even tapped his foot.'

'Did you know all the words to these songs?'

'Yes, we sing them on the way home from work, after listening to them on the radio.'

'Clever girls,' said Hector thoughtfully.

'Marlene Dietrich is very popular these days,' Marie enthused. 'She made her name as Lola-Lola, a cabaret singer, in *The Blue Angel*.'

'Ah,' said Hector, nodding, 'I've heard of her, of course, and seen the posters outside the cinemas. In my day it would have been the young Mary Pickford who everyone followed.'

'Yes, but now talkies are all the rage,' said Marie, her eyes wide.

'This is 1934 now,' Vesta agreed. 'It's different from when you were young, Dad.'

Hector gave a hearty laugh. 'I'm lucky to have you two girls to keep me young.' He frowned. 'Can't say I took to Scoresby, though. And your mother, well, she'd not like him at all. Oh, no!'

'Oh!' Vesta drew to a sudden halt. 'Please, Dad, don't tell her that. If we get a job at the Duke's it will mean so much to us.'

'You can twist me round your little finger,' Hector said, half frowning, half smiling. 'We'll see, eh?'

Vesta pouted. 'Anyway, we haven't got it yet. He said he'd think about it.'

They didn't have to wait long to find out as Teddy's car appeared. It honked loudly, causing other drivers to move over as he drew in to the kerb.

'Mr Scoresby sent me after you,' he called breathlessly as he leaped across to the pavement. 'Would you like to sing at the Duke's next Saturday?'

'Oh, yes, yes!' Vesta jumped up and down, clapping her hands.

'Wait a minute,' interrupted Hector, placing a restraining hand on her shoulder. 'Your mother has to give her approval.'

'Yes,' said Vesta, suddenly anxious, 'but she will, won't she?'

Once again, Hector frowned. 'This is very sudden, young man.'

Teddy looked impatient. 'Mr Scoresby doesn't make the offer to everyone, you know.'

'Please, Dad, say yes.'

Hector nodded slowly. 'Only if I can come with you.'

Teddy gave a cold smile. 'You can speak to Mr Scoresby about it.' He paused. 'In fact, Mr Scoresby told me to tell you there's a job going at the club for someone like yourself.'

Hector frowned, his eyebrows meeting over his nose. 'A job – for me?'

'Yes.'

'But I didn't perform,' Hector protested. 'I was sent out.'

'Mr Scoresby doesn't like any distractions.'

Hector gave a little mutter, but finally nodded. 'I suppose it's understandable.'

'However,' continued Teddy hesitantly, 'if you don't want to take up the offer . . .?'

'Not at all,' responded Hector eagerly. 'I'd like to see what it's all about.'

'That's settled, then. Please be at the club for nine next Saturday.'

'Thank you for coming to tell us,' Vesta called after Teddy as he jumped back in the car.

When he'd driven off, she threw her arms around Hector. 'Isn't Teddy wonderful, Dad? Oh, I can't believe this is happening to us!'

Holding his daughter gently, Hector drew his fingers over his walrus moustache. 'Scoresby must have been impressed by my appearance and posture.' He drew a smooth hand down the front of his cape. 'Remember, girls, it always pays to keep yourself in trim.'

'What will you say to Mum?' Vesta asked her father, a suspicious expression on her face.

'That I'll be with you and she has no need to worry.'

'Oh!' Vesta hugged Hector tight. 'I love you, Dad.'

Marie looked into Hector's shining face. He wore a very happy expression as he held Vesta close. Could all this be happening, Marie wondered, as he drew her into

his arms too. They all started to talk and laugh at the same
time. But Marie couldn't help wondering what interest
Mr Scoresby had in her father. Had Teddy told him
Hector was a busker? If so, what kind of songs would Mr
Scoresby want him to sing?

As, in very high spirits, they continued their walk
home in the dusky summer's night, they listened to
Hector's plans of what he would sing at the club.

'Perhaps,' said Marie cautiously, 'it might be better to
find out what Mr Scoresby wants.'

But Hector gave a rumble of laughter. 'You were
always the careful one, my love. Just like your mother;
solid as a rock. But tonight we've all had a stroke of luck,
wouldn't you say?'

'Yes,' agreed Vesta immediately.

'The Haskins family are about to make their mark on the
East End,' said Hector with a broad grin. 'And let me do the
talking when we get in. I know just the thing to say.'

As Marie met Vesta's gaze, they both silently acknowledged they doubted this. Though neither of them would
hurt Hector's feelings by saying so.

Teddy jumped cheerfully down the steps of the basement
and entered the dimly lit club. This time he had a genuine
smile on his face. Wally would be pleased with him. Getting
the two girls on board was a feather in his cap. And his
suggestion regarding their father had brought an ugly smile
to Wally's face, as they both realized the old boy could be
of use to them. Luckily, his plan had worked very nicely.

Teddy looked around the deserted club and saw Irene attempting her work behind the bar. Her listless movements told him that the bosses were not around. After the departure of Sid Rigler, the hired hand, Irene had been told to clear up the place. Teddy had also been allotted some of Sid's duties, which hadn't gone down at all well with Teddy. He hated sweeping the dusty floors and cleaning out the lavatories. He didn't mind attending to the stage and the lights, but he was above more menial jobs.

'Drink?' asked Irene, wiping the bar top with a cloth. She removed the cigarette from between her lips and ground it out in the still full ashtray.

'Where's Wally?'

'Out the back with Leo.'

Teddy perched himself on one of the tall stools, making sure his gaze was directed at the door that led out into the passage and the office. He wasn't taking any chances. If Wally caught him sitting around, it wouldn't bode well for him.

'A quick one.' He nodded to the brandy. 'A double.'

Irene smiled, her normally garish red lips distinctly pale. Teddy studied her slim figure as she turned and poured his drink. Nice legs and a good arse. She called herself a dancer, like the other girls did. He smiled to himself. Blonde Shirley was next on his list, but he'd have to wait as she was amusing Leo at the moment. Not that she would last long; Leo's women never did. Perhaps it was because Wally used them first; it was share and share alike for the Scoresbys. Amusing to Teddy, and quite enjoyable, when he was left to pick up the crumbs.

Irene turned back to him, her turban covering her thick, dark hair, which matched her exotic dark eyes. Sadly the rest of her face was plump and her mouth set in a disagreeable pout. The last time they had gone to bed, he'd made a note to finish with her. If she'd kept her mouth shut, their affair might have gone on longer. But she drove him crazy with her gossip. The last people he wanted to think about when he was in the mood were the Scoresbys.

Pulling back his shoulders and tugging the white cuffs of his shirt below the jacket sleeves, he lifted the tumbler and sucked down the hot amber liquid. He had a thing for brandy. Especially when it was free, when Irene poured him one.

'When are you gonna come round?' Irene placed her elbows on the bar and cupped her chin in her hands seductively. Teddy wanted to tell her she looked ridiculous in the turban, trying to make eyes at him. But he was careful. He didn't want to make an enemy of anyone here at the club.

'Not yet,' he told her. 'Wally's on the prowl.'

'I'm over him.' Irene tossed her head, another silly movement. 'He can't treat me like a common tart.'

'But he's not over you.' Teddy gave her a helpless shrug. 'You're too pretty to forget. I saw him watching you. And we both know what that means.'

Irene fluttered her dark eyelashes. 'Teddy bear, I do believe you've got a case of the green-eye.'

He smirked. 'Could be.'

She laughed, squirming on the counter. 'He ain't a patch on you.'

Teddy lowered his voice confidingly. 'Listen, I don't want to risk it. Not when Wally's just outed Sid. You won't see him back here again.'

This bombshell made Irene's jaw drop. 'Sid's really gone?'

Teddy nodded slowly. 'Keep it under your hat.'

'How do you know?'

'I drove Sid to Hoxton last night. On Wally's orders.'

'Hoxton?'

Teddy watched the penny drop slowly.

'You mean, to that bookie he was ducking?'

Teddy nodded again. 'Wally didn't want the bookie coming on his turf. And Sid was up to his eyeballs.'

'So what happened to Sid?' Irene had stopped moving and was staring at him.

'I told you, he won't be coming back.'

Irene's mouth fell open slowly. 'Christ, Teddy, you mean Wally – he—'

'Watch it!' muttered Teddy, downing the last of the brandy as the door opened. 'Wally's back.'

Irene turned sharply away and Teddy slid off the stool. The alcohol gave him a buzz, but it didn't stop the blood draining from his face as he hurried round to Wally Scoresby.

'I told the girls, Mr Scoresby, and their father. I said exactly what you told me to say.'

Wally Scoresby stared at him and slid a cigar from the inside pocket of his hand-made Savile Row jacket. Teddy felt his blood freeze as he stared into Wally's disfigured face. Teddy knew he deliberately used the burn scars from the acid attack a few years back to intimidate, but that didn't mean he was immune to Wally's power. The man was terrifying. He exuded threat, unlike his brother, Leo, who had the brains and beauty that Wally had missed out on. Leo had a knack for money and fictionalizing the accounts. Teddy knew that Wally's greed added up to a violent, cold-blooded individual, whilst Leo was by far the deadlier. He was good-looking, suave and charming; and possessed a killer instinct with a selective, intelligent force behind it. You couldn't fool Leo. But you stood a chance with Wally, if you played him right.

'Get me a drink,' Wally said.

Teddy returned to Irene, who was busying herself behind the bar. 'Quick, Irene, Mr Scoresby's usual.'

Irene glanced fearfully at him as she poured the whisky. Teddy grasped it, following after Wally, who had walked across the room to the stage.

'Here you are, Mr Scoresby.'

'I told you I wanted the women on their own.'

Teddy stopped dead. 'I'm sorry?'

'You will be if you don't listen in future.' Wally turned and pointed the lighted end of the cigar close to Teddy's face. 'What was their old man doing here?'

'I . . . I don't know,' faltered Teddy, momentarily unnerved. 'He just appeared when I collected them.'

'And you told him to clear off?'

'Well, I did try to—'

'You spineless little bleeder.' Wally snatched the tumbler from Teddy's hand. 'Do I have to spell everything out for you?'

'I'm sorry, Mr Scoresby,' Teddy said again, desperately.

Wally threw the drink back, then stared unblinkingly at Teddy. He pushed the empty glass into Teddy's chest. 'This time you're forgiven, Romeo. What age did you say those girls were?'

'Eighteen.'

'They're just acts, right, hired to sing and dance, if the law comes sniffing around? No booze, no mixing with the men, not this lot, anyway. I'm saving them for something else.'

'Yes, Mr Scoresby.'

'And, Teddy, get shot of Irene. She's a nosy cow.'

Teddy felt the blood pump at his temples. 'Me?' he repeated hoarsely.

'Yes, you Sonny Jim. You found her, you get rid of her. She knows too much. I don't trust her to keep her gob shut.'

'But what shall I tell her?'

Wally screwed up his face, making the disfigured side even more grotesque. 'That's your problem.'

'What if she . . . well, refuses?'

Wally gave him a deadpan expression. 'Learn from your mistakes, boy. You don't have no said to you. If you do, then you deal with the problem. And I mean deal with it. Right?'

Teddy swallowed. He felt as though he'd been hit by a truck. What did Wally mean? He'd delivered Sid to the bookie, but all in one piece and still breathing. He wasn't a killer. He couldn't take a life.

'Cheer up.' Wally poked him in the chest with his thumb, whilst his cigar smoke streamed into Teddy's eyes. 'This is just the beginning of your illustrious career in the entertainment business. You got talents, you have. Pretty ones. A nice clean boat race, no marks – yet. And I take it that's the way you'd like to keep it?'

Again Teddy swallowed as the lighted end of the cigar passed inches away from his face. He had nothing to say – he knew Wally wasn't looking for an answer.

'Now, run along, cos I'm the boss and though I'm enjoying meself standing here giving you grief – and you're standing there taking it cos you're too shit-scared to do anything else – I've got other things on my mind. Piss off and get the action ready for tonight. Tell the girls they do three numbers, then change and come out and mingle. They get the blokes plastered and make sure it's cash up front. Pedro's running the bar. He'll see the women's cocktails are water. If I catch any of the cows drinking, they're out the door that very minute. Got it?'

Teddy nodded again. He watched Wally walk to the bar and lean against it, stretching across to stroke Irene's shoulder. There was fear in her eyes as she looked up at him and he trailed his finger over her skin. The same kind of fear that was now inside Teddy's stomach.

Chapter 12

Marie and Vesta rehearsed their songs when they came home from work each night. They wanted to show Wally Scoresby that the Haskins girls had something special.

'Are you sure this man is a decent sort?' Ada asked again on Friday evening as she served up the supper. Hector had assured her when they'd returned from the audition that everything was all up and above board. Since then, he had embellished the truth, Marie noticed, by singing Wally Scoresby's praises.

'He definitely has an eye for talent,' Hector said as he tucked into a slice of meat pie and mash. 'Must have as he offered me a job too.'

'It sounds very odd to me,' Ada concluded, as she placed the girls' meals before them. 'Fancy offering you a job without seeing what you do!'

'You haven't much faith in me, Ada,' Hector replied mildly. 'I'll have a real job, like you've always wanted. I thought you would be pleased. I shall be there to keep an eye on the girls whilst doing my bit as well.'

'Hector, love,' Ada smiled patiently as she sat down at the table, 'you must have your head in the clouds. Even I know that your singing and reciting is now out of date.'

'Yes, Dad, Mum's right.' For once Vesta agreed with her mother. 'Can't you sing something modern?'

Hector put down his knife and fork with a sombre frown. 'Yes, perhaps I should.'

'Why don't you sing a Harry Lauder song?' asked Marie quickly. 'Your voice is just like his.'

Hector nodded. 'Good idea.'

'Now eat up, everyone.' Ada swiftly changed the subject. 'Whatever happens, you need to keep up your strength.'

After supper, Vesta put her arms around Ada. 'Thank you, Mum. I didn't think you'd be so encouraging.'

'You're big girls now. And anyway, your dad will be with you.'

Marie laughed. 'Or rather, we shall be with him!'

They all began to laugh as they washed and dried the dishes. But Marie could see that Ada was trying not to show her concern, whilst Hector was back to clearing his throat and puffing out his chest, fiddling with the knob on the radio in case Harry Lauder was being broadcast.

'I was afraid Mum might spoil things,' Vesta whispered that night as they lay in bed. 'But for once she encouraged us.'

'She wasn't expecting all three of us to get jobs.'

'Especially Dad, who is a bit old to take up performing again, don't you think?'

'Just goes to show it's never too late,' Marie said eagerly.

'But it's men like Teddy who catch a girl's eye.'

'One girl in particular,' Marie laughed as she lay back on the pillow.

Vesta sighed longingly as she, too, lay down. 'I haven't seen Teddy all week. Nor has Elsie.'

'Did you ask her, then?'

'Yes. She said he goes out early and comes in late. Some nights she doesn't think he comes home at all.'

'Where would he go?'

'To the club, of course. Oh, Marie, can you believe we are really going to sing and dance there?'

'It hasn't sunk in yet.'

'I wonder if there will be lots of people watching us.'

'There were plenty of tables and chairs.'

'I wonder what the other girls are like.'

'They were all very pretty and could dance. Now, I'd better turn off the lamp or else we'll never get to sleep. And tomorrow is our big day.'

'I'm too excited to sleep.'

But it was Marie who remained awake, wondering what would happen on their first performance at the club the following night. Mr Scoresby hadn't said anything about their costumes, so they planned to wear the pink dresses again. Their act was now word- and dance-perfect; the only thing missing was the sheet music for the piano player to follow.

This problem had been discussed with Elsie, who had

a friend who owned a music shop in Bethnal Green. But nothing had come of that yet.

Marie turned restlessly towards the open window. It was a hot summer's night, the last in August. As the warm breeze blew in, it carried all the scents of the river. She remembered the day at the park with Bing when the same smells had felt exciting and new, and she had challenged Bing to sing for her. She couldn't forget the way he had looked into her eyes and sung 'I'm Through With Love'. His voice had given her sweet chills. And yet the magic had seemed lost as soon as he'd talked about settling down.

Marie finally drifted off. She dreamed of sparkling costumes, the mellow lights of the Duke's and the attentive audience who, in her dreams, were sitting at the tables watching the twins' act. She saw their dressing rooms with little lights all around the mirrors. In her imagination she could smell the make-up and perfume of the artistes in the air. And the applause . . . she could even hear that too.

The next day they hurried home from work at twelve thirty. As soon as they got in, Elsie stopped them. 'Come in, I've got something for you. Your mother has gone to the market, so I'll make you a cuppa and we'll have some cake.'

'We'll just change into something cooler.' Marie and Vesta hurried into their bedroom and took off their heavy, uncomfortable working overalls. Their cool summer dresses felt much better. When they returned to Elsie, she had a tray of tea and cakes ready and waiting.

'Sit down and tuck in, girls.'

Marie loved Elsie's part of the house. They were sitting in two big, tub-shaped chairs made of leather. The room was full of old, quality furniture, heavy drapes and thick carpeting. Elsie had hundreds of mementoes of the theatre all over the shelves and on the walls. Being the landlady of the Cubby Hole, she had been given these over the years by artistes appearing at the Queen's and other London theatres.

There were all sorts of programmes, pamphlets, posters and postcards scattered over the surfaces. A tall glass-fronted cupboard was full of china pieces, and silver and gold from royal celebrations and distinguished theatrical events. Like the twins, she had a Victor phonograph in one corner, but the horn on Elsie's was like a big open flower, whilst theirs had a long, conical brass cone. There were piles of heavy Victor records next to this, and placed on the wall behind the cushion-strewn sofa was a bevelled mirror with decorative fans etched on either side. It was not just an interesting room, but a cosy one, furnished with memories from Elsie's past. Her collection of many photographs recorded her life with Joe in the East End. Joe had looked like their father with a big, drooping moustache. He had been a thespian in his early days, so Elsie said. She loved to talk about their years at the pub and the variety of people they met there.

But now Elsie was rooting around in her big Gladstone bag where she kept her important papers. 'I've managed to get you what you wanted for tonight.'

'Did your friend with the music shop have our music?' Vesta asked excitedly.

'No, I didn't have time to go up to Bethnal Green. So I popped into the Cubby Hole instead. I knew Bing would be able to help us.'

'Bing?' Marie and Vesta said together.

'Don't look so surprised. He is a musician, you know.'

'I wouldn't have called him that,' said Vesta.

'Then you'd be wrong, ducks,' said Elsie, passing them the sheet music. 'He's a very talented young man.'

'But he only plays in a pub,' protested Vesta as she sipped her tea. 'On an old honky-tonk piano.'

'Don't look down your nose at him, dear,' said Elsie warningly, giving Vesta a long stare. 'A lot of talent is discovered in places like the Cubby Hole. Joe and me saw many a good singer and dancer begin their career with a knees-up.'

'Sorry,' said Vesta, going red. 'I forgot you and Joe were the landlords.'

Elsie shrugged. 'It was different in those days, I'll grant you. Everyone could have a go. They all stood the same chance if they had talent.'

Marie smiled. 'Bing has got a lovely voice.'

'Not as good as Teddy's,' challenged Vesta quickly. 'But then Teddy has sung on the stage and at the Duke's.'

Seeing the colour rise in Marie's cheeks, Elsie held up her hand and changed the subject. 'Now, now, you two. Are you all set for tonight?'

'Yes,' said Marie excitedly.

'Behave yourselves and keep your father in line too.'

Marie knew that would be impossible. Once Hector was into his stride, no one could stop him.

'Watch this Scoresby fellow,' said Elsie, wagging her finger and making her gold bracelet jangle.

'Why?' giggled Vesta.

'There are rogues out there.'

'You sound like Mum.'

Elsie's smile disappeared. 'Your mother is being very brave letting you do as you want. I've tried to reassure her, but you girls must understand she worries about you.'

'And now she's worried about Dad too.' Vesta rolled her eyes.

'Now, now, Vesta,' said Elsie reprovingly. 'One day when you are mothers yourselves you'll know what worry is all about.' She smiled again. 'Finish up the last cakes, now. They're nice and creamy.'

'I'm afraid I feel too nervous,' admitted Vesta. 'Right here in the middle of my stomach.'

Marie had butterflies too and suspected it wasn't just down to thinking about tonight. A little flutter began inside her as Elsie had talked of Bing. Marie would never admit to it, but she had missed him. He and Charlie hadn't appeared after work, nor had Bing called round. If only Bing had more ambition and wanted to better himself. But all he could do was think about settling down.

And Marie didn't want that!

As they had missed the bus and walked all the way to the Duke's, Marie knew Hector was feeling tired. He wasn't as young as he used to be, and he had insisted on wearing his heavy black coat, which looked very dramatic with its half-cape, but was meant for winter wear. Underneath this he wore a velvet smoking jacket and a white frilled shirt. The song he had chosen to sing was Harry Lauder's 'Keep Right On To The End Of The Road', which had been a great hit in 1926. It was very patriotic, although Harry Lauder himself was Scottish. But his deep voice resembled Hector's and everyone knew the words.

As they walked arm in arm up Westferry Road, they all sang a chorus or two, and people turned to smile and laugh, and sometimes even join in. Hector was very well known for his busking and almost everyone they came across had a word to say to them. When he told them he was to sing at the Duke's, several patted him on the back and wished him luck.

Marie loved being with her father; he was so colourful and lively. Although not a born East Ender, he loved everything about the cockney life and had passed this love on to his daughters.

When they reached Poplar High Street and the Queen's, the crowds had dispersed as the late performance had long since started. It was getting on for nine o'clock. There were only a few minutes to go before meeting Wally Scoresby again.

'It would be wonderful to perform here,' said Hector, raising his voice above the rumble of traffic that still passed by.

'You're already a star to us,' said Marie. She was very proud of her father.

'And always will be,' nodded Vesta.

He patted their blonde waves gently. 'I brought my lucky charm with me.' He slid from his pocket a small nugget of coal worn smooth over the years. 'This has never let me down. And it won't tonight.' He slipped it back in his pocket and held out his elbows. 'Hold on to me, my lovelies, fame and fortune await us.'

Marie held tightly to her father's arm as they continued on to the Duke's close by. She could hardly believe their dreams were coming true. And although she felt very nervous, Hector had assured them that nerves could be used to inspire a performance.

She dearly hoped that was so.

Chapter 13

There was a buzz of excitement as Marie followed her father and Vesta down the basement steps to the club. The Duke's was filling up with well-dressed men and women taking their places at the tables; some of the men already had drinks in their hands and were talking at the bar. The piano player was with two other men dressed in dark suits; one sat behind a set of drums and the other held a bass.

'I didn't expect to see musicians,' Marie whispered as they peered through the smoky atmosphere. 'I'm pleased we brought our music.'

Vesta nodded. 'Just look at these people: the men all have bow ties and the women are all young and pretty.'

Marie noticed there was a lot of laughter coming from the bar. A tall, slim young man wearing a white shirt, bow tie and waistcoat was shaking cocktails and pouring out drinks. The girl that had been there on the night they came for their audition was helping him. This time she had a smile on her face as she talked to the male customers.

'Look, here's Teddy,' said Vesta with a sigh of relief.

'I'll take you straight through to the dressing room,' Teddy said as he came up to them. 'Follow me.'

Marie thought he looked very handsome in his formal suit, bow tie and polished shoes. She knew that Vesta must be thinking the same as they made their way through the crowd. One or two men turned to stare and smile. Marie blushed. She felt as though they stuck out like sore thumbs in their old coats. No one in the club looked like they did and she was suddenly ashamed of her appearance.

Soon they were ushered through a door beside a wide sweep of steps. Marie guessed they must lead to the main entrance. The passage Teddy took them into was long and narrow, and, in contrast to the club, dark and dingy. Several doors led off; one was marked 'Office', the other he pushed open.

'This is where you girls go.'

'And what about me?' said Hector, looking down the passage.

'The boss wants to speak to you,' answered Teddy hurriedly. 'Girls, you'd better go in and get yourselves ready.'

'Here's our music,' said Marie handing over the papers.

Teddy raised an eyebrow. 'Where did you get this?'

'From Bobby Brown, a friend of ours, and Elsie's. He's known as Bing and sings at the Cubby Hole.'

'Oh, *him*,' scoffed Teddy dismissively. 'It's a wonder his sort can read a note.'

'What do you mean by "his sort"?' Marie demanded. 'He's a very good singer.'

'I've had a drink or two there, but can't tolerate the rowdy noise for long. Now, the dancers are on first and you're on after them,' Teddy instructed as he bundled them into the room.

Marie was angry at Teddy's comments. She knew Vesta didn't care, but she did. And she was about to comment to Vesta when a girl with very long legs walked over to them. 'You must be the twins,' she said. All four dancers in the room had sparkly green costumes and low necklines that showed a lot of cleavage. They wore high heels and fishnet stockings, and one or two had feathers in their hair.

'My name's Bev,' said the blonde girl that Marie remembered had sat on the bar stool at their audition. 'Teddy said you'd be along. What are your names?'

'Marie and Vesta,' they both said together.

Bev grinned. 'You sound like parrots.'

'I'm Sal,' said a tall brunette.

'And I'm Rose and this is Joanie,' said another dark-haired girl, indicating her red-headed friend on the next chair.

'Hello,' Vesta and Marie said together.

All the girls laughed. 'You're funny,' said Rose. 'Who is who?'

'I'm Marie,' said Marie.

'And I'm Vesta.'

'You two are certainly good-lookers,' said Bev. 'No wonder Wally liked you.'

Marie smiled. 'I hope he did.'

All the girls exchanged glances.

'You'd better take off those awful coats,' said Bev. 'What are your costumes like?'

Marie went crimson as they slipped off their coats and was very relieved when all four girls nodded.

'Not bad,' said Joanie. 'You've both got great figures.'

'Thank you,' said Marie and Vesta together.

This caused another ripple of laughter. 'Don't take any notice of us,' chuckled Bev. 'We haven't had much to do with twin performers. Now, about those costumes, they will do for tonight, but next time you can borrow something glamorous from the wardrobe over there.'

Marie looked to where Bev pointed. There was a long rail with dozens of dresses and costumes hanging from it of all shapes and colours.

'There's not a lot of time left so you'd better put on your make-up,' said Sal, shuffling round the chairs that were covered in stockings and underwear.

'We haven't brought any,' said Marie weakly. 'We didn't think we'd need it.'

'Blimey, haven't you ever done anything like this before?'

The twins shook their heads.

'Come on then, sit down and we'll help you,' grinned Joanie, producing a slim tray of block mascara and spitting in it, then mixing it with the brush. Bev took the powder and rouge from a box and began to powder Marie's face.

'Christ,' she gasped, 'you two are just kids. How old are you?'

'Eighteen,' they chorused.

Marie saw Bev glance at the other girls. No one said anything more until Bev put the last dab of powder on Marie's face. 'Just to let you know, the most important rule here is, don't ever let Wally or Leo catch you drinking. You've always got to have water or lemonade.'

'We don't drink,' said Vesta and Marie together. 'We don't like the taste.'

'Do you smoke?'

'No,' they said again together.

Bev cackled. 'Blimey, you two really are innocent.'

'We might be, but we've always dreamed of going into show business,' said Vesta indignantly as Sal clipped a silver bow in her hair.

'Is this what you call show business?' Joanie laughed. 'Well, that's a first. I've never heard this dump called that before.'

'Don't dishearten them,' reproved Bev sharply. 'They're just babies.'

Marie studied their made-up faces in the mirror. What would Ada say if she saw them like this?

As she kept still for Sal to arrange a bow in her hair like Vesta's, Marie had time to look around. There were no bright lights on the three cracked and rust-pitted mirrors, just bulbs that dangled from the yellow, peeling ceiling. A long mirror was nailed up at one end of the room beside the clothes rail. A big, battered bamboo screen stood on the other side, presumably to change behind. Clothes and shoes were scattered everywhere. She could understand why Joanie had referred to it as a dump. But that didn't seem to matter. For her and Vesta, it all just added to the excitement of the place.

'What you gonna sing tonight, then?' asked Bev as she turned to add a feather to her own headdress.

' "Falling In Love Again" and "Million Dollar Baby", ' said Marie, fascinated by the quick movements of each girl to get herself ready.

'At least you're up to date,' chuckled Sal. 'The blokes will really like seeing double. No wonder Wally got you lined up quick. You'll be in dem—'

In the mirror, Marie saw Bev nudge Sal.

'Are you nervous?' asked Bev.

'Yes, a bit.'

'Don't worry, you'll knock 'em dead.'

'That's what our dad says.'

'He ain't wrong.'

Just then a loud bang came at the door. 'Five minutes, girls!' It was Teddy's voice.

'That's it, we're on!' said Bev, making a last adjustment to her bodice and heaving up her big bosoms.

Marie looked at Vesta, who was staring wide-eyed in the mirror. Marie turned to do the same.

'Oh, Marie, we're finally looking grown-up,' breathed Vesta, staring at herself, then drawing a finger under her eyes and blinking under the heavy mascara. 'Our dream is coming true at last.'

'Mum wouldn't approve,' Marie said with a rueful grin.

Vesta laughed. 'She's not here to see it, thank goodness.'

'I wonder what Mr Scoresby has in mind for Dad.'

'Dunno.' Vesta picked up their bag. 'Quick, we'd better put on our tap shoes.'

Marie could hardly breathe for excitement. She had loved everything that had happened to them from the moment they'd come down the basement steps and entered the dressing room.

Vesta was right. Their dream *was* coming true.

'Are you all right, Ada?' Elsie stuck her head round the door of Ada's front room. She had knocked lightly, but had no reply. Chancing that Ada was in the kitchen and couldn't hear, she was surprised to find no one in the kitchen either.

'Ada?' she called more loudly, slowly making her way into the hall. Standing still for a moment, she called out again. After a few moments, Ada appeared from the bedroom.

'I thought you might like a port and lemon, ducks.'

'No, thanks, Elsie.'

'Are you worried about your girls?'

Ada sunk her head. Elsie hurried along to where she stood. 'Ada, you've been crying.'

'No, I haven't.'

'Come and sit down.' Elsie led her friend into the front room and drew her down onto the sofa. 'Tell Elsie all about it.'

'You know all about it. You're the one person who does.' Ada wiped her eyes with her handkerchief.

'It was in the past, love, a long time ago.'

'Not long enough, Elsie. I don't want my daughters to be in danger.'

Elsie patted her hand. 'Why should they be? Look, nothing you could say or do would have changed their minds about tonight. Your girls have got performing in their blood. If this hadn't happened sooner it would have later.'

'The later the better, as far as I'm concerned. Oh, why did Hector keep on encouraging them?'

'Because performing is in his blood too.'

'But he was the one who . . . who . . .' Ada gave a huge sob and closed her eyes. 'Oh, Elsie, I've tried to forgive and forget. Well, I can forgive, but I can't forget.'

'Is he up to his old tricks again? Is that why you're so worried?'

Ada looked down to her lap. 'Not as far as I know. But I'm always on edge wondering – wondering . . .' She frowned into Elsie's concerned gaze. 'Hector is so easily led. We know nothing about these two brothers, do we?'

'But he's with the girls, at least.'

'That should make me feel better, but it doesn't.'

'He learned his lesson, Ada. No reason for something like what happened before to happen again.'

Ada sighed and looked into the distance. 'All I ever wanted was my girls to find themselves decent husbands. Lead happy, normal lives with children and homes. Why do they have to be different from everyone else?'

'Because they *are* different, Ada,' Elsie remarked. 'They have class as well as talent, and you gave it to them.'

'So it's me that's at fault, is it?' Ada said bitterly.

'No, love. Don't twist me words. It's just you can't live their lives for them.'

Ada nodded sadly. 'I was hoping Marie might bring home that young man from the Cubby Hole.'

'She could do a lot worse, that's true.'

'But Teddy!' Ada exclaimed. 'There's something about *him* that worries me.'

Elsie made no comment, for she felt the same. He had latched on to Vesta a little too quickly for Elsie's liking. Set up that audition without letting Ada know. Now, if he was a decent sort, he'd have gone and asked their mother first.

Elsie smiled at the memory of the girls as leggy seven-year-olds, sitting on the bench outside the pub, that first day Hector brought them to the East End. A right pair of little ragamuffins! Didn't look as though they or their mother had eaten a decent meal in a week! No wonder she'd offered Hector the rooms above the pub to tide them over. She couldn't have lived with her conscience if she'd not helped them out. And Hector being the double of her late husband, Joe, well, it hadn't been difficult to take the little family under her wing. Perhaps she had seen a reflection of herself and Joe, with the kids they'd never been lucky enough to have . . .

'Elsie?' Ada's voice brought her back to the present.

'Sorry, gel, I was off on one, then.'

Ada smiled weakly. 'Look, it's late. Off you go to bed.'

'I was going to stay with you till they came home.'

'No, don't worry about me. I'll send them in to you in the morning.'

Elsie nodded. She fancied a quick port before she went to bed. A good sherry or port made the perfect nightcap.

'Goodnight, then, love.' She kissed Ada's cheek.

''Night, Elsie. And thanks.'

Elsie got up and left, closing the door quietly after her. She stood in the hall for a few seconds, glancing up the stairs to the rooms above and then back to the front door. She was about to go into her rooms, when she heard the whisper of a soft voice.

Gradually the front door opened and Nina stepped in. She didn't see Elsie at first. When she did, she gave a little gasp. 'Oh, you're still up, Mrs Goldberg.'

'Hello, ducks.'

Nina's expression was hidden under her long hair.

'Late night at work, was it?' asked Elsie casually. ''Spect you're all in.'

Nina was about to reply when Elsie spotted a figure behind her. Nina followed her gaze. 'Oh, er, you know my Uncle Ivor,' Nina said hesitantly. 'He saw me home as I missed the bus.'

Elsie studied the short, well-dressed, bespectacled and balding man who she had seen once or twice before. He now seemed eager to depart and stepped backwards into the darkness.

'Goodnight, Uncle.'

Elsie watched Nina close the door quickly. Had the young woman been going to take her uncle upstairs? But the house rule was, after ten, no guests were allowed.

Elsie felt sorry for this young girl, although Nina never gave very much of herself away. Like Teddy Turner, she was a model lodger. She was also a loner. Her only relative, it seemed, was this strange little man whom she called Uncle Ivor. Elsie had no liking for him. She had a knack of weighing up people at a glance. And, usually, she wasn't far wrong.

'Well, I'm off to me bed,' said Elsie pleasantly. 'But I'll warn you that Hector and the girls ain't come in yet and there may be a bit of noise.'

'Another visit to the Queen's?' said Nina softly.

'No. As a matter of fact, the twins got a chance to sing and dance at the Duke's. That club over Poplar way.'

Nina looked shocked. 'I wouldn't have thought they would like that sort of place—' She looked awkward. 'I mean, they are still very young to work in a—' Once again she stopped, going red.

Elsie smiled. 'Well, this club is supposed to be very posh.'

Nina nodded uncertainly. 'Oh, I see.'

'As I said, if you do hear anything, don't worry. It'll only be them. Goodnight, ducks.'

'Goodnight, Mrs Goldberg.'

In her room, Elsie put her ear to the door. She heard Nina go up the creaky stairs, but she continued to listen for the front door. If that old sod tried to get in again, she'd catch him in the act. But all was quiet, and after a while Elsie went to her late husband's cocktail cabinet and took out a bottle of port.

She then made herself comfortable in Joe's favourite chair, an old, chintzy relic that was worn on the arms, and the polished wooden frame had long ago lost its shine. In places, the upholstery was quite threadbare. The seat had sunk a little too, but with a cushion spread there, and one at her back, it was as comfortable as a bed.

She sipped the mellow liquid and sighed deeply. Now what had that been all about with Nina? It was no business of hers, of course. Had Nina acted strange because she'd been caught in the act? Bringing in a visitor after hours was understandable if it had been a young man. A kiss and cuddle with a boyfriend was only natural, and she wouldn't blame Nina for trying. But an old codger like him, even if he was her uncle . . .?

Elsie gave a shudder. She didn't like that set-up at all. She didn't want to admit to herself what she was really thinking. The girl couldn't be on the game, could she? If she was, she was hiding it well. But when the Duke's was mentioned, Nina's comment – that it wasn't right for the twins – had struck Elsie as more worldly-wise than her looks gave her credit for.

Elsie's thoughts went to the future. If push came to shove and she ever found Nina trying it on under her roof, what would she do?

Elsie took another sip of her drink. A landlady always had trouble with her lodgers in one way or another. Some paid up, some didn't. Some were noisy, dirty and drinkers. Others couldn't be bothered to give you the time of day. She'd had a few since Joe died. But her present residents were the best of the lot.

Coming to a decision, Elsie reckoned that if Nina followed the rules of the house and kept her business away from here, then that was all right by her. A living was hard enough to make these days and some didn't even bother to try. Even if the supposed Uncle Ivor paid for her rent, who was Elsie to judge anyone? Least of all a hard-working, quiet and decent sort who never said boo to a goose. Besides which, she had a soft spot for the girl. And that counted for a lot with Elsie.

Chapter 14

'Everything turned out wonderful!' Vesta hurried over to Ada who had fallen asleep on the couch. 'Mum, we've got the job two nights a week.'

Marie sat on the other side of Ada. 'Friday and Saturday. Teddy said Mr Scoresby was very pleased with us.'

Ada wiped her eyes with her knuckles. 'What time is it?'

'Not much past eleven.' Vesta tugged off her coat and did a little dance. 'You should have seen us, Mum. We sang "Falling In Love Again", followed by "Million Dollar Baby". We were very nervous at first and couldn't see a thing as the lights blinded us. But when we finished everyone clapped loudly.'

Marie knew Vesta was still on cloud nine and, as usual, was exaggerating. There had been a brief and rather weak applause, which had been very disappointing. But the dancers had said the customers needed to get to know them.

'So, you were successful.' Ada's voice was flat. 'I'm very pleased for you both. But it's very late hours to keep.'

Vesta shrugged. 'The club doesn't get going till ten. The dancers are on first, then it's us. After us, the band plays and Teddy sings. Although we didn't stop to listen to him as we came home to see you.'

Ada blinked her tired eyes. 'You sang with a band?'

'Yes, three musicians, one playing the piano, another the drums and the third a bass.'

Ada nodded slowly. 'What about your father?'

Marie glanced at the door. Hector was still in the hall. His evening hadn't gone so well. They knew he was preparing himself to face Ada. When he walked in, he had a bright smile. 'Hello, Ada, dear. There, you see, I returned your daughters safe and sound.'

He took off his black coat and folded it over his arm. 'They sang and danced very well, I understand.'

'Didn't you see them perform?'

Hector cleared his throat. 'No, Mr Scoresby had other work for me to see to.'

Everyone went silent. Marie looked at Vesta, who was lost in a world of her own.

'What sort of work?' Ada asked suspiciously.

'This and that,' Hector answered vaguely. 'When one of the acts leaves I shall take their place. I'm in the wings until then and am quite prepared to start at the bottom of the ladder.' Hector smiled even wider under his moustache and, bracing his shoulders, he added, 'The pay is very good, you'll be pleased to hear. Two pounds and ten shillings for only four nights a week.'

'Have you accepted?'

'Of course,' said Hector, sounding surprised. 'A regular job is what you've always wanted me to have. And I hope to make you proud of me again.'

They were all silent when he went into the kitchen to make cocoa. Finally Ada spoke. 'I suppose you are going to tell me you will be paid good money, too?'

'Yes,' said Vesta proudly. 'We get two pounds, and if we're good enough, much more.'

'So you'll keep your jobs at the factory?' Ada asked anxiously.

Marie glanced at Vesta. On the way home they had decided that if by Christmas they were still working at the club, they would leave Ellisdon's. But neither of them wanted to tell Ada that.

'Don't worry,' said Vesta quickly. 'We promise not to do anything rash.'

'I hope not.' Ada looked doubtful. Then turning her head towards the kitchen, she said in a whisper, 'Perhaps things will work out for the best, after all.'

Marie couldn't bring herself to tell Ada that she had seen Hector at the end of the long corridor, sweeping and clearing rubbish. His sleeves had been rolled up and he was mopping the sweat from his brow. It was humiliating for a man like Hector, with all his acting experience, to be made to do such work.

'I wish you could have been there tonight,' said Vesta, encouraged by Ada's remark. 'You should have seen the other girls in their costumes. They're called Bev, Sal, Joanie and Rose. There was another girl too, Irene. But we didn't see much of her. She was helping the barman, Pedro.'

Ada nodded, pushing herself up from the couch. 'All this excitement has made me tired.' She bent and kissed them both, cupping their faces in her hands. She gave a deep sigh. 'Elsie was asking after you. I said you'd drop by tomorrow.'

'We will,' they said together, but it wasn't long before they too were yawning.

'Goodnight, Dad,' they shouted.

'Goodnight, my clever girls.' Hector appeared from the kitchen. He drew them into his arms. Kissing the tops of their heads, he whispered, 'Your mother and I are very proud of you. I hope you know that.'

'We do.' They hugged him tight.

Marie knew they had two wonderful parents who cared about them. She hoped dearly that, in the weeks ahead, they could make them even prouder.

'I've never been so happy,' sighed Vesta as they lay in bed. 'Tonight we sang with a band, something we've never done before. And those girls seemed to like us.'

'Yes,' agreed Marie. 'But they did give us strange looks.'

'Because of our silly clothes,' Vesta giggled. 'With our old coats and no make-up we must have looked very old-fashioned. But soon we'll have lovely clothes, new shoes, and powder and lipstick.'

'We can't afford all that.'

'With the money we earn, we will.'

'Having two jobs won't be easy,' Marie reminded her sister. 'Especially going to work at Ellisdon's early on Saturday.'

'Joanie said we need new songs,' Vesta said thoughtfully. 'You'll have to ask lover boy for more music.'

This woke Marie up. 'I can't ask favours from Bing. I've told him I don't want to see him.'

'He's mad keen on you.'

Marie stared into the darkness. 'I don't want to lead him on.'

Vesta turned over. 'You know you like him.'

'He's just a friend.'

'I saw your face when Teddy said something about him.'

'Teddy was very unkind.'

Vesta gave a long sigh. 'Listen, just ask him the next time we meet. You don't have to marry the man.' She glanced at Marie and adopted a more persuasive tone. 'I'm sure he would be the first in line to offer his help, if he knew what you needed.'

'Do you think so?'

'Yes, I'm sure of it. That's the kind of nice person he is.'

'Well, yes, he is nice.'

'There, so we both agree and our problem is solved,' Vesta said with a contented sigh. 'Now, sleep tight, little songbird.' She kissed Marie's cheek and was soon snoring softly.

Marie stayed awake, lost in thought. Although she was

'No one told you to dress them up like tarts,' Teddy was shouting at Joanie.

Marie wanted to drop through the floor. She had never felt so humiliated. So they had looked like tarts!

Teddy whipped round and glared at Marie and Vesta. 'Get those costumes off,' he yelled angrily. 'And take that stuff off your faces too. You're lucky Mr Scoresby didn't sack you on the spot.'

Marie felt Vesta tremble beside her. When he strode past them and banged the door, Vesta burst into tears.

All the girls gathered round. 'Don't cry, love. He's had a rollicking from Wally, that's all.'

Vesta sobbed loudly. 'But it wasn't our fault.'

'I know, and I owned up,' Joanie admitted at once, her cheeks the colour of her red hair. 'I just thought the dresses were the same size and would fit. Didn't give much thought to them making you look like—' She stopped and faltered. 'Well . . . too old.'

'You are a stupid mare,' accused Bev angrily. 'You could have got us all into a lot of trouble.' She patted Vesta's shoulder. 'Don't worry, Wally won't hold you responsible. That was just a threat on Teddy's part.'

'I told you, it's mostly war in this game,' said Rose as she unlaced the front of her costume. 'You two will have to toughen up if you want to stay in the business. You may have got on the wrong side of Wally tonight, but he didn't sack you, be thankful for that.' She looked at the other three girls. 'Wally never asked us to help out with these kids. Let's hope Teddy manages to smooth things over.'

Marie looked at the four girls and was shocked to find they all wore the same expressions. Was it fear in their faces?

'It's not fair,' Vesta kept on mumbling as they unhooked one another and slid off the scarlet dresses and stockings.

'We should have had more sense,' Marie insisted.

'We'll keep our noses out of your business,' Bev called across the room. 'Wally obviously wants you to keep the innocent look. Anyway, take no notice. Wally and Teddy can blow hot and cold. You just have to go along with it.'

Vesta sniffed. 'Teddy's never shouted at me before. He's always been so nice.'

'You'll learn a lot about human nature in this place, love,' said Joanie as she took off her feathered headdress and flopped down on a chair.

As they looked in the mirror and wiped their faces with grease, Marie saw the other girls behind them. They were talking in whispers. She couldn't hear what they were saying, but she guessed they were talking about them.

The look on their faces when Teddy had shouted at them had not escaped Marie. Yes, it was definitely fear she had seen in their eyes.

Chapter 15

Work the next day came hard. The twins were put in the cutting room and made to complete a large order that had to be finalized that morning. The air was full of dust and debris, the noise of the machines sounded deafening. When they clocked off, they both had sore throats.

'This isn't a good start to our career,' Vesta complained as they began to walk home. 'First those dresses and now me throat is so dry I don't think I can sing.'

'We'll gargle with salt water and soon feel better,' Marie tried to encourage as they approached the dock gates. She felt dispirited after last night's events. Her confidence had fallen to an all-time low. She wasn't looking forward to returning to the club that evening.

'I wanted to hear Teddy sing last night,' Vesta continued to complain, dragging her feet. Her shoulders looked as though she carried the weight of the world on them. 'But I couldn't wait to get out of there.'

'I'm just glad our dad never saw us in those dresses.'

'Do you think he likes standing at the club's front door?' Vesta asked gloomily.

Marie hadn't said that she'd seen him sweeping up. She hoped that was just an exception. 'Mr Scoresby told him the job is important.'

'But it's only keeping out the riffraff—' Vesta stopped, staring straight ahead. 'Well, look who it is. Lover boy and his daft pal.'

Marie's heart sank. Bing and Charlie were coming out of the dock gates.

'Our luck has changed.' Vesta straightened her shoulders and smiled, patting her curls into place. 'This is the chance to get our music.'

Marie glared at Vesta. 'We can't do that.'

'Not "we", but *you*. He'll do anything you say.'

'No,' said Marie resolutely, beginning to panic.

'Why not?' Vesta clutched her arm. 'Oh, please, Marie. All you have to do is ask nicely. I'll keep Charlie occupied while you do it.'

'Hello, girls,' said Charlie as they approached.

'Hello,' said Vesta in a flirtatious manner.

'Nice day, ain't it?' said Charlie, smiling.

'Which way are you going?' asked Vesta, which made Marie want to curl up and die.

'Your way,' said Charlie. The smile on his face was so wide it showed up under all the grime.

Vesta slipped her hand through his arm. 'Come on then, handsome.'

Bing stared after them, then turned to Marie. 'What's up with your sister?'

'She's just being friendly.' Marie blushed.

Bing gave a puzzled frown but then said, 'I saw your dad at the Cubby Hole. He was celebrating your success at the Duke's.'

'It's only twice a week,' Marie shrugged. 'Not like a full-time job.'

'So you're going to become a big star?'

She blushed again. 'I don't know about that.'

'If I'd had any sense I would have kept me trap shut about the club,' Bing said regretfully. 'That way you might not have turned me down.'

Marie began to smile. 'I said I wanted to be friends.'

The September sun streamed through his hair, making it look like bristles of gold. 'Did you sing them songs I gave to Elsie?'

'Yes, thank you. They were very good.'

'Would it put me back in your good books if I got you some more?'

Marie felt he was reading her thoughts and felt guilty. 'You don't have to do that.'

'It's the least I can do. I've got lots of music at home. Shall I bring a couple round?'

Marie lowered her head. 'That would be nice.'

He slung his jacket over his shoulder. 'And if you see my mate, remind him he's got a girlfriend already, will you?'

Marie watched him walk off. She was disappointed he hadn't offered to walk her home. Had she hurt his feelings again when she had said he needn't give them any more songs? Would he really call round?

She began to walk home, considering carefully what she was going to tell Vesta.

'Did you ask?' Vesta was eager to know after she had sent Charlie off.

'Not exactly.'

'What? After all the time I spent on Charlie?'

'You've never shown any interest in him before.'

'And I'm not interested now,' Vesta replied in a huff.

'I didn't ask, because I didn't have to,' Marie said after a long and awkward pause. 'Bing offered himself.'

'He did?' Vesta threw her arms around Marie. 'I told you! He's really crazy about you.'

Marie waited until Vesta let her go. Her sister's mood had changed and her eyes were gleaming and bright. 'What song are we getting?'

'We'll have to wait and see.'

'Did you tell him how important it is?' Vesta pressed.

'I didn't have to. And besides, he has lots at home, gathering dust.'

Vesta jumped up and down and clapped. 'All our problems are solved!' She slipped her arm through Marie's. 'When can we have them?'

Marie decided to change the subject. 'Vesta, I hope you'll remember Charlie has a girlfriend.'

Vesta laughed. 'I'm just larking around.'

'But you don't like him.'

'No, but I'd like to make Teddy jealous.'

'Don't play with people's feelings, Vesta,' Marie warned, stopping to look into her sister's face. 'You could hurt Charlie. And his girlfriend.'

Vesta stared at her. 'Hark at you! I'm not the one playing with people's feelings. You're only being nice to Bing because he's useful.'

'That's not true. It was you who encouraged me to get the music.'

'Let's not argue about men,' Vesta dismissed, taking Marie's arm again as they went up the steps to the house. 'Girls should stick together. Especially girls like us.' She laughed.

Marie glanced at her sister. Vesta had a familiar expression on her face. She looked like she was planning something.

That night's performance went better than Marie had expected. They wore their pink dresses and tap shoes, and the songs were sung without fault. The musicians, whose names they learned were Benny, Jeff and Walter, all gave the girls the thumbs-up as they left the stage.

'Sorry again about last night,' said Bev when the twins returned and began to take off their make-up.

'Yes,' said Joanie quietly. 'Mr Scoresby says we're to mind our own business.'

'I hope you didn't get into trouble,' said Marie. She didn't want to fall out with them.

'No,' said Joanie, glancing over her shoulder. 'It was Irene who got the sack instead.'

'The girl behind the bar?'

'Yes. Wally's ex.'

'I didn't know that,' said Vesta as she brushed her hair in the mirror.

Marie saw Bev nudge Joanie hard. 'If you two want to hear Teddy sing,' Bev said quickly, 'he's on now. You'd better be quick if you want to catch him.'

Vesta dropped the hairbrush and hurriedly pulled on her coat. 'Come on, Marie, I don't want to miss him tonight.'

'I haven't changed yet.'

'All right. I'll meet you at the back of the stage.'

Marie had no desire to hear Teddy again. She took her time in removing the little make-up she wore, then went behind the screen. As she took off her clothes, she overheard Irene's name. In the mirror she could see the girls talking together. Their faces were very serious. What was it they didn't want to say in front of her?

When she had hung her and Vesta's costumes on the rail and put on a blouse and skirt, she slipped her coat over her arm and went to the door. ''Night everyone.'

'See you next week,' Bev and Joanie called, but the others were still talking in whispers.

Marie stood in the draughty passage outside. She tried to listen to what was being said in her absence. But Teddy's droning made it impossible to hear. Once again Joanie had been silenced by Bev, and Marie suspected she had been on the point of talking about Irene.

Marie looked along the passage. A pale light flickered at the end of it. She walked along slowly and turned left into yet another passage. The air smelled as though that part of the club hadn't be used in a long time.

Finally the passage came to an end. A door was slightly open and she pushed it.

'Dad, what are you doing?' she asked in surprise as she saw the bent figure of her father behind some crates.

'Marie! I might ask you the same.'

She walked over to where he stood. There was a door to his left, with two heavy bolts drawn across it. 'Does that lead outside?'

'Yes, but it's not for general use. You shouldn't be here. Did anyone see you come down?'

'No. The door was open slightly and I could hear noises.'

'This is a private area.' He wiped the sweat from his face with a rag. 'Wally has asked me to clear the rubbish and put a new lock on the door.'

'What's in those crates? They look heavy.'

'They are a bit,' Hector said quickly. 'It's mostly drinks for the new bar.'

'New bar?' Marie repeated.

Hector looked over her shoulder. 'Yes, Wally and Leo intend to open one here for their most select trade.' He smiled nervously, which seemed unusual to Marie. Her father was always so full of confidence. She saw how hard he was breathing and sweating. His clothes were all dusty too. 'Dad, I don't like to see you doing this work. It's heavy labouring.'

'It's only temporary, my dear,' Hector dismissed, wiping his forehead again. 'I've agreed to fill in as their handyman until there is a spot for me in the cabaret. Now, not a word to anyone about this. I don't want your mother to worry.'

Marie nodded. 'We'll wait for you in Duke Street.'

He caught her arm. 'No, I may be longer than usual, so go on home.'

'What shall I tell Mum?'

'Just that I was given overtime.'

Marie didn't want to leave him. Hector might look strong, but he wasn't used to hard physical work. He wasn't cut out to be a handyman.

'Go along, love.' He shooed her off and reluctantly she made her way back down the dark passage.

'Where have you been?' demanded Vesta as they stood in the wings, listening to Teddy's pathetic attempts at crooning.

'I took me time to get changed.'

'I should think you did!' whispered Vesta. 'You've missed the best part. Just listen to him. Isn't he wonderful?'

Marie could see that Vesta was besotted by Teddy's performance, as she stood with a dreamy expression on her face.

Chapter 16

The next morning, Sunday, Marie was first to answer a knock on the front door. When she opened it she was surprised to find Bing standing there. 'I thought these songs might do,' he said as Vesta joined them.

Vesta looked at them and frowned. '"Tiger Rag" and "Where The Blue Of The Night"?'

Bing nodded. '"Tiger Rag" is by the Mills Brothers, a good tune to dance to. The other is from Bing Crosby's radio show, but I warn you, it could take some practice.'

'We can ask Benny, the piano player at the Duke's, to play it for us,' suggested Vesta.

'I'd offer myself,' Bing said, 'but I'm driving some friends out to Epping Forest. Doubt there will be many more nice days like this.'

Marie wanted to ask who his friends were. Were they Charlie and his girlfriend?

'Let me know if I can help,' he called as he ran down the steps.

They stared after him as he climbed into the car. Marie was surprised when she saw him slide a straw boater onto his head. She noticed he was wearing immaculate white flannels and a blue blazer; was he looking as smart as that for someone special?

'Who's he taking out, I wonder,' said Vesta when they went back in.

'Don't know,' shrugged Marie. 'And I don't care.'

But Marie found herself thinking about Bing. Would she have liked to be the one who was sitting next to him in his car? Still, she couldn't expect the offer as she had made it quite plain that she wasn't interested. Perhaps another girl had been given the opportunity and had taken it.

Teddy was trying to make a quick getaway. He'd done his fair quota tonight. This being a Wednesday, the club was closed and it was poker night. All evening the stakes had been high. A group of nine hard faces sat at the table with Wally and Wally was a bad loser. The Scoresbys' addiction to gambling was a problem here in the East End, where rival gangs all vied to be top dog. Not so up West in the brothers' gentlemen's club, where the wealthy were willing to take big losses and not make a fuss. They had too much to hide, what with their fresh totty provided by the Scoresbys, guilty secrets that could end a political career or ruin a marriage. They always allowed the brothers to indulge themselves when Wally or Leo took to the tables. The wealthy liked to say they had rubbed shoulders with the East End's roughest and toughest, knowing the game had been rigged from the first hand.

Teddy shook his head in wonder at the punters' foolishness. Life must be so uneventful for them that they were quite willing to risk their careers and standing for a night's excesses.

Teddy slipped quietly to the wings of the stage. He intended to go along the passage to the end room, Wally and Leo's secret project, where there was a hidden exit. He'd go through it and out into the night unobserved.

Uncomfortably aware that he had bitten off more than he could chew with Irene, Teddy didn't want a repeat. And he was very much afraid he might be saddled with one. Last month, Wally had paid a backhander to the Law to turn a blind eye to the late-night gambling and drinking. That backhander had led to Irene's downfall. Screwing around with Wally had given her an inflated ego and sealed her end.

Teddy shuddered. There had been no way he could do it. He'd had to get someone else to do the job for him. It had cost an arm and a leg, and he begrudged taking it from his savings.

Thinking of arms and legs, Teddy hurried on his way. And he almost made his escape – would have, if Pedro hadn't called him back.

'Teddy bear, you're wanted.' Pedro's high-pitched voice drifted along the passage. Teddy froze, then turned slowly round. Pedro blew him a kiss from the palm of his hand. 'You're too pretty to leave the party early.'

Teddy groaned inwardly. His shoulders fell forward and, as if he were being pulled by an invisible chain, he retraced his steps.

As he entered the club, the air was dense with smoke. Wally's fearful disfigurement still made Teddy squirm as he stood at Wally's side. Wally sat at the table with Joanie on his knee, her arms around his neck. Teddy felt the urge to slap her. She hadn't learned from Irene, who was supposed to be her best mate. Instead, she had taken Irene's place. And now Wally was making the most of it.

'Get me a drink,' Wally ordered without looking up. The other players, all guarding their hands, glanced up at Teddy. They knew, as he knew, Wally's run of luck was sure to be contested. The hands he had played all evening stank like bad fish. Which was why Teddy had been trying to make an exit before he was told to step in and stop trouble.

Teddy walked over to the bar. Pedro raised his eyebrows and blinked his long black lashes. He handed a clean glass to Teddy. 'He didn't want me to pour it for him, sweetheart, though I did offer.'

'I'll bet you did.'

'Don't be like that, Teddy bear. Green ain't your colour.'

Teddy ignored the remark; Pedro enjoyed playing to his effeminate side, even though he was tall and had a good physique. But Teddy never underestimated the barman. Wally hadn't hired Pedro for his ability to make cocktails; Pedro was insurance. He came with his own lethal speciality: a knuckle duster with a razor built into the metal, which made him almost as danger-ous as Leo.

Teddy heaved a fatalistic sigh. He was part of the Scoresbys' machine. For now. But there was a day not too far off – a day he had been planning since Wally and Leo had set him up at the Duke's.

Pedro's dark eyes gleamed as he leaned close. 'Haven't you noticed the looks on the faces of the three idiots opposite Wally?'

Teddy nodded. He'd noticed all right. That was why he had been trying to make himself scarce.

'South of the river mob,' continued Pedro under his breath as he poured Wally's drink, 'and they must fancy their chances on Scoresby turf. So if Wally's next hand is a flush, be prepared.'

Teddy nodded gratefully. He knew that if he was in a tight spot, despite their bickering, Pedro would be the one he'd look to.

Taking a deep breath, Teddy took the whisky over to the table. He managed – just – to keep his hand from shaking as he passed it to Wally, who downed the drink in one.

Teddy's heart dropped as Wally threw down his cards. An ace, a king, a queen, a jack and a ten. All hearts. And Wally's fourth lucky flush of the evening.

Minutes seemed to drag by, although Teddy knew it could only be seconds. All the players sat still. Then one by one, they left the table, leaving only the bald punter and his two mates. Teddy saw Wally grin, urging Joanie off his knee, then lean forward to claim the pot.

But a fat hand got there first. 'I reckon you've got more than your dick stuffed down your trousers, pal,' said the bald-headed idiot with a mouth and nose that had lost direction in his fat face. 'You don't strike me as having enough nous to play four flushes in a row, so you must be having a joke, right?'

Teddy closed his eyes in distress. These were the words he had dreaded to hear. He glanced nervously over towards Pedro, who reached out to knock lightly on the partition wall.

Wally stood up. Teddy took a nervous step back. The bald-headed contender rose to his feet, as did his mates. One of them tried sliding a hand inside his jacket, but Wally shook his head. 'Stop right there,' he said in a malevolent whisper, 'or that move will turn out to be your last one.'

Once again time seemed to stand still for Teddy. Until a tall, dark-haired figure wearing a hand-tailored suit emerged by the bar.

Teddy wished he was a million miles away, marooned on an island where Wally and Leo could never ever get to him. He looked at the three bolshie South Londoners and almost felt sorry for them. They had smiles on their faces and were puffing up like turkeys at Christmas.

And everyone knew what happened to turkeys at Christmas.

Although they'd had all week to learn their new routine, Marie had to admit that Bing was right. Without a musical accompaniment, 'Where The Blue Of The Night', was tricky. On Friday, they decided to revert back to their old songs and went to the Duke's hoping that Benny would help them.

After they had left Hector at the office, they went into the dressing room, to be greeted by four long faces.

'Where's Teddy?' asked Vesta worriedly.

'Gone out,' answered Bev evasively.

'Where to?' Vesta looked disappointed.

'It's not our business,' said Bev, keeping her voice down.

Marie glanced at Vesta. Without speaking they changed into their costumes. It was Benny's voice they heard in the corridor, shouting to tell the chorus line they were on.

When the dancers had filed out, Marie looked at Vesta. 'What do you make of that?'

'Do you think Teddy's all right?' Vesta was very pale. 'He's always around normally.'

'I'm sure he's all right.' Marie sat down on one of the chairs.

'I wonder if Elsie's seen him?'

Marie was thinking about this when she noticed a newspaper folded on the top of Bev's make-up box. She picked it up and read the headlines. The police were having trouble in separating the Fascist and anti-Fascist marchers in the city, but at the bottom of the page, some-one had drawn a large circle.

'What is it?' asked Vesta. 'What are you reading?'

'I can't believe it,' said Marie on a soft gasp. 'Listen. "The body of a young woman has been recovered from the Millwall Dock and identified as Irene Wallis of Ebondale Street, Isle of Dogs. It is believed she had spent the night in the local tavern, drinking."'

'Irene Wallis? Who's she?'

'The girl who worked behind the bar is called Irene.'

'There must be hundreds of Irenes in the East End.'

'"Witnesses have come forward to say they saw her in the Quarry public house, close to the dock, shortly before the body was recovered. The coroner has recorded death by misadventure."' Marie looked up. 'Do you think this is why the girls were quiet?'

'Could be.'

Marie placed the newspaper back on Bev's box. 'There is the circle drawn round it – did Bev do that?'

'Or it could be a coincidence,' said Vesta, leaning forward to inspect her face.

'We'll ask Dad if he's heard anything,' Marie decided.

But Vesta didn't reply. She was concentrating on her reflection as she mimed the words to their song.

'Yes, I did hear something,' said Hector in answer to their question, as they made their way back to Sphinx Street. 'It was the girl who worked at the club. The police came early this evening and took Teddy away to make a statement.'

'So that's why he wasn't there,' breathed Vesta with relief. 'But what's Teddy got to do with Irene?'

'He told the police he had employed her.'

'But he wouldn't know anything personal about her.' Vesta sounded indignant.

Hector hurried them on. 'Let's go a little faster. This fog looks like it could be a peasouper.'

Marie thought that Hector had quickly got off the subject of Irene. Was there something he didn't want them to know?

When they arrived home, they put their wages on the table in front of Ada. 'This is for you, Mum,' said Marie proudly.

Ada shook her head. 'It's your money, not mine.'

'But our two pounds will help. You can give up work,' insisted Marie.

'I don't want to give up my job.' Ada looked at the money disdainfully. 'Your factory money is enough.' She kissed them on the cheek. 'Goodnight and God bless. Don't stay up late.'

Hector sat down at the table and sighed.

'What's the matter, Dad?'

'Your mother's got her pride.'

'We don't mind,' said Vesta, grinning. 'There's lots of clothes I want to buy.'

'We'll save it,' Marie suggested, 'for a rainy day.'

'Not all of it,' said Vesta disappointedly. 'I'm rich! And I want to enjoy that wonderful feeling.'

'Well, some of it's going in the Post Office,' said Marie. 'for a rainy day.'

'Yes, you never know when we'll get one of those.' Hector looked troubled.

'Dad, do you really like your job?' Marie asked. 'You could always go back to busking.'

'Busking doesn't pay as well. And there is always a chance at the club that I'll—' He dredged up a smile. 'Now off you go to bed, like your mother said.'

That night, Marie couldn't sleep. Although she hadn't known Irene, she kept thinking about her. How dreadful a death; to die in the murky waters of the dock. Did Teddy know anything about it? And if not, why had the police taken him away?

'I didn't sleep a wink last night,' said Vesta as they left the factory the next day and set off for the market.

'Nor did I,' agreed Marie. 'That poor girl, Irene.'

'Oh, her.' Vesta shrugged. 'I was thinking about buying a coat.'

'Irene was so pretty.'

'She shouldn't have been drinking,' said Vesta, as they passed the dock gates. She paused. 'No sign of Laurel and Hardy.'

'Don't call Bing and Charlie that.'

'Well, it suits them.'

'Vesta, I'd rather you—' Marie began, but found herself pulled along at breakneck speed.

'Come on, we've got two whole pounds to spend, a fortune!'

When they arrived at the market, it was very busy. They had to push their way through the Saturday crowd.

'This ain't bad,' said Vesta, lifting up a blue coat.

'You'll need a few bob if you want to buy it,' warned the toothless old woman behind the stall. 'I've just robbed it off a toff's missus. She was hard up and needed the money.'

Vesta nodded eagerly. 'It don't look like it's ever been worn.'

'Come into an in'eritance, 'ave yer?'

'Not at all.' Vesta lifted her chin and said in an exaggerated voice, 'Our theatrical career has just begun at the Duke's.'

Instead of looking impressed, the old woman laughed scornfully. 'That 'ouse of ill repute?'

'What do you mean?' Vesta snapped. 'The Duke's is high class.'

'Yeah, pull the other one.'

Vesta dropped the coat and turned to Marie. 'I shan't bring my custom here again,' she said in a loud voice as she marched Marie off. 'All you ever get is sour grapes. And I can't abide those!'

Vesta's mood switched quickly on their way home. 'The old gas bag doesn't know what she's talking about. No, I'll get Charlie to take me up West.'

'Charlie? But he's got a girlfriend.'

'I know, I know! You've said before. But I'm not asking for a ring on me finger,' huffed Vesta crossly.

Nina Brass was coming down the stairs when they arrived home. She looked elegant and sophisticated, dressed in a biscuit-coloured coat, matching buttons and scarf, and a smooth-brimmed hat.

'Hello,' Marie and Vesta said together.

'Oh, I love your coat, Nina,' said Vesta enviously. 'It's beautiful. Where did you buy it?'

'Up West,' said Nina quietly.

'That's where I'm going to buy all me clothes,' Vesta retorted. 'No more markets for me, thanks to working at the Duke's.'

Nina stared at her. 'You really are going to work there?'

'Yes. Ain't it exciting?'

'But you're both so . . . well, young, to do a job like that.' Nina hesitated. 'Are you sure that's what you both want?'

'We ain't that young,' Vesta replied. 'Teddy says it doesn't matter how young you are if you've got real talent.'

'We're still working at the factory,' explained Marie quickly. 'We know the club might not work out. But we thought we'd give it a try.'

Nina began to answer, but the front door opened and Teddy walked in.

'Well, goodnight,' said Nina, as she hurried past Teddy and out of the front door.

'What was all that about?' asked Teddy, glancing after her.

'Search me,' Vesta said with a frown. 'I always thought she was a bit strange.'

'What did she say?'

'Don't let's waste time talking about her.' Vesta's voice softened as she went to stand beside him. 'I missed you last night.'

'I suppose you heard about Irene?'

'Yes. Did she really fall in the dock?'

'She was drunk.'

'How do you know that?' Marie asked curiously.

'The landlord of the Quarry told the police.'

'Was she a friend of yours?'

Teddy threw Marie a cold glance. 'Course she wasn't.' He quickly changed the subject. 'Listen, Wally's told me to warn you that, in case you fancy a tipple on the quiet, you're not to drink or smoke on the premises.'

'Oh, we wouldn't do that,' said Vesta at once.

'Good. As the brothers don't want trouble with fires from forgotten cigarettes or dog ends. After all this with Irene, and the rozzers coming round again, it's been bad for business.'

'Irene didn't seem like a drunk,' Marie insisted, receiving another glare from Teddy.

'Looks can be deceiving,' he muttered. 'And anyway it's none of your business. Just make sure you stick to the rules.'

Marie watched him go up the stairs. She was thinking that if anyone was deceiving, it was Teddy. How could he talk of the dead in such an irreverent way?

'Why did you say that about Irene?' Vesta asked angrily. 'It's no business of ours, like Teddy said.'

'She is — was — a dancer, like us.'

'Obviously a bad one. Now, for goodness' sake stop asking Teddy silly questions. He got us the job, remember? And you're just making us sound ungrateful.' Vesta threw back her head and strode away.

Marie wasn't ungrateful, but neither was she under Teddy's spell. As she followed her sister, she tried not to breathe in the smell of Teddy's hair oil that hung in the air. She and Vesta might be twins and have a lot of things in common, but their choice in men certainly wasn't one of them.

Chapter 17

By the end of September, the Haskins sisters were still perfecting their new songs. Benny had no time to help them and they hadn't seen Bing again, much to Marie's disappointment. She would have asked him to play for them on Elsie's piano.

'The band is too fast for us,' complained Vesta on the last Saturday of the month as they hurried from the stage towards the dressing room. 'It's not our fault that we can't keep up with them. Do you think Wally will give us the sack?'

'No, he would have done so by now. Teddy hasn't said anything, has he?'

'He's too gentlemanly to do so,' argued Vesta crossly. 'It's Bing's fault for giving us such difficult songs. He don't even bother to play them for us.'

'You told him you would get Benny to.'

'Yes, but how was I to know that Irene would get herself killed? Everyone has been in a bad mood since.'

The chorus girls barely looked up as the twins walked in. They seemed to be discussing their routine and it sounded to Marie as if it hadn't gone very well. Sal flopped on a chair, whilst Bev and Rose kicked off their high heels, blaming one another for missing the steps.

'It wasn't me,' Bev insisted, 'you danced out of step tonight.'

'Only because everyone else did,' replied Rose angrily.

'It was her fault,' said Sal, pointing at Joanie. 'And we all know why.'

Joanie made a rude gesture and stood up. Marie saw her steady herself as she threw off her headdress. With shoulders slumped, she shuffled behind the screen.

'Well, you've been here almost a month now; how do you like working for the Scoresbys?' asked Bev.

'It's our dream come true,' said Vesta with a blush.

'It don't take much to please you, then?' Bev smirked as she rolled down her stockings. 'But I'll give you two credit, you ain't done bad. Wally would have had you out by now if he wasn't pleased.'

'We don't see him much,' Vesta shrugged. 'And we never see Leo.'

'You don't want to neither.'

'Teddy's very nice, though.' Vesta blushed.

'He's lives at your place, don't he?' said Bev curiously.

'Yes, on the next floor.'

'Bet that's convenient,' said Rose sarcastically.

'Teddy is always the perfect gentleman.' Vesta looked offended.

'You'll learn,' Bev sighed wearily. 'In this big, wide world of temptation there ain't many gentlemen left. And our Teddy certainly ain't one of 'em.'

Suddenly Joanie stumbled out from behind the screen. 'Leave them alone,' she shouted in a slurred voice as she tried to grasp the back of a chair. 'They're just kids. Like we all were once. Just like Irene was before—'

Immediately the other girls stood up. Bev went across and grabbed Joanie's arm. 'Keep your voice down, you fool!' she snarled.

'Why should I?' yelled Joanie, her eyes wild and unfocused. 'I'm sick of seeing this happen time and again when we could do something about it.'

'It's too late,' whispered Sal, poking a finger towards her. 'We're all in the same mess and bawlin' your head off won't help.'

'I don't care. I've had enough of lies,' yelled Joanie, as Bev tried to calm her.

Marie watched open-mouthed as Joanie began to cry.

'Stop it, for God's sake, Joanie!' exclaimed Bev.

Suddenly Joanie crumbled, as though all the life had gone out of her. She lay in a heap on the floor. 'She was drinking before she got here,' whispered Bev as she knelt beside her. 'She was supposed to be on the wagon, but Irene's death set her off again.'

'They were good pals,' nodded Sal, as they all crowded round.

'What did she mean about having enough of lies?' Marie asked.

'It was the drink you heard talking,' Bev muttered. 'Let's get her into her ordinary clothes. Somehow we'll have to get her out of the club. You and Vesta, drag the screen round us, in case someone looks in. Better still, when you've done it, go and guard the door.'

'What if someone tries to come in?' asked Marie.

'You'll have to think of something to stop them,' shrugged Bev, returning her attention to undressing Joanie.

Silently Marie and Vesta walked to the door. 'What did they mean about Teddy not being a gentleman?' whispered Vesta after a while.

'I don't know and I don't care,' said Marie, listening to the shuffles, groans and whispers coming from behind the screen. 'I'm more worried about what will happen if that door opens.'

'Joanie should have known better than to get drunk.'

'But Irene was her best friend, it's understandable.'

Suddenly there was a hammering on the door. 'What's going on in there?' a voice demanded.

'Oh my God,' Vesta breathed, clutching Marie. 'It's Teddy.'

Marie's knees turned to jelly as the door opened. Teddy stood there, narrowing his eyes. 'What's all the racket about?'

Marie was filled with fear. She could hear her heart pounding loudly and wondered if Teddy could too. One step more and Teddy would be in full view of the screen.

'It's her!' exclaimed Marie, turning to Vesta. 'She keeps taking my things.'

Vesta's eyes flew open in fright.

'Give me back me new shoes!' Marie grabbed a handful of Vesta's hair and pulled.

Vesta screamed, holding her head. 'Stop it, leave me alone! I ain't got your shoes.'

Marie took another lunge and caught Vesta by the shoulders, shaking her roughly.

'You're hurting me!' shrieked Vesta, trying to get away.

'Stop that!' ordered Teddy, sliding his hands around Marie's waist. She shuddered as his fingers squeezed her.

Teddy held Marie against him. A smile formed on his face as she tried to wriggle out of his arms. 'Well, well, I never thought you had it in you,' he drawled, taking the opportunity to press her into him. 'I must say I like to see a bit of spirit.'

Marie stared into his eyes defiantly. 'Let me go, I wasn't doing anything wrong.' She felt sick at the smell of his hair oil. He held her even tighter.

'Get out of here, Teddy, we'll sort it,' said Bev, coming up.

Teddy smiled, trailing his hands over Marie's hips. Keeping her pinned against him, he muttered, 'You'd better, or else you'll have Wally to answer to.'

'I told you, we will,' insisted Bev. 'Now get out, Teddy, as we're all trying to change.'

Marie held her breath as Teddy hesitated. It seemed an eternity before he released her.

When he'd gone, Marie felt dizzy with relief. She smiled at Bev. 'Thank you.'

'What you did was quick thinking.'

Marie rushed over to Vesta who had collapsed on a chair. 'I'm so sorry, Vesta. I had to make it look real.'

'You could have warned me first,' Vesta said angrily.

'I didn't know I was going to do it.'

'Well, you pulled hard enough.' She examined her head in the mirror. 'I think I've got a bald patch.'

Bev laughed. 'Don't worry, it'll grow again.'

A moan came from behind the screen. They all rushed back to find Joanie trying to stand up. Her coat was half off her shoulders. She fell back again, her head rolling sideways.

'What are we going to do?' whispered Sal fearfully. 'We'll never get her out in this state.'

'She's legless,' agreed Bev worriedly. 'Even if we carried her between us, they'd see.'

'There's a door in the room at the end of the passage,' suggested Marie.

They all turned to stare at her. 'How do you know that?' demanded Bev.

'I went up there by mistake one day.' She couldn't say that she'd seen Hector in the room working, as he'd asked her to keep it a secret.

'Blimey, you risked it.'

'I saw a door with two bolts on it. It must lead out onto the alley.'

'I think we should tell Teddy,' said Vesta suddenly. 'He might help us if we told him the truth.'

Bev stared at her. 'That bit of hair coming out of your head must have loosened your brains, love. No, your *gentleman* would go straight to Wally.'

Vesta gave a pout. 'If you say so. But it sounds very dangerous to me, when it isn't even our fault, it's Joanie's. I've had enough frights for one night.'

'Yeah, me too,' agreed Rose.

Sal nodded. 'Joanie will just have to take what's coming to her.'

'Charming,' said Bev in a cold voice. 'And you two are supposed to be her mates? Well, thank God it ain't me stretched out there.' Turning to Marie, she raised a pencilled eyebrow. 'Do you feel the same?'

Marie shook her head. 'The two of us could do it.'

Bev grinned. 'You're on.'

As soon as Teddy began to sing, Marie and Bev dragged Joanie out into the passage. With her arms slung round their shoulders Joanie moaned loudly as she tried to stumble along.

'Shut up, you silly mare, or we'll drop you right here,' Bev hissed.

Marie tried not to inhale the damp and musty smell of the passage as it grew darker and more suffocating near the end.

'You know we'd be brown bread if Wally caught us?' said Bev, trying to catch her breath as they hauled Joanie along.

'I know, my dad warned me before.'

'Your dad?'

'Yes, he's the handyman now.'

'What, like Sid was? But don't your dad act or something?' Bev puffed.

'Yes, but Wally got him to clear the rubbish instead. That's how I came across the room. Only I couldn't let on to Vesta as Dad asked me not to say he's just the hired help. He knows Mum and Vesta would worry.'

Bev stopped and took a deep breath. 'Blimey, that's rotten of Wally. Your poor old man is living in hope for nothing.'

Marie didn't answer. She was too busy trying to support Joanie's weight as she slumped between them.

Finally they came to the room at the end of the passage. 'Blimey, we're done for if this door is locked,' gasped Bev.

'Dad said he was going to fit a new lock. But he might not have done it yet.' Marie reached out to grasp the handle.

'Thank Gawd your old man ain't on the ball,' sighed Bev when the door opened and they dragged Joanie inside.

Marie slid her hand down the wall to find the light switch. The plaster was damp and peeling and the room smelled of decay.

'Where's the door gone?' Bev asked when the light went on. 'I can't see one.'

'It must be behind those crates.'

'We'll never shift all them.'

Just then, there were footsteps. Marie froze. Joanie groaned loudly. Marie heard Bev's angry rasp, trying to keep Joanie silent. Marie was too frightened to turn round. They held their breaths, waiting to see if it was Teddy or Wally.

Chapter 18

'Marie, what are you doing in here again?' Hector's voice was shocked as he gazed at the three of them.

'Oh, Dad, thank goodness it's you.'

'I told you before, you mustn't come here. What's this?' He pointed to Joanie.

'She had too much to drink. And you know Wally's rules. We can't take her out through the club and we can't leave her in the dressing room. We thought whilst Teddy was singing we'd try this way.'

Hector shook his head. 'I piled the crates in front of the door as Wally told me to.' He wiped his brow with his sleeve. 'It took me ages.'

'I'm sorry,' said Marie, 'but we didn't know what else to do. You see, Joanie is Irene's friend. She was terribly upset when Irene died.'

Hector nodded slowly. 'Yes, that was very sad indeed.' He stroked his moustache as he considered the problem. 'Well, I'll just have to move the crates again. Lay your friend on the floor there. Then, please, both of you go back to the dressing room or else you'll get into trouble, and me too.'

'But you can't move all those again, love,' said Bev anxiously.

'I'll manage. Now, hurry up and go, the pair of you.'

They lowered Joanie carefully to the floor. Marie went to her father and hugged him.

He patted her cheek. 'Quickly now. If I'm caught in here, I can say I'm cleaning. But there's no excuse for you.'

They crept back through the passage. Marie knew they were both too frightened to speak. As they arrived at the dressing room, Teddy's voice faded at the end of his number.

'Quick, we'll just make it,' urged Bev.

'What happened?' All the girls came rushing over as they shut the door behind them.

'Her old man is gold,' said Bev excitedly. 'He's getting Joanie into the alley for us.'

'You mean Dad?' said Vesta in surprise.

'Yes, he heard us and came to see what the noise was.' Marie looked at Bev.

'You were dead lucky it wasn't Wally,' said Rose. 'Listen, is that his voice outside?'

They all gathered at the door and listened.

'Quick!' whispered Bev. 'Look busy! If anyone asks where Joanie is, we'll say she slipped out as she was sick.'

Clothes flew everywhere, Bev began to hum, and Rose and Sal began talking loudly as they clattered the chairs around.

Marie felt herself caught up in a burst of action. All the time she was praying that Teddy and Wally wouldn't go along the passage to the room at the end. At the same time she didn't want them to come in the dressing room either!

Teddy was feeling pleased with himself as he walked off the stage; there had been a mild applause, which was something to be grateful for, as the customers rarely bothered. The men were too preoccupied with their drinking. And their paid escorts, some of whom were the Scoresbys' tarts, had false smiles on their hard, painted faces as they tried to maintain their air of respectability. Not that this lasted long; the moment they opened their mouths it was obvious what they were.

Nevertheless, the twins were making their mark quickly, which had surprised him. They could actually sing! Wally had given him a generous handshake for finding them. But Teddy was beginning to wish he hadn't. In no time at all they had been promoted to prime position. It was a place usually reserved for him, along with the extra cash it afforded.

Teddy felt a moment's deep loathing for the Scoresbys. He needed them and feared them in equal measure. Swallowing down the bitter taste of disgust, he straightened his spine. Nothing and no one would spoil his plans or threaten the stash he was secretly saving. When he'd had enough, he was going to leave this country and disappear. He refused to live the rest of his life at the brothers' mercy. His tart of a mother and the bullyboys she mixed with had had their pound of flesh from him. Now the

Scoresbys would take what was left of him, if they could. But Teddy had other ideas. One day, he would be free of them and leading the life he truly deserved.

Teddy was halfway to the girls' dressing room when Wally stepped out of the office. He froze.

Wally stabbed a finger in his chest. 'Stop right there, a minute.' Wally's breath was sour from the whisky. Teddy swallowed and formed the same obedient expression he'd worn for the last six months.

'Yes, Mr Scoresby, how can I help?'

'Where do you think you're off to?' Wally demanded. 'Trying to do a bunk like you did when them South Londoners got a bit stroppy?'

Teddy had a feeling in his bowels that Wally was not best pleased with him. 'No, of course not!' Teddy pulled at his bow tie nervously. 'You know I'm not so handy when it comes to the physical, Mr Scoresby.'

'Shut your trap.'

'Yes, Mr Scoresby.' Teddy tried not to study the awful disfigurement of Wally's face. It looked like two different people staring at him. One half bore a sneaking resemblance to his brother, Leo, the other to a monster that had curled inside his skin and taken up residence there.

'You didn't think I would notice you trying to do a bunk,' said Wally in the kind of hushed, malevolent tone that Teddy knew was the hallmark of an approaching fit of temper. 'That's why I sent Pedro after you.'

Once again, Teddy kept quiet. He knew the worst was to come.

'And then, what happens?' Wally drew closer and Teddy's breath almost stopped. 'Pedro is all over you like a rash, like he was your mother or something. And what do I see next? Pedro is cutting that Bermondsey geezer, before the ugly sod gets to you.'

Teddy's thoughts were running along the same lines and he hated to admit it, but Wally was right. Pedro had saved him from a very nasty pasting. And though Teddy had been grateful for it, he could see retribution in Wally's menacing expression.

'What is it with you and him?' Wally demanded in the same threatening whisper. 'I didn't take you for a pansy too.'

'I'm not,' objected Teddy before he could think what he was saying. 'Pedro's just a good friend. We don't—'

'I don't give a flying fart what you two are,' Wally interrupted, his tone contemptuous. 'But he ain't your minder, he's mine. That's what I pay him for. To cover my arse and ignore yours.' Teddy thought Wally's eyes looked mad. 'Now, I've given him a rollicking and he knows he's on his last breath. And I'm telling you the same: when it comes to a bundle, you put yourself in the front line, right? If there's a blade coming at me, you take it, or he does. Not like the other night when you fainted away like a bleedin' fairy princess.'

Teddy felt himself go scarlet. His blood pumped humiliatingly into his face. How he hated this man who degraded him.

'Got it now, have you?' The punch to his shoulder made him fall sideways. Another clout around his jaw and he was reeling against the wall. He could hear Wally laughing and all Teddy could do was pray this was just a moment's anger.

'This little slap,' sneered Wally, snatching Teddy's lapels and pulling him close, 'is just to remind you about your terms and conditions of working for the firm. Right?'

Teddy nodded silently as Wally tightened his grip.

'And now you can get rid of that dozy cow Joanie, who thinks she's God's gift to men. I could have danced better than she could tonight, the clumsy bitch. And then you can start upping the ante with the twins. We've had the all-innocence bit and the men are lapping it up. Now it's time to give a sneak preview of what our goods really have to offer.'

Teddy felt his head being forced back into an unsustainable position. 'Y . . . yes, Mr Scoresby.'

'Get 'em new costumes. And not them red tarts' outfits they had on before. Let's have a bit of decorum, as it don't take a genius to know we need to work up the demand, not give everything away all at once.'

Teddy stared into Wally's eyes. Would he ever escape the Scoresbys? They were killers, violent thugs who stopped at nothing to get what they wanted. He still couldn't get the mental image from his mind of Leo splitting open the South Londoners' faces whilst Wally had broken their arms. They had enjoyed every moment and revelled in the screams.

'Well, what are you waiting for?' Wally demanded, roughly pushing him along the passage. 'Go and give them two girls the good news that we're rigging them out with new clobber. And don't forget that tart Joanie.' Wally smiled evilly, stretching the ugly red scars on his face and drawing an index finger across his throat.

Teddy backed away as Wally watched him. Who was to be next, Teddy wondered. First Sid, then Irene and now Joanie. It was a growing list. And Teddy knew that Wally savoured every violent act, almost for the sake of it.

Marie was putting on her coat as Teddy entered the dressing room. The girls all stopped what they were doing.

'What do you want this time?' Bev demanded, glaring at him.

Teddy looked at Marie and Vesta. 'You'll be pleased to know that Mr Scoresby says you can have new costumes.'

Vesta jumped up from the chair where she had been sitting. 'Oh, Teddy, that's wonderful!'

'It's been left up to me to decide the style.'

'Could we have one like that Kay English's, the Ziegfeld girl in that lovely photo?' asked Vesta.

'We'll see.'

'Oh, Teddy, thank you.'

'Have you learned any new songs yet?'

Vesta was already nodding. 'Oh yes,' she said eagerly. 'We're practising all the time.'

'And is the boss buying us new costumes too?' interrupted Bev in a bitter tone. 'Or do we have to make do with what's on the rail?'

'If you've any complaints you'll have to speak to Mr Scoresby.' Teddy looked past her, to Rose and Sal, who were hurriedly packing their bags. 'Where's Joanie?' he demanded, looking round the room.

Marie's heart gave a lurch. Bev closed the lid of her make-up box with a snap. 'She buggered off whilst you were singing,' Bev answered with a toss of her head. 'The poor cow was sick and couldn't dance properly.'

'What was wrong with her?' Teddy asked.

'Must've eaten something.'

Teddy frowned. 'Her dancing was terrible. Mr Scoresby noticed.'

'You'd dance terrible too, if you'd been on the lav all night.'

Teddy was silent for a moment, then walked up to Bev and pointed a finger. 'I want to see her and quick. So make sure she gets the message.'

'Yes, your lordship,' nodded Bev as she ignored him and wiped off her lipstick. 'Any other errands you'd like me to run?'

'You're a lippy cow,' he growled, meeting her gaze in the mirror. 'Just do as you're told.' The atmosphere in the room was tense as he turned and walked over to Marie. His eyes went over her, slipping down to her breasts. Marie was glad she was wearing her old coat as it covered her figure.

'You need a new image,' he told her in a smooth voice. 'Mr Scoresby likes his girls to set an example. I'll take you up West to buy some quality clothes.'

Marie felt her skin crawl. 'No thanks,' she told him coldly. 'I'm not one of Mr Scoresby's girls. I'm just an employee.'

Teddy laughed. 'Have it your way. But Mr Scoresby pays you, remember that. And handsomely too.' He shrugged, walking back through the dressing room, kicking from his path the shoes scattered over the floor. Then suddenly he stopped.

Marie saw Bev stiffen as she watched him warily.

Slowly turning, Teddy frowned at her. 'Joanie's never gone off early before. Are you sure she's not pulling a fast one?'

'She's never had the shits so bad before,' said Bev casually.

'Does she still live in that dump at Whitechapel?'

'No.' Bev's voice betrayed the first sign of fear. 'That was Irene's place. They shared a room together.'

'Where is she living now?'

Bev rolled her eyes. 'Christ, Teddy, how should I know? I ain't her mother.'

Teddy glared at her. 'You'd better pass on what I've said or *someone* will pay for it,' he threatened, then left the room.

Bev sank down on a chair. Her face was white and her hands were shaking. 'I could do with a fag.'

Rose and Sal came over. 'You shouldn't have spoken to him like that,' said Sal, pushing her brown hair away from her face. 'He knows something's up.'

'What else was I to do?' demanded Bev crossly. 'Neither of you two stepped in to back me up.'

'No, because we've got more sense than you,' muttered Rose, sliding her arm through Sal's as though speaking for both of them.

'He gives me the creeps,' Bev mumbled, 'but I won't kowtow to him. He just likes to throw his weight around.'

'Teddy isn't like that!' Vesta burst out. 'You're just upset because we're getting new costumes and you're not.' She looked at the others. 'None of you seems to give Teddy any credit for what he does. He has to manage all the acts as well as look after Mr Scoresby. And you, Marie, had the nerve to turn him down when he offered to get you some decent clothes. I wish he'd asked me, because I would have grabbed the chance.'

Bev's lips trembled as she looked at Vesta. 'I ain't jealous, love. The fact is, he scares me, although I put on a front. And he scared me even more tonight, wanting to find Joanie so badly.'

'He probably guessed she was drinking,' said Vesta shortly. 'You should have told him the truth.'

Bev laughed. 'Yeah, you think so?'

'Yes, I do.' Vesta turned to Rose and Sal. 'If Joanie has got herself into trouble, it's not up to us to get her out of it. Tonight we could have all been blamed for what she did. Even our dad.' She crossed her arms and faced Bev. 'As from now, Joanie has to look after herself.'

Bev got up slowly. She walked over to Rose and Sal. 'Do you two feel the same?'

Rose went crimson. 'She has got a point.'

Sal nodded. 'If you and Marie had got caught, we could have lost our jobs.'

Bev gave a mirthless laugh. 'So I take it that none of you is prepared to help me with the poor cow out in the alley?'

The two dancers shrugged. 'Sorry,' said Rose, glancing at Sal. 'But we think Vesta's right.'

Bev shook her head in dismay. 'And to think, I once thought of you as friends, just like Joanie did.' She turned and snatched up her bag, striding to the door.

Marie hurried after her. 'Wait, Bev, I'll help you.'

'No, love.' Bev smiled gratefully. 'You've done enough. It took guts to do what you did, dragging Joanie up that passage with me. And I won't forget that. Nor will Joanie when she sobers up. I'll see the poor cow's all right, don't worry.' Bev threw a glance of contempt at the other girls as she left.

Rose and Sal soon began telling Vesta that they thought Joanie had always been after Wally, like Irene.

'They made themselves cheap,' pointed out Sal, her eyes narrowing vindictively, 'and didn't give a tinker's cuss about us. So why should we help?'

Marie knew that Rose and Sal were finding excuses to make themselves feel better. But it was Bev who had been the one who cared enough to help a friend. Vesta had spoken her mind and the others agreed with her. Marie felt distanced from her twin. She knew that things were changing.

Chapter 19

The following Friday evening, a girl stopped the twins at the factory gates. 'You're Vesta Haskins, aren't you?' she asked.

Vesta nodded. 'Yes, what do you want?'

'I work over there, in Ellisdon's offices.' She nodded to the tall building at the side of the factory. Her pretty face was flushed as she looked at them, her dark brown hair drawn back from her face and clipped over one ear. 'I've heard you're seeing Teddy Turner.'

Marie looked at Vesta, who had gone pale. 'What business is that of yours?' Vesta demanded.

'He's trouble, that's what. I thought it was only fair to give you a warning.'

'You must have the wrong Teddy,' Vesta said, taking a sharp breath.

'He works at a club up Poplar called the Duke's.'

Vesta gave a soft gasp, as the girl stepped closer.

'Listen, he's bad news,' said the girl in a whisper. 'I wouldn't believe it either once, when someone warned me. But now I'm expecting. He dumped me as soon as I told him about the baby. Gawd knows what I'm going to do.'

'I don't believe you,' said Vesta, regaining her breath. 'The jealous cows here are just making mischief.'

'Well, it's up to you,' shrugged the girl, 'makes no difference to me.'

Marie called after the girl as she walked away. 'Wait a minute, what's your name?'

'Flo Davis,' she replied. 'But I'll bet he says he don't know me.'

Marie took Vesta's arm. 'Go after her, Vesta. Give her a chance to tell you what she knows.'

'It's just gossip.' Vesta pulled away. 'She's jealous, like all the girls who follow him around. This kind of bitchiness is one of the reasons why I hate Ellisdon's and want to leave.' Vesta's face was now flushed red. 'If it wasn't for Mum, I'd give in me notice right now.'

Marie watched the small figure disappear, but Vesta walked off in the other direction. Marie was torn; should she go after Flo Davis? But it was Vesta who should be asking the questions, not her.

Finally the girl disappeared. Marie caught up with Vesta. She knew her sister had made up her mind to stick her head in the sand. Once she had done that, there was no persuading her to listen.

That evening as they were getting ready to go to the club, Vesta turned from the mirror and looked at Marie. 'You're not going to say anything to Teddy, are you?'

'What about?'

'That girl, Flo Davis, of course.'

'It's not up to me to ask him if he's got a girl in trouble.'

'I don't believe her,' Vesta shrugged. 'And I don't want to spoil our day tomorrow.'

Marie stopped brushing her hair. 'What's happening tomorrow?'

'Teddy's taking me to choose our costumes.'

'When did he ask you to do that?'

'I saw him on the stairs yesterday.' Vesta frowned as she saw the startled expression on Marie's face. 'Don't look at me like that. You had your chance, Marie. He asked you first.'

'Vesta, you should think about what Flo said.'

'Why? Teddy has never overstepped the mark with me. Until I find something to complain about, I'll keep me mouth shut.'

'Can't you ask if he knows a Flo Davis?'

Vesta looked angry. 'I told you, no. Now, cheer up, for goodness' sake. We're getting ourselves new costumes and one of us, at least, will be there to choose them!'

When they arrived at the club a tall, leggy blonde was standing in the dressing room talking to Rose and Sal. She wore the sparkly blue outfit that looked to Marie as though it might have been Joanie's. Rose and Sal were laughing at what she said, whilst Bev sat at the mirror, applying her make-up.

'This is Shirley,' said Rose, taking hold of the girl's arm. 'Shirley, meet Vesta and Marie, our twins.'

'Hello, Shirley,' said Marie and Vesta together.

Rose and Sal laughed. 'They always do that,' giggled Rose.

'Nice to meet yer.' Shirley smiled, showing a row of rather uneven nicotine-stained teeth beneath her red lipstick.

'Shirley is Joanie's replacement,' said Sal, glancing across at Bev.

'Replacement?' echoed Marie and Vesta.

'Yes, as Joanie seems to have disappeared, the silly cow. So Teddy took on Shirley and we had a quick practice this afternoon and she's done just fine.'

'Oh, the routine ain't no problem for me,' said Shirley, waving her hand. 'I used to dance at the Folies in Paris.'

'Paris!' Vesta exclaimed. 'Did you really? Oh, that must have been so exciting.'

As Vesta talked with Shirley and the two girls, Marie went over to Bev. She seemed to be taking extra care with her make-up and wouldn't look up. Finally Marie put her fingers gently on Bev's arm. 'Did you get Joanie home safely?' she whispered.

Bev became still, though Marie saw her hand shaking. 'Yes, I let her stay at my place. Then she went out the next day and never came back.'

'But where could she have gone?'

Bev slowly looked round. 'Don't ask no more questions, please.'

Marie gasped. 'What's happened to your eye? It's all black and blue.'

'I walked into a door.' Bev turned back to the mirror. 'Now, if you know what's good for you, you'll piss off.'

'But—'

'Do as I say,' Bev muttered, not turning to look at her. 'Talk to the others or they'll oust you as well.'

'I don't care about them. It's you I'm worried about.'

Bev stared at her in the mirror. 'If that's true, love, just leave me alone.'

Eventually Marie went over to their costumes and began to undress. What had happened to Bev? Would walking into a door have caused such an injury? It looked more as if someone had hit her.

When Teddy's knock came and the girls lined up to do their number, Bev wouldn't look at Marie as they filed out.

'Shirley's nice,' said Vesta when they'd gone. 'She's danced at the Folies, you know. And met a lot of famous people.'

'Did you see Bev's black eye?' Marie asked as she did up the side of her costume.

'No. How did she get that?'

'She said she walked into a door. But I don't believe her.'

Vesta sighed. 'There you go again, poking your nose into someone else's business. She probably had a fight with her boyfriend and doesn't want to say.'

Marie was thinking that someone may have picked a fight with Bev instead. But she knew it would sound as if she was accusing Teddy, whose last words to Bev were that if she didn't give his message to Joanie then someone would pay for it. And as Joanie appeared to have vanished, had Teddy followed up on his threat?

The chorus girls came back, Rose and Sal full of praise for Shirley's dancing. When Marie and Vesta returned after performing their routine, Rose and Sal were still telling Shirley how good it was to have a 'proper' dancer amongst them.

Marie looked across at Bev. There was sadness in her face. Marie was certain she knew more about Joanie, and it was only Marie who bothered to say goodbye to Bev when she left.

'How do I look?' asked Vesta the next day after work. She was wearing a floral dress and a black bolero that looked very pretty, with her blonde hair freshly washed and waved around her face. They had rushed home from work so that Vesta could be ready to go out with Teddy by two.

'You'll need a coat,' said Marie, frowning.

'I'd rather freeze than wear that old thing.'

'You probably will freeze as it's October now.'

'Yes, but Teddy's car will be warm.' Vesta rolled her eyes and put her hand on her stomach. 'My insides are going over, I'm so nervous. And oh, I haven't got a proper handbag!'

Marie slid a small, hand-embroidered purse from the bottom of the wardrobe. 'We got this from Cox Street last year, remember?'

Vesta snatched it. 'It will have to do as I've got nothing else.'

'Have you told Mum you're going out with Teddy?'

'No. She's out all afternoon at the school, cleaning up after the jumble sale this morning. Now, are you going to wish me luck?'

'I'll tell you what Mum would tell you,' Marie smiled. 'Just behave yourself.'

'Yes, and I'll tell you what I couldn't tell Mum,' giggled Vesta, 'that I won't have any fun if I'm good.' She pecked Marie on the cheek. 'Bet you wish you was coming now!'

Five minutes later, Marie was looking out of the window as Teddy opened the car door for Vesta, then drove them away.

Half an hour later, another knock came.

A pair of brown, smiling eyes greeted Marie as she opened the door.

'Bing, what are you doing here?'

He grinned from ear to ear. 'You could sound a bit more pleased to see me.' He looked very smart in casual dark trousers and sports jacket, with a white handkerchief corner poking up from his breast pocket.

'I am pleased of course. Just surprised.'

'Thought it was about time I brought you more songs,' he said, holding out a bundle of papers.

Marie grinned. 'I hope these are not as difficult.'

'I could play them for you? Elsie will let us use her joanna.'

A SISTER'S SHAME

A SISTER'S SHAME 183

'Vesta's not here.' Marie hesitated.

'You could learn them and teach her.'

Marie didn't want to miss the opportunity. 'I suppose I could.'

As they knocked on Elsie's door, Marie wished she'd had a chance to change. She was wearing an old skirt and blouse. Bing looked very handsome. She wondered if he was going to take out those friends again to Epping Forest. Or could it be one particular friend?

'Course you can use it, son,' Elsie agreed immediately, and led the way to the upright piano. Taking a pile of old newspapers from the stool, and brushing the seat, she frowned. 'It needs a bit of tuning, mind.'

'Good enough for us, Mrs G,' said Bing as he seated himself and placed the music in front of him.

'Right, you two, I can't stop to listen,' said Elsie, winding her gold turban around her head. 'I'm off to my friend Sophie, at Bethnal Green. The Rabbi is calling to discuss help for our friends who are fleeing from Germany. Since President Hindenburg died in August, Hitler has given himself the title of Führer. He is making life very difficult for all those who don't conform to his ideas.'

'Elsie, that's terrible. But surely he won't be allowed to continue in that way?' Marie asked.

'I'm afraid that he will,' sighed Elsie as she turned to pick up her bag. 'Anyway, nothing for you two to worry about. Just close the door when you leave, my darlings.'

When Elsie had left, Marie looked at Bing. 'Do you think that Elsie's right about Hitler?'

'Ramsay MacDonald should have the measure of him,' Bing said hesitantly. 'After all, it's only sixteen years since the last bash.'

They were silent for a moment, but soon Bing's face broke into a smile. 'Come on, let's give this one a try. It's called "Crazy Feet".'

Marie was surprised at how easy it was to pick up the tune as Bing played. He seemed to know exactly when to pause and race on, so that when she tried a few steps, it was easy to perform them.

'Very nice,' he grinned when she'd finished. 'Fred Astaire, eat your heart out.'

Marie laughed. 'What's the next one?'

'"All Of Me" by Ruth Etting. Do you know it?'

Marie nodded. 'I like her singing very much.'

Bing turned the pages of the music. 'Do you want me to run through it first?'

Marie leaned on top of the piano. 'Yes, please.'

Placing his fingers lightly on the keys, he began to play. As the opening chords gave way to the rhythm, much slower than 'Crazy Feet', he began to hum, glancing up at her from time to time, until at last, in his rich baritone voice, he began to sing the words.

Marie closed her eyes. This was a beautiful song. It was about someone who was so lovesick, they had decided to give themselves to the one they loved, even though this love couldn't be returned. Suddenly it reminded her of Vesta and she opened her eyes.

Bing stopped playing. 'Is something wrong?'

'The words remind me of someone.'

'Then perhaps it isn't for you?' he asked uncertainly.

'No, I'd like to try to sing it.'

He turned back to the music and Marie took her position behind him, looking over his shoulder so she could easily read the words. The melody was soft and gentle, and although she was nervous, soon Bing's voice carried her along. Finally, when she was confident enough, he let her sing alone.

It was a song she knew would always remind her of that moment, when Bing sat at Elsie's piano and there seemed no one else in the world but them. Just as she remembered the day by the river when Bing had first sung to her.

When it was over, he closed the sheet of music. 'You'll be all right now. I'm sure you'll be able to teach Vesta.'

Marie wanted to say she could listen to him playing and singing for ever, but he stood up to go, and smiled. 'You have a good voice, Marie. Don't ever forget that.'

'Thanks.'

He looked around the room. 'Well, don't want to outwear me welcome.' They left Elsie's and went into the hall. 'See you around then,' he said as he opened the front door.

'Have you been to Island Gardens lately?' she asked.

'The last time I was down that way, I was with a friend. But she's been too busy to come out again.' He grinned. 'I might call on her sometime.'

Marie smiled. 'I hope you do.'

'Do you?'

'Yes.' Marie couldn't bring herself to say that she missed his company and hoped that he would ask her out now. That would be much too forward. She was very disappointed when he walked away.

Back indoors, she curled up on the couch. Bing had told her she had a good voice and, taking the sheet of music, she hummed 'All Of Me'. She could hear his voice in her head and remembered the way he had looked up at her as he played. Was there a message in his eyes? A warm feeling inside her told her there might be. But was this really what she wanted? She felt confused and excited all at once.

She closed her eyes and soon drifted off.

Marie woke in a cold sweat, her heart thudding violently. The woman in her dream cowered fearfully in the corner, away from the man who threatened her. Each time Marie tried to see her face but it was always hidden. The baby in her belly was what she was protecting and Marie knew how precious this infant was to her. As much as Marie willed someone to come to their rescue, the dream always ended with her terrible cries.

Marie shivered, trying to clear her mind. How long had she been asleep? Slowly she got up and walked to the window. Outside, Teddy's car was parked there, its engine rumbling, and Vesta stood on the pavement waving goodbye.

Marie was still trying to throw off the unpleasant feelings the dream had left her with when Vesta walked

in. She was wearing a new coat and carrying two
parcels.

'Just look at me!' she exclaimed, dropping the parcels
on a chair. She began to parade around the room. 'Do
you like my coat? Black astrakhan is the latest fashion.'
She lifted the collar to her face. 'Just like you see on the
films.'

Marie rubbed her eyes, finally coming awake. 'It must
have cost a fortune.'

'Teddy didn't mind.'

'Did Teddy buy it?'

'Of course.' Vesta pointed her toe. 'See? New shoes as
well. Not those horrible common shoes like we make at
Ellisdon's, but smart fashion shoes with high heels. And
you should see our new costumes!' Vesta drew out two
green sequined costumes from the bags. The first thing
that Marie noticed were the low-cut necks and flimsy
straps. 'Aren't they gorgeous?' Vesta said, holding one up
to her. 'The assistant in this shop said they are just like the
Ziegfeld Follies dancers wear.'

'But we're not a vaudeville act,' Marie reminded her.

'No, but Teddy liked them.'

'They're not our style.'

Vesta laughed, shaking her head. 'You're as bad as
Mum, you are!'

'She definitely won't like them.'

Vesta rolled her eyes. 'Grow up, Marie! This is what
we have to wear to get noticed. As for Mum, she won't
even be seeing them. Teddy said he'll drive us to the club

tonight and we can take them in these bags. I'll put every-thing away till we leave. And when you see Teddy, try to be grateful. He spent a lot of money on us today.'

'Mr Scoresby's money, you mean.'

Vesta pouted. 'And what's wrong with that? We're young, pretty and talented. So why don't you just enjoy our success? Think what this means for the future. Now, I'm going to hide these before Mum comes in and starts nagging.'

Vesta hurried to the bedroom and Marie sat down with a sigh. What was happening to Vesta? She didn't seem to be the same person any more. She would never have lied so easily in the past. What would they look like in those costumes? The last time they had been laughed at when they wore those red outfits. These green ones didn't seem much better. Should she refuse to wear hers or would that only cause more trouble?

Chapter 20

Marie was surprised that night when Mr Scoresby, and not Teddy, entered the dressing room.

'You did good,' he told Shirley, who gave a nervous laugh as he walked across and peered at her. 'You ain't no oil painting, gel, but you're a marked improvement on that clumsy tart Joanie.'

He turned to Vesta and nodded. 'I'm glad to see me money wasn't wasted in forking out for new gear.'

'Thank you, Mr Scoresby,' said Vesta, her eyes wide and fluttering. 'They're really lovely costumes.'

Marie didn't think they were lovely at all. She had felt naked and self-conscious after she'd changed into the new costume, with its low neck and high-cut legs. To keep from exposing too much of her breasts she had managed to pin it tighter. Wrapping a sparkly green scarf from the clothes rail around her waist, she had felt able to sing and dance without embarrassment. Vesta wouldn't hear of any changes to hers. Rose, Sal and Shirley had encouraged her, saying how much better she looked.

Wally Scoresby puffed on his cigar as he moved slowly round the room. Marie had forgotten how ugly he was until he came closer. He narrowed his small eyes, one side of his face showing up under the light, as though he had shiny red worms under his skin. 'What's that?' he demanded, pointing his cigar.

'A scarf, Mr Scoresby.'

'I know it's a scarf, but it ain't on your head.'

Marie felt her knees tremble. She couldn't think of anything to say, she felt so frightened.

'Well?' he demanded, frowning at her.

'I . . . I thought the audience might like to see me and Vesta dressed a bit different,' she stammered. 'We did get more of an applause,' she ventured to add.

Wally stared at her, tilting his head as he scrutinized her. Marie knew the girls were all waiting to see what happened. She could feel Bev gazing up from the stool where she sat as if begging her not to say more. Marie knew she couldn't let any of them see how intimidated she felt.

'So you're the brains of the act, are you?' he said at last, his tone derisive. 'Well, I don't pay you to think, I pay you to sing and dance. And as long as the punters are happy, I'm happy.' He stepped very close so that she felt his breath on her face. 'But you were lucky tonight; you gave 'em a bit of a tease and they seemed to like it. Just don't forget that the moment you lose me any trade, you'll have Wally Scoresby to answer to.'

Marie felt the colour burn in her cheeks as she looked down, away from his aggressive gaze.

Wally straightened his back and, very slowly, went over to Vesta. 'As for you, darlin', you got the thumbs-up from the gaffer. Carry on as you are and the Duke's will take good care of you.'

'Oh, thank you, Mr Scoresby!' Vesta gushed. 'I'm very grateful for all you've done for us.'

Wally gave her an ugly grin, then turned his attention to Bev. 'What are you staring at, you ugly cow?' he demanded.

Marie saw Bev look quickly away.

'You'd better smarten yourself up, gel,' threatened Wally, moving across to where she sat. 'Cos the same applies to you. If the customers don't like you, then you'll take the consequences.' He swivelled and looked at Rose, Shirley and Sal. 'The same goes for you lot. Right?'

All three nodded silently. Glaring at them once more, he blew the smoke from his mouth and left the room. Sal, Shirley and Rose let out sighs of relief.

'You lucky bitch, Vesta,' said Rose in a voice filled with envy. 'Wally will see to it you get on now. He's got lots of connections in the entertainment world, so they say.'

'Do you think so?' Vesta asked coyly as they gathered round her.

'You're his favourite, it's obvious.'

Marie went over to Bev, who sat ignored by the others. 'I don't give a flying fart what he thinks of me,' muttered Bev. 'If I could get out of this place, I'd go right this minute.'

'Why don't you just leave?'

Bev laughed emptily. 'Because he won't let me. He might not want me, but he won't let me go, neither.'

A sudden dread filled Marie as she blurted, 'But what if you gave in your notice?'

'No one leaves Wally.' Bev stared at her pityingly. 'He likes the pair of you, just as he liked me, Irene and Joanie once. We were the first three girls here, but he got tired of us . . .'

'What do you mean?'

'I've said too much already.'

'Bev, did Wally and Teddy have something to do with what happened to Irene and Joanie?'

Bev's voice was muffled as she looked back at Marie. 'You don't want to know.' Bev's face became hard. 'Listen, I admire you, gel, for taking on Wally like you did tonight. But he won't forget that in a hurry. As for your sister . . .' she glanced at the four girls talking and laughing together, 'she's playing with fire and can only get burned. My advice to you both is to get out of this dump whilst you can. Your old man too, if he knows what's good for him.'

With that, she stood up, ending the conversation as she slipped on her coat and gathered her things. Without glancing back, she left, once again with her head bowed.

Marie tried to think calmly about Bev's warning. She had to consider if it was to be taken seriously, or if Bev was just jealous of Vesta, like Flo Davis at the factory.

Chapter 21

It was almost a month later, on a cold November Sunday, when Bing called round again. 'I was wondering if you'd like a ride out?' he asked Marie as he stood on the door-step, dressed in a smart overcoat and a trilby hat, which he slid off his head as he spoke.

Marie heard Ada and Vesta's raised voices coming from the front room. There had been nothing but rows since Vesta had got it into her head she was Wally's favourite. Marie nodded quickly. 'Yes, I'll just get me coat.'

'You sure I ain't come at the wrong time?' Bing asked, looking uncomfortable as the quarrelling became louder.

'No, it's perfect timing.' Marie hurried in and took her coat from the peg, calling to Ada that she was going out with Bing.

Soon he was driving them down the Commercial Road. Marie was relieved to be away from the bickering.

'Ain't your mum and Vesta getting along?' Bing asked after a while.

'Mum doesn't approve of Teddy. But Vesta won't hear a word against him.'

'What does your dad say about this?'

Marie lifted her shoulders on a sigh. 'He's taken to staying out late again.'

'Can't say as I blame your mum,' said Bing quietly. 'As you know, Teddy and the club ain't my cup of tea either.'

'You were right,' Marie admitted, putting aside her pride. 'And I wouldn't listen.'

Bing turned briefly, an eyebrow quirked.

'One of the dancers called Irene went missing and was found dead in the docks,' she faltered. 'But the police think it was an accident after Teddy gave them a statement. Then another dancer, Joanie, also disappeared.'

'That's a big coincidence,' Bing nodded as he drove.

'I didn't know Irene, but I did know Joanie.' Marie paused. 'I helped her friend, Bev, to get Joanie out of the club one night when she was drunk. There's a back door in a room we're not supposed to go in.'

'But you did?'

'Me dad helped us. Wally has made him the handyman. I don't believe he ever meant Dad to perform at the club. He just wanted a dogsbody.'

Bing growled under his breath. 'Wally really is the animal they say he is.' He paused. 'Marie, I reckon you should leave that club.'

'I promised Mum I wouldn't without Vesta.'

'And she won't because of Teddy?'

Marie nodded. 'I didn't mean to tell you all this. It's not your problem.'

Bing gave a long sigh. 'You're wrong there, Marie. You might not know this, but Vesta is seeing my pal Charlie. And is about to cause him and his girl, Dolly, a lot of grief.'

'What?' Marie gasped.

'Charlie is going to leave Dolly.'

'But Vesta's mad about Teddy.'

'Then what's Vesta's game?'

'Perhaps it's to make Teddy jealous,' Marie guessed with a heavy heart. 'Working at the Duke's is changing her.'

Bing slowed the car in traffic, his expression grim. 'I've told Charlie he's a right chump, but he won't listen neither.'

'I'll speak to Vesta,' Marie offered, 'but I don't know if it'll do any good.'

'Thanks. It's worth a try.'

After a few moments of silence, Bing threw her a smile. 'Do you fancy dropping in for a cuppa with me mum and dad?'

'That would be nice.'

'I said I might bring a friend.'

As they drove to Aldgate where Mr and Mrs Brown lived, Marie gazed out at the street vendors and pedestrians beginning to fill the Sunday streets of the East End. The smells from the taverns and the hot chestnuts cooked on the barrows mingled pleasantly in the winter's air. It would be nice to meet Bing's parents. But her mind was still on Vesta and Charlie. What would Teddy do if he found out that she was seeing Charlie? It could only spell trouble. Marie didn't think Vesta would heed her warning, but she had promised Bing she would try.

'Is that cup strong enough for you, Marie, love?' asked Ivy, Bing's mother, as she poured rich brown tea into a dainty white china cup.

Marie sipped the delicious brew. 'It's just right, thank you, Mrs Brown.'

'It's Ivy and Johnny to you, dear. We don't go on formalities in this house. Now, Johnny, do the honours and cut the cake.' Ivy sat down at the big square table covered in a starched cream linen tablecloth. The cutlery shone, the speckled knitted tea cosy was put over the teapot and the home-cooked caraway seed cake was sliced up by Johnny.

Marie liked Bing's father. He was an older version of Bing. Johnny was tall and lean like his son, with hair that Marie imagined had once been the identical shade of gold to Bing's. Now it was blended with grey, yet it still stood up on end, as energetic as ever, in what seemed to be the trademark of the Brown family. Johnny also had Bing's big brown eyes and generous mouth. But it was from his mother that Bing got his smile. Ivy was a neat, plump lady with short fair hair, styled into finger waves around her head. She had a smile that, like Bing's, stretched from ear to ear.

The four of them sat in the parlour of the small terraced house that backed onto a row of shops and pubs. The room had a flower-tiled fireplace and over-mantel, a button-back leather couch and two matching easy chairs. There was a brown carpet on the floor neatly bordered by lino. Marie thought it was a solid house, just like Johnny and Ivy, who told her they had lived at Aldgate all their lives and raised two sons there.

'Archie's older by a year,' Ivy explained as she watched Marie turn the pages of the large family photograph album. 'That's my boys when they were nine and ten. Little devils, they were, but they turned out all right, didn't they, Johnny?'

'Too right, love,' Johnny agreed, pressing tobacco into the bowl of his pipe. Though not lighting up, he puffed at it; Ivy had explained to Marie that smoking was only allowed after tea.

Marie looked up from the sepia photograph of two young boys standing in a back yard. They both wore school uniforms and big grins. Their skinny arms were strung around each other and their hair stood up at all angles.

'I can't tell the difference,' Marie said as she looked at Bing and Archie.

'Everyone thought they were twins,' nodded Johnny. 'And you should have seen the scrapes they got into and blamed each other! We never worked out who was the culprit.'

'I brought Marie round here to impress her,' said Bing with a chuckle, 'not to put her off.'

'My two sons were thick as thieves as kids,' said Ivy

proudly. 'Just like you and your sister, no doubt. Bing's told us all about how talented the Haskins girls are.'

Marie looked at Bing. He was now the colour of the red chintz cushion on the couch beside him.

'Mum, don't give away me secrets,' he said, quickly swallowing his cake.

'Oh, he don't stop going on about you,' Ivy continued eagerly. 'And he says what a lovely voice you've got. And of course, how pretty you are, though I have to say in person, dear, you've exceeded all expectations.'

It was Marie's turn to blush. Had Bing really been singing her praises? 'Bing is the one with the good voice,' she answered, glancing shyly across the table.

'Oh, don't we know it,' agreed Ivy. 'Mind you, he's used to family knees-ups and parties. Once, me two sisters and brother lived close by, but now they've moved to all parts of the country and we don't see much of them. Still, we have lovely memories, don't we, Johnny?'

'Yes, and hopefully a lot more to come in the future as our boys' families expand.' Johnny winked at his son.

Marie saw Bing roll his eyes in embarrassment.

'I've got a good idea. Why don't we all go in the other room for a bit of a singsong?' suggested Johnny eagerly. 'This house ain't seen a good knees-up since our Archie's leaving do before he went to Australia three years ago. And we rarely get down the pub these days.'

'No, Johnny, sit down,' said Ivy, waving her hand. 'Marie is used to professional entertainment, not an amateur banging about on a piano.'

'I'd love to hear you play,' said Marie eagerly.

'Would you really?' Ivy looked surprised.

Marie nodded. She looked at Bing, who gave her a mischievous smile. In the short time she had been with Bing's parents, she had managed to forget all about her problems, surrounded by the warmth and harmony in the Browns' cosy home.

Marie glanced through the lace curtains to the early evening outside. She had spent such happy, laughter-filled hours, singing, dancing and having fun with the Browns, that she felt as though she had always known this kind and talented family. They reminded her of how life had once been in her own home before they had discovered the Duke's. She didn't want the day to end.

Ivy closed the sheet music in front of her and replaced it on the pile on top of the piano, mopping her forehead with her handkerchief as she did so. Johnny replaced his ukulele in its case and sat down heavily on the chair, a big grin on his face. Bing and Marie had sung to Ivy's excellent rendition of 'Chinese Laundry Blues', the last of the many other popular songs in her repertoire.

Ivy swivelled round on the piano stool and smiled at Marie. 'I hope we haven't worn you out.'

'Not at all,' Marie said a little breathlessly as she sat on the couch by Bing.

'Nothing like a good family singsong to bring people together,' said Johnny. 'Kids never forget them as they grow up.'

Ivy laughed. 'Once upon a time we would have all gone down the pub and carried on there. The Cubby Hole was our favourite, and now our son plays there.' She looked across at her husband. 'Whoever would have thought that, eh?'

'How's Elsie?' Johnny asked as he slipped his tie from his collar as he sat in the easy chair. 'Me and Ivy ain't seen her for ages.'

'She's very well,' Marie answered. 'I'll tell her I've seen you.'

'Give her our best. The pub was never the same after Joe died and she retired. Kind of lost its character.'

'Well, don't let's get maudlin,' said Ivy firmly, lifting the tray full of dirty crocs that had been ignored during the afternoon of merrymaking. 'You'll stay for supper, Marie love, won't you?'

'No, Ivy, thank you all the same.' Marie rose to her feet. 'I must get home as Mum didn't know where I was off to.'

'Next time, perhaps.'

Johnny helped his wife take the things out to the kitchen and Bing brought in Marie's coat. 'It's a shame you can't stay. Mum does a tasty bubble and squeak for Sunday supper.'

'Don't tempt me,' Marie sighed. She wasn't looking forward to going home. If Ada and Vesta weren't speaking, the house would be very quiet and tense. On the other hand, they could still be going at it hammer and tongs. Marie looked up at Bing as he helped her on with her coat. 'I've had a lovely afternoon, thank you.'

'Me mad family ain't put you off then?'

Marie laughed. 'You've got a lovely family. I can see now where you got your talent from.'

'They're all right,' he agreed with a grin, 'not bad, as families go.' He tilted his head and drew a hand through his hair. 'Next Sunday?' he asked. 'Reckon you could stand my company again?'

Marie looked into Bing's big brown eyes and knew that she couldn't refuse him. He lifted her chin, his fingers soft and gentle on her skin. He looked into her eyes, a clear message written there. She gave a little shudder of delight. Her heart was being stolen and she knew he was about to kiss her.

Then suddenly, Ivy and Johnny's voices could be heard in the hall. Bing let her go as Ivy bustled in to say her goodbyes.

It was the following Saturday afternoon, as they were walking home from work, that Marie brought up the subject of Charlie. She knew it would upset Vesta but she had promised Bing she would try.

'Are you seeing Charlie?' she asked as they walked by the dock gates.

'Who told you that?' Vesta snapped. She had been in a bad mood all morning after Teddy had promised to take her out shopping this afternoon, then said he couldn't.

'Bing is Charlie's friend and he also knows Dolly.'

'You can tell Bing to mind his own business.'

'Charlie might leave Dolly for you. Have you thought about that?'

Vesta tossed her head. 'It's just a bit of fun, that's all.' Nevertheless, Vesta hurried past the dock gates. Marie knew she didn't want to bump into Charlie in front of her.

'Vesta, stop.' Marie caught her up.

Vesta laughed, pushing her dirty turban away from her face. 'It's only Teddy I'm interested in.'

'Are you trying to make him jealous?'

'Course I am,' admitted Vesta brazenly. 'I want him to know that he's not the only fish in the sea.'

'But what Flo Davis said about him might be true.'

Vesta laughed. 'It was all lies, as I thought. I asked Teddy and he said he hadn't heard of her before. I could see he was telling the truth.'

Marie shook her head slowly. 'You don't know for sure.'

Vesta turned away in a huff. They walked on in silence, and although Marie tried again, Vesta wouldn't listen. To make matters worse, when they got within sight of home, a familiar figure was standing on the doorstep. Tall and dressed in a smart herringbone overcoat, scarf and gloves, Teddy was unmistakable.

Vesta ran up the steps and threw her arms around him. 'Teddy, darling, you're waiting to take me out after all?'

Marie saw Teddy disentangle himself, a scowl on his face. 'I'm afraid not. I'm leaving.'

Vesta gasped. 'What? Leaving here?'

'Yes, for good.' He lifted the suitcase on the steps beside him. 'The people in this house have finally driven me away.'

'Do you mean Mum?' Vesta's voice was a hoarse whisper.

Teddy's nod was sharp. 'Amongst others, yes.' He glanced bitterly at Marie. 'I can't live here any more.'

'Oh, please don't go, Teddy! What will I do without you?' Vesta gave a cry of despair as she clutched his arm.

'I'm sorry. I'll see you at work this evening.'

'But where will you live now?'

'I've found other rooms more to my liking.'

'Teddy, don't go, I love you.'

Teddy shook her off and hurried down the steps, ignoring Marie. He strode to his car parked in the road and put the suitcase in the back. With a slam and fierce roar, the vehicle sped off.

Vesta turned on Marie. 'You see what you and Mum have done? I'll never forgive you.'

'We haven't done anything.'

'You hate him, you always have. Well, now he's gone and I hope you're satisfied!' Vesta ran inside.

Marie followed, wondering what had happened to cause Teddy to leave today. The answer soon came when she found everyone in the hall.

Wippet held Kaiser in his arms. The little animal was trembling, his leg stuck out at a strange angle. Elsie stood beside them, trying to comfort the frightened creature. Ada faced Vesta, who stood shaking with anger.

'What did you say to make Teddy leave?' Vesta demanded.

'It wasn't us who made him leave,' Ada replied, her face thin and tight as Vesta glared at her. 'I saw him being cruel to Kaiser, and he left rather than admit it.'

'You're lying!' Vesta exclaimed, tears brimming in her eyes. 'You just want to get rid of him!'

'That's not true, love,' Elsie interrupted, laying a hand on Vesta's arm. 'Your mother ain't a liar. She saw what she saw, and so did Wippet. Teddy kicked Kaiser down the stairs, because he was chattering outside Teddy's room.'

'My poor Kaiser,' whispered Wippet, his big head and small body crouched on the stairs as he tried to comfort the monkey. 'He's hurt your leg.'

'Teddy would never do such a thing,' shouted Vesta. 'Your monkey probably just fell from the banister. He's always doing silly things and everyone encourages him by laughing. Teddy was easy to put the blame on as none of you like him.'

'If you think that, then you're daft, girl,' said Elsie sharply. 'Teddy has got a flamin' temper on him and took it out on a defenceless animal. Not only that, but he was very rude to your mother.'

'He had reason to be,' pouted Vesta, ignoring Ada. 'You don't know the half, Elsie, so don't interfere.'

Elsie's dark eyes glittered. 'Ducks, I have known you since you were seven years old and your mother is my best friend. She wouldn't hurt a fly and she didn't deserve to be spoken to the way she was. And if you've any sense at all, you'll steer clear of that arrogant bugger, and wake up to reality. All that bloomin' fame and fortune rubbish has turned your head. And not for the better, may I say.'

Marie watched Vesta pull back her shoulders and walk away as the painful chattering of the little monkey filled the hallway and Wippet tried to ease its suffering.

Marie didn't want to go to the club that night, but at home no one was speaking. Wippet had put Kaiser in his small cage and taken him to the animal hospital. To hear Kaiser's continual screeches had been very upsetting.

'Mr Scoresby wants to see you,' Teddy said to Vesta when the twins arrived at the club. He looked at Marie. 'But not you.'

Vesta gave Marie a smirk and followed Teddy into the office.

'Where's Vesta?' the girls asked when Marie went into the dressing room.

'Mr Scoresby wanted to see her.'

Shirley, Sal and Rose all looked at one another. 'Wonder what he wants,' said Sal, frowning.

'It might be to do with the new room he's opening up,' Rose said as she pulled on her costume. 'It's for Wally and Leo's rich friends and private parties. There will be lots going on, like gambling, cabaret and drinking, which is why Wally and Leo have kept it under wraps.'

'But what's that got to do with Vesta?' asked Marie as she began to undress.

'*She's* Wally's favourite, ain't she? Pedro told me things are changing round here.' Shirley tossed her head, slyly winking at Sal and Rose. 'He hears all the gossip behind the bar.'

'Don't take no notice of her,' muttered Bev, glancing angrily at Rose. 'She's winding you up, that's all.'

'Why don't you just shut up, face-ache?' muttered Rose, pushing past Bev's stool and managing to tip it over. 'Oops, just look at her,' sneered Rose as Bev sprawled on the floor. 'Plastered, like her mate Joanie!'

Marie could hardly believe what happened next. Bev scrambled to her feet and launched herself at Rose. They fell together on the clothes rail, pulling each other's hair as blue feathers flew around them and sequins scattered over the floor. Screams pierced the air and Bev's long nails flew viciously at Rose's face. The next moment, Bev was on her back and Rose was on top of her. Marie stumbled forward, her feet caught in the tangle of costumes, headdresses, feathers and underclothes. She tried to separate the two women, but at that moment the door opened and Teddy rushed in.

'Look what she's done to me!' Rose cried, holding her scratched face. 'She's scarred me for life! And only because I was telling her to stop spreading gossip.'

'You bloody liar! You're the one with a poisoned tongue!' Once again Bev flew at Rose. Teddy stepped between them and pushed them apart.

'I gave you women a warning, and still you act like a bunch of wild animals. So now you can answer to Wally. You two, go into the office and wait for me there.'

With her head hanging low, Bev stumbled out of the dressing room, followed by Rose.

Teddy glanced at Sal and Shirley. 'Well, what are you two gawping at? You've got a job to do. And pick up those costumes. Mr Scoresby doesn't pay out a fortune to have it trashed.'

'Yes, Teddy,' they said obediently.

Teddy turned to Marie. 'As for you, Mr Scoresby wants you to dance with the girls from now on. He has other plans for Vesta.'

'What do you mean?' Marie asked, her jaw dropping.

'Your sister will be singing before a selected clientele and you won't be needed. Think yourself lucky that Mr Scoresby has given you a place in the chorus line.' Teddy's eyes held a cold contempt as he added, 'This will serve as an example to anyone who even thinks about making trouble.'

'But you can't—' Marie began, only for Teddy to turn his back on her and leave the room.

'See? We told you so,' said Sal, looking at Shirley knowingly. 'Wally has taken a shine to your sister. And you needn't look down your nose at us like that. You're lucky you've still got a job.'

Marie stared at them as they giggled and whispered together. She knew that they were enjoying her humiliation and she also knew that Teddy had taken his revenge for this afternoon.

'What happened in here?' demanded Vesta, as she rushed in. 'Mr Scoresby has got Bev and Rose in the office. Did they really have a fight?'

'That silly cow Bev attacked Rose,' nodded Shirley. 'She went at it hammer and tongs. Rose could be scarred for life.'

'Vesta, did Mr Scoresby tell you he's separating us?' Marie asked as Vesta took off her coat.

'Yes,' nodded Vesta sheepishly.

'What did he say?'

'That he's giving me a chance in the new part of the club.' Vesta held out her hands. 'I'm sorry, Marie, but he don't like your voice as much as mine.'

'He's never heard it. We always sing together.'

'I can't help that.'

'Leave the kid alone,' said Sal archly, slipping her arm through Vesta's. 'There ain't no use taking it out on her. Wally's chose her out of the two of you and that's that.' She narrowed her eyes at Marie. 'You'll have to make do with dancing with us.'

Shirley patted Vesta's cheek. 'Congratulations, kiddo, you're going places. I, for one, wish you good luck.'

'Me too,' nodded Sal, glancing triumphantly at Marie.

Marie shook her head slowly. 'You don't know anything about this room, Vesta. Or what it will be used for.'

'Blimey, that's just sour grapes,' Shirley remarked as she turned to Vesta and smiled. 'Make the most of it, I say, while the going's good.'

'I am,' said Vesta defiantly, looking into Marie's shocked gaze. 'It would have helped if you'd been nicer to Teddy,' she continued in a resentful tone. 'You'll have to go home on your own tonight as Teddy is taking me up West to show me a really posh club. He says I'll be able to learn a lot from watching the cabaret.'

'You lucky cow. What are you going to wear?' said Shirley, before Marie could reply. 'You ain't got nothing for a party.'

'Oh, yes, I have. I brought me new coat, and a dress and shoes. They're over there behind the screen tucked away.' Once again she turned to Marie, a sulky expression on her face. 'I'm sure Mum will have something to say when she knows you've let me go off on me own. But you can tell her she might as well get used to it. I'm a big girl now and don't need you to look after me.'

The door opened and it was Rose. Her dark hair framed her scratched face as she hurried in. 'I need a fag,' she said as she sat down with a sigh. 'Wally gave me a grilling and was furious when he saw what she'd done to my face. But I had to fight me corner to end up on the right side of him.'

'You know Teddy'll go mad if he catches you smoking,' warned Shirley. 'A place like this would go up in a blink if ever it caught fire.'

Rose took a roll-up from her bag, lit it and closed her eyes in satisfaction. When she opened them, she looked at Marie. 'So I hear you'll be dancing in the chorus line?

Well, that's a turn up for the book!' A look of contempt filled her eyes.

'Where's Bev?' asked Shirley as Rose puffed out smoke into the air.

'She's got the sack. You won't see no more of that stupid cow.'

Marie felt sick. 'What do you mean?'

'She was trouble and they've got rid of her.'

Everyone went silent. 'But what about her things?' Marie asked.

'We're to give them to Wally.' Rose turned to Sal. 'Here, get Bev's things together, will you?' Rose stretched out an arm and pointed the cigarette at Marie, narrowing her eyes as she spoke. 'You'd better watch your step or else you'll be going the same way as Bev. She never knew when to keep her mouth shut and nor, it seems, do you.' Her eyes were full of triumph as she held up the bag that Sal handed her. 'Say goodbye to your friend.'

Marie watched Rose drop the cigarette on the floor and put it out with the tip of her shoe. Swinging her hips, she left the room, taking the bag with her.

Marie looked back at Vesta, but she was talking to Sal and Shirley. What was going to happen now, Marie wondered. A cold shudder went through her as she thought of poor Bev. Marie knew that Rose had managed to get rid of Bev and take the lead over the girls. Through Rose, Teddy had managed to have his revenge after all.

Chapter 22

'Oh, no!' Ada gasped when Marie told her the news that night on her return home. Ada stood in her dressing gown, looking exhausted.

'Mum, she's a big girl now.'

'No, she ain't, she's a baby.' Ada sniffed back her tears. 'Where was your father in all this?'

'He was doing jobs for Mr Scoresby.'

Ada buried her face in her hands and sank down on the hard kitchen chair. 'I was going to have it out with Vesta tonight; try to make her see that Teddy is the guilty party, not us. I waited up specially.'

'She wouldn't have listened.' Marie wearily took off her coat and sat beside Ada. 'Mum, try not worry.'

Ada jerked up her head. 'I should have refused to let her work at that place. I knew it would bring trouble to our door. Vesta can't be reasoned with and your father is like a stranger. I can't remember the last time we all sat down and ate a proper meal. The Duke's has driven us all apart. We ain't a family no more.'

Marie knew her mother was right. They hadn't listened

to the warning she had given them and now Vesta was turning against them.

Ada looked distraught. 'What are we to do, Marie?'

Marie held her mother's cold, thin hand. 'We must hope Vesta sees Teddy for what he is.'

'But will she?'

Marie couldn't bring herself to tell Ada about Vesta going into the new part of the club. She couldn't add to the worry that was now heaped on Ada's tired shoulders. She had to put on a brave face. Ada was unhappy enough.

'It will be all right in the end. Vesta will come to her senses.'

'I only pray she does.'

'Go and get some sleep now. I'll wait up for Vesta.'

Ada nodded reluctantly, her face a picture of despair. 'I used to worry about your father going off the rails and now it's Vesta. Marie, you won't ever go the same way, will you?'

Marie stood up and folded her mother in her arms. 'We're going to be a family again, Mum. One day this will seem like a bad dream.'

'I hope so, love.'

After her mother had gone to bed, Marie waited up, hoping either Hector or Vesta would come in. But neither of them did. Marie went to bed in the early hours and fell asleep listening for Vesta, hoping she would climb into the bed beside her.

★   ★   ★

In the morning, Marie woke alone. She hurriedly washed and dressed and went into the front room. Her mother was sitting by the window, looking very pale.

'Mum, Vesta didn't come home.'

'I know. I looked into your room to see if she had.' Ada clenched her thin fingers together in her lap. 'But your father returned, saying that Mr Scoresby had kept him late.'

'Did you tell him about Vesta?'

'Yes.' She sighed. 'He was very upset. This morning he went out early for a walk to clear his head.'

Marie sat quietly with her mother. It felt very lonely without Vesta. Even though Vesta never woke in a good mood lately, at least she was there. But Vesta was always thinking about Teddy and he knew Vesta liked the finer things in life. To keep her under his thumb he gave her what she wanted, and Marie was afraid that his plan was working.

The hours seemed to go slowly. Marie and Ada kept looking out of the window. When Hector returned, it was almost midday. Ever since he had become a handyman at the Duke's, he cared less about his appearance. His shirt was crumpled and open at the neck and there were stains down the front of it. His old trousers hung from him, revealing the weight he had lost.

'Where have you been?' demanded Ada crossly.

'Has Vesta come home?'

'No.' Ada's voice trembled as she sucked in a sob. 'You should have watched out for her at that club.'

Hector shuffled forward, his shoulders slumped. 'You don't understand, Ada. I—'

'I understand very well,' broke in Ada tearfully as she jumped to her feet. 'I don't want to hear any more excuses. I'm going in to see Elsie.'

The door slammed and Hector groaned. 'I don't want to upset your mother. I love her too much to hurt her.'

'Then why don't you spend more time at home, Dad? She needs you here.'

Hector lowered his head. 'Yes, I know. Marie, there's something I must tell you.'

'Are you in trouble?'

His eyes met hers. They were filled with the same expression of fear that she had seen in Bev's. 'We all are, Marie. This might seem like madness to you, but you must take your sister away somewhere – somewhere they can't find you – can never find you.'

'Dad . . .' Marie hesitated. 'What are you talking about?'

'The Scoresbys. They are evil people and have no intention of furthering your careers. They are opportunists of the worst kind . . .'

Marie went to him as he wiped his hand across his sweating forehead. 'Dad, you're frightening me.'

'I know, and I am sorry. But I should have given up this business years ago and supported you, like a proper father. But I was deluded, my dear, blinded by ambition, and didn't see the dangers, not even after—' He stopped and turned away. 'You would have all been better off without me.'

'Oh, Dad, please don't say that. And what do you mean about the Scoresbys being evil opportunists?'

'They're corrupt,' he said passionately, 'and will soon draw you both into their underworld.' He closed his eyes briefly. 'I dread to think of it. And I blame myself for not seeing the danger before.' He turned, his eyes filled with tears. 'But it's not too late for you and Vesta. Believe me when I tell you the reason I'm absent from home is not because I'm drinking again, but because I've been trying to save up a little money. I perform on every street corner, anywhere I can, at all hours, so that I can at least send you away with a nest egg.' He took her hands, clasping them tightly. 'The money will provide for you and Vesta to start afresh.'

Marie shook her head in confusion. 'But we couldn't leave you and Mum. This is our home and we love it.'

'You must go. You are in danger, my dear. The Scoresbys are powerful and even have some of the police in their pay.'

Marie felt as though she was trapped in a bad dream. It had the same feeling as the one she always had about the pregnant woman. 'Are you sure, Dad?'

'Yes, I've overheard the brothers talking. They give backhanders to the bobbies and even blackmail people in high places to get what they want. The only way for you and Vesta to be safe from the Scoresbys is to leave the East End.'

'But where would we go?' Marie asked bewilderedly. 'We only know the island.'

'Perhaps Elsie could help us.'

'Even if she can,' Marie pointed out, 'Vesta won't leave Teddy. She says she's in love with him.'

Marie looked at the pitiful sight of her father as he thrust his hand wearily through his untidy hair. Like her, he knew that Vesta's feelings for Teddy would set her against any plan they could make to leave the island. Just like the dream she had had so many times, the feeling of dread was surrounding her.

Ada had been right all along.

And none of them had listened.

Bing struggled yet again to tame his wilful mop of hair, which refused to sit flat on his head for very long, despite his attempt to force it into place with a wet comb. After a few minutes, his thick golden hair was standing on end again.

He glanced out of the window at the Blackwall rooftops and smoking chimneys, which were slowly becoming eaten by the pale grey mist that was descending over the docks. November was proving to be cold and dreary, and the fog that now loomed spoiled any chance of a pleasant afternoon with Marie. A trip to the West End would prove impossible if the visibility worsened. The furthest they might get in the car would be Poplar, and perhaps a coffee stall open for a hot drink. But undeterred, Bing lifted the sheet music he had selected and slid it into the inside pocket of his overcoat, taking one more glance in the mirror. Straightening his tie and giving himself an encouraging wink, he left his small room and hurried down the steps of the tenement block and out to where he had parked his car.

During the short drive to Sphinx Street, he wondered if he should chance even the short journey to Poplar. The fog was coming down thickly. But his heart sank when he arrived at number two. A large black vehicle he recognized as Teddy's was parked in the road.

As Bing climbed out of his car, Marie ran down the steps. 'Oh, Bing, something awful's happened,' she blurted as he met her. 'I . . . I must go after her—'

He held her shoulders gently as the damp yellow mist swirled around them. 'Hold your horses, what's up?'

'Vesta stayed out all night with Teddy. Then when she came in today, she said she was leaving.'

'Leaving home?'

Marie nodded, pushing strands of wavy hair from her eyes. 'Dad tried to stop him, but Teddy just pushed him aside. Mum begged her not to go, but she wouldn't listen. I've got to try again before he drives off.'

Bing glanced at the car, then led Marie back to the steps. 'Go inside in the warm.'

'What are you going to do?'

'Talk some sense into her, if possible.' Bing gave her one last gentle push. When he reached the car, Teddy climbed out.

'What do you want?' Teddy demanded, moving cautiously round to where Bing stood.

'I want a word with Vesta.'

'What business is it of yours?' Teddy sneered, poking a finger in Bing's shoulder. 'Get lost and don't interfere again.'

Bing felt his anger rise. He pushed Teddy's hand out of the way. 'Listen, you lowlife, you don't scare me. I ain't an old man you can push around. Or a woman you can threaten. Your first mistake was getting out of that motor and the second was opening your big gob.'

Teddy lunged at him, but Bing snatched his collar and dragged him round to the side of the car. Vesta's white face appeared at the glass.

'Leave him alone!' she screamed as she wound down the window, her eyes wide in fright.

'Let go of me—' Teddy began, only to cower as Bing pressed him back against the car.

'Are you really intending to go off with him?' Bing demanded as he gazed at Vesta.

'Course I am. I love him. Now let him go.'

'This is your chance – your last chance – to change your mind,' Bing muttered, exerting pressure on Teddy, who was going red in the face as Bing held him fast.

'Why would I do that?' Vesta demanded, sticking her head out to look at Teddy. 'You're hurting him, you monster!'

'He'll live,' growled Bing angrily. 'Vesta, get out of the car and come with me. Your family loves you, and wants you back.'

'Leave us alone!' Vesta said, pulling the collar of the expensive-looking coat around her pale face. 'They drove

Teddy away and I'll never forgive them. You can tell them that Mr Scoresby has offered me a part in his new cabaret and I'll never go back to Ellisdon's.'

'I'll have you for this, Brown, and that's a promise,' Teddy snarled as Bing reluctantly released him. As he stumbled into the swirling layers of fog, Bing could hear him cursing.

The car soon sped away into the yellowing mist and Bing could only watch helplessly. Teddy was a coward at heart, full of bluster, and an opportunist. How could Vesta be so blind to the truth?

Sighing heavily and pushing his hands in his pockets, Bing walked back to number two, his heart heavy. He feared for Vesta but, more than that, he feared for Marie.

'How could she go off with him like that?' Ada cried as she sat on the couch, her eyes red raw and a crumpled handkerchief in her hands.

'Now, now,' soothed Hector, his once handsome face creased with worry lines as he put his arm gently round her. 'She'll soon tire of being away from home – you know our Vesta.' He looked across to where Marie sat with Bing on the easy chairs beside the fire. Marie saw the secret agony in his eyes.

'It's *him*, that Teddy, who's turned her against us.' Ada stood up, pacing the room as though she was trying to think aloud. 'Where is she living? Is it with him? But she couldn't! Living in sin would be against all we've taught her. Oh, Hector, you must get her away from him. It's your responsibility as her father.'

'But, my dear, what can I do? She says she loves him.'

'She don't know what love is. All she has is these big ideas that you gave her; never a day went by when you told her she could be famous if she went on the stage.'

He nodded, sinking his head on his chest. 'And for that I am truly sorry, Ada. I should have listened to you.'

'Sorry won't help our daughter now,' Ada said, angry tears filling her eyes again. 'As a mother, I know she's in danger, I feel it!'

'I'll speak to her on Friday,' Marie said quietly.

'And I shall be beside you when you do,' Hector nodded, squaring his shoulders in a fresh attempt to look positive. 'With a little diplomacy, we'll persuade her to come home, I'm sure.'

'She didn't even say where she'd been last night,' croaked Ada, threading her handkerchief between her fingers as though she hadn't been listening. 'She just came in and announced she was leaving. Just like that. As though all the years before didn't matter. As though we were nothing to her. She ain't even taken her clothes. Just said *he* was going to buy her new ones. Like that coat she had on today. I've never even seen it before. Dressed up like a little madam, she was. No, not a madam, but someone that I didn't recognize . . .' Ada held her face in her hands and began weeping. Hector went to her and held her in his arms.

The room was silent as no one knew what to say.

Marie looked at Bing. 'I'll make some tea.'

After a while, he joined her in the kitchen. 'Marie, I don't want you to go back to the club,' he told her firmly.

'I don't want to, either. But—' She stopped as she put the kettle on to boil. Turning to Bing, she whispered, 'Mum doesn't know this, but Dad says he's been saving up for me and Vesta to go away. Like you, he believes the Scoresbys are bad people, but now it's too late. Vesta's gone with Teddy. If I leave the club, how will we see her if she don't come home? As it is, they've separated us. I'm in the chorus line, and Vesta is to sing in this new room that's specially for Wally's rich friends.'

'Did Vesta go along with this idea?'

'Yes, I'm afraid she did.'

'Christ, that ain't good.' Bing pushed a worried hand through his hair. 'But how can I protect you at the club?'

She smiled. 'Is that what you want to do?'

He nodded. 'If you'd let me.'

She felt his arms go round her, pulling her gently against him. 'Marie, listen, I understand you feel responsible for Vesta, but it sounds like they ain't about to make it easy for you at the club.'

'I know. But I've got to stay till we know about Vesta.'

'Then I'll be there to meet you after you finish. I want the Scoresbys to know that someone is in your corner.'

'You'd do that for me?'

He lifted her chin tenderly. 'That and a lot more. This ain't the time to tell you, but I love you, Marie. Always have. Always will.'

'Oh, Bing, I—'

'You don't have to say anything.'

Marie's eyes filled with tears. 'I don't deserve you.'

'I just want you to know the truth. I can't keep saying I'm only a friend. What I feel is more than friendship. Much more.'

He bent his head slowly and kissed her full on the lips. She found herself kissing him back, her heart pounding. 'Oh, Bing,' she mumbled, her body quivering as he held her.

'I love you, Marie,' he told her again.

She looked into his eyes. 'And I love you too.'

He smiled, tracing a finger over her cheek. 'Then whatever lies ahead, we'll face it together, right?'

She nodded, but what could Bing or anyone do, if the Scoresbys were as powerful as Hector had said?

'Let's have a smile now and try to cheer your mum and dad up,' he whispered, taking her hand. 'Tomorrow is another day. Things won't look as black as they do now.'

Marie hoped that was true. Dare she let herself have hope? For a few short moments, the icy feeling inside her disappeared and a comforting warmth replaced it.

Chapter 23

'I'll hold your sister's job until Friday,' said Mr Morton the following week. 'But after that, I'll find someone to replace her.'

'Thank you, Mr Morton.' Marie stood alone in his office before his large desk. The offices were in a building adjacent to the factory and very clean compared to the dirty, dusty and noisy shop floor.

Folding his hands in his lap, he rested back in his chair. His long, stern face wore an expression of curiosity. 'And you, Marie, do you intend to remain here at Ellisdon's?'

'Yes, Mr Morton, of course.'

'You've been here since you left school?'

Marie nodded, looking down in her lap and remembering the days that she and Vesta had shared at Ellisdon's. They hadn't all been happy, but they had been together and had a laugh. That was, until the job at the Duke's came along.

'Have you thought about your own future?' Mr Morton asked.

Marie looked up, surprised at his question. 'No, Mr Morton.'

'There will be a position free in the clerical department soon. I would like to place someone there whom I can trust and engage someone new for the cutting room.'

'But I can't type or do shorthand,' she blurted.

A kind smile broke over Mr Morton's stern face. He sat forward, adjusting the glasses on the end of his long nose. 'This particular post requires a runner between the factory and the offices, delivering parts and correspondence. Also you will be required to check off the leather as it is brought in by the barges to the warehouse. It's a responsible job, requiring good timekeeping. Do you think you could do that?'

'Yes, I think so, Mr Morton,' Marie nodded.

'Good. You're a bright girl. And you've been with us long enough for me to believe that you will be suitable for the job that Miss Davis did.'

'Miss Davis?' Marie repeated in surprise. 'Flo Davis?'

He frowned. 'Do you know her?'

'Only in passing.' Marie felt her cheeks grow warm.

'Well, she was a good employee and I'm sorry we lost her due to her unfortunate circumstances. Now, I think that's all. Think about the offer I have made you and let me know by the end of the week.'

'Thank you, Mr Morton.'

She left the office and hurried across to the factory. The chimneys were belting out smoke across the docks and the cold November wind was blowing the dust from the open containers across the bare yards. The hoots and sounds from the river, along with the cry of the gulls, added to the lonely feeling of the day without Vesta to talk to.

As Marie put her coat in the cloakroom and wrapped her coarse apron around her waist before going to the cutting room, she looked in the mirror. A wave of sadness engulfed her. She missed Vesta so much. Not even the offer of the new job had helped, although it would be a fresh start if Vesta truly wasn't coming back. She didn't like to think about that. Perhaps by Friday, Vesta would be home.

Marie looked at her reflection in the cracked, rusty cloakroom mirror. Her abundance of blonde waves and her big blue eyes stared back. So Flo Davis had been telling the truth.

'Unfortunate circumstances', Mr Morton had said. Marie shuddered at the thought of Flo having Teddy's child, with little hope of marrying the father.

On Friday, when Marie arrived nervously at the club, neither Teddy nor Vesta was to be found. 'Teddy said you're to wear Bev's old costume,' said Rose in the dressing room as she smeared red lipstick over her lips. 'You've seen us do the routine enough times. So you'll easily pick it up.'

Marie listened as Rose repeated the steps and saw Sal and Shirley smirking in the mirror. She knew the girls didn't like her, but she wasn't going to let them see that she cared. She didn't ask about Vesta either, as she knew they wouldn't tell her.

Their performance that night was brief, as a brawl started at the bar. Pedro dealt with the drunks but the club was left empty, and the cabaret and band was dismissed for the night.

'I told you it won't be the same round here,' complained Rose to Shirley as they took off their costumes. 'Wally is going to save Teddy and his star acts for the posh lot. We're the mugs who'll have to put up with the gropers and the drunks.'

Marie hung her costume on the rail, quickly putting on her coat. She wanted to try to find Vesta.

'Goodnight then,' she called as she slipped her bag over her shoulder.

''Night,' answered Shirley and Sal, barely glancing her way as they listened to Rose's fierce complaints.

'No use going up there,' shouted a voice as Marie made her way along the dark passage.

Her heart leaped. She turned quickly to see the familiar figure of the piano player. 'Oh, it's you, Benny.'

'There's no point in going up there, gel.'

'I want to find Vesta.'

Benny slid on his battered trilby. 'Wally's had the door removed and a wall built there instead.'

Marie frowned. 'But why do that?'

'There's a new club on the other side now. Come on, I'll tell you on the way out.'

They made their way past the dressing room and office, where the door was open. The office was cleared out, except for a table and chair in the corner.

'It's empty!' she gasped as they paused to look in.

'Pedro is running the show here,' Benny explained as he guided her across the deserted club and into the cold night. 'Keep it under your hat, but the club failed to meet expectations and is in debt.'

'And so they've just left?' Marie asked bewilderedly.

Benny nodded. 'Wally bungs Pedro a wedge, of course, to front what remains of the business. Meanwhile, the new club is called the Blue Flamingo. I hear it's very up-market.'

'But what about us?' Marie asked. 'Is Pedro our boss?'

Benny shrugged. 'Dunno, love. We'll have to wait and see what happens. Now, do you want me to walk you up to the High Street? It ain't healthy to be out here on your own.'

'I was hoping me dad would meet me.'

'No chance of that.' Benny grimaced. 'That nutter Pedro sent him down in the cellars. It ain't right an old bloke like him should have to shift all that booze.'

Marie's shoulders slumped. 'Poor Dad.'

Just then, headlights appeared and a vehicle drove slowly down the alley. It stopped and Bing climbed out.

'This is Benny, one of the band,' Marie said as Bing approached. 'Benny, this is . . .' Marie hesitated as the two men eyed each other suspiciously.

'Let's just say I'm someone in Marie's corner,' Bing muttered, sliding an arm around her waist.

'Good on you, son,' Benny approved, nodding. 'Just you take care of her, eh?' He tipped his hat and disappeared into the darkness.

Marie smiled up at Bing. 'Don't worry, Benny is to be trusted.'

'If you say so,' said Bing uncertainly. 'Did you see Vesta?'

'No. Benny told me that they've had the door sealed up and opened a club on the other side, called the Blue Flamingo. The Duke's is in debt and the Scoresbys have left Pedro in charge.'

'So the rats are jumping from the sinking ship?' Bing growled.

'Looks like it.'

'What's worse, Pedro's made Dad go down in the cellars to work.'

'Christ, Marie, he's too old for that. In my book, the two of you are better off quitting the club right away.'

'I can't yet.'

'Because of Vesta?'

She nodded.

Bing took her in his arms and sighed. 'What am I going to do with you?'

'You could kiss me.' She slipped her arms around his neck and he kissed her, for a moment dispelling all her fears.

Marie's thoughts were scattered as they drove home. She knew that Bing was right about leaving the club, but she still felt close to Vesta there and was sure Hector felt the same way.

The curtains in the front room were drawn against the

cold night. Marie sat by the fire with her mother and Bing; Ada wore her dressing gown, a cup of cold tea by her side. Her hands moved restlessly as she listened to Marie.

'You should try to get some rest, Mrs H,' Bing said gently. 'Won't do no good to worry.'

'But my daughter is missing,' replied Ada fiercely. 'I want her home, where she belongs.'

'We all want that,' agreed Marie. 'Except Vesta.'

'So what is the name of this place she's gone to?' Ada asked again.

'The Blue Flamingo,' Marie and Bing said together.

'Your father is to blame for spoiling her,' Ada accused. 'But he always gave in.'

Marie wanted to defend her father but Ada was in no mood to listen.

Bing reached for his overcoat and stood up. 'I'd better call it a night and get home to me bed.'

Ada pushed herself up from the chair. 'Goodnight, Bing.' She added as always, 'Don't stay up too late, Marie.'

On the doorstep, Bing drew her into his arms. 'Give me a moment to look at you, beautiful.' He lifted a lock of blonde hair from her forehead and twisted it behind her ear. 'Marie, I don't reckon your sister will want to come home.'

'Why? Because of Teddy?'

'No, because she'd have your mum to face.'

'Mum only wants to see Vesta happy.'

'Yes, but being happy is down to Vesta.'

Suddenly tears filled Marie's eyes. 'Bing, it's all such a mess.' He held her close and she laid her head on his chest.

'Listen, Mum and Dad want us to go round to tea on Sunday.' He ran his fingers through her hair. 'Do you fancy that?'

'Yes, of course.' She knew he was trying to act as if everything was going on as normal. But with Vesta gone, it all felt far from that.

It was a cold Monday in early December when Marie started her new job at the factory. The girls in the cutting room had wished her good luck, but she missed Vesta. To her surprise the clatter of keys in the typing pool was almost as deafening as the noise on the factory floor.

She was given a large box on four wheels. In it were the correspondence and parcels to be delivered to the rest of the factory. The trolley was heavy and had to be left at the bottom of each staircase. Sometimes, she had to wait for the head of the department to reply; other times she was directed elsewhere, with more parcels and packages and even small sheets of leather.

The office staff ate in a room on the top floor. There were comfortable tables and chairs, unlike in the works canteen with its hard wooden benches. There was also a tea-making trolley with real china cups and saucers. Marie received a few smiles and nods, but eventually her loneliness became too hard to bear and she had to go to the cloakrooms and shed a quiet tear for Vesta.

At one o'clock, the manager, Mr Morton, told her to put on her coat. He led her out through the big doors and onto the cold and windy wharf. Here, the tugs off-loaded their cargo. Afterwards, it was collected by the labourers who stacked the warehouse. It was Marie's job to check everything off on her list; when an item was missing, she had to find it, going through all the crates, containers and boxes again. She didn't mind it, though, as the waiting bargemen and impatient warehouse staff kept her busy. She also discovered she was good at figures. Adding up the totals in her mind was easy and she received a smile of approval from Mr Morton. But when she went back to the small room she had to herself, no larger than a cupboard, she missed Vesta so much that once again tears were close.

By the end of her first day, her back ached unbearably and, though she knew she would get used to going up and down stairs, the backs of her legs had cramp. As no one had warned her that flat shoes would have made her job easier, she had worn her one pair of fashionable strapped heels. But although they went well with her navy-blue skirt and blouse, the following day they would have to be exchanged for lace-ups.

'Well, how was it?' asked Elsie the moment Marie stepped in the door that evening. Elsie was talking with Nina and Wippet, but the little monkey was very subdued. It clung to Wippet, his big eyes blinking sadly.

'It's different from the factory,' Marie answered, smiling at Nina and Wippet. 'But I'll get used to it.'

Nina looked very pretty as usual, in her pale green beret and coat of the same colour. 'I'm sure you'll do very well,' she said.

'You never came to see me escape my chains,'

interrupted Wippet, running his stubby fingers comfortingly over the animal's back.

'Sorry, there wasn't time,' Marie apologized. 'How is Kaiser?'

Wippet shook his large head. 'He is very nervous now. His leg hasn't mended properly, you see.'

Marie reached out to stroke the monkey, but it cowered away.

'After what Teddy did, Kaiser doesn't trust humans any more. I wonder how that cruel man would feel if someone broke his leg?'

'Come in and have a cuppa,' said Elsie, giving Marie a wink. 'You've had a long day.'

Everyone said goodnight. A few moments later, Marie was sitting in Elsie's front room, drinking tea.

'Wippet ain't stopped moaning,' Elsie confided as she made herself comfortable in the easy chair. 'He's got a bee in his bonnet about Teddy still.'

'I'm not surprised.'

'It was a terrible thing to do.'

'Yes, poor Kaiser.'

'Now, tell me your news, love. What was your day really like?'

Marie looked down. 'I missed Vesta.'

'Bound to, she's your twin.' Elsie leaned forward. 'Your mum told me all about this new club, the Blue Flamingo. So the Scoresbys have left the Duke's?'

Marie nodded. 'Benny, one of the band, said it's because of the debt it's run up.'

'That's an old trick of the trade.'

'Perhaps Vesta is better off after all.'

'Maybe,' Elsie said hopefully. 'I can't help thinking she'll be bored after a while. Without you, she ain't got no one to complain to.' Elsie grinned. 'My money's on her packing it in, and soon.'

'Yes, but will the Scoresbys let her go?'

Elsie sat up. 'Why shouldn't they?'

'It was something one of the dancers told me.' Marie hesitated as she didn't know whether to tell Elsie. 'That no one leaves unless the brothers let them.'

'What did she mean?' Elsie frowned.

'I don't know; she was dismissed after that.'

Elsie patted her hand. 'Look, you know what Vesta's like about Christmas – she won't want to miss out on the presents or singsong we all have on Christmas Day.'

Marie looked up. 'I hope you're right.'

Elsie smiled brightly. 'So, you say this new job they've given you at Ellisdon's is all right?'

Marie put out her hands. 'It's the first time I've come home without brown stains all over me fingers.'

'Why was you offered the job?' Elsie asked curiously.

'A girl called Flo Davis was leaving.' Marie went red. 'Due to "unfortunate circumstances".'

'You mean she was up the spout?'

'Vesta was surprised when she claimed the father was Teddy.'

Elsie put her hands to her mouth. 'What did Vesta say about that?'

'She thought the girls at the factory were just jealous.'

'I don't put anything past that charmer,' Elsie said bitterly. 'I rue the day he ever came here and I let him have lodgings.'

'You weren't to know.'

'Listen, why don't you leave the Duke's now? There ain't no reason to stay.'

'There might be a chance I'll see Vesta. And anyway, Dad has been made to work in the cellars. I wouldn't leave without him.'

Elsie gasped. 'Does your mum know?'

'Don't think Dad would say, as it would worry her.' Marie drank the rest of her tea. 'I never thought our dream would tear the family apart,' she said, emotion filling her.

'Come along, lovely,' Elsie said kindly, leaning forward. 'Cheer up.'

'I can't be happy without Vesta.'

'Now you do sound like your sister, a drama queen!' Elsie exclaimed with a rueful grin. 'Listen, the parting of the ways was bound to happen.'

Marie shook her head firmly. 'We wanted to sing and dance and go on the stage. Neither of us knew it would lead to this.'

'What's done is done,' Elsie pointed out as she raised a black-pencilled eyebrow. 'It just wasn't what you imagined it to be.'

'And neither was it for Dad,' Marie whispered hoarsely.

'Ah, well, my love, that's show business.'

'Is it?' Marie asked in surprise.

'Everyone wants a bit of that cherry. It looks red and sweet as it hangs from the tree, but it's bitter when you taste it.'

'You sound like Mum.'

'She has her reasons.' Elsie lifted a warning finger. 'Your dad and Vesta have chosen their paths and you, yours. One day they'll cross again, but until then, have no regrets. Regrets are a waste of time and spoil the here and now. They are just hurtful thoughts you torture yourself with.'

Marie smiled. 'How did you get to be so wise, Elsie?'

Elsie winked. 'You don't get to look as good as I do at my age without knowing a trick or two.'

Marie giggled. 'You always put me straight.'

'Then remember this, gel. You can either wake up and be happy. Or wake up and be miserable. Now which do you choose?'

Again Marie laughed. 'I'd be daft not to want to be happy.'

Elsie beamed her a smile and stood up. 'There you are then. Now off you go, and, Marie . . .' She grabbed Marie's arm.

'Yes?'

'Success in life ain't come as you wanted, but a part of your dream has come true. A pat on the back for your new job, in case nobody ain't given you one.'

Marie had a big smile on her face as she left. She felt very different from the unhappy girl who had walked in earlier tonight.

Chapter 24

As the days went by, and after her talk with Elsie, Marie began to enjoy her new job. She made friends and used her brains to do the necessary calculations. This was very different from hammering leather in the dusty, noisy cutting room. Every day she felt an improvement.

The same could not be said of the Duke's. Marie hated it. None of the customers paid any attention to the dancers. The heavy drinking caused brawls so that it was often impossible to perform. Sometimes the dancers had to run from the stage as chairs and bottles whizzed through the air.

On the Friday before Christmas Pedro told the girls that they wouldn't be needed until New Year's Eve. Rose, Shirley and Sal complained bitterly. Walter and Jeff, the drum and bass players, were dismissed, leaving only Benny.

'You needn't worry about your sister,' said Benny that night as they left the club. 'I heard from Pedro, who was told by Teddy, she's bringing in trade.'

'Is she happy?' asked Marie, her teeth chattering as they stood in the freezing cold alley, both shivering as the wind blew the rubbish against the walls and over the cobbles.

'You'd hear if she wasn't.'

'That's true. But I still want to see her and hear it with me own ears.'

'Take my tip and leave well enough alone, girl. Don't go chasing her. Look after number one.'

Later, as Bing was driving her home, Marie told him what Benny had said. 'I just hope she turns up at Christmas and puts everyone's minds at rest,' Marie ended on a sigh.

'She will. As Benny says, if Vesta ain't happy with something, she'll soon let you know.'

Marie thought about this. It was true that Vesta never suffered in silence. She was a girl who wanted her own way and usually got it.

'Have you thought any more about leaving the club?' Bing asked her.

'Yes. If things go on as they are, there's no point in staying. Now the Scoresbys have gone, I don't think Pedro cares.'

Bing smiled. 'That's music to my ears.'

But Marie still wasn't certain. What if Vesta went to look for her? But wouldn't she have done that by now, if she was unhappy? Perhaps she was waiting until Christmas, when, in true Vesta style, she would make a dramatic appearance.

Bing took her shopping the next afternoon. They strolled round the market and Marie bought presents: a pair of plaid slippers for Hector, a scarf and gloves for Ada, and a shiny pair of dangling earrings for Elsie.

When they walked past the fruit and veg stall Fat Freda called out, 'You're looking good, girl. Not still working at that dive, are you?'

Marie only nodded.

'Heard it's been dumped by them brothers.'

Marie looked at Bing, who stretched across and turned over the cabbages. 'Got any bargains, Freda? We ain't got all day to natter.'

Freda laughed loudly. 'Nor have I, love. Now what would you like? I've got a few apples and pears on the cheap.'

'That'll do,' Bing nodded. 'And don't forget to knock a bob off for me smile.'

'You'll be lucky, you cheeky devil.'

When they had finished shopping, Bing took Marie to the coffee stall. Despite the cold day, they put down their parcels and sat on the crates provided.

'Even Freda knows about the Duke's,' Marie said with a sigh.

'Cheer up, it ain't the end of the world.'

Marie grinned. 'No, that's true.'

'Listen, can I come round to your gaff on Christmas Day? I've got a special present to give you.'

'What is it?'

'Why, a Christmas kiss, of course!' He grinned, his lovely smile making her tummy turn cartwheels. He wore his smart heavy coat and a dark blue scarf tucked into the turned-up collar, which was all the fashion. His hair still stuck up, and there was twinkling mischief in his eyes.

Marie giggled under her new hat, a beige and white shell-like beret that she had bought to go with a beige coat from the second-hand stall. The coat hadn't been worn very much. And though she could afford to buy something new, she was being careful. The dancers were still waiting to be paid for last week, a development that Marie felt, after speaking to Benny, was not unexpected. If they weren't paid again before Christmas, she would only have her wages from the factory. Not that Marie cared. The money from the club had brought them only sadness.

'Drink up, and then we can buy your present to me.'

He said it with a straight face and Marie laughed. 'You've got a cheek!'

'Nothing like asking.'

'I'll give you the same, a kiss.'

'That'll do. Can I have it now?'

Marie pushed him away as he pursed his lips. As the passers-by smiled at them, Marie felt proud to be his girl. And, as he drew her against him, she sipped the last of her coffee, trying to hide the wonderful feeling inside her. She knew that the more she saw him, the more she liked him. He was a big part of her life, always eager to make her smile and lift her spirits.

When Bing and Marie arrived back, Elsie had decorated the tree. It stood in the hall, a sight to behold; glass balls and trinkets, a lot of them resembling gold, hanging from the branches. Elsie had kept all her and Joe's decorations from their days at the pub. On the top of the tree was a sparkling star, tied on with ribbon. The edges were a bit battered and the white ribbon had turned yellow from age and smoke, but it still looked wonderful.

'Blimey, where are we, the North Pole?' Bing grinned as they stood in the hall, staring at the tree, its branches draped with white fringes and balls of white knitting wool.

'Each year Elsie decorates a tree,' Marie explained. 'We used to help her when we were kids. See, there's a star on the top that we made at school.'

'Look at what the tree's standing in,' Bing chuckled. 'A pail from the Cubby Hole.'

'How do you know that?' Marie stared down at the bucket that Elsie had tried to cover with red crêpe paper.

'It's got "Ladies" painted on it under that paper. You can just see the top of the L. There's another one just like it that's still in the Gents.'

Marie burst out laughing. In the end they were laughing so much that Marie knew it was, for her, both a release and a relief. This Christmas was certain to be mixed with different emotions, but she knew Bing would be by her side through it all. And as he drew her into his arms and slowly kissed her, she knew she couldn't ask for more.

*   *   *

It was Monday, 24 December – Christmas Eve. Marie was surprised when Mr Morton allowed the staff to leave at twelve thirty. He wished them all well and gave them each a card.

'They must think a lot of you,' Ada commented when Marie arrived home. 'You never got a card before.' Ada was stuffing the chicken, forcing in the sausagemeat with a look of determination on her face. Marie knew she was trying, as they all were, to enjoy Christmas.

Ada had hung the hand-made paper-chains in the front room and put holly on the mantel. A sprig of mistletoe hung from the ceiling. The cards they had received depicting Father Christmas and his reindeers and sacks full of presents, the three Wise Men and the Shepherds were placed on the shelf by the window, lined up against the books. Though the front room looked very festive, Marie knew that the decorations were a painful reminder to them all of Vesta's absence. Christmas was supposed to be the happiest time of the year.

'I sent your father on an errand,' Ada continued as she pushed at the chicken. 'Buy a nice bottle of port, I told him, with lemon. Your sister might be glad of a glass of something fortifying.'

Marie put down Mr Morton's card. 'Mum, you mustn't be disappointed if she doesn't turn up.'

'I know.' Ada's voice trembled.

'You'll push that stuffing out the other end if you're not careful.'

Ada ignored this, her face set. 'You can start on the vegetables, since you're home early.'

'Give me a moment to take me things off.'

'And you can bring the pudding from the pantry. We'll have custard to go with it.'

Marie slipped off her coat and hung it on the peg. She felt like resting her legs for ten minutes after all the stairs she'd been running up and down at work. 'Christmas Day isn't till tomorrow.'

'I want to have everything ready for her.' Ada reached for the big china plate. In the next instant it had slipped from her hands.

The crash on the floor echoed noisily. Ada stared down at the broken pieces, scattered far and wide. 'Oh, that was my best plate!' Suddenly she burst into tears.

'Mum, it's only a plate. I'll clear it up.'

'I don't care about the china. I keep thinking of all those Christmases when she was here. You two in the kitchen with me. My beautiful daughters, helping to prepare for tomorrow.' Ada wiped her eyes with her handkerchief. 'Oh, what's the use of pretending, Marie? She ain't gonna come tomorrow, is she?'

'She might.'

Ada wept again, the tears falling on her apron.

Just then, Hector walked in. He looked thin and gaunt, and wore the dirty old coat he used for work.

'What's the matter?' he asked, blinking.

'Nothing,' said Ada sharply.

He stared at the broken china. But before he could speak, Ada snapped, 'Hector, you're letting yourself go. Vesta won't want to see you like that.'

'Have you heard? Is she coming tomorrow?'

'How should we know?' Ada shrugged.

Marie went towards him. 'Is this the port, Dad?'

'Yes, but I forgot the lemon.' He handed her the bottle.

'Your father can't be trusted with the smallest thing lately,' Ada muttered as she began to clear up the china.

Marie thought her father looked ill. All his good spirit had vanished and he wore a forlorn expression. Ada's sharp tongue was getting on even Marie's nerves.

Christmas Day would be miserable if Vesta didn't show up. As Marie kneeled down to help her mother, she said a silent prayer that Vesta would.

'Teddy, how do I look?' Vesta turned sideways, her hand sliding down the soft pink chiffon of the gown that she and Teddy had bought in the West End. It was a stunning dress, small pink and silver sequins scattered over the heart-shaped bodice and a few hidden in the folds of the full skirt. When she moved the dress caught the light. Vesta had never worn anything like it before. In the six weeks since she had left home, Teddy had made her so happy! He catered for her every need, and had introduced her to so many wealthy, friendly people at the Blue Flamingo that her head was still spinning. And tonight they were invited as a couple to a party, somewhere in the country, where, Teddy had told her, she would be introduced to many people in the entertainment world.

How lucky she was to have Teddy! There was nothing he wouldn't do for her. Since she had moved into his rooms on that terrible Sunday in November, when that bully Bing Brown had tried to stop her leaving, her life had changed unbelievably.

Teddy came to stand beside her. He was the most handsome man she had ever met. Ever seen! And tonight in his black dinner suit, white shirt and bow tie, with his dark hair brushed smoothly back across his head, he looked like an actor from one of those Hollywood films. This thought sent even more shivers along her spine.

'You look perfect,' he told her, running his dark eyes over her and making her go weak at the knees. 'Just remember, tonight you must make a good impression. This is your chance to meet some influential people. Actors, directors, producers; the type who will give you a start in show business.'

'You and Mr Scoresby have done that already,' she murmured gratefully, linking her arms around his neck. 'I love singing at the Blue Flamingo. Though I do feel a bit rotten about Marie.'

'She had her chance.'

'I know, but she is me sister.'

'Vesta, watch your language. It's not "me", but "my".'

She giggled. 'Oops, sorry.'

'You've been drinking, haven't you?'

She giggled. 'Only one to calm my nerves.'

'There's a time and place for everything,' he told her, kissing her nose.

'Like when we're in bed?' Vesta was shocked at her boldness, but she didn't care. Teddy had liberated her, made her a woman. His lovemaking had been incredible; he'd taught her well and she had loved every moment. He had also shown her what to do for him, which had at first embarrassed her. Nevertheless, after a few drinks, she had soon lost her shyness. There had been other women who wanted him too, but he had chosen her. She still couldn't believe it! Perhaps flirting with Charlie had worked. When Charlie had turned up at the Blue Flamingo a few nights ago, demanding to see her, Teddy had instructed the doormen to get rid of him.

A mischievous smile played on her lips as Teddy studied her critically. She had pinned up her hair to one side to show off the diamanté earrings that were his most recent gift to her. He took a great interest in her appearance, buying her clothes, shoes and jewellery that now filled their large white wardrobe in the bedroom. Some of his choices hadn't been quite what she would have chosen, but that didn't matter. If he told her she looked beautiful in them, then that was enough to make her happy. She loved their life together in the apartment that Wally had given them off the Commercial Road. Though the district was a bit shabby the interior was luxurious, with art deco furniture, carpets and even a bathroom with a bath in it so big that they could both fit in it together.

Vesta blushed. Teddy had certainly taught her how to have pleasure. What would Marie think of all this? What would her family say if they could see her now?

Vesta felt a tremble of misgivings as she thought of them. She hadn't even written to Ada to let her know how she was. But her mother and Marie had made her very angry, treating Teddy in the way they had. She would never forgive them for nearly causing her to lose out on her biggest chance in life.

And yet, she missed her family. She had never been apart from them at Christmas. She knew exactly what they would be doing now: preparing dinner for tomorrow and wrapping presents. Ada would be fussing about with Elsie in the hall, decorating the Christmas tree.

Vesta didn't want to miss them or to feel guilty. Marie was her twin; they had never been separated. Six weeks was the first and longest time in their lives. But, as Teddy pointed out, Marie had had her chance too and had refused it.

Comforted by this thought, Vesta slipped her fingers around Teddy's smooth neck. She wanted reassurance. She wanted love. She wanted him, not her family.

'Don't do that, Vesta. We must go to the party now.'

'Kiss me quickly, then.'

He laughed, his dark eyes assessing her. 'You're like a little girl, always wanting attention.'

'What's so bad about that?'

'Nothing, in fact you'll get plenty of it tonight.'

'You're the only man for me.'

Teddy smiled at her in a strange way she hadn't noticed before. 'Once you meet Wally and Leo's friends, you'll be too busy enjoying yourself to think about me.'

It was a remark that made Vesta feel a little uncomfortable. Teddy kissed her, running his fingers down the bare skin of her back and teasing the little place on her spine that he knew made her want more – so much more. She wanted to meet all these rich and famous people who could prosper her career. But she wanted Teddy most of all. She was worried about the other women at the party, who would be more beautiful and educated than she was. Women who took one look at Teddy and wanted him too.

A painful dart of jealousy went through her. She kissed Teddy so fiercely that soon her straps were falling around her bodice and he was peeling the soft, slippery material away from her skin.

Chapter 25

'Happy Christmas, Mum.' There was an hour to go to midnight and Ada was, at last, going to bed.

'Happy Christmas, Marie.' Ada kissed her cheek. 'Thank you for staying in and helping me.'

'Where else would I be on Christmas Eve?'

'You could have gone out.'

'Bing said he'd call round tomorrow night after he's seen his mum and dad.'

Ada smiled and pulled the collar of her dressing gown closer. 'Don't get cold. The fire's almost out.'

'I want to put my presents by the tree.'

Ada smiled wistfully. 'You girls couldn't wait to get up in the morning on Christmas Day to see what Father Christmas had brought.'

'I hope he turns up tonight.' Marie grinned.

'The best present he could bring me is your sister.'

'Perhaps he will.'

Ada nodded sadly. 'Goodnight then, love.'

'Goodnight, Mum.'

Ada turned to go, then stopped. 'If you see your father, tell him he can sleep on the couch.'

'Mum, don't make him do that.'

'He'll only disturb me. And I'm finding it hard enough to sleep as it is.'

When Ada had gone, Marie heaved a big sigh. The rift between Hector and Ada was growing. They had quarrelled bitterly earlier that evening over Hector going to the club.

'So you'd put that club above your family?' Ada had demanded as he was about to leave.

'No, my dear, that's not true.'

'Then stay home.'

Hector had looked desperate as he stood at the door. 'I promise things will change after Christmas, Ada.'

'I'm not interested in promises,' Ada had called over her shoulder as she went to the kitchen. 'You just can't bear to be away from what you think is the limelight.'

'That may have been true once,' Hector had mumbled, 'but not any more.'

Marie knew the truth. Her father was exhausted from the heavy work in the cellars. He was no longer smart and well-dressed. His spirit had been broken. He looked like a frail old man whose dreams had fallen by the wayside.

When Ada went to bed, Marie took her presents to the tree. She laid them under the branches, listening to the church bells pealing for the midnight service. Families would sing carols and hear the story of the Nativity once again. The cold weather and problems of the past year would be forgotten in order to celebrate the birth of Jesus.

Marie remembered how, when they first came to the island, Ada had taken them to church. As children they had enjoyed the feeling of unity, when people celebrated the special time of year. But Ada had never been a strong churchgoer and the habit had died.

Smiling at the sight of the little pictures of Christmas that she and Vesta had drawn many years before, Marie swallowed on the lump in her throat. 'Bring our family together tomorrow,' she whispered, 'and let Christmas be like it once was.'

Marie shivered as she stood in the hall. The house was very quiet. It was Christmas Day.

Vesta blinked through the crowded room, searching for the smooth, dark hair of Teddy, who seemed to have disappeared in the throng of partygoers. Someone, a young man whose name she had forgotten, with a cut-glass accent and a lot of fair, wavy hair that fell into his eyes, had danced with her after Teddy had introduced them.

'Drink up, darling,' he had told her, pressing a glass into her hand. 'It's gone twelve and Christmas Day!'

Since then she had had more dances and another glass – or was it two? – of what she now knew was the best champagne. Lots of people had spoken to her. She had hardly seen Teddy.

'Vesta, are you all right?' Teddy was suddenly beside her.

'Where have you been?'

'Just circulating.'

She giggled.

'What's so funny.'

'Nothing. It's the long words you use.'

'Do you want a breath of fresh air on the balcony?'

Vesta turned, following Teddy's nod to the two large doors that led into the big room overlooking a green wooded space outside. She had been in that room with Teddy when they'd first arrived. Wally and Leo Scoresby had been there and were talking with other men in dress suits and smoking cigars. It had seemed very exciting as they'd all turned to look at her and smile. Even Wally's face hadn't seemed so ugly as he'd actually given her a nod.

'No, I don't want any fresh air. I'd rather go on dancing for ever.' She laughed, sounding silly even to herself.

He smiled. 'Yes, I saw you enjoying yourself.'

Vesta felt a little disappointed. 'Weren't you jealous? Why didn't you come and rescue me?'

'You didn't look as if you needed rescuing.'

Vesta thought that her head felt very strange and her own voice sounded a long way off. But the feeling was not unpleasant. In fact, she liked it.

'Do you want something to eat?' Teddy asked, touching her bare back above the zip of her dress. She shivered. He could make her feel so excited with only one touch. 'Wait here, I'll go and get you something.'

She wanted to stop him. Food didn't interest her, although she had been amazed at the variety of food placed on a long buffet table under the big windows. She didn't recognize some of the dishes and Teddy had said

names she'd never heard before. He knew so much and
she knew so little. Like this wonderful place, she thought,
as she gazed around. To come here with him and to be
introduced to all these people was amazing. Above her,
the low-beamed ceilings were strung with expensive-
looking decorations and silver and gold banners that
twirled and waved above their heads. Teddy had told her
the Christmas tree on the lawn outside was sixteen foot
high and cut down from the acres of woodland that
surrounded the old house. It was covered from top to
bottom in different-coloured lights.

As Teddy had paraded her around, all the men seemed
very imposing in their dinner suits, accompanied by
glamorously dressed women who looked a lot younger.
There were sultry brunettes and dazzling redheads and
one very beautiful blonde who wore a backless silver
evening gown that perfectly moulded her reed-slim
figure. She had spoken to Teddy softly, kissing him
briefly on the mouth, which Vesta hadn't liked at all.
Another woman also did the same a little while later, but
then Teddy had explained it was the custom amongst
people who knew each other well in these kind of circles.

'Do you know these girls well, then?' Vesta had asked,
causing Teddy to smile and raise his eyebrows.

'It's part of my job. Leo and Wally expect me to be
charming to their guests.'

Then she had been full of envy for the women. She
wanted to be like them: confident and sure of herself. She
knew she was beautiful and young – Teddy always told

her that – but, more than that, she wanted an air of poise
and sophistication that she knew was lacking.

Vesta drank the last of her champagne. She began to
smile as the warm sensation swirled inside her. The drink
was making her feel confident, exactly what she had
wished for.

'What's so amusing?' Teddy asked when he returned,
a small plate in his hand filled with odd-looking pieces of
food.

'Your face is all funny.'

'You'd better eat this.'

'Can I have another champagne?'

'After you've eaten.'

She took the food to please him. He always had her
best interests at heart. She loved the way he looked after
her, and showed her off, giving her all the attention.

'These people must be very rich,' she said after swallowing a few scraps. Quickly she put the plate down on
a side table.

'Yes, they are.'

'How do you know them?'

'I told you, it's my job for the Scoresbys to know
people.'

'But, I mean, when did you—'

'I'll get you another drink.' She saw Teddy turn and
stop a waiter. He took a long glass from the tray. She had
never seen so many waiters and waitresses in one room.
She giggled. 'I love champagne.' The bubbles were going
up her nose again.

'How would you like a part in a West End show?' Teddy asked casually.

'Really?' Vesta gasped.

'That man over there is a director. I could put a good word in for you.'

Vesta looked up into Teddy's handsome face. 'But I don't even know if I can act.'

'You can sing and dance. You can probably act too.' He grinned, touching the skin of her arm with his fingers. 'It's worth a try.'

Vesta took another sip of her drink. She felt scared and excited all at once. She looked at the man with silver hair that Teddy had said was a director. A tall, exotic-looking girl with black hair was with him. Although he was much older than she, his silver hair and elegant posture set him out from the crowd.

'What's his name?'

'William Dearlove. You should recognize his face from the magazines you spend so much time reading.'

Vesta saw the funny side of this. 'Dearlove? What a silly name!'

'Don't say that out loud,' Teddy told her sharply. 'Not if you want to impress him. Come along, I'll introduce you.'

'Teddy, are you sure he'd be interested in me?' she blurted, looking at the beautiful girl again.

'Just relax and enjoy yourself.'

Vesta felt herself being guided towards the group of people now gathered round William Dearlove. Their faces all turned in her direction as they approached. The silver-haired man smiled politely, making her feel quite special as he took her hand.

A moment's embarrassment filled her as Teddy said, 'Bill, I'd like you to meet Vesta, the singer at the Blue Flamingo I was telling you about.'

'Why, I'm charmed, my dear.' He kissed her hand.

Vesta stared into his piercing gaze – very blue eyes that didn't blink. Teddy gave her arm a squeeze. In panic, she glanced round, trying to behave like the other girls did. They all looked like the models standing in the West End shop windows. She straightened her back and gave a dazzling smile. Since singing at the Blue Flamingo, she had learned how to make herself more attractive as Teddy always told her she must look her best. Now she knew why. Mixing with these famous people meant that she might fulfil her dream one day.

'Please call me Bill.'

'Yes . . . oh . . .' She fumbled for words.

'Tell me about yourself, Vesta.' He took her arm and gently steered her away from the others, leaving Teddy to talk with the beautiful dark-haired girl. Vesta didn't like that much, as Teddy was admired by so many women. But Bill was taking the glass from her hand and replacing it with a full one. 'We can't have you going thirsty, my dear. Now, tell me, what kind of songs do you enjoy singing?'

Vesta found that, after a few minutes, she was talking easily to him and her shyness faded. He really was nice. Her worries soon slipped away and the conversation didn't falter as she told him how she had started at the

Duke's with Marie and then gone on to the Blue Flamingo on her own. Bill didn't seem to find this strange and he asked no difficult questions, as though he assumed she was adult enough to make her own decisions. When she had finished her champagne, he asked her if she would like to dance. She looked round for Teddy, but he'd gone. Fear gripped her. Had he gone off with the girl?

'Don't worry about Teddy,' Bill said easily. 'He knows you'll be safe with me.' He laughed and Vesta smiled. He was very gentlemanly.

On the dance floor, Bill's hand slipped round her waist. As he took her in his arms and held her close, she felt as though she was treading on soft, spinning clouds. He told her about the theatre and his work and the amazing life that he led amongst actors and actresses. As they danced, it seemed as if she had known him for ever.

When the music stopped, he seemed in no hurry to let her go. Vesta couldn't help hoping that Teddy was watching from somewhere. And that he was jealous, just like he had been about Charlie. And if he was with the girl, he'd soon drop her and come over to the dance floor. But he didn't. Vesta was angry and frightened. Angry that he'd left her and frightened he was enjoying himself without her.

'Another dance?' Bill asked.

Vesta looked round again. There was no sign of Teddy. She nodded. Bill smiled, drawing her close once more. She decided she was going to enjoy herself with Bill, just as much as Teddy obviously was with someone else.

Chapter 26

'We'd better start dinner, or the chicken will be cooked to a crisp,' Ada warned as the four of them sat in the front room on Christmas Day. Elsie had arrived and now it was half past two.

'Good idea!' Elsie adjusted her glittering bolero and scarf over her dress. Her black velvet turban framed her face and made her eyes look like two dark beads as she smiled.

'I'll help you dish up, Mum,' offered Marie, but Elsie shook her head and nodded to Hector.

'No, you did your bit yesterday, gel. I'll muck in with your mother.'

'You don't want to get that outfit dirty,' warned Ada, wrapping an apron around her grey suit, which she had last worn on that night in August, when they had all gone to the Queen's to see Teddy. It seemed like a lifetime ago, and the thought of it gave Marie a sad feeling. Then, they were all happy. It was before it had become clear that Teddy was a wolf in sheep's clothing, who was to have a devastating effect on their lives.

'Don't worry about me, gel,' Elsie chuckled as they went to the kitchen. 'Though I could do with another port and lemon.'

Marie hadn't wanted a drink and was surprised that Hector hadn't either. He always liked his Christmas tipple. But now he sat in the chair, dressed in his Sunday suit, which had once seemed so smart but now hung from his thin body. Even the neck of his white shirt and attached collar was too big. His baggy waistcoat exaggerated the space where his paunch once used to be. Even the sleeves of his shirt seemed too long under his jacket.

'Dad, shall I pour you an ale?' Marie asked when they were alone.

'Not now,' Hector said quietly in a distracted voice. 'I'll wait till your sister comes. She wouldn't miss Christmas with us.' He turned slowly to meet Marie's gaze. 'They won't let me see her, you know.'

'Who?'

'I went to the Blue Flamingo the other night but they turned me away.'

Marie reached out and took hold of his hand. Even though they were sitting in the warm room, beside a roaring fire, he felt cold. 'Did you tell Mum?'

'No, love. I didn't want to worry her.'

'Vesta will come home soon.'

'I hope so. I miss her. And so does your mother.'

Marie put her arms around him. 'It's Christmas, and even if she doesn't come, she'll be thinking of us.'

'Yes, and the day's not over yet.' He smiled, patting her shoulder.

Marie felt the tears prick her eyes. They all missed Vesta so much, especially now, at Christmas, when they had always been together. It was going to be difficult to eat their meal and feel happy. But, as Elsie shouted to Hector that the meat was ready to carve, Marie knew they would all try.

Vesta woke, feeling sick. She had a pain in her head that felt as if it was about to split her brain in two. She had never felt like this before. She opened her eyes slowly. Waves of nausea rolled over her. She looked for the white wardrobe that was always the first thing she saw in the morning at Teddy's. Instead, she saw a pair of long curtains. A beam of daylight flowed in. Automatically reaching out for Teddy, her hand felt an empty space.

Sitting up, she regretted the sharp movement. Her head spun and whirled. It was all she could do not to be sick. When her stomach had settled a little, she looked around her. The bedclothes were rumpled and thrown back. Where was Teddy?

Pushing the bedclothes aside, she lowered her bare feet to the floor. The only garment she was wearing was her slip; her bra and panties were absent. A cold chill filled her.

The room was silent, except for a faint gurgling of water. Her toes landed on a thick, luxurious carpet. Where was she? Certainly not in the bedroom at Teddy's.

She groaned. Her head hurt too much to think. She stumbled towards the curtains and pulled them open.

A set of French doors opened onto a long balcony and beyond this was the biggest green lawn she had ever seen. Around its edges were tall fir trees. A memory came back. They were the same trees that she remembered from last night as she'd gazed from the big room.

Another scene appeared in her mind. She was dancing and laughing with the older man with silver hair. He was making her laugh and guiding her expertly round the dance floor, holding her very close.

Where was Teddy in all this? Steadying herself on a chair, she felt the curve of hard, sculptured wood. Quickly she drew her hand away, as if she had no right to touch it. The chair stood in front of a polished dark wood dressing table. Its surface was filled with silver-backed brushes, perfume bottles and delicate glass pots.

Her gaze travelled to a set of imposing doors with brass handles. Next to these was an elegant pink couch, which went up at one end and down the other. Its short, stumpy legs were like huge bird's claws.

Vesta gazed at the oil painting above. A tall, ugly woman, wearing an old-fashioned riding habit, looked down on her. Vesta shuddered. The picture reminded her of school and the history books they had been made to study.

To her left was a long marble-topped cabinet and on it a painted china jug and big bowl. Marie went back to the dressing table and looked in the mirror. A cry escaped her lips. Her face was white, like a ghost's. Her eyes looked smudged from last night's make-up and her hair was a mess, hanging down in tangled clumps. One strap of her slip had fallen over her arm, revealing her breast. She pulled the strap up quickly. Where was her underwear? Where was her lovely pink dress? Where was Teddy?

'Good morning,' a voice said.

Vesta spun round. The tall, silver-haired man from last night stood there. His chest was naked and a white towel was wrapped round his waist.

'Where am I? Who are you?' she mumbled.

'Don't tell me you've forgotten already?' An amused smile played on his lips. 'William Dearlove is the name. Last night you called me Bill.'

'Bill?' Vesta's heart was racing. She looked round. 'What am I doing here?'

'Don't you remember?'

Vesta tried to think back, but her head ached too much.

He stepped towards her. 'You and Teddy had rather a frightful argument. After which he left.'

'He wouldn't leave without me.'

'I'm afraid he did.'

Vesta fought back the waves of sickness. 'What happened?'

Bill tilted his head. 'You really don't remember?'

'No.'

'Perhaps you should use the bathroom and freshen up, first?' He gestured to the room behind him.

'I want to go home.'

'You are free to leave,' he shrugged. 'Though I thought we could enjoy breakfast together – after such an enjoyable night.' He glanced at the bed.

Vesta followed his gaze. The rumpled covers were strewn everywhere. 'You mean I . . .?' Had she slept in that bed with this man? She couldn't have. But why was he standing there half naked and she had no clothes except her slip? She began to cry.

'Come now, Vesta, calm yourself.'

She wiped her eyes with her fingers as he stepped close. 'Stay away from me. I want to leave.'

He gave another casual shrug. 'Go ahead. If that's what you want. But wouldn't it be best to wait for your clothes?'

She looked around, at the floor and the chairs and back to the bed. 'Where are they?'

'I asked the maid to clean them. I'm afraid you spilled rather a lot of champagne over your dress last night.'

Vesta's head hurt each time she tried to think. She was confused. She couldn't have slept with this man. She couldn't!

'Meanwhile, please do as I suggest and use the bathroom whilst you're waiting for your clothes. There's a robe in there and a selection of toiletries at your disposal.'

Vesta felt trapped. She couldn't run away without her clothes. But was this some kind of trick? Oh, why had Teddy left her in all this mess?

Bill Dearlove seemed to read her thoughts and grinned. 'Don't worry, you will be quite safe, I promise you.'

She ran to the door. Once inside the bathroom, she slipped the lock. Her breathing was fast as she leaned her back against the cold wood. Sharp flashes of memory returned: the silver hair and charming smile. Hands on her, touching her. And then, the most awful memory of all: him lying beside her, removing her clothes, kissing her and making love to her.

She wanted to die, and ran to the big white toilet to be sick. When she'd finished, she turned on the golden tap of the basin. Waiting for the nausea to subside, she splashed water over her face. Once again she was shocked when she saw herself in the gold-framed mirror. Her ashen, mascara-streaked face belonged to a stranger.

Vesta turned unsteadily and looked at the bath. Perhaps she would feel better if she bathed and tidied herself. She had never seen golden bath taps before, or such a big bathroom. Whoever this man was, he must be very rich. She remembered him telling her about his work in the theatre. Slowly it was all coming back.

Everything, except what had happened between her and Teddy. It was as if it was so bad, she hadn't wanted to remember it.

'At last, I've got you all to myself,' said Bing as they stood by the tree on Christmas night. Marie thought he had never looked more handsome than he did tonight. He wore a white open-neck shirt, a V-neck sleeveless jumper with coloured stripes, and smart grey Oxford bags with turn-ups. He had also grown his hair longer and managed to smooth it down. Though it looked very neat, Marie liked the natural way it always stuck up.

'Thank you for our presents,' she told him softly. 'They must have cost a lot.'

'Who else have I got to spend me money on?'

'You're not Father Christmas.'

'No, but with Vesta not turning up, they put a smile on everyone's faces.'

'Yes,' she sighed sadly, 'it wasn't the same without her.'

'Did you like the record I gave you?' he asked. Marie knew he was changing the subject deliberately. It had been a long day and Vesta's absence had been keenly felt.

She nodded. 'When I hear Bing Crosby singing "It Must Be True" I'll always think of you.'

'That was the idea.' He laughed.

'Did you like the wallet I gave you?'

'Yes, and me lucky penny inside.'

Marie sighed again. 'Well, it's the end of the evening now.'

'No, the best is yet to come.' He gave her a squeeze.

'Go on then, kiss me,' she teased.

'Look under the star first.'

She looked up to the top of the tree where the star twinkled. 'When did you put that box there?'

'Just now, when you weren't looking.'

He stretched up and took hold of it. Placing it in her hands, he whispered, 'Happy Christmas, beautiful.'

Marie undid the bow. With a curious smile on her face, she opened the lid.

'Oh!' she gasped.

'Do you like it?'

Marie stared at the gold ring, with a ruby-red stone set in the clasp. 'Is this for me?'

'It's me gran's engagement ring.' Taking her left hand he slipped it over her finger. 'And now it's yours, if you'll have it.'

Marie gazed at the blood-red stone and gold band. 'It fits perfectly.'

'I know this ain't a good time, but I figured if I don't get me oar in first, some other blighter will get in theirs. Especially as you've got that new job an' all, with all them clever bods in the offices making eyes at you over their desks. One day, one of 'em is gonna make his play and I might lose you for ever.' He pushed his hand through his hair, causing it to spring up straight. 'But if you've got a ring on your finger that says you're mine, we can wait as long as you like to get hitched. I mean, I'd wed you tomorrow if I had my way, but that's only wishful thinking.'

'Are you asking me to marry you?'

'Didn't I say?'

'Not in so many words.'

He went down on one knee. 'Marie Haskins, would you do me the honour of becoming my wife?'

She laughed but her smile soon faded. 'Are you sure?'

He frowned, his eyes full of surprise. 'I've wanted to marry you from the first moment I saw you. But I ain't being pushy. It's why we broke up last time. I've learned my lesson since then. I want you enough to hang around. If you still want to tread those proverbial boards, I won't stand in your way. Just keep me ring on your finger.'

'I didn't expect this.'

'There ain't a price I wouldn't pay to have you as me wife.' He stood up and held her close. 'What makes you happy, makes me happy.'

'You are such a good man.'

'I'm handsome and rich too, don't forget,' he teased, lifting her face between his hands. His kiss was urgent and demanding and for a brief moment she felt frightened at the thought of such a commitment. Was this love they shared enough to make them both happy? Would it last for ever, through thick and thin and all the ups and downs of life? Ada and Hector had been happy once but now they had drifted far apart.

'I love you, Marie,' Bing whispered, dispelling her doubts as he touched her cheek softly.

'And I love you.'

Marie closed her eyes as his lips went warmly over hers. It was the first Christmas that she and Vesta had ever been parted. And now she was going to be engaged. She wanted to tell Vesta. She wanted her to be here so that she could share her happiness.

Chapter 27

Vesta managed to calm down a little as she ran a hot bath. The luxury of endless hot water spilling from the gold taps and the bubbles that sprang to the surface made her feel much better. As she lay in the sweet-smelling water, she began to look around. The bathroom was pure luxury, all black-and-white tiles with two carved figures of almost naked women sculptured into the marble walls. There were many different bottles of perfume and bath oil on the glass shelves. The long mirrors and soft lighting made the room look big and spacious. Even the towels were huge, white and fluffy, like nothing else she had ever seen before.

She stayed in the bath for a long time, feeling her body under the water. It didn't seem any different, thank goodness. Whatever had happened last night, Bill hadn't hurt her. She remembered more things now: the feeling of confidence the champagne gave her; the soft words of praise that Bill had spoken; and then Teddy leaving her. She had gone to find him. And when she had, he was with the beautiful dark-haired girl.

Vesta gave a sob. He was kissing her! Not just a peck on the cheek, or lightly on the mouth as she'd seen him do before. But in a room on their own, with the girl tightly in his arms. It had been a passionate kiss. Tears of anger crawled down her cheeks and dropped into the bath. She had pulled Teddy away and slapped his face.

Vesta closed her wet eyes. That was their quarrel. It all rushed back. Teddy had been furious. But he had betrayed her. That was why she had slept with Bill!

Vesta sat up and washed off the soft bubbles. Why had Teddy been kissing that girl? But then, he had kissed others that night. Teddy had told her it was part of his job for the Scoresbys. But if kissing girls like that was what he had to do in his job, then she would never have him to herself!

After wallowing in self-pity for a while she felt the water begin to grow cold. She climbed out of the bath and dried herself, then slipped on the white robe. There was, as Bill had said, a selection of toiletries in one of the drawers under the basins. There were toothbrushes and toothpastes, creams and lotions. She used everything, forgetting for a short while what had happened with Teddy, as the expensive cosmetics took her interest. Bill must be very rich indeed if he owned all this.

As she brushed her hair, she wondered if he was married. He was an older man, so he was likely to be. Not only had she slept with a stranger but he could have a wife and family too.

When she found the courage to go out, he was standing outside on the balcony. The French windows were thrown open allowing the cold winter breeze to flow in. His back was turned to her and she saw how broad-shouldered and tall he was against the bright winter light. He was dressed in slim grey trousers, one hand casually slipped in a pocket, his silver hair shaped smoothly above his pearl-grey shirt. He cut a very imposing figure. For a moment, Vesta hesitated. She didn't know what to say. There were too many thoughts whirling around in her head.

He turned and gave her an intimate smile. He had very blue, steady eyes and a long, lean nose. His mouth looked both cruel and attractive. She didn't want to think of him kissing her with those sensual lips, but she knew that he had.

'Did my clothes come back?' she asked, looking around.

'The maid hung them in the wardrobe. Come and have some fresh air first. It will blow the cobwebs away.'

'No, I want to get dressed.'

He narrowed his eyes and leaned back against the balcony rail. The cold breeze didn't seem to affect him as he balanced a cigarette between his long fingers. Vesta had never been so close to anyone with such a sense of power and wealth around them. Despite feeling frightened, she was intrigued.

'Have you thought about how you'll get home?' he asked. 'And what you will say to Teddy? It is, after all, Christmas Day.'

Vesta managed to stop herself from bursting into tears again. She had completely forgotten that! This morning she had intended to go back to Sphinx Street. She'd never been apart from her family on Christmas Day. At this thought, a tear trickled down her cheek. She was unhappy, confused and sick at heart.

'Dry your tears,' Bill said as he walked towards her and pressed a large white handkerchief into her hand.

'Th-thank you.' She blew her nose. 'I wish I'd never come here.'

'I'm afraid I have to disagree.'

As she looked up into his eyes, she felt a little shiver. He was old, but still handsome, with skin that looked like a young man's, and he smelled very expensive. Like the lotions in the bathroom.

'You and I had a very good time.'

She pulled away. 'I don't want to talk about it.'

He looked unruffled. 'In that case, perhaps you'd better get dressed. And join me for breakfast.'

'I don't want any breakfast.'

'Oh, yes, you do. Now, make yourself look beautiful.' He pointed to the dressing table and closed the French windows. 'You have no reason to be ashamed, Vesta. You are young and lovely and, I am sure, very talented. I shall be interested in hearing your reading voice.'

Vesta felt suddenly like living again. She had forgotten he had asked her to read for him. He had said he thought that she might get a part in a play. 'I . . . I . . .' she began, her mind spinning.

'I can see you are upset. We'll talk later.' He walked to the big door. 'When you're ready, pull this cord and the maid will come for you.'

When he'd gone, she hurried to the wardrobe. To her relief, her dress was hanging inside it. All her underwear was arranged in white tissue paper on a shelf. She blushed. Did the maid know she'd slept with Bill?

Her clothes smelled sweetly of fresh laundering. Her dress was as good as new, though she couldn't remember spilling champagne over it. She checked in her purse, also on the shelf. There was no money, of course. Teddy had said she didn't need any. But her cheap lipstick, and small white handkerchief, which suddenly looked old and worn, were still safely there. Ada had embroidered her initial, 'V', in the corners. The thought of Ada and home brought a lump to Vesta's throat. She missed her family suddenly and wouldn't be able to see them now. What would Ada say, if she knew she had slept with Bill? But then she remembered what Bill had said. What was it? She had nothing to be ashamed of. She was grown-up, an adult, and last night it had been Teddy who was at fault. Thinking of Teddy made her angry and sad at the same time.

She dressed and then sat at the dressing table, using the silver-backed brush to tidy her hair. In one of the drawers were lipsticks, mascaras, powders and skin creams. Were these Bill's wife's?

She felt ill again. Even so, she used them.

When she was ready she pulled the cord. Her hands were still shaking as the tall, slender-as-a-reed maid arrived seconds later, dressed in a black dress, her dark hair coiled on top of her head.

'Follow me, please,' she said, and Vesta felt frightened again.

'Where to?'

'The dining room. Breakfast is served.'

'I'm not hungry.'

'No, but Mr Dearlove is.' The maid gave her a sharp look.

Vesta had no choice but to follow. As she was led through the big house, she could hardly believe all she saw. A series of high-ceilinged, magnificent rooms were furnished with antiques and oil paintings. Vesta wished she could stop and gaze around, but the maid was hurrying on down a purple carpeted staircase. The curve of the long, smooth banister led them into an entrance hall. It was as big as a room itself. Christmas decorations had been strung across the walls and glittered like jewels. Was this the way she and Teddy had come in last night? She couldn't remember. It was all so strange and unfamiliar this morning, when last night it had seemed like a magical palace.

The next set of doors led into the dining room. Here, the light streamed in from a row of tall windows. A roaring log fire glowed under an ornate mantel. Bill sat at a long, polished table, his attention taken by a newspaper in front of him. On the table's surface were silver dishes and starched white napkins folded beside plates the size of frying pans. The smell of fresh coffee filled the air; not the cheap, bitter kind that Vesta was used to smelling at the stall on the market, but something far richer and more enticing.

'Ah, you're here.' Bill looked up and put aside the paper, patting the elaborately carved chair beside him. 'Sit beside me.'

'I'm not hungry,' Vesta insisted again as she sat down.

'No matter. Some fresh orange juice, coffee or water perhaps?'

Vesta drank the water he poured for her. Then, without speaking, he served himself with sausages, eggs and bacon from one of the dishes.

'Thank you,' he told the hovering maid. 'That will be all.'

'Are you sure I can't tempt you?' he asked after the maid had gone. Vesta closed her eyes at the sight of all the food.

'Then try this,' he said as he stood up. Taking a bottle from a silver bucket, he poured a little of the bubbling liquid into a fluted glass. 'When I was your age, I suffered dreadfully with hangovers. However, I soon discovered that a few sips of the hair of the dog is unequalled for settling the stomach.'

He placed the glass at her side. Then he drew his fingers down her arm. She jumped, but he only chuckled again.

'Where am I?' she faltered, shrinking away from his touch. 'What is this place?'

'Don't you know?'

'Teddy said we were going to somewhere in the country to a party given by Wally and Leo.'

'You could say that.' Bill resumed his seat.

'But this place don't belong to them?'

He smiled. 'No, it's called Ossmingley Manor. An extremely wealthy friend of mine owns it, as you may guess. He lives abroad and is happy for his friends to use it.'

'Are we the only ones here?'

'No. Some other guests left earlier and some have gone out walking in this beautiful countryside.'

'Are we far from London?'

He chuckled softly. 'Didn't Teddy tell you where you were going?'

She looked away. She couldn't remember.

'This is Surrey.'

Vesta didn't understand. Why had Teddy left her here, so far away from home? She began to panic. 'What was Teddy doing with that girl?' she asked.

'Oh, so you do remember.'

'A bit. What were they doing?'

'What your boyfriend does best – enjoying himself. As we were.'

Vesta felt close to tears. 'Teddy's not interested in other women.' But as she said it, she knew the words didn't ring true.

Bill raised an eyebrow. 'Is that what you think?'

Another tear trickled down her cheeks. She didn't want to hear anything bad about Teddy. And yet she had

seen it with her own eyes. Even now, she was remembering the way he looked at women, the hushed whispers
she'd caught through the evening and the dark-haired
beauty in his arms . . .

'Vesta,' said her host patiently, 'I'm not in the business
of telling lies. The truth hurts sometimes, but you must
wake up to the fact that you are leading a very precarious
life, by virtue of the fact that you are living with someone
like Teddy.'

'I don't know what you're talking about.'

'Then all I can say is, if you choose to stay with him,
you will learn very fast.'

Vesta sniffed back her tears. She reached for the champagne. It was the only thing that helped.

'Are you married?' she asked on a stifled sob.

Bill's lips twisted wryly. 'No, my dear. I am not. Thrice
spliced and thrice divorced.'

'You've been married three times!'

He grinned. 'Yes, for my sins.'

'Why did you do what you did last night and—' She
gulped, unable to say the words.

'Why did I make love to you?' His smile was not
unkind. 'You refused to leave here with your errant
lover. I took you under my wing and you were not
unwilling to enjoy my company. It was quite natural for
us to end up in bed. And you seemed to enjoy yourself
very much, which rather dispels any illusion of loyalty on
your part to Teddy.'

Vesta drew in a bitter breath. 'But I love him.'

'Then how do you explain waking up beside me this morning and not Teddy?'

'I don't know,' she choked. 'It's all a muddle and a mess.'

At this his face hardened. A pair of steely blue eyes fixed her with clear contempt. 'Vesta, please stop this. You're no naive virgin. Indeed, you proved very satisfactory in bed. Whether schooled by this young man or others, you made the most cooperative lay. Be proud of your accomplishments, not ashamed of them.'

Vesta's heart almost stopped. She jumped to her feet, pushing her hands over her ears. She hadn't slept with other men! 'I don't want to hear any more!' Hot tears of humiliation scorched her cheeks. She hated this Bill! What right had he to accuse her of being a loose woman?

'Sit down,' he told her abruptly.

'No.'

'You'll do as you're told. Do you want to leave this place looking a wretched fool? Or do you want to keep your pride and regard this as one of life's helpful lessons? With a little discussion between us, you might find this experience very enlightening.'

Vesta glared at him. She snatched a napkin and sat down heavily.

Slowly pushing away his cup and saucer, Bill leaned his elbows on the table. 'Your childish behaviour, Vesta, is unacceptable. Remember, we came to know each other quite intimately last night. You were a willing young woman between the sheets. And despite your dramatics this morning, I find you quite charming. I like you, Vesta. You are refreshing and have spirit. Therefore I would rather you leave here not as a silly schoolgirl, but rather a woman knowing what she is about and, most importantly, who her friends are. Believe me when I tell you, there is nothing more important in this line of business than your friends.' He paused, eyeing her with caution. 'Now, dry your eyes. Put on a pretty smile and I shall be happy, knowing my lovely companion is not here under duress but is eager to learn – as *all* must learn who enter the entertainment industry.'

Vesta stared at him. Did he mean, if she tried she could really go on the stage? She could see that he was a rich and powerful man. He had rich and powerful friends. Even though she hadn't understood half the words he'd used, she realized he was trying to help her. He wanted to be her friend. Was that what she wanted too?

Teddy had left her. She couldn't get home without money. She was in the middle of Surrey, miles away from home, on Christmas Day. There was only Bill.

He held up his glass and raised an eyebrow. 'A toast to new friendships, Vesta. To your undoubted fame in a very lucrative and exciting world.'

Vesta felt breathless. Her tears all seemed to dry as he spoke those words. She reached for her glass. Gazing into his eyes, she felt a curl of excitement inside her. Taking a deep breath, she said nothing and sipped the champagne.

He smiled approvingly. 'Now, when I take you home, as I most certainly will, I shall tell Teddy that a room was arranged for you here last night. And only for you.' He raised his eyebrow again. 'How does that sound?'

Vesta found herself nodding.

'Then presumably Teddy will offer you his apologies for leaving you in the wilds of Surrey, and you will offer yours for embarrassing him in front of his friends. A lovers' quarrel. A tiff. And soon over.'

But although Vesta nodded again, she wasn't as certain as Bill that she wanted to make up with Teddy. He had hurt her and hurt her deeply. What kind of future could they have together if he was always going off with other women? Even if it was his job, could she put up with that?

'Good,' said Bill happily. 'Now try a little scrambled egg with your champagne. Very important to have the right balance in life.'

She did as she was told, forcing down the hot food, slowly beginning to feel better now that Bill seemed to be clearing up the dreadful mess she had landed herself in.

She glanced at him as she was eating. Everything about his movements was graceful and well-mannered. He might be an older man, but there was something about him that, although she didn't want to admit it, she felt attracted to in a strange sort of way.

On Saturday, Marie went to the market with Ada. The fogs and mists of the previous month had left and the last weekend of the year was unseasonably mild.

'This is for you,' said Ada, returning from the jewellery stall. Marie stood watching the tradesmen selling off the last of the year's wares; the fruit and veg were rock-bottom prices.

Marie gazed at the silver locket that Ada placed in the palm of her hand.

'A gift to celebrate your engagement, love.'

'It's lovely, Mum.'

'It was only cheap.'

Marie unfastened the clasp. 'Help me to put it on.'

Ada put down her bag and, pushing her daughter's hair gently to one side, linked the chain around her neck. 'You can keep a picture of Bing inside.'

Marie knew that Ada was putting on a brave face. There had been no word from Vesta, not even a Christmas card.

Marie hugged her mother. 'Yes, I will.'

Ada looked wistful. 'I'm glad you're not working tonight.'

'So am I.'

'Have you changed your mind about finding fame and fortune?'

'I've changed my mind about a lot of things.'

'You're growing up fast.'

Marie smiled. 'I'm older and wiser now.'

'I wish your sister was.' Ada lifted her bag and slid her arm through Marie's. 'If only I could see her, talk to her, I might be able to persuade her to come home.'

Marie glanced at her mother's thin, apprehensive face and the faint spark of hope in her eyes. Though Vesta had fallen in love and left home, there was no excuse for not sending word to Ada. A letter or card would have given them all peace of mind.

On Sunday, Bing took Marie to see Ivy and Johnny. Ivy had cooked a special roast with apple pie and cream for afters, to celebrate their engagement. But all the time she was enjoying herself, Marie thought of Ada at home, missing Vesta deeply.

Chapter 28

Rose, Shirley and Sal all had long faces as Marie walked into the dressing room on Monday. Although it was New Year's Eve, the club was half empty. The few who had turned out were drinking heavily and rowdy.

'It was a waste of time turning up,' said Rose as she pulled on her costume, barely giving a glance to Marie.

'And we ain't been paid,' agreed Sal, as she tried and failed to replace a broken feather in her headdress, then threw it aside in disgust. 'This place is bad news. No one appreciates our dancing, they only shout abuse. The rate this goes on, we might not ever get our money.'

'And there's no use hoping for tips,' continued Shirley. 'The drunks out there wouldn't give us the drip off their noses, let alone a quid or two.'

Rose gave a cackle of laughter. 'Suits me, as I don't want none of their filthy paws grabbing me and trying to kiss me.'

As Marie changed into her costume, she listened to the

conversation with interest. But no one said anything about the Blue Flamingo.

As usual, they did their routine without receiving a word of appreciation. The punters looked fed up and miserable, stringing out their drinks, ignoring the dancers as they left the stage.

'Ignorant sods,' announced Rose as they filed back to the dressing room. 'Anyway, I've got meself another job, so what do I care?'

The other girls looked at her in surprise. 'Doing what?' asked Sal, frowning.

'I'm going somewhere I'm appreciated.'

'Where's that?' Shirley asked suspiciously.

'Never you mind. But it's good pay.'

Sal gasped. 'You ain't going on the game, are you?'

Rose looked indignant. 'Course not. If you must know, Pedro gave me this posh geezer's name up West. A friend of Wally's. All he wants is someone to take out and dance with. It's money for old rope.'

Shirley poked her in the arm. 'Christ, Rose, you ain't falling for that old chestnut, are you?'

Rose turned on her spitefully. 'Trust you to think the worst!'

'Well, I don't like the sound of it neither,' Sal said cautiously.

'Only because Pedro offered me the job and not you,' argued Rose, throwing back her head and studying herself in the mirror. 'Sorry about that, but all's fair in love and war, girls.'

Marie was tired of hearing Rose repeat this. And when she saw Shirley and Sal glance at one another behind Rose's back, she knew they were too.

It was half past eleven when Pedro let them go. The club was cold and empty. The air stank of stale booze and damp. The girls complained bitterly about not being paid and were only pacified when Pedro promised to pay them the following Saturday.

Benny had already left by the time Marie made her way out. She was relieved to see the shape of Bing's car drawing up in the darkness.

He rushed to meet her and pulled her into his arms. 'You're early,' he whispered. 'I was prepared to wait until after midnight. Sort out the drunks who pester you.'

'The drunks went home early.' She was so happy to be safe in his arms.

'Shall we wait for your dad?'

'No. He could be a long time clearing up.'

As he drove Bing turned to her. 'Any mention of the Blue Flamingo?'

'The girls spent all their time complaining about drunks and not being paid. No one said anything much about the club. And Rose has got herself another job.'

'Doing what?'

'Keeping company with a rich man, she says. Someone Wally knows. All he wants is to dance with her.'

Bing's eyebrows shot up. 'Then she ain't the savvy sort she thinks she is.'

'She wouldn't listen to Shirley either, who tried to warn her.'

Outside the house, Bing turned off the engine and drummed his fingers on the steering wheel. 'Tonight I went round to see Charlie as he ain't been at work. His arm is broken and in a sling.'

'Did he have an accident?'

'After a few jars one night before Christmas, he went round to the Blue Flamingo. Course, the Scoresbys' heavies stopped him and Charlie cut up rough. He decked a couple of 'em and gave them a mouthful.' Bing hesitated. 'On his way home a car pulled up and some blokes got out and returned the favour.'

Marie gasped. 'Poor Charlie!' She shuddered at the memory of Vesta saying she wanted to make Charlie jealous.

'He'll live. But his pride is dented.'

'What's he going to do now?'

'Stay out of trouble, I hope.'

'Can he get his girl back?'

'Dunno if she'll have him.'

They sat in silence, until Bing looked at his watch. 'Happy New Year, Mrs Brown.'

'I'm not Mrs Brown yet.'

'Give me a kiss. No one is looking.' As he pulled her close, a light flooded out from the front room. He groaned and sat back. 'Caught in the act.'

Marie sighed softly. She wanted to be kissed too. 'Come in, if you like.'

'Don't think I will. See you tomorrow, sweetheart.'

Reluctantly, Marie left the car. She watched it turn the corner and listened as the engine noise died away. Touching the ring on her finger, she felt close to Bing. One day they wouldn't have to part. And on this happy thought she went inside to Ada.

Marie woke in the middle of the night. Her nightdress was stuck to her skin and her heart was thumping. She turned to the place beside her, only to find it empty. Then, as the nightmare came back with full force, the pictures seemed clearer than ever: a brute of a man standing over a small woman cowering against the wall. Her arms were folded protectively across her bump to shield her precious baby. Then, as he struck her, a piercing cry echoed in Marie's head.

Marie waited for the drumming of her heart to slow as she sat up in bed. This time there was no one to share the dream with. Images kept forming in her mind: the red-veined eyes of the monster about to attack a defenceless woman; her screams and feeble protests as he grabbed her and threw her across the room.

Marie pushed away the bedclothes, desperate to free herself from the cold fear still chilling her skin. She drew back the curtains, hoping to see the dawn lighting the sky above the roofs. But it was still dark. The stars twinkled in a vast, ebony universe. She pulled on her dressing gown and went to the front room. Once again her heart leaped. For a moment she froze as she saw a figure in the chair.

And then, in the light of the embers, she saw who it was. 'Dad, what are you doing sitting there?'

'I don't want to disturb your mother.'

She could smell the musty odour of the club on his coat. 'You look all in.'

'I am a bit.'

'The work at the club is too hard for you.'

He nodded. 'You're right, love. I'm not the young man I once was.' Pausing, he asked in a muffled voice, 'Is there any news of Vesta?'

'No, the girls didn't say anything. Nor did Benny.' Marie placed a blanket over him and poked the embers. Quickly she added a little kindling. When the dry wood caught, the fire flared into life. 'You'll soon be warm.' She saw his head droop sideways. Very soon he started to snore. Marie gazed at the hunched figure in the chair. If only Vesta would come home. She always put a light in his eye; the light that had seemed to have gone out these days.

She sat in a chair too and gazed into the flames of the fire. It was now Tuesday, the first day of January 1935. The New Year had begun. What lay in store for the Haskins family? Would it bring Vesta home? As the warmth made her drowsy, Marie thought of her twin and hoped Vesta was thinking of her.

By dawn's early light, Marie washed and dressed and trod softly back to the front window. There was no one about.

Her father still slept, so she went to the kitchen. Here she prepared a saucepan of milk ready to mix with the porridge oats, together with two generous slices of bread and dripping. After a good breakfast he would feel more like his old self. Placing Hector's shaving soap and blade on the draining board, she folded a clean vest and shirt from the ceiling rack over the chair. With luck there would be time for him to wash and shave before Ada got up.

Returning to the front room, Marie heard the first signs of life outside. From the window she could see children playing on the cobbles: the girls with their skipping ropes and the boys their footballs. One little girl was chalking lines on the pavement for hopscotch. An older boy threw a rope over the lamp-post to swing on.

Another tiny girl fell over. Her knickers had fallen round her ankles. Had she wet herself? Nobody seemed to care. Plonking herself on a doorstep, she let out a loud bawl. Eventually the door opened and she was hauled inside.

Marie smiled at the familiar sight. She and Vesta had done just the same when they were younger. Though their favourite game had been dressing up and putting on little shows, they loved playing out in the street. Sometimes all the kids would come in the back yard and watch them. It was nice when they clapped, but the boys often made rude noises. She smiled. Vesta had got very annoyed at the disturbance and told them to go away. Marie sighed. Their childhood had been very happy.

She thought of Bing. He had called her 'Mrs Brown' last night. What would it be like to be a wife and mother?

Gazing at the ring on her finger, and the pretty red stone in its clasp, she knew her life was about to change. The ring was a sign of her loyalty to Bing, not to a career on the stage, although he'd said she could still have one if she wanted. What did she want? If she married him, one day her children would be playing in the street too. She knew so very little about babies. Would she be a good mother?

'Is that you, Marie?' her father mumbled.

'Yes, Dad.'

He gazed up at her, scratching the stubble on his chin. 'What happened? Why am I sitting here?'

'You came home late.'

'Ah, yes,' he nodded, and sat back with a sigh. 'I remember now. I didn't want to disturb Ada.'

'Dad, if I left the Duke's, would you leave with me?'

He looked at her sadly. 'They wouldn't let me.'

'The brothers aren't there now, just Pedro.'

'Yes, but they still have a finger in the pie.'

Marie sat beside him. 'Don't worry, we'll find a way out.'

He nodded and patted her hand. 'I hope so. Happy New Year, love.'

'The same to you, Dad.'

Once again he looked at her with sadness in his eyes. She knew he missed Vesta as much as any of them. Was he staying at the Duke's because it was close to where Vesta might be? But Marie was worried that the work might eventually kill him.

*   *   *

Elsie knocked later that morning. 'Happy New Year, everyone.'

'The same to you, Elsie.'

She held up a bottle. 'I've brought a nice drop of port to celebrate.'

'Come in,' said Marie softly.

'How are your mum and dad?' Elsie asked.

'There's been no word from Vesta.'

Elsie rolled her eyes. 'That girl needs her bottom spanking.'

'Even if she didn't visit,' agreed Marie, 'she could have sent a card.'

Elsie touched Marie's shoulder. 'Come on, chin up, gel.'

In the front room there was silence. 'Happy New Year, everyone!' Elsie stood the port on the table and went over to Ada. 'Let's have a smile, Ada. And Hector, for Gawd's sake stop poking that fire. You'll put it out if you're not careful. Now where are the glasses?'

'I don't want a drink,' Ada said.

'No thanks, Elsie.' Hector sat on the couch.

'Blimey, what long faces this morning! You'll have a drink whether you like it or not,' Elsie decided. 'Look at the pair of you, you'd think there'd been a death in the family.'

'There has in a way,' Ada sighed. 'I don't suppose I'll ever see my daughter again.'

'Rubbish!' exclaimed Elsie. 'Your Vesta will be round. The trouble is, Ada,' she continued firmly, 'you spoiled that girl and now you're paying the price.'

Marie saw her mother sit up in the chair. 'I never spoiled her. There was no money to spoil her with!'

'I don't mean with money.' Elsie flipped her hand at Marie. 'Go on, girl, get some glasses. The bottle won't pour into thin air.'

Marie hurried to the kitchen and returned with the glasses. Elsie was still lecturing Ada. 'Vesta knew how to wind you and Hector round her little finger. When she couldn't get something she wanted, there would be tears and tantrums. You'd always give in, because you didn't want to get on the wrong side of her. Now, if that ain't spoiling, I don't know what is!'

Ada stood up, her cheeks flushed. 'You've no right to speak to me in that way.'

Marie put down the tray. 'Mum, Elsie is only trying to help.'

'A fine way of helping,' Ada said bitterly. 'I don't need advice from someone who ain't ever had kids.' Ada's hands trembled. 'Have you ever looked after a husband and children and worked all the hours God sends?'

At this, Hector stood up. 'Ada, think what you're saying. Elsie has been a second mother to our girls.'

'And you!' Ada exclaimed, turning on her husband. 'Call yourself a good father? Our Vesta would still be here if it wasn't for you!' She sank down on the chair and wept.

Quietly, Elsie sat beside her. 'Come on, love, it's New Year's Day.'

Ada shook her head, sniffing. 'I'm sorry. I didn't mean what I said.'

'I know you didn't.'

'I dunno what come over me.'

'We ain't going to let a few cross words come between us.'

Ada sniffed loudly again. 'No, course not.'

Elsie lifted her glass. 'Well, here's to us all, old friends, good and true.'

Ada wiped her cheeks. 'Elsie, I could bite my tongue out.'

'Don't do that, love.' Elsie chuckled, smacking her lips as she sipped the strong spirit. 'I'd miss our long chats.'

Ada glanced at Hector. 'I'm sorry, Hector.'

He gave her a grin under his moustache.

Marie listened to the loud tick of the mantel clock. Though peace reigned again, none of them could think of much to say as the minutes dragged by. It was Vesta who was on their minds.

When there were footsteps in the hall, they all looked up. The door opened. Dressed in a beautiful coat, with a pill-box hat sitting on the side of her head, as if by some miracle Vesta appeared and smiled widely.

'Happy New Year, everyone!'

Marie jumped up and ran into her arms. It was as though their thoughts had brought her back home.

Chapter 29

Bing looked around his small gaff in Blackwall. It was just one room full of his clobber. When he was married, their home would be very different from this. His boss at the PLA had a house on Manchester Road, with rooms for rent. Though not having discussed the date of their wedding yet, Bing fancied the spring. Last week, his mum and dad had offered them two rooms upstairs. But he'd seen too many of his docker pals start married life that way and regret it. Not everyone got along with each other. He loved his mum and dad dearly, but he liked his independence better.

Bing thought of the mid-Victorian house he had earmarked. Two ground-floor rooms, a scullery and back yard, with basement rooms that could be let out to lodgers to earn a few extra pennies. Manchester Road was acknowledged to be a cut above the rest of the island districts. Its broad width and elegant houses, accessed by flights of steps, and clean-cut black-painted railings were not dissimilar to Sphinx Street.

He knew Marie would feel at home here. And he would do all he could to see she was happy; she meant the world to him and, if he could, he would make her the happiest girl in the world.

He took a brand-new sheet of music from his pile by the bed. He had sung 'Let Me Call You Sweetheart' a few times at the pub. It was easy to carry off the famous crooner's drawl. Not that the patrons of the Cubby Hole gave him any credit. They preferred the livelier tunes. But this was special. 'Sweetheart' was his favourite word; one he would only use for the girl he loved. And that, of course, was Marie.

With a smile on his face and tucking the papers into his breast pocket, he glanced in the mirror and gave himself a wide grin. For a docker, he scrubbed up well. Nodding his approval and humming a few bars of 'Let Me Call You Sweetheart', he left his room, hurrying down the flight of concrete steps, setting off to call on his new land-lord before seeing Marie.

'Well, how do I look?' Vesta twirled around, happy to have her family's full attention. She had dressed for the part and, showing off the brown velvet fur-trimmed coat that Teddy had bought her, she felt confident and sophis-ticated. The coat was a gift from Teddy to make up for the way he had left her at the manor. For this, she had Bill to thank. He had brought her home in his chauffeur-driven car. True to his word, he had told Teddy that he'd arranged an overnight room for her at the manor. To her surprise, Teddy had thanked him, then when Bill had gone, said their quarrel had been a storm in a teacup. He wanted to forgive and forget.

And, when Teddy bought her the coat and a beautiful evening dress to match, she had given in. She had also felt guilty about Bill. But, as no more was said about that night at Ossmingley Manor, she was trying to forget it.

'You look beautiful,' said Ada, as she helped her daughter off with the expensive coat. Vesta pressed her hands down over the slim-fitting green dress and looked at her sister. After her initial welcome, Marie didn't look very pleased to see her. Nor did Elsie.

'We thought you'd come on Christmas Day,' said Marie in a flat voice.

'Yes, it didn't seem the same without you,' added Hector as he took the coat from Ada and folded it carefully over the couch.

'Teddy took me somewhere special, a party, in fact,' Vesta said quickly. 'I meant to visit, but time just flew.'

'We missed you,' said Ada. 'But now you're here, it doesn't matter.'

'Is there anything to drink?' She didn't want a lecture. After all, she wasn't to blame for what happened on Christmas Day.

'Yes,' said Ada eagerly. 'I'll go and put the kettle on.'

Vesta was about to say it wasn't tea she wanted when Elsie said, 'I'll see to that, Ada. Vesta, your mother has one or two questions she'd like to ask you. She hasn't seen you since you walked out, remember?'

'It wouldn't have happened if you'd been nice to Teddy.'

'He hurt Kaiser,' Elsie reminded her.

'He didn't mean to.'

'Let's forget all that,' Hector reasoned, plumping the cushion on the couch. 'Come and sit down. Tell us all your news.'

Vesta sat close to her father. She knew he was her ally and always had been. To her, he was the voice of reason in this family.

'So, are you happy at this new club?' said her mother as she sat down beside the fire.

'Yes.' She didn't say that she hadn't sung at the club since before Christmas. Teddy had got another act to sing there for the New Year celebrations. Her guilty conscience had caused her to wonder if he was punishing her for the embarrassment she caused him at the manor. 'I'm certainly not missing the factory,' she said instead. 'In fact I can't believe I stuck it out so long. My nails are actually growing.' She held out her long red nails that she'd taken hours to manicure and colour last night. 'The Blue Flamingo is very choosy. The members are all rich people who are never rowdy and always applaud.' She glanced at Marie. 'It's not a bit like the Duke's.'

Marie smiled. 'I'm glad you're happy.'

'What's been happening here, then?' Vesta hoped Elsie would hurry up with the tea. This was more difficult than she'd thought. Expecting to find everyone pleased to see her, she was surrounded by critical faces.

'Well, your sister got engaged,' Ada said.

'What?' Vesta felt her insides tightening as she looked across the room to where Marie sat.

'Yes, Bing asked me to marry him,' Marie answered quietly.

'And you agreed?' Vesta swallowed, trying to hide her shock that Marie hadn't been moping about missing her.

'Yes, I did.'

'Is that the ring?' Vesta stared at Marie's hand.

'It was a Christmas present.'

'I thought you didn't want to get married.'

'I didn't once.'

Vesta narrowed her eyes. 'I suppose you blame me for ruining your career.'

To Vesta's surprise, Marie only smiled. 'I fell in love and that changed things.'

'So it seems. Congratulations.' Vesta forced a smile on her lips but the emotions inside her were painful. Marie was her twin and they always shared everything. Well, they couldn't share men, of course, but being the last to know about Marie's engagement made her, once more, feel left out. 'I hope you'll be very happy.'

'Thank you.' Marie looked down and touched the ring, as though she was thinking of Bing.

Ada reached out to squeeze Vesta's hand. 'Now, dear, tell us more about yourself and of course . . .' Her mother hesitated. 'Teddy. Are you still seeing him?'

'What a daft question, Mum!'

'I only asked. We know so little about what goes on in your life. Does he sing at the Blue Flamingo too?'

Vesta rolled her eyes. 'You know he does.' How many more questions were to be fired at her, she wondered.

'We have important people to please, like I said. So Teddy acts as a host when Wally and Leo are busy. Like at the Christmas party I told you about, Teddy introduced me to lots of famous people. Have you heard of William Dearlove?'

Vesta was disappointed when they all shook their heads. None of her family appreciated how much she'd come up in the world. 'He's a director,' she explained, 'a very well-known one in the world of theatre. Bill says I'd make a good actress. I'm going to read for him soon.'

'Who's Bill?' asked Ada.

'William Dearlove. Bill's what he's called by his friends.'

Ada's expression was bewildered. 'But you don't know anything about acting.'

'Me and Marie were always putting on shows.'

'Yes, but you was only kids.'

'That doesn't mean I can't do it.' Vesta thought of all the occasions in her life that Ada had discouraged her. Now she was doing it again. Well, it wasn't going to work. She was free to do as she wished and that was the way it was going to stay. She could look after herself now. After all, she'd managed to put things right between herself and Teddy, and keep Bill as a friend too. In fact, he'd called round the house this week when Teddy was at work, to see how she was. At first, she hadn't wanted to let him in. She didn't want to talk about that night at the manor. But he hadn't mentioned it. Instead, he reminded her he was going to do all he could to help her.

'Bill is going to get me elocution lessons,' she said, tossing back her blonde waves. 'As he says I have promise.'

Ada's mouth opened on a gasp. 'But he don't know you and you don't know him. Why's he doing that?'

'I told you, I show promise.' Vesta wondered irritably what more she had to say to make an impression.

'But why should he be interested in a young girl who ain't never acted before?' Ada persisted.

Vesta was close to tears. It was only her pride keeping them from falling. Why did her mother always have to spoil things?

'Your mother only cares, love, she's not having a go,' Hector interrupted. 'We're sure you could do anything if you really wanted.'

'Stop that, Hector,' Ada admonished. 'It was you that gave her all them big ideas before.'

Vesta saw her father's shoulders droop. It was still Ada who always had the last say. Her father never seemed able to defend himself.

'Here's the tea,' said Elsie, coming in with a tray. Setting it down on the table, she arranged the cups, saucers and plates. 'There's a slice of Christmas cake for everyone. So you won't go hungry, Vesta.'

That all sat in silence as Elsie served the cake. Vesta looked at Marie and the ring on her finger. She felt the painful stirrings of envy. She wanted Teddy's ring on her finger. But would she ever get it? 'So when's the big day, Marie?' she asked curiously.

'We haven't decided yet.'

'Are you still going to work at the factory when you're married?'

'Your sister got promotion,' Ada said before Marie could reply. 'To the offices.'

Vesta was shocked. 'You can't type or do shorthand.'

'No, I check in the goods, mostly, from the barges. Then take the paperwork to the offices.'

'How did you manage that?'

'I filled in Flo Davis's place.'

'Flo Dav—' Vesta stopped. She glanced at Ada, who didn't know anything about the girl who said she was having Teddy's baby. She met Marie's eyes, who looked away quickly.

'Where are you living, Vesta?' Ada asked. 'We haven't got your address. You left without giving me one.'

'You know very well I'm with Teddy.'

Everyone was silent again. Vesta glared at them defiantly. 'What's wrong with that?'

'You're only eighteen,' Ada cried. 'You don't know what life is about.'

'Would you still say that to me if I was married and had a couple of kids hanging round my ankles?'

'Vesta, come home to where you belong,' her mother begged. 'You can't live in sin.'

'Mum, that's an old-fashioned idea. One day me and Teddy will be married. But it's my career that comes first.' Vesta pushed away her tea and stood up. 'I've got to go now.'

Ada tried to stop her putting on her coat. 'Please don't leave.'

'Ada, calm down,' Hector said, as Vesta walked to the door.

'Don't let her go. You're her father. Put your foot down.'

Hector stood in the middle of them. 'Vesta, don't leave like this. Let's try to work things out.'

'It'll only end up in a row,' Vesta grumbled. 'As long as I'm with Teddy, Mum will never be happy.' She shrugged him off and grabbed her bag.

'At least leave us your address, love, somewhere we can write to.'

'Just write to the club.' She didn't want her family turning up on their doorstep. Teddy would go mad.

Vesta hurried out. She didn't look at Marie as she knew the pleading expression in her eyes would drag her back. She loved her sister, father and mother, but she had her own life to lead. And it wasn't the life they wanted for her. If Ada had her way, she would be leading a drab and boring life that would eventually drive her crazy.

Marie caught up with her on the steps. 'Vesta, come in the bedroom. It will be better on our own.'

'Mum wouldn't like that.'

'It will take time for her to understand.'

Vesta drew away. She didn't want to speak to Marie alone. She might let out her big secret. And even Marie wouldn't understand about Bill. 'I have to go now. Here's Teddy.' Vesta hurried down the steps as his car drew up.

She opened the door and sat in. She couldn't resist calling back, 'After all, you wouldn't want Teddy darkening the doorstep, would you?' But the moment she said it, she was sorry. She had wanted to hurt and she had. Marie was staring after her with watery, sad eyes.

Vesta forced back the tears as Teddy drove off with a powerful roar.

It was early evening when Bing and Marie walked down to Island Gardens. His arm lay lightly around her shoulders as they gazed over the dark waters of the Thames. On the other side of the river, the lights of Greenwich sparkled like tiny diamonds. The air was cold but not frosty and the sky above a cloudless dark blue.

'So Vesta turned up after all,' he murmured after listening to all Marie had told him. 'That was a surprise.'

'I think she felt guilty about Christmas.'

'Your mum must have been upset when she left.'

'Yes. She doesn't approve of them living in sin.'

'Your mum ain't religious, is she?'

'No, but it's what people will think.' She leaned her head against his shoulder. 'Things might have been different if Vesta had listened to Flo Davis.'

'Teddy would never admit to being the father of her child.'

'No, I suppose not.'

'Talking of living in sin,' Bing said slowly, 'what would you say to a spring wedding?'

'What, ours?'

'My boss is letting out rooms in his house in Manchester Road and has given us first refusal. If you give the nod, I'll move in and do it up, ready for, say, April or May.'

'I don't know. Mum might be lonely.'

'We could wait for ever for others to get sorted.' He bent to kiss her, his hands moving over her back and pressing her against him. 'I have a new song to sing you but I'm gonna save it till the day we're married.'

As a lone vessel hooted somewhere out on the river, he kissed her again; a kiss that reminded her just how much she loved him.

Chapter 30

It was a Saturday in the middle of January when Pedro stormed into the dressing room.

'Where's our money?' demanded Shirley, as she put on her coat. 'We've not had a penny for weeks.'

Pedro ignored her.

'Come with me,' he told Marie.

She quickly did up her blouse. It wasn't often that Pedro ventured into the dressing room, and she wondered what he wanted.

'What are you up to?' demanded Rose, standing in his way. 'Are you paying her before us?'

'No, you silly cow. It's nothing to do with that.' Pedro pushed her back and glared at Marie. 'Hurry up!'

Marie picked up her coat and bag. She knew they were all staring suspiciously after her.

Striding through the empty club, Pedro led the way to the small room behind the bar. A long wooden draining board was cluttered with unwashed glasses. Stacks of wooden crates stood next to an opening in the floor. Marie saw the draymen's boards beneath. It was the entrance to the cellars.

'Is Dad down there?' she asked anxiously.

'He's so drunk he's fallen over.'

'Me dad wouldn't do that.'

Pedro pointed a finger in her face. 'If he's not up them stairs quick he gets locked in for the night.'

Marie went to the trap door. She didn't want to go down in the dark. The smell was awful.

'Well, what are you waiting for?' Pedro demanded.

Stepping down to the first wooden stair, she held on to the draymen's boards. The only light below came from a lantern nailed to a pillar. As she descended, the air reeked of decay. There were scuffling noises all around and she knew there must be rats.

When she reached the bottom, she stood still. Cobwebs hung from the pillars and cast deep shadows. To her right a big barrel was turned on its side. Her father was sitting beside it on the wet sawdust.

'Dad, what happened?' She went on her knees beside him.

'The barrel fell on top of me and the ale spilled out.'

'Pedro said you'd been drinking.'

He shook his head wearily. 'No, my strength just gave out. That's why I dropped the barrel.'

Marie pulled his arm round her shoulders. 'I'll help you to stand.'

Marie managed to help him to his feet, but he soon sank down again. 'It's no use, my dear. My legs are too weak.'

'Don't worry, I'll go and get Bing.'

He grasped her hand as she went to leave. 'Be careful. Pedro is unpredictable.'

She nodded, giving a brief smile. 'Bing will know what to do.'

'Well, where is he?' Pedro demanded when she climbed out of the cellar.

'I need help to lift him.'

'If he's too drunk to get himself up those stairs, a night on his arse sobering up will teach him a lesson.'

Marie wanted to slap his face. Her hands folded into fists as she said defiantly, 'He's not drunk. He's exhausted. The work you make him do is too heavy.'

'He's lucky to have a job.' Pedro gripped her arm and pushed her out of the room.

'I'm going to get a friend to help.'

Pedro just shrugged. 'You'll have to be quick as I'm closing up and the trap door's going down.'

With a smirk on his face, he returned to the room.

Marie felt her blood run cold. She turned and ran out. Her heart was thumping as she hurried into the cold night. She looked around for Bing's car and saw the dark shape under the lamplight.

'Bing, is that you?'

A car door banged. 'Marie, what's wrong?'

'Dad's fallen over in the cellar,' she gasped. 'I tried to help him, but he's so weak he can't walk.'

'Didn't anyone help him?'

'Pedro accused him of being drunk. He said a night down there would teach him a lesson.'

Bing slipped his arm around her. 'I'll soon put a stop to his tricks. Where is the cellar?'

'In the room behind the bar on the floor by some crates. There's a trap door the draymen use for the barrels.'

He nodded, pushing her towards the car and opening the door. 'Get in and keep warm. I won't be long.'

'Please be careful,' she shouted from the open window. She didn't want Bing to get into trouble like Charlie had. But, neither did she want her father locked in a cold cellar all night.

Bing made his way through the narrow door and down the steps into the Duke's. The room was deserted and in darkness, except for a pale light shining from a room behind the bar. A tall man, wearing a dirty half-apron, appeared in the doorway.

'Who the hell are you?' he demanded, as Bing strode towards him.

'A friend of Hector Haskins.'

'Then you ain't welcome here.'

'Don't worry, chum, I ain't planning to stay.'

The man, who Bing took to be Pedro, reached behind the bar. The blade of a knife glinted.

Bing froze. 'I'm not after trouble,' he said, but the hair on the back of his neck stood up. 'I just want the old man.'

'He ain't going nowhere.'

Bing stared steadily into his dark eyes. 'Don't sound like a bright idea to me.'

'You've got a big mouth, mister.'

'So they tell me.' Bing watched the tip of the knife point towards him. He wondered how handy Pedro was with it.

'You ain't a copper, are you?'

Bing shrugged. 'No, I take care of my own business.'

The barman moved forward, the knife at waist level. Bing stepped back, lifting his hands from his sides. 'Listen, Hector's ruffled your feathers, right? But do you really want to land yourself in hot water with your boss?'

'What do you know about that?' Pedro demanded sourly.

'Enough to guess that, if the old man died, Wally wouldn't thank you for the trouble of dumping him. Wally's a busy man and a corpse turning up on his doorstep will give him aggro.' Bing held his breath. He could almost hear Pedro's mind working. 'Or you could step aside and let me take him.'

Bing glanced left and right. What escape route was there if Pedro should attack him? He looked for a chair he could grab to defend himself with, but they were all stacked by the tables.

To his surprise, Pedro retreated a few steps. He jabbed the knife towards the room. 'Don't try nothing clever or you'll both regret it. I'll give you five minutes.'

Bing made for the room and, as Marie had said, found the trap door by a stack of crates. As he lifted it, the stink made his eyes water. A wooden flight of steps ended in semi-darkness on the cellar floor.

'Hector?' he yelled, as he made his way down. A lantern flickered and gave light to the shadows. He looked up the stairs. Was Pedro planning to trick him?

'Help!' a voice shouted, and Bing hurried the last few steps. Making his way to an overturned barrel, he found Hector beside it.

'Bing, is that you?' Hector asked weakly. 'Thank God. I thought that Pedro had done something to Marie.'

'No worries there, she's safe in the car,' he whispered. 'And you're gonna be sitting beside her in no time at all.'

'Be careful of Pedro.'

'I've clocked him, don't worry.'

Hector's face was ghost-like in the eerie gloom. 'I'm afraid I'm too weak to walk very far.'

'Don't worry, it's a fireman's lift for you.'

Before Hector could reply Bing thrust his hands under Hector's limp body and hauled him up. Without pausing, he shoved his shoulder into Hector's middle. One good pull and he was over his shoulder. Standing up straight, right arm locked on Hector's legs, he made his way back to the stairs. The smell of the rats and filth choked him and he paused for one last breath.

The stairs creaked as he went up. A rat shot out from the crumbling walls. He took a sharp breath as his knees and thighs knotted. Cuffing the sweat quickly from his eyes, he found himself at last in the room above.

Pedro was waiting for him, and he pressed cold steel to Bing's throat. 'I don't know who you are, but you're trouble.'

The palms of Bing's hands filled with sweat. He felt the tip of the knife slide up to his jaw. He waited for the rip of skin, knowing that, with Hector on top of him, he was helpless.

Pedro laughed. Then, kicking hard at Bing's backside, he sent him sprawling. It was only by luck that Bing didn't fall, managing to steady both himself and Hector. The effort cost him dearly as, winded and half-blinded by the sweat in his eyes, he shuffled his way out and across the room.

One day, he promised himself, he'd pay another call here and it wouldn't be to shake the man's hand. But it was Hector he was concerned for and, finding the short flight of steps, he fumbled for the latch and let himself out.

Chapter 31

Vesta walked around the room that she was rapidly beginning to tire of. Once, she had admired Teddy's taste, now she was beginning to see its flaws. The dark-coloured drapes shut out what sunlight could creep through the small windows, and the bare walls were bereft of family photographs or pictures. Teddy seemed to have no family or friends, and now, it seemed, she didn't either. She missed working at the Blue Flamingo and meeting people. But Teddy insisted she was destined for better things, which was why he approved of Bill.

Vesta looked out of the window and down onto the street to see if the big, chauffeur-driven car had arrived. It was a miserable January day, cold and gloomy. Why did Teddy have to leave her today of all days? He said it was to go on business, but she suspected he was seeing other women again. They had quarrelled last night, and this morning Teddy had left without even waking her to say goodbye.

The unhappy scene was still on her mind. 'Can't you go some other time?' she had begged him when he told her that he had to be away. 'I can't read for Bill on my own.'

'Don't whinge,' he'd told her as he packed his bag. 'All you'll have to do is learn a few lines. What could be simpler? Even for you.'

'What if I go wrong?'

'You won't.'

'When will you be back?'

'I don't know.'

'Teddy, do you love me still?'

He'd turned, looking very angry. 'If you let Bill down, you won't get your chance again. I've put a lot of work into getting your career off the ground and all you can do is complain. Do you want to go on the stage or not?'

She had tried not to cry. Tears only made him more angry. 'Yes, I do, but—'

'In this business there are no "buts",' he'd bellowed at her. 'If you find a golden goose, you look after it. And Bill is your golden goose. I've done all I can for you. Now you have to stand on your own two feet.'

She could smell him on the pillow. It was all she could do to talk herself into getting ready. She didn't really want to be on her own with Bill. She still couldn't forget what had happened at Christmas.

Vesta took a sip of the gin and lime she had mixed. Did she look glamorous enough? Were these the right clothes to wear? 'Teddy, are you with someone else?' she whispered aloud.

Moving quickly across the room, she gazed into the long art deco mirror. The dress fitted her like a glove, just as Teddy had said it did. She loved it when they went up to the West End and to the big stores. After their last shopping spree at New Year, Teddy had taken her to Bill's apartment in Bloomsbury and shown her off.

His apartment was sumptuous. It was modern, unlike Ossmingley Manor, with paintings on the walls she didn't understand at all, like squiggles and shapes, and lots of shiny floors that had big furry rugs on them. During the evening, she had been introduced to some wealthy businessmen. At first, she had felt out of place and shy. But in no time at all, after their flattering compliments, she was soon at ease. Sipping one of Bill's famous cocktails, and smoking a cigarette that Teddy had inserted into a long cigarette holder for her, she had revelled in the attention.

Vesta gazed once more in the mirror. How different she was from the shabbily dressed girl of last year! The deep crimson dress had a flirtatious flare to the skirt and draped in folds over her legs. The shoulders were padded, just like the Hollywood actresses wore. She'd had her blonde waves permed fashionably, allowing the small, plate-shaped hat, the very latest in fashion, to sit elegantly on her head.

Teddy gave her all she asked for. There was no one to scold her for being vain or wasteful, like Ada was always doing. She could have all the expensive hairdos, clothes and shoes she wanted. Her underwear was pure silk and very feminine. Today she was wearing the very latest in nylon hosiery. No more baggy stockings like those she had to share with Marie.

Vesta thought of Teddy's hands sliding over her legs. Her skin would shiver as he expertly undid her suspenders and removed her underwear. He had taught her that men liked different things from women, and how to use her hands and tongue to arouse him. He assured her that making love was nothing to be ashamed of. It was what people did to have fun and enjoy themselves. Vesta couldn't imagine Ada and Hector ever doing what she and Teddy did. And poor Marie! How would she find out how wonderful lovemaking could be if she married a common docker like Bing?

But her thoughts soon turned again to where Teddy had gone. Lately, he hadn't seemed so interested in making love. That was why she was suspicious. Did he still see the dark-haired girl from Ossmingley Manor? Is that who he was with today?

Vesta tried to stop her jealousy. She drank some more gin. As the alcohol warmed her inside, she slipped on her fur-trimmed coat. She had asked Teddy for enough money to get a taxi back from Bloomsbury, if Bill's chauffeur wasn't on hand. Vesta had tried not to look into his eyes. She was afraid he would see the guilt in her own.

Returning her attention to the mirror, she sunk her chin into the collar of her coat. She *did* look glamorous! There was nothing to be worried about. After all, this was the beginning of her career. She remembered what Teddy had said: Bill was her golden goose.

Going to the window, she was just in time to see Bill's car draw up. Her heart jumped as the chauffeur held open the door and Bill climbed out.

The top of his silver head gleamed in the pale morning light. Dressed immaculately in a long, tailored navy-blue coat, he could have been royalty. Vesta thought how handsome he was for his age, tall and broad-shouldered, with that mane of hair. She could sense his wealth and power, even from this distance.

She rushed to the door. Then, feeling anxious, she hurried back and drained her glass. Taking a deep breath, she made herself walk slowly to the door and wait for his knock.

Ada opened the door and stifled a cry. Her eyes protruded in shock as Bing and Marie dragged Hector in. 'Oh, what's happened to him?' she gasped.

'Dad fell over at the club,' Marie said breathlessly.

'How?'

'A barrel fell on him.'

Ada stood back, her hand to her mouth. 'I knew no good could come of him working at that place.'

'We'll put him to bed, Mrs H,' Bing said as they struggled across the room.

Ada rushed to the bedroom and, drawing back the bedclothes, she helped Bing and Marie to lower Hector onto the bed.

'Has he broken anything?' Ada's voice was shaky as she began to undo Hector's coat.

'Don't think so,' Bing muttered. 'But being carted around like a sack of potatoes don't help.'

'Perhaps we should go for the doctor,' Marie said as Ada began to undo Hector's shirt buttons.

'Are you in pain, love?' Ada bent close to Hector, pushing back the greasy strands of hair from his dirty face.

'No,' Hector mumbled, 'just need to sleep.'

Ada nodded, gently releasing the stud in his collar to reveal his grimy vest. She looked up at Marie and Bing. 'After he's slept, I'll wash him and change his clothes. He'll be right as rain after a good meal.' She pulled herself upright and smiled at them gratefully, though Marie could see she was afraid to say more as tears were close.

'I'd better be off now,' Bing said.

In the hall he held Marie close. 'Your dad is tough and will pull through,' he assured her. The house was quiet and dark. Only the lamplight from the street flowed in.

'I don't know what I'd have done tonight if you hadn't been there,' Marie whispered. 'Pedro would have left him in that cellar all night.'

'Marie, you can't go back to the Duke's. Neither can your dad. It's finished.'

She nodded. 'I know.'

'This is 1935, a new year,' he continued. 'Your mum has got your dad back and he'll be well again. You and me have a home of our own to make, and, although I know life ain't the same without Vesta, it's us that counts. I promise to make you happy, Marie.'

Marie knew she was so lucky to have Bing by her side. Tonight could have ended badly if he hadn't been there. And she *did* want to be married, and have a home of her own and babies. But even though her heart belonged to Bing, her thoughts were still with Vesta.

That night, she had the dream again. She woke bathed in sweat. She was certain she had heard Vesta calling her name. In the early hours of the morning, she found herself writing a letter to Vesta. It was only a few lines, but it told her they all loved and missed her very much.

Chapter 32

Teddy hated January – the bleak weather, the cold and the fogs. One day he would be away from the Smoke and living in style in a warm, exotic climate. He had nothing to stay for in England; he was a loner and he knew it. The Scoresbys were just a means to an end. He would make enough money from their rackets to pay for a passage across to the other side of the world. They had used him for their own purposes for long enough, but soon it was going to change.

Wally was getting crazier by the minute and Leo mixed with the theatrical scene and even the politicians and police to further their business. They had set up the Duke's with the aim of turning it into a money box. But because of their rampant gambling, they soon ran into debt. Their idea to move to the Blue Flamingo and run it as silent partners, making him, Teddy, their front man, was a poisoned chalice. He'd seen what had happened to Pedro. And he knew the brothers' addiction to gambling and avoiding their creditors could end only one way. He now had the uncomfortable sensation that in a short while he would be expected to clean up their mess yet again.

Teddy walked into the Duke's and inhaled the stale air. It made him sick to think of what he had done for the Scoresbys. It started with that poor old codger Sid, who hadn't known how to keep shtoom, and then Irene, the mouthy cow. Then those South London boys – and a few more loudmouths since – he'd had to do all the dirty work. Well, one day it would end and that day was not far off.

Teddy pulled back his shoulders under his hand-stitched jacket and made his way to the bar. He gave a Pedro a brief nod, and was returned a sharp glance that could mean only one thing: a warning.

Teddy shivered. He approached with caution the single table at which Wally, Leo and two other men were sitting. Their drinks were positioned by the central deck of cards and the pile of paper money beside it. Wally's repulsive face was set in a grimace as he studied his hand. Leo's handsome features were unreadable as he sat quietly beside his brother.

Teddy knew he wouldn't be addressed until the game was over. He stood still, aware of Pedro to his right. The two other players were dressed in shabby dark suits and looked like the Scoresbys' usual victims: idiots who fancied themselves as hard men but, after being caned by the brothers, discovered they were not. With Wally's short fuse and Leo's sadistic tendencies they would be well advised to accept their losses.

The seconds crept by as the cards went down. Slowly a leer formed on Wally's distorted face. And just as slowly he placed his cards, all hearts, on the table: an ace, a king, a queen, a jack and a ten. Teddy felt hot with apprehension. It was Wally's party trick. The flush he literally kept up his sleeve and, in every case, the winning hand.

'I'm a lucky bastard, ain't I, Leo?'

Leo nodded, giving the evil eye to the two defeated players. 'Fancy another game, boys?'

'Yeah, go on,' urged Wally, though as he pushed the overflowing ashtray aside and drew the pot towards him, it was clear this was no invitation.

There was a muttered protest from one of the visitors. Wally's head jerked up. 'What was that, old son?'

The man quickly sank back his drink. It wasn't long before the two players were on their feet.

'Not got the balls for it?' taunted Wally, narrowing his eyes.

There was no reply and the two losers, defeated and morose, turned and made their way out. Pedro moved sharply to follow them, so fast on his feet that even Teddy was surprised.

'Better luck next time, boys,' Wally shouted, his stretched pink skin glistening as he laughed and managed a few last obscenities.

Teddy's legs turned to jelly as Wally swivelled round to look at him. 'Look who it ain't, Leo, standing all alone by himself in the corner.' Wally put up a meaty hand and waved him forward. 'Sit down, Teddy, make yourself comfortable.'

Teddy did as he was told, though he would have preferred to keep as far away from Wally as possible. He had witnessed Wally's unpredictable reactions – broken glass bottles, a slap or a punch – according to his mood.

'Fill us in, then, 'andsome,' Wally mocked, watching Teddy closely. 'Have we got the old geezer sorted?'

Teddy nodded. 'Yes, so far, Mr Scoresby.' It had been a week since he had last seen Vesta. He was certain that Dearlove would have done his part and won her over, so sealing her fate as a toy for his amusement.

'What's that supposed to mean?' Wally's face quickly lost its distorted smile.

'It hasn't been easy . . .' Teddy mumbled.

At this both Wally and Leo looked at him. Teddy shivered under their cold gazes.

'Has he got the girl or hasn't he?' Leo asked in a low, smooth tone, which frightened Teddy most of all.

'Yes,' Teddy said quickly. 'I've set it all up.'

'You were supposed to do that at Christmas,' Wally barked, and reached for his cigar. Narrowing his eyes, he blew smoke through the twisted side of his mouth, causing Teddy to blink and stifle a cough.

'I know, but Vesta wasn't as easy as the others.'

'Listen, we pay you good money to deliver on time,' Wally muttered angrily. 'We don't want this old sort disappointed. His mates are our livelihood too, remember? The other tarts didn't take you half as long.'

Teddy adjusted his tie. He was feeling hot and uncomfortable. 'I'm sorry, but those girls had no family or friends so it was easy to do the business. But with Vesta—'

'Stop there,' Leo interrupted in his cold, husky voice. 'I don't want no excuses. We were expecting what was arranged. You get the punters the girls they want, and they pay us the earner.'

'Yes, yes,' nodded Teddy, his gut twisting so painfully he could hardly draw breath. 'And I'm sure Mr Dearlove will be quite satisfied. His friends too.'

'They'd better be,' said Leo threateningly. 'Or else we'll find someone who can do the job properly.'

Teddy felt his throat constrict. There was no spittle left in his mouth. He took out his handkerchief and dabbed at his forehead.

'Listen,' muttered Wally malevolently, 'you ain't taking a liberty with us, are you? Keeping this bit of skirt for yourself?'

'No, no,' Teddy protested. Little did they know how tired he was of Vesta; she was a liability, a drag, and after that episode at Christmas where she'd acted like a common trollop, no one would be happier to see her go than he.

Wally did a bad mimic of this answer, making Teddy feel humiliated. Then to mock him even more, Wally's hand shot out and grabbed him. He pushed his disfigured face into Teddy's. In a blinding flash of pain Teddy's was knocked sideways. The slap had caught him off guard. He should have seen it coming.

Wally laughed as he clutched Teddy's collar so tight, Teddy thought he would stop breathing. His eyes felt as though they were being squeezed out of their sockets. His

Adam's apple was rammed against Wally's hand. The air in his lungs had gone and he was beginning to feel dizzy.

Wally pushed him back in his chair. Spreading out his hands, Teddy held the table. He ducked, expecting another blow. But all that came was Wally's laughter whilst Leo stared at him.

At the back of Teddy's mind, behind the fear, he swore he would soon be gone from this madhouse. He had worked hard to get the Scoresbys the right women and turn them into an investment. It was through his efforts the plan had succeeded. And yet all they could do was slap him about.

'Just remember what you are,' Leo threatened. 'You're nothing, just a go-between, a lowlife. If it wasn't for us finding you, you would have nothing. There ain't a stroke you can pull that me and Wally don't know about. If you cross us once, you'll never do it again.'

Teddy stared at him, his heart beating fast. He knew what Leo was capable of, and once more he vowed the sooner he was shot of the Scoresbys the better.

Leo stood up and, coming round the table, he stroked Teddy's thick black hair. Running his fingers through its well-combed thickness, he traced his thumb down the side of Teddy's cheek. 'Nice looks, good accent, a few bob in your pocket . . . it's a good life, ain't it? Don't forget, it's us that give it to you.'

Teddy was shaking and Leo was clearly enjoying the feel of his fear. He daren't look up. The look might be his last. According to the whims of the Scoresby brothers, his life hung in the balance.

Just then there was a noise at the bar. A figure that Teddy knew must be Pedro moved close. An unopened bottle of malt whisky was lowered to the table. Pedro's long fingers untwisted the cap and set down two tumblers. 'Thought you might like to end the evening on a chaser, Mr Scoresby. The best we've got in the house.'

Teddy silently blessed Pedro. Leo's hand grasped the half-filled glass. With Wally and Leo's sarcastic taunts in his ears, Teddy waited. He was the butt of their jokes and there wasn't a damn thing he could do about it. But at least he was here. He was still breathing.

Teddy listened to Pedro turning the lock of the front door. The Duke's was now closed and Teddy felt as though the life had been drawn out of him. With shaking hands he poured himself a whisky. He threw it back and poured another. He wasn't a big drinker but he had to have something to help him gather his thoughts.

'You were sailing close to the wind, my friend,' Pedro whispered and, like Leo, drew his hand down the back of Teddy's dark head.

Teddy flinched, pushing him away. 'Leave off, Pedro.'

'So that's all the thanks I'm going to get for saving your pretty arse?' The barman sat on the chair that Wally had just left.

Teddy turned sulkily towards him. He knew Pedro had distracted Leo but, not wanting to admit he owed Pedro anything, he shrugged. 'I can handle them.'

'You ain't in their league, Teddy bear.'

'We'll see,' rasped Teddy irritably. 'I'll get away from them somehow.'

Pedro laughed. 'That'll be the day.'

Teddy forgot his anger and frowned. 'What do you mean?'

'They own us, lock, stock and barrel.'

'Not me, they don't.' Teddy gulped his drink. 'As soon as Dearlove and his cronies are fixed up, I'm off. What the Scoresbys don't know is that those twins have cost me dearly. I planned to get the two of them, but only got one. Her sister was the full goods – a better voice and looks and altogether a rich man's brass – but I had to settle for second best.'

Pedro looked at him slyly. 'I had trouble with that very same tart on Saturday.'

'What? Marie?' Teddy frowned in puzzlement.

'The old geezer was pie-eyed and fell over. The girl sends this right mouthy joker in to face me up.'

'Who?'

'Dunno. Someone who knew that Wally still runs the Duke's.' Pedro described what had happened and Teddy's face darkened.

'Stroppy sort with a loud mouth?'

'That's him.'

'He's caused me trouble before.'

'I can soon put a stop to that, Teddy bear.' Pedro reached across and stroked Teddy's hand. 'Just give me the word.'

Teddy started and clutched his drink. 'Not yet. I've got to think it all out.'

'Don't leave it too late,' Pedro warned.

'Does Wally know this?'

'Course not. He don't give a monkey's about the Duke's now. Listen, if you really want to get shot of the Scoresbys, why don't we shack up and leave together? Cut our losses while we can. I know a few people on the boats. We could be on the other side of the world in a couple of months. Think about it. I've always looked after you, Teddy bear. You can trust me.'

Teddy turned slowly to the barman and saw another madman staring across at him. The light in Pedro's eyes was disturbing. Teddy groaned inwardly. How had he got himself into such a situation? He was swimming with sharks. But as Pedro had reminded him, he could count on him in a tight spot. And, Teddy decided anxiously, there may be more of those to come before he had saved enough to cut loose.

Teddy forced a smile, though his stomach revolted. He was holding a candle to the devil. 'All right,' he murmured. 'We'll bide our time. I don't intend to come out of this with nothing. The Scoresbys are raking it in at the Blue Flamingo. And before we leave, I want some of it too.'

Pedro grinned, touching him. Teddy recoiled again. 'That's what I like about you, Teddy. You're a greedy bugger, the same as me.'

Chapter 33

It was over three weeks since Marie and Hector had left the Duke's and there had been no word from anyone. Marie hoped that that part of their lives was now over. She had begun to enjoy the weekends again. It was Friday and after leaving the factory she walked towards the dock gates. Although it was early, she hoped that she might see Bing and Charlie.

But as she came into sight of the gates, another figure about her own size and dressed in a fawn coat with a fur collar, gloves to match, and high heels hurried towards her.

Marie stood still. Her mouth fell open. 'Vesta?'

'Oh, Marie, I hoped you'd be walking this way.' Vesta hugged her.

'What are you doing here?'

'I've come to see you, of course. It's early knock-off from the factory on Fridays. I still remember, you know.'

Marie gazed at her sister. 'Have you seen Mum?'

'No.' Ada linked her arm through Marie's. 'I wanted us to talk alone. Can we go and sit somewhere?'

Marie glanced at the dock gates and Vesta frowned. 'Or are you meeting Bing?'

'No, I've no special plans.' Marie didn't want to miss the opportunity of talking to her sister and she hadn't arranged to meet Bing.

'Island Gardens?' said Vesta.

'Yes, all right.' Marie was very surprised. She had never expected to see Vesta anywhere near the factory again, even if it was just to speak to her. They took the next turning that led away from Ellisdon's and Vesta glanced over her shoulder. 'I didn't see any old faces.'

'Mr Morton let me off early.'

Vesta glanced down at Marie's coat and shoes. 'Course, I thought you looked smart. You're in the offices now.'

'Yes.' Marie was glad she'd given her shoes a good polish last night and worn a decent herringbone coat to work.

'You've had your hair cut,' Vesta said, glancing at Marie's new short style.

'Yes. I went up to Poplar to the hairdresser's.'

'It looks nice. I've grown mine.' Vesta touched her long bob.

They met each other's gaze and laughed. 'It's just like the old days,' said Vesta, squeezing Marie's arm as they walked. 'Do you remember which one of us first did our hair differently?'

Marie nodded. 'You did, on our eighteenth birthday. You pinned your hair up. And it did look lovely.'

Vesta's smile faded. 'Do you ever think of when we were kids?'

Marie nodded. 'All the time.'

'So you miss those days too?'

'Yes, but now we're grown-up and our lives are very different.'

Vesta gave a sharp nod. 'I suppose you blame me for ruining your career?'

'Why should I do that?'

'Because I left you at the Duke's.'

Marie shook her head. 'No, I don't blame you for that. But I wish it could have been different. That place could only bring trouble.' She paused. 'Dad and me have left there now.'

Vesta stopped dead. 'You have?'

'Yes. Come and sit on a bench and I'll tell you all about it.'

They walked into Island Gardens and past the entrance to the foot tunnel that led under the river to Greenwich. The light was going now, but the red sun still shone above the river, glowing softly on the water and sending shafts of light through the bare trees. The smell of salt and tar rose up from the river, and the hoots were loud from the tugs and ships that were going in and out of the port.

When they were seated, Marie told Vesta everything that had happened since Pedro had taken over. 'If it hadn't been for Bing, he would have left Dad down in the cellar.'

'Teddy never told me about it,' said Vesta in a whisper. She looked hard at Marie. 'I suppose that's something else you blame me for, nearly getting Dad killed?'

'No, I don't blame you for anything. Nor does he. We all decided to work at the Duke's.'

'Yes, but as I said before, I left you and Dad behind.'

'Are you still happy?' Marie asked.

'Yes, course,' Vesta nodded quickly but her eyes soon filled with tears and her lips trembled as she looked away.

'What's wrong?' Marie touched her arm.

'Nothing.' Vesta gave a little choke. Her chin dropped onto her fur collar. 'That's not true,' she mumbled, wiping away a tear with her gloved finger. 'Everything's wrong. And I've only myself to blame.'

'You mean you aren't happy with Teddy?' Marie's heart lurched.

'He sees other women. And although he says it's his job, I don't believe him.'

Marie listened to the story of the Christmas party and how Vesta had caught Teddy kissing another girl and slapped his face.

'But you told us you had a wonderful time.'

'I was just pretending as I didn't want you all to see how unhappy I was.' She took out a hanky and dabbed at her eyes. 'So awful I can't tell you about it.'

Marie took her wrist. 'Of course you can. Remember, we tell each other everything.'

'Not this I can't.'

'Vesta, you're frightening me.'

'I'm frightened too. Teddy ain't the same any more. He goes off for days on end and is never in. He won't let me work at the club and makes me . . . well, he says I have to go with this other person, Bill, I met at the party.'

'Go with him?' Marie repeated, puzzled.

'To his place in the West End.'

'What to do?'

Vesta shrugged. 'At first it was to read for him, like I told you. He said if I had a nice reading voice, as good as my singing voice, then one day I could be an actress. It was what Teddy told me too, and like a fool I believed them.' She looked away again. 'It never worked out that way. Marie, please don't ask any more.'

'I won't if you don't want me to. But what can I say to convince you to leave Teddy?' Marie pleaded. 'It's not too late to start afresh and leave this part of your life behind. If only you would!'

But Vesta turned and hid her eyes. 'I can't,' she mumbled.

'Why did you come to the factory today?' Marie asked, pulling her back round.

'I needed someone to talk to.'

'Someone?'

'You, of course.'

'Vesta, come home.'

She hung her head. 'I don't know if I could.'

Marie leaned forward. 'You don't mean Teddy would try to stop you?'

She shrugged. 'I don't know.'

'He can't force you to stay with him.'

Vesta looked into Marie's eyes. 'That's the thing, I don't think he wants me any more. Yet, I don't know if—' She stopped, putting her hanky to her mouth. 'Oh, it's all such a mess.'

Marie drew her into her arms. 'It's all right, don't cry.'

'It's all I do these days.'

Marie waited for the tears to subside. 'Vesta, me and Bing have set the date.'

'What?' Vesta looked shocked as she sat back.

'Please don't be upset.'

'I'm not. What's the date?'

'Friday, April the 26th at St Luke's. Charlie is going to be our best man and Dad will give me away. Would you be my bridesmaid?'

'Oh – oh!' Vesta looked as though she was going to cry again. 'You'd really want that when I've treated you so badly?'

'That don't make any difference.' Marie felt hopeful as Vesta didn't refuse. 'Then you could come and stay for a few days.'

'I couldn't stay with Mum and Dad, though. I've missed you all so much, and I know what I've lost by pushing you all away. But if I was to go home, even for a short while, Mum would get the truth out of me and that would make both me and her very sad. It might even spoil the happiest day of your life.'

'You could stay with me and Bing, then. We've got a place in Manchester Road.'

'What, your own house?'

Marie felt guilty. 'It's nothing special. Just rooms that Bing found, and he's doing up before we move there.'

'I don't think so,' Vesta mumbled. 'With a new husband you wouldn't want me around.'

'Course I would.'

'Ain't you having a honeymoon?'

'Not till September. It would be lovely to have you with us. And then you would be able to see how you liked being on your own again. Well, you wouldn't be on your own, 'cos you'd have us. Will you at least think about it?'

Vesta nodded sadly. 'Yes, all right.'

'There's a girl at work who's selling her wedding dress. It's cream satin and only six months old. She has two bridesmaid's dresses as well. They're blue and very pretty.'

Vesta was close to tears. She mumbled something and stood up. 'You won't tell Mum and Dad you've seen me, will you?'

'Not if you don't want me to. Can I come to visit you?'

Vesta looked alarmed. 'Teddy wouldn't like that.'

'Can I write to the Blue Flamingo? Will you get the letter?' Maire thought of the letter she had written, still at home.

Vesta frowned. 'I might. There's a drawer they keep the post in.'

'Vesta, I miss you.' Marie held her tight.

'I've got to go.'

Marie wanted to take her sister home, back to the safety of Sphinx Street and their old way of life. But she knew that Vesta would never go back to the factory, even if she did leave Teddy. And with what Vesta had said about Teddy not allowing visits from her family, it sounded as if he controlled her life. Marie was very worried about how much danger Vesta had put herself in.

As dusk fell, Vesta left. Marie longed to tell her everything could be put right if only she had the courage to leave Teddy. But Vesta still had feelings for him and Marie knew that nothing would be resolved until these died.

'What's next on our list?' Bing asked as they strolled to the market the following afternoon.

They were shopping for things for Manchester Road. Marie loved their cosy nest into which Bing had already moved. He had painted it from top to bottom, and even bought a new mattress for the iron bedstead from a reputable West End dealer. Marie didn't want to find any bugs between the springs, a common occurrence for newly-weds in rented accommodation. But Bing had found it comfortable and clean and completed their bedroom with an eye-catching bird's-eye maple wardrobe and chest of drawers. The last to be decorated was the small scullery. Elsie had given them a decent set of pots and pans and Marie was searching for cutlery. But most of the knives and forks on the stalls were bent or tarnished. Bing had found four small, round pudding bowls with no chips or cracks, though they did look rather worn. The painted flowers were faded, but it was still a matching set.

'I'm not sure,' Marie answered distractedly. She was trying not to think about her offer to Vesta yesterday. What would Bing say if he knew she had seen Vesta and offered to have her at Manchester Road? They weren't even having a honeymoon until September. The wedding weekend was meant to be very special and spent on their own. Now she had told Vesta she was welcome to stay there.

'What's up?' he asked suddenly.

'I've done something you won't like.'

'Won't know till you tell me, will I?' He stopped and looked at her.

Marie explained how Vesta had turned up at the factory and they had gone to Island Gardens. When she told Bing about Teddy and the wealthy man, Bing rolled his eyes.

'What's she got herself into?'

'I don't know. And there's something else. I asked her to be my bridesmaid.'

'What did she say to that?'

'She wasn't sure, as she didn't want to stay with Mum and Dad. So I said she could come to us at Manchester Road.'

'What?' bellowed Bing.

'I know I should have talked to you first.'

'But we'll have only just got spliced.' Bing held out his gloved hands. 'Blimey, Marie, what were you thinking?'

'I thought it might encourage her to leave Teddy.'

'She's got a home to go to, if she wants.'

'I know.'

Bing closed his eyes and sighed long and deep. He turned and walked on, his breath curling up in the cold air. Marie knew he was a kind and thoughtful man who would do anything for her and, as she caught him up and slid her hand through his arm, she hoped that if Vesta did come to their wedding he would reconsider and let her stay with them.

When they reached the market Bing looked over to the coffee stall. 'Fancy a hot drink?'

'Yes please.'

Marie sighed. She felt as though she was being pulled in all directions. But she understood why he was angry. She went over to the first stall, full of bric-a-brac. Her mind was churning. She would soon be Mrs Brown – would they have many arguments like these when they were married? Bing was easy-going and nothing seemed to ruffle his feathers. Marie feared she had taken advantage of his good nature.

She looked around for something they needed for Manchester Road. Even the girls at work had got together to buy them beige chenille curtains for the front room. Bing's mum and dad had got them a posh set of china from Petticoat Lane. And Elsie, Ada and Hector were also contributing to their bottom drawer. Marie looked at the many items: tea strainers, picture frames, lavender bags, bits and pieces of jewellery and dozens of ornaments. But her mind kept straying back to the quarrel they had just had.

Then someone nudged her elbow. 'Hello, ducks, remember me?'

Marie looked at the woman; a long, lined, pale face framed by tight black curls trapped under a floral head-scarf gazed back at her. Her crumpled raincoat smelled strongly of mothballs. 'Bev, is that you?' Marie gasped.

'Yes. It's me. I ain't a ghost, though I expect you thought I might be, after that night at the club.'

'It's a relief to know you're still around.'

'Only just.'

'What happened?'

Marie saw Bev look around nervously before she answered. 'I dyed my hair to change my looks after the quarrel with Rose.'

'You dyed it because of that?'

'Rose was in with the Scoresbys. She was paid to tell them what was being said amongst us. She had it in for me from the start cos I was friends with Joanie. After Wally fired me that night, Pedro forced me out in the alley and gave me a slap. He tried to make me tell him where Joanie was, but I truly didn't know. I thought I'd had me chips, but luckily a copper came along. I managed to get away, but I knew if I didn't get out of the East End, I'd wind up like Irene.'

'I thought she fell in the dock.'

'She fell in, but with someone's help. See, once or twice she got stroppy and bad-mouthed Wally, the silly cow. It was only a matter of time after that.' Bev looked around again, her eyes flying here and there. 'After that pasting from Pedro I'm always looking over me shoulder. I ain't been back to these parts till today and, blow me down, I bump into you. What's going on in your life now? Where's Vesta? Is she still as daft over Teddy?'

'She's living with him now,' Marie explained.

'Christ!' Bev rolled her eyes. 'She always liked him. Think that was only a matter of time.'

Marie felt a stab of pain. It was true.

'I saw Sal over Greenwich,' Bev continued in a whisper. 'Did you know that Pedro kicked the girls out without a penny? Wally's only interested in his new club.' She touched Marie's arm. 'Is your dad still working there?'

'No, and neither am I. Dad fell over in the cellars and couldn't get up. Pedro threatened to shut him in down there.'

'What!' cried Bev.

'If it wasn't for Bing, my husband-to-be' – she pointed to the tall figure at the coffee stall – 'coming to help us, Dad might have been down there all night.'

'Pedro is a sadistic sod. Him and Teddy are a heartless pair.' She glanced quickly at Bing. 'But your bloke looks a good 'un.'

'Yes, he is.' Marie suddenly realized how good Bing was. Why had she hurt him? She wanted them to be on their own on their wedding night as much as he did. But

she also loved Vesta and was afraid she wouldn't leave
Teddy without somewhere she could go.

'I hope that sister of yours sees sense,' warned Bev. 'Tell
her from me, Teddy's a bad 'un.' Bev adjusted her head-
scarf, pulling it over her face. 'Listen, as much as I'd like to
catch up on old times, there's always a chance someone
might recognize me. It was nice seeing you, gel.'

Marie watched her leave; a round-shouldered, dowdy
figure in an old raincoat and flat shoes. What had
happened to the bubbly Bev with the glamorous make-
up and blonde hair? The Duke's had changed her, just as
it had Vesta.

Marie walked over to Bing, who was paying for the
coffee. He turned round. 'Was that our first ding-dong?'
he asked with a grin.

'I think so.'

'We'd better put things right, then.'

She looked into his brown gaze. 'I'm sorry about what
I said to Vesta.'

'Any other time wouldn't have mattered.'

'It just came out of me mouth.'

He grinned. 'And what a lovely mouth it is.'

She blushed as he looked at her with love, all trace of
anger gone.

They sat on the old wooden seats close by. 'Guess who
I've just seen?'

'Go on, surprise me.'

'Bev, the dancer from the Duke's who Wally fired.'

'What did she have to say?'

'Pedro hit her to make her tell him where Joanie was. She didn't, as she didn't know herself. After that, she left the East End. Now she has dark hair and wears no make-up so she's not recognized.'

'One day that Pedro is going to get his comeuppance.'

'She told me to tell Vesta that Teddy is no good.'

'A bit late, don't you think? And anyway, once Vesta wouldn't have listened to a word against Teddy, as your mum found out.'

'That's all changed now.'

'Then she's got to make the break. People like Teddy and the Scoresbys are bullies, the worst of their kind. They build their trade on fear and are successful at it. Vesta has to leave whilst she can or else I'm concerned it will be too late.' Bing took her hand. 'Sorry I lost me rag. Your sister will never be turned away from our door, and that's a promise. I'll always do what I can to help her because I know how much she means to you.' He bent and kissed her.

Marie's heart filled with love. She knew they would have quarrels and life would have its share of ups and downs. But she also knew Bing would always be there for her.

Just as she would be for Vesta.

Chapter 34

Vesta gazed from the window. The rain had stopped and the March wind was blowing the skirts of the women who walked by. Some held their hats. Others tugged at their scarves, pulling them closer round their chins. The clouds were grey above and although she couldn't see clearly from her swollen left eye, she could still see from her right. Lifting her hand to touch the swollen skin of her cheek, she jumped. Even the pressure of her finger-tips hurt. But it wasn't her black-and-blue face that was troubling her, it was something much worse than that. She had missed two periods now. Was she pregnant? The thought of it made her feel sick. What would Teddy do, if he found out?

Vesta left the window and walked round the small room. It was her prison now, until she was released to see Bill. The thought of this made her feel much worse. Why had she been so gullible? Why had she believed that Teddy and Bill had wanted to further her career? She had been so stupid. She'd even decided that if Bill had asked her to move in with him she would have. After all, Teddy didn't want her. She knew that now. Neither man wanted her. They only wanted to use her.

Vesta sat down on the couch. She was trapped. She had to sit within these four walls each day, wondering what she had done with her life. After the beating Teddy had given her last week, because she had refused to go to Bill's, she was trying to think of a way to escape. But where could she go? She wanted to see Marie again. She wanted be Marie's bridesmaid. She wanted to be part of the family again and forget her terrible past. But she couldn't see Marie like this. She couldn't walk out in the street like this. And would Teddy follow her? He'd told her she was their possession now, that she could never go back to working in a factory. She liked the good life too much. Was that true, she wondered as she thought of Ellisdon's, the dust, dirt and grime and the life she had always resented. What man would have her now? Even a man like Charlie.

Slowly she got to her feet and went to the cocktail cabinet to pour her favourite drink, gin and lime. Waiting to feel it warm her inside, she caught sight of herself in the mirror. She looked like an old hag. Peeping out from the swollen mounds around her eyes were two tiny, pale blue moving marbles. The contrast of purple and mauve skin surrounding them was shocking. The split above her eye was healing. Thank goodness it wasn't visible below her hairline. But her hair! She put her fingers through it. Lank and colourless, it clung to her head. She hadn't been able to raise her arms properly to wash it. Her right arm had been bent back when Teddy threw her to the floor.

Vesta gave a sob and sank down on the couch again.

What was going to happen to her? At least, looking like this, she wouldn't be forced by Teddy into seeing Bill again. She shuddered as she thought of his hands exploring her. All his wealth and status didn't change the fact it was only sex he wanted from her. She had been sold, tricked into believing Bill was her friend, then given some awful drink that had gone to her head and something else – a pill. And, just like at Christmas, she had woken up in Bill's apartment, unable to remember anything clearly. Vesta closed her eyes. She wanted to cry, but she couldn't. She had shed so many tears.

And now she lived in fear. Fear of waking up in this place on her own, fear of Teddy arriving. She stiffened as she heard the key in the door. It opened suddenly. Teddy stood there. Vesta wondered how she could ever have loved him. She looked into his dark, menacing eyes that she had once thought were so handsome.

'So you've bothered to get up at last.' He looked around. 'This place is a dump. You live like a pig in a sty.'

She took a step back and said nothing. She had learned that silence was better than opening her mouth. Everything she said seemed to annoy him.

'Here,' he said, dropping a bag on the table. 'There's some make-up in there to cover your face. You don't seem to have done a very good job of it so far. And look at the state of you. Next week, I've told Bill you'll be ready to see him again.'

Vesta was wearing her dressing gown and slippers. She couldn't put on her bra or slip as it was too painful to move her arm. Teddy walked towards her. 'Your hair's a mess.'

'Teddy, it's my arm. I—'

'Not more moans and groans?' he snapped, pulling the dressing gown apart. 'It was those that got you into trouble before.'

Vesta put her lips together to force herself not to cry out as Teddy held her breast. She couldn't stand his touch. But she had to. If she refused to let him do what he wanted, he got angry. That was how she wound up like this.

'Go in the bedroom whilst I pour myself a drink.'

Vesta felt sick again. Not just the normal sickness that happened when Teddy or Bill touched her, but another type. A sickness she was even more afraid of.

'Well?' He glared at her. 'Go on, you silly cow.'

She turned and went to the bedroom. She hadn't bothered to make the bed. She knew Teddy would be angry when he saw it. She pulled the cover over quickly.

When Teddy came in, she watched him take off his clothes and stand naked before her, a surly smile on his face. He took his drink in one gulp and handed her a glass.

'Drink it down.'

She did, hoping it would soon put her out of her misery.

Teddy came towards her. She felt her skin crawl as he guided her fingers to his body. She knew what he wanted her to do. And there was nothing else to be done, but do it.

At last Easter Sunday was here, celebrated by Marie and Bing at St Luke's, where they were to be married and their banns had been called. As it was Easter, the Reverend had asked them to attend the service. The tall spire had glistened as though welcoming them as they walked arm in arm through the big wooden doors. The stained-glass windows shed rays of coloured light as the couple walked down the aisle. Although they weren't regular churchgoers, everyone seemed very friendly. The organ pealed and the choir sang stirring hymns; age and history seemed to rise up from the polished pews as they sat there.

'Imagine, Marie,' whispered Bing, looking handsome in his dark grey pinstripe suit and blue spotted tie. 'We'll be standing at that altar in five days' time. And Charlie will have your ring in his pocket. My mum and dad and your parents and Elsie and all our friends will be here to see us get wed. And you're gonna be the most beautiful bride on God's earth.' He gave a long sigh of satisfaction. 'And, although we won't be going away, we'll have our honeymoon in September to look forward to.'

Marie smiled up at the man beside her. In September they were going to Southend for a week, when they both had two weeks' holiday from work. Southend was by the sea, with all the fun of the fair. At the end of the season it wouldn't be too crowded for them to find a nice bed and breakfast place.

As much as she was looking forward to the day, Marie was beginning to lose hope that Vesta would be her bridesmaid. She'd heard nothing, receiving not even a letter. So she had written to Vesta care of the Blue Flamingo, to remind her about the wedding. Had she got the letter? And if she had, why hadn't she written back? Even if it was only to say no, that she had decided to stay with Teddy, it would have been better than nothing.

As she'd walked home from the factory each day, Marie had hoped she'd see her twin. She told herself that, as usual, Vesta would appear at the last minute.

But that hadn't happened. And now there were only five days to go until the 26th.

'Happy?' Bing whispered again.

She nodded. She *was* happy. But was Vesta?

When they arrived home, Elsie and Ada were discussing the reception that was to be held after the service.

'You two look pleased with yourselves,' Elsie grinned as Bing and Marie walked in.

'We are,' Bing nodded. 'By this time next week we'll be Mr and Mrs Brown.'

Ada smiled, pushing a stray lock of her hair under her turban. 'I hope you said a prayer for us, Marie, and Vesta too?'

'Yes, I did.' Marie looked into Ada's eyes. She saw the sadness that Ada had been careful to hide during the months they had been preparing for the wedding. Vesta was never far from their thoughts. And though Marie had kept her letter to Vesta a secret, Vesta turning up to be her bridesmaid had been her one hope of making Ada happy.

'Elsie and me are preparing the food and drink the day before,' Ada hurried on as she looked down at her list. 'Your bouquet and the buttonholes will be delivered by Freda on Friday morning. She's putting some flowers in the church too.'

Marie had chosen lilies for her bouquet and, as Freda had a son who worked at Covent Garden, they had got them at a knockdown price.

'Now, is your dress ready?' asked Ada for the hundredth time, and Marie nodded. 'It's in my wardrobe. I didn't even need to have it cleaned, as the girl I bought it from had already done that.' Marie had tried on her wedding gown and found it fitted perfectly. She and the girl at work were about the same size. Marie knew that the blue bridesmaid's dress would be just right for Vesta. She hadn't shown it to Ada. She didn't want her to get up her hopes and then be disappointed. Instead she had hung both dresses in the wardrobe at Manchester Road.

'On the day, we're going to have both our doors open.' Elsie puffed on one of the long, brown cigarettes she had taken to smoking lately. 'The food's going to be in your mum's and the drink in mine. No doubt there'll

be a bit of noise, with the knees-up, but there's only
Nina and Wippet to worry about and they'll both join in,
I'm sure.'

Marie smiled as the two women nodded in agreement.
Ada and Elsie were growing closer; with Hector helping
out more in the house since he'd left the Duke's, Ada
liked to sit in Elsie's kitchen, putting the world to rights.
Marie knew they talked about Vesta and were hoping
that somehow she'd come to the wedding. At the weekends, they went to the market or sometimes caught a bus
to Poplar. Lately they had been occupied writing invitations and making long lists. One of those invitations had
gone to the Blue Flamingo.

'And you, young man.' Elsie jabbed her cigarette at
Bing, coughing as she inhaled the strong smoke. 'I hope
that car of yours don't conk out. You'll have a lot of
delivering to and fro, that day.'

Bing smiled. 'Don't worry on that score, ladies. My
mate Charlie is helping with the driving. And, as I'm not
supposed to see the bride on that day, he's coming round
for you girls first.'

'Is the groom riding a bike, then?' Elsie chuckled.

'No,' laughed Bing with good grace. 'I'm sporting out
for a taxi as I'm staying with Mum and Dad the night
before, and we'll all come in that.'

'Don't let Charlie lose the ring,' warned Elsie. 'You
know what he's like when he's had a few.' They all
remembered the story of Charlie getting drunk and being
beaten up.

'What are you wearing, Elsie?' Marie asked, knowing full well that Elsie would put on a show.

'Oh, a nice little two-piece I picked up down the Lane. But it don't compare to your mother's dress and coat. She looked like a girl of twenty-one when she tried it on in that little shop up Poplar.'

Marie looked at Ada, who was going pink. 'Mum, you never said.'

'Oh, Elsie's exaggerating!' Ada was trying to hide her blush as she added quietly, 'Your dad and me don't want to let you down, love. This is an important day in your life. Time to get out the glad rags.'

Marie had wanted to buy both Ada and Hector their wedding outfits. She had saved enough from the club to pay for her wedding. But Ada wouldn't hear of her spending her money and had gone out with Elsie to buy something special herself.

Suddenly Ada sniffed.

'Oh Gawd,' muttered Elsie. 'What's wrong, gel?'

'I'm sorry, but I can't help wishing your sister was here, Marie. It don't seem complete without her.'

Marie was silent. If only she could tell Ada that Vesta *was* coming!

'Ada, you ain't gonna spoil it for Marie, are you?'

'No, course not.' Ada wiped her eyes.

'This is Marie's day,' Elsie said firmly. 'And if Vesta has got any sense, she'll be there, with us, in the front row.'

'But what if she ain't?' Ada was tearful again.

Elsie shrugged. 'Then there's sod all we can do about it.'

Marie touched her mother's hand. 'You've sent an invitation, don't forget.'

Ada got up and drew Marie into her arms. 'I won't let you down on the day.'

'I know you won't, Mum.' Marie hoped that, even if Vesta didn't get the invitation and letter, she would remember that Friday the 26th was her wedding day and would turn up.

Vesta found a moment to slip into Wally's room, whilst the men were talking in the club. Teddy had brought her with him to the Blue Flamingo, as he wanted the Scoresbys to see her. He now openly called her 'the goods' and told her that she had to use make-up to cover her bruised face, as the Scoresbys wouldn't be happy to see damaged goods. Her reflection in the mirror before she had left had made her wince. The bruises were all covered and the mascara looked heavy and thick over her eyes. He had told her to wear bright lipstick and jewellery and more new clothes that he'd bought her. She felt like the tart Teddy had accused her of being.

Vesta looked around Wally's room. The last time she had been here, she had been happy. Wally had told her how well she had sung. How the customers had liked her. Little had she known then what these evil men had planned for her.

Her heart raced and she tried to quell the feeling of sickness. Once Teddy had finished his business with the

Scoresbys, he would come to find her. After that he would take her back to her prison.

If only Marie had written to her! Vesta gazed around the room she had once thought was lavish and spectacular. But now she hated the gold and black décor and naked figurines. The ugly paintings on the wall of half-clothed men and women weren't classy. They were crude.

She went to Wally and Leo's desk. Quickly she opened the top drawer. It was here the correspondence was kept; she'd seen Wally open it and take out his papers. Now, as she rummaged through, she saw documents of all kinds.

Someone's loud laughter drifted into the room. She could hear Teddy and Wally talking. Someone said Bill's name. She shivered as she thought of what was being discussed, closing her eyes in shame.

She pulled out the drawer beneath. Her heart raced. There were two letters with her name on. She picked them up. They had been opened. One was in her mother's handwriting. The other was Marie's. Inside the first was a pretty card. It was an invitation to Marie's wedding on Friday. The other was a letter from Marie. Tears filled Vesta's eyes. She wanted to be with her family. Then her eyes caught something else at the back of the drawer and she gasped. It was a gun.

She froze. She had never seen a gun before. What was it doing there? The cold, hard metal caught the light. In the drawer it was just an object but when used it became a weapon of violence and of death.

The voices outside had stopped. Reaching down to close the drawer, Vesta paused. She couldn't believe what she saw next. It was a photograph. Although her fingers touched it, her eyes couldn't believe it was real. The man in it was Bill, the woman, her. They were both naked.

Vesta felt dizzy and sick. She tried to clear her head and stared once more at the couple, their bodies twisted together. Could they really be her and Bill? Was she imagining it?

Vesta's throat tightened. She could hardly breathe. Someone had been watching them, hidden from their view as the photograph was taken. She felt terribly ashamed. The photo brought back all her feelings of desperation and guilt as she had begun to realize what Bill had wanted her for. Her eyes were closed as if she had shut herself off from reality.

Vesta felt a moment's terror. Why had she not known about – or even suspected – that hidden camera?

She knew the answer to that. It was because of the drink and the pill she had been given. It had helped to blot out everything. She hadn't cared about her actions, nor had she suspected the evil that was around her.

'You little fool, what are you doing?' It was Teddy. He snatched the letters from her and put them in his pocket. 'It would be the end of me if Wally caught you snooping in here.'

'That's me and Bill in those photographs,' she blurted.

Teddy glanced down and shrugged. 'It's called insurance. The Scoresbys have their way of getting people to pay up or do what they want, if they prove to be tricky.'

To her surprise Teddy picked up the gun. He pushed the cold steel up and down her arm. 'Do you like the feel of it? Does it excite you? Well, I hope it will remind you that you're the Scoresbys' property, all bought and paid for. We'll have no more tantrums or dramas. You don't want that pretty face messed up again, or' – he raised the gun to her cheek – 'something worse.'

Vesta trembled as he drew the tip of it over her sore skin. He laughed at her fear, a cruel laugh that now sounded crazy. She knew then that he was capable of carrying out that threat.

He slid the gun in his overcoat pocket and closed the drawer. 'Leo and Wally want to see you. Just smile and leave me to do the talking.'

Vesta choked back her terrified sob. Everyone had warned her against Teddy. Even Flo Davis. Ada was right; she hadn't known anything about the world. Teddy's good looks and charm had dazzled her. His promises had made her believe he could give her everything she wanted.

What a fool she had been!

Teddy bundled her out of the door, and her legs hardly had strength to move as he propelled her towards Leo and Wally.

Chapter 35

On the morning of 26 April, Marie stood in her wedding dress, examining her reflection in the mirror. On Wednesday night Bing had helped her to bring the dress round to Sphinx Street. Since then it had hung in the wardrobe. The blue bridesmaid's dress was wrapped up in a bag and hidden in a drawer. Marie knew that if Vesta was to have arrived in time to be her bridesmaid, it would have been before this moment. Had she decided that it would be too painful to meet her family again? Or had Teddy stopped her? Suddenly doubts and fears whirled in her mind, threatening to spoil the happiest day of her life.

Marie turned her thoughts to Bing and their future together. She was marrying a wonderful man whom she loved and trusted. Bing wouldn't want to see any trace of unhappiness on her face. She pulled back her shoulders and took a deep breath.

Once more, she studied her image with care. Her dress was ankle length, the modern fashion for brides; the pointed sleeves matched the pointed waist of the bodice. Ada's silver locket hung round her neck. The stone in her engagement ring sparkled and the small blue bow on her cuff reminded her that she was wearing something old, something borrowed and something blue.

Marie reflected on the beautiful lilies and buttonholes that had arrived early this morning. Elsie and Ada had taken them into the kitchen before setting the buffet on the dining table. Hector had arranged the drink to his liking, as he and Charlie would be giving the toasts.

When Marie put on her dress, Ada had gasped.

'You make a beautiful bride,' she'd whispered, quickly wiping away a tear. 'Shall I help you with your veil?'

Marie felt her heart beating fast as Ada lifted the veil and secured the satin band of pearls that held it in place. Ada tucked her blonde waves under. 'It fits just right.'

Marie stared at her reflection, wondering if all brides felt so nervous. Would Bing think she looked beautiful? 'Is Dad ready?'

'He's all fingers and thumbs this morning. But he still cuts quite a dash for an old-timer.'

Marie knew if it hadn't been for Bing, this day might not have come. He had rescued her and Hector from the Duke's. She loved him dearly and knew that he was the right man for her.

Ada kissed her cheek. 'I know you and Bing will be very happy.' A horn sounding outside made them jump. 'That's Charlie!'

Marie went out to the front room. Hector beamed her a smile and held out his arm. In his formal grey suit and grey bow tie, with his moustache trimmed neatly and his shock of dark hair smoothed down over his head, he looked like the old Hector that everyone knew and loved.

'Don't worry, love, you'll knock 'em dead,' he whispered. There were tears in his eyes. It was his old saying to her and Vesta. Marie knew they were all thinking of Vesta. They missed her and it wasn't the same without her. But now it was time to go to meet her groom, who would be waiting at St Luke's for his bride.

Marie walked slowly down the aisle on her father's arm as the organ played the Wedding March. Bing turned and smiled at her. His smile made all her worries fade away and her heart fill with love. He stood tall and handsome in his black dress suit. The light from one of the tall windows fell on him and Charlie, who also was dressed in black. Marie's heart beat very fast as the congregation turned to look at her and Hector. Marie felt Hector press her arm against him. At the front, Ada and Elsie were smiling, all traces of sadness gone. Ada looked elegant in her new coat, a slim-fitting light grey woollen dress and matching wide-brimmed floppy hat. Elsie was wearing a green tailored skirt and matching jacket, while Nina was dressed in a pale pink coat and pretty box hat, and Wippet was wearing a grey suit and tie. Some of the girls from work sat behind them, along with Elsie's friend from Bethnal Green. Charlie's new girlfriend, Madge, a pretty brunette from Dublin, sat beside her.

Bing's parents were seated on the other side. Ivy was dressed all in cream and brown with a feather in her hat.

Johnny looked tall and smart in a suit, his hair standing on end, just like Bing's. Marie smiled at them. There were faces she didn't recognize, but all were smiling as Hector stood aside to allow Bing to take his place.

She looked up at the man who would soon be her husband. She loved him so much. The Reverend David Hughes, the clergyman who was to marry them, had a kind, smiling face. The organ finished playing and for a moment the church was very still. Marie thought the thud of her heart was so loud, everyone could hear it.

'Dearly beloved,' said Mr Hughes, his voice echoing clearly, 'we are gathered together here in the sight of God, and in the face of this congregation, to join together this man and this woman in Holy Matrimony.'

As he spoke Marie looked at Bing. Love spilled from his eyes. She wanted to be with him for the rest of her life.

Her voice felt very small when she made her vows. Bing's was strong and solid. Mr Hughes led them: '. . . to have and to hold . . . from this day forward, for better, for worse, for richer, for poorer, in sickness and in health, to love and to cherish, till death us do part . . .'

They were beautiful words. Marie knew she would honour them always, and though there may be ups and downs in their marriage, she knew they would be happy. Fleetingly she thought of Vesta. Her twin was not here to see her married. Marie looked into Bing's eyes again. Love filled the empty space that Vesta had left.

Charlie handed over the ring. Bing took Marie's hand.

'. . . With my body I thee honour you; and all my worldly goods with thee I share: In the name of the Father, and of the Son, and of the Holy Ghost. Amen.' He slid on her ring. The golden band gleamed on her finger.

'I pronounce that they be man and wife together,' said Mr Hughes when the blessings spoken. 'Robert, you may kiss the bride.'

Marie knew that, as Bing placed his lips on hers and told her he would always love her, this was the happiest day of her life. She had dreamed of another life once; but that dream could not compare to the way she felt today.

The organ boomed out again and Bing led her to the vestry to sign the register. She was now Mrs Bobby Brown and her husband was beside her and had promised he always would be. It was a promise that she knew Bing would keep.

Marie and Bing stood outside on the church steps. The sun shone down on them and people cheered. The photographer adjusted the camera on the tripod, and friends and family crowded round. A slight breeze lifted Marie's veil. Everywhere smelled fresh and new. All through the service, there had been a breathless hush, but now everyone was talking and laughing. Bing squeezed her arm as she leaned against his tall, strong frame. She was now Mrs Brown and wanted to shout it to the world.

As they went to Bing's car, where Charlie was in the driving seat, confetti showered over them. First Ada and Elsie, and then Bing's parents hugged Marie. She knew she would remember this day all her life: the smells, sights and sounds of the East End on her wedding day – hoots from the river traffic, the sirens and the cries of the gulls – the silence as Bing slipped on her ring; the Vicar's clear voice and the organ's beautiful music.

Everyone waved as Marie and Bing sat in the back of the car. Marie couldn't stop smiling. She was sitting beside her new husband and was the happiest girl in the world.

Bing took her in his arms and kissed her. He whispered, 'I love you, Mrs Brown.'

'And I love you too.'

'No canoodling in the back seat!' shouted Charlie, giving a toot on the horn. It was only a short distance to Sphinx Street, but everyone stopped to look at the red car with white ribbons tied to the bonnet.

It was only when Marie glanced down at the lilies in her lap that she was reminded of that one special person missing, and for a short while her thoughts went to Vesta, who would have looked beautiful in the blue brides-maid's dress.

'I can't believe I'm married,' Marie sighed much later that day, as Bing carried her up to the newly painted black door in Manchester Road. 'And this is our new home.'

'I'll prove it.' He set her down and unlocked the door. He pressed the key into her hand. 'It's all yours.' She went to step in, holding her wedding dress up from the floor, but Bing grabbed her and swung her into his arms. 'Hold on a minute. I've got to carry you over the doorstep.'

She giggled as she held tightly to his broad shoulders. All afternoon she had longed to do this, to be alone with him. The reception had been wonderful, with plenty of eating and drinking, whilst Bing played requests on Elsie's piano. The music, dancing and singing had kept everyone entertained until finally darkness had fallen.

'I'm only ten minutes' walk away,' Marie had reminded Ada as they left. But all the same, Ada's tears had fallen. It wasn't until now, with her arms around Bing's neck, that she could truly take in all that had happened.

Bing set her slowly down. He pressed his hands down over the sleeves of her dress. 'I don't know how I kept me hands off you today.'

Then he kissed her long and hard as they stood in their new home. 'I'll build a fire,' he told her, kissing her again.

'No, don't do that.'

'Don't want my wife to get cold.'

'We won't if we're in bed.'

Bing gave a lusty growl. 'Do you mean that?'

'We've only got the weekend together.'

'We've got all our lives. But I like your idea. Thought that you'd want to do something else first, though. Like unpack your suitcase or have something to eat.'

'Most of my clothes are here. There's only a couple of things I had to bring with me. The suitcase isn't going to hurt in the car for one night. As for eating, yes, I'm hungry. But not for what we've got in the larder.'

He took her in his arms again. 'Mrs Brown, you know how to drive a man crazy.'

She grinned. 'I'm learning.'

Bing was kissing her and whispering as he took her to the bedroom and they fell on the bed. 'September ain't that far off for our honeymoon.'

'I'm counting the days.'

He tipped up her chin. 'Did you miss your sister?'

'Yes, but I have you.' She didn't want to be unhappy. And she knew if she thought about Vesta, she would be. This was her wedding night; she wanted to lose herself in the happiness she had found with Bing.

He kissed her long and passionately. In the darkness, he began to undress her. As he touched and caressed her, she gave herself up to the lovemaking of the husband who would now be her partner for life.

Marie opened her eyes to the unfamiliar sight of the open sash window with its flowered drapes and gleaming white lace. A shaft of late April sunshine flowed over the maple chest of drawers beneath, identical in rich texture to the wardrobe beside it. The gentle breeze drifted in the river air and she smiled. From the scullery she could hear her husband singing, clattering around and making tea.

Sitting up in bed, she folded her hands over the beautiful damson counterpane that Ada and Hector had given them as their wedding present. Marie still couldn't believe she was now married and kept repeating her married name over and over, revelling in the warm, wonderful feeling of joy and happiness. Bing had made a passionate and thoughtful lover. She blushed at the thought of their first night together. If she had had any worries before, Bing had soon dispelled them.

How many times had he whispered he loved her? That she was beautiful and the woman of his dreams? Just trickling his fingers over her bare skin had made her want him. She hated the thought of Monday when they would part, he to the docks and she to the factory. She wouldn't be able to wait to get home from work to see him.

Now, as she listened to Bing humming softly, she smiled. So much had happened since they'd made their wedding vows. Images came to her mind of Ada and Hector dancing together. Elsie had got a little tipsy and flirted with one of Bing's friends. The big, burly docker had insisted on lifting her up and whirling her round the floor. The girls from work had given her a card from Mr Morton, wishing her every happiness. Wippet had persuaded Kaiser to light a cigarette and even Nina had joined in with the singing.

Marie watched the dust motes, bright in the sunlight, flow down to the foot of the bed. Soon Bing would carry in their tea and lie beside her again. She trembled at the thought of his strong, lean body, muscular in all the right places, firm and yet yielding under her touch.

Marie reached out for her mirror on the bedside table. In the oval glass, she saw a different Marie to the girl who had walked down the aisle. Now a woman gazed back, happy and fulfilled. Under her blonde hair, her blue eyes were serene. Even her freckled nose seemed to shine healthily.

'How's my girl this morning?' Bing strolled in, placing a cup and saucer beside her. He sat on the edge of the bed. She still couldn't believe that she was married to this man. He wore only his white pants, his toned chest and muscular arms evidence of the hard work he did in the docks. His arms were sprinkled with fine light hairs, which caught the rays of the sunshine. There wasn't an inch of spare flesh on his body; she had run her fingers over it a thousand times last night, unable to believe this man was all hers.

Her heart raced as he leaned forward and kissed her. His lips were tender, inquisitive and exploring. After their night of passion they now shared a lingering, confident delight. Marie was amazed at each little revelation, each discovery they made between them.

'What were you singing?' she asked as she sank her head back on the pillow.

His eyes were filled with a teasing sparkle. 'I was tuning up. Did you recognize it?'

'No, but I can guess.'

'Come here then, snuggle against me and I'll sing it to you.'

Eagerly Marie wrapped herself around him, resting her head on his chest. She tried not to giggle as he coughed softly and cleared his throat. But her smile soon faded as he began to sing 'Let Me Call You Sweetheart'. Not only was he note-perfect, but his soft, husky voice was so beautiful that it brought tears of love and joy to her eyes. His fingers stroked her bare arm as he sang, entwining in her hair and running down the curve of her neck to the sensitive knuckle of bone on her shoulder. Each word, she knew, was meant for her. It was their song: a song of hope and endearment that seemed perfectly right for lovers.

When he had finished, she lifted her head from his chest and put her mouth close to his. Her lips were wet with tears and he drew away the moisture with his finger, tracing their full curve. No words could be found between them. The song would always remind them of this moment, the first day of their life together and, they hoped, many more to come.

It was hours later when they woke. Bing's arm was thrown across her and, as he opened his eyes, he smiled, his hand sliding down to pull her against him.

'Who is this beautiful woman in my bed?' he teased, sliding the strap of her slip over her arm and kissing her shoulder.

'You'd better stop that, or we'll be here all day.'

He gazed at her with a deep longing. 'Another good idea, Mrs Brown.'

'I'm full of those, you wait and see.'

'I'm no fool, marrying a genius.'

She took hold of his ear and tweaked it. 'That's for being cheeky.'

'Can you do it again, please?'

She laughed and he reached out again and lifted the strands of her hair, trickling them through his fingers. Then sliding his thumb slowly over her chin and down to her neck, he pressed his lips on the soft skin of her breast.

She shivered in anticipation. 'You'd better not do that again.'

'I can't believe you're my wife.'

'Even Mr Morton forgot to call me Mrs Brown and wrote "Marie Haskins".'

'Damn sauce! I'll have words with him about that.'

Marie laughed. 'That's one person I don't want you to upset.'

'Do you really want to work at the factory? My wage is enough for us to live on.'

She smiled. 'I'll give up my job when something happens.'

A tremble seemed to go through him as he drew her very close. 'I hope that something will be soon.'

'It's only been one night! And, well . . . today.' She stopped, her face crimson.

'Yes, and there's twins in the family, don't forget.'

Marie nodded sadly. She hadn't forgotten.

'Oh, me and my big mouth,' Bing muttered, banging the heel of his hand again his head. 'I didn't mean to remind you of—' He paused before he blurted Vesta's name. 'I was just thinking of babies.'

'Doesn't matter.' She kissed his cheek softly. 'Mum always said she thought there was a chance that one of us girls might have twins.'

'Are you happy, sweetheart?' Bing asked, bringing her out of her troubled thoughts.

'Course I am.'

'It won't be long before you see Vesta again.'

Marie tipped up his chin and frowned. 'What makes you say that?'

'She'll turn up if she's missing you like you're missing her.'

'Yes, but is she?'

In answer, his hands drew her to him, and she found release from her doubts as he caressed and kissed her. Marie knew she would forget any sadness in their love-making and, for a time, her world would be perfect.

Chapter 36

The smell of baking came from the kitchen, where Ada was working, as Marie walked into the house in Sphinx Street. The aroma of mixed spices reminded her of the hot cross buns Ada baked every Easter, though if her family had been given a choice, it was Ada's apple pie they preferred, with its rich golden pastry and thick custard. Although Ada worked, she had always found time to cook.

All the memories from childhood tumbled back as Marie heard the clatter of baking. Today the radio was turned up and the news was all about the next day, Monday, 6 May: King George V's Silver Jubilee. The King and Queen Mary would be riding in a carriage to St Paul's Cathedral for the Thanksgiving Service. Many people had been given the day off work. Already the nation was preparing, and Marie and Bing were looking forward to joining the party at Sphinx Street.

'Mm, smells delicious!' Marie poked her head round the kitchen door. There were scales on the table, very old ones, which had been with Ada through the years. And there was flour, sugar, butter, stewed apples and milk, with a little bowl full of currants.

Ada almost dropped the rolling pin. 'Marie! What are you doing here? You're a day early.'

'I thought I'd just call in.'

Ada rushed over and hugged her, keeping her floury hands outstretched. 'How is married life suiting you?' She turned off the radio.

'I've no complaints,' Marie smiled mischievously. 'Bing is painting the scullery, so I thought I'd escape for an hour. Do you need any help?' She hung her bag on the peg.

'Not in that lovely frock, I don't. Pour yourself a cuppa. There's one in the pot. You can fill my cup too.'

Marie did so, carrying the teas back to the table.

Ada glanced down at her pinafore, speckled with flour. 'Just look at me! I would have changed if I'd known you was coming. Oh, you do look a treat. I haven't seen that dress before.'

'It's from the same girl at work who sold me my wedding dress.' Marie had bought several cheap summer frocks from her friend. This one had a pretty pale green collar and short sleeves, with a flared, darker green skirt and bodice.

'Why is she selling her clothes?'

Marie pulled out a chair and watched Ada roll the pastry. 'She's having a baby.'

Ada frowned. 'You might be in the same position yourself soon.'

'Oh, Mum, we've only just got married.'

'These things happen, love.' Ada crooked an eyebrow. 'Unless of course, you've other ideas?'

'Such as?'

'Young people these days find ways and means to avoid having children.'

'Well, I'm not one of them.' Marie had thought a lot about babies ever since that day she had watched the children playing in Sphinx Street. She knew she didn't want a dirty and neglected little girl or boy, with a running nose, holed shoes and a grubby face. The streets were full of children looking like waifs and strays. She would keep their baby clean and take care of it and never let it be bullied.

Marie had already decided to use the box room, which was, at the moment, used as a store cupboard, as the nursery. Nurseries were unheard of on the island. There were too many kids in every household to ever think of such a thing. Often the parents had children of all ages sleeping in the same room as themselves. Bing had wisely made two rooms of one very big one. He and Charlie had nailed up a false wall and found a door at the scrap yard. This made two large bedrooms and a small room. One window had to be halved for two rooms, but Bing had done a good job of disguising the alteration. After which, Marie had put up some nice floral curtains in both rooms.

'I'm glad to hear it as I'd like to be a granny. Now, tell me all about married life.'

Marie rested her elbows on a clean space and sunk her chin into her hands. 'I go to work and come home every day. But now I do the cooking and housekeeping with a husband in mind.' She grinned. 'Bing is always up first at six and makes a cup of tea. He brings it in and we – well, drink it together.' Marie blushed. The mornings were very rushed, but they liked to spend those few precious moments in each other's arms.

Ada pressed the pastry edges into a pattern. 'Your father used to do that.'

'Yes, I remember. Me and Vesta would listen to Dad in the kitchen. It felt cosy, especially on dark mornings.'

Ada smiled wistfully. 'Your dad would tell me all the exciting things he was going to do that day. Where he was going to sing or recite. Or he'd have some idea about going to a theatre and talking the manager into letting him perform. He was always certain the next big thing was just around the corner.'

Marie nodded. 'Dad made us feel anything was possible.' It was Hector's stories about the theatre that had given them their dream.

'That was your father's charm.' Ada suddenly sat down. 'I loved him very much. It was only when . . .' She looked at the dish she had just made and sighed. 'Things change, I'm afraid.'

Marie leaned forward. 'But you still love each other?'

Ada looked slowly into her eyes. 'We've spent too many years together not to forgive and forget.'

Marie felt a chill run through her. What did Ada mean, when she said things like that?

Ada gave a little start as though coming back to reality. She stood up again and began to trim the pastry. She continued to ask Marie many questions about her new life at Manchester Road. It was as if she didn't want to speak about the past with Hector. Marie wondered if there was a secret she kept hidden well out of reach.

At last the apple pie was in the oven. Ada took a crumpled piece of paper from her apron pocket. 'All our neighbours are providing something for tomorrow's celebration. Elsie went round with the list.'

Scones, angel cakes, fruit cakes and cherry cakes had all been crossed off. There was a line drawn under the cheap cuts of meat and loaves. Elsie was providing all these. The apple pies and custard were down to Ada.

'On my way home from work yesterday,' said Marie, wanting to contribute, 'I bought pies and sausages. I thought we could cut them into small portions for the kids.'

'Thank you, love.' Ada smiled. 'Seeing as you're newly married, you needn't have gone to the trouble.'

'I want to do me bit.' Marie was excited about the Silver Jubilee street party. Secretly she wanted Bing to see her being capable and organized. With all the women filling up the tables in the street, it would be quite chaotic. 'Is there anything else I can do?'

Ada nodded. 'I've made plenty of small cakes to go with the pies. They're in the big tin over there. They just need icing.'

Marie got up and opened the big tin. A familiar confectionary smell wafted out. Once again, memories of her childhood returned. She began to mix the powder that Ada gave her in a bowl. As she spread the cakes with icing, she remembered how Vesta would always lick the spoon. Then, unable to resist, she would stick her finger in the bowl. Marie would follow, only to be caught by Ada. All three would end up laughing as they tried to hide their sticky fingers.

Marie felt a little girl again. Vesta was beside her and they were giggling. They never had straight faces for long.

Ada turned on the radio again. The broadcaster's voice soon dispelled any nostalgia, explaining that tomorrow's temperature would reach seventy-four degrees in the shade. Forty members of the Royal Family and four thousand leading citizens of Britain and the Empire were to be at the cathedral service. According to the news, the Jubilee was to be a momentous occasion. People were expected to sleep out in the street that night to reserve their places to catch sight of the Royals.

The forecast was that there were to be more crowds on the streets of London, including the East End, than at any time since Armistice Day in 1918.

'You'd never believe on a day like this that just across the Channel, old Hitler is beginning to beat the drums of war again,' reflected Elsie as she stood with Marie by the long, decorated tables, overflowing with food. She leaned forward and clipped the ear of a little boy who was stuffing cakes into his mouth without stopping. 'That's your lot for now, Sonny Jim,' she scolded. 'Give others a chance to enjoy the party.'

The little boy looked up at Elsie with a scowl. His grubby mouth, big rebellious eyes and dirty clothing made Marie's heart soften. She didn't recognize him. He was one of the many street urchins of the East End that were making the most of the free food and drink.

'But there can't be another war,' protested Marie. 'Our government wouldn't allow it.'

'Our bunch are toothless watchdogs,' Elsie retorted, still with an eye on the little boy. 'They choose to ignore Himmler, the bloke in charge of the concentration camps. My friends at the synagogue hear terrible things. To repeat them on a day like this would be a crime. But mark my words, the Nazis are only just beginning to show their true colours.'

'Elsie, I haven't heard you talk like this before.'

'Well, this all may change in the coming months.'

Marie hadn't taken much interest in politics. Bing sometimes came home with some news that was discussed amongst the dockers, but mostly they just wanted to be with each other, in their own little world, usually tucked up in bed with their arms around one another. Still, marriage was making Marie think about the nation's future as a whole. The rumours of Germany's rearmament was very worrying. But could this really mean another war?

'I'm off to see my friend at Bethnal Green. Yesterday she received sad news. One of her cousins who lived in

Germany fled with his family to Austria. They were caught at the border and taken away.'

'But can't someone do something?' Marie asked.

Elsie looked up at her in surprise. 'And who will help the Jews, my dear, against this madman?'

Marie felt another shiver of dismay.

'I'm sorry, I should not have said this,' Elsie told her, patting her arm. 'But now I must go. Watch that little devil there. He's eaten more in five minutes than you or I could put away in five days. Oh, and tell your mother I'll see her later.'

Marie watched Elsie make her way through the crowds, a small but determined little figure, who had looked out for them for all the years she had been in their lives. Marie knew that she was beloved by one and all, from her many friends from the Cubby Hole years with Joe, to the Rabbi and his community in Bethnal Green. Yet she had always had time for Marie and Vesta as they grew up and she was their mother's best friend.

Marie looked about her. Sphinx Street was packed full of celebrating people. Men, women and children were eating, singing and dancing. There were two upright pianos, one at either end of the street. The tunes were battling one another, but nobody cared. The kids were stuffing themselves at the tables. The men had hung bunting from every ledge they could find. Union Jacks and bunting flapped in the warm breeze. Every door was open, as was every window.

Just then, Marie saw Bing carrying a plate of sand-
wiches, flying it over the children's heads to the table. He
was wearing a Union Jack around his waist and a boater
with red, white and blue ribbons. She smiled and waved
as he glanced up. She was so proud to be his wife. To
think that such sadness as Elsie had spoken of could be in
the world on a day like today!

The little boy suddenly leaned over and was sick. All
the other children let out screams. Marie bent down and
gave him her handkerchief. 'I think you had better stop
eating now.'

He looked very pale. 'Yes, missus.'

'Go inside that house.' She pointed to the open front
door. 'Ask my mum, Mrs Haskins, for a brush and pan to
clear it up.'

'Yes, missus.' He went off holding his stomach.

'Marie?'

The voice made her start. She looked round and could
hardly believe her eyes. It was Vesta.

'I don't want anyone to see me.'

Marie glanced over at Bing, who was now surrounded
by children as he sat at the piano, playing requests.

'Why not?'

'I've got something to tell you.'

'What is it?'

Vesta looked around. She looked thin in a pale blue
frock that was a bit crumpled. Her hair was cut short but
it wasn't permed in her usual fashionable style. Her eyes

seemed sunken, with big, dark rings around them, and she fidgeted nervously with her bag. 'Not here, Marie.'

Marie looked over at Bing again. 'You could come home with me. But I'll have to tell Bing, in case Mum asks.'

'Please be quick. I'll meet you round the corner.'

With that, Vesta disappeared. Marie hesitated. There was only one thing she could do. She wove her way across to Bing and managed to whisper in his ear. He stopped playing and frowned up at her.

'Is she with Teddy?'

'No. And she doesn't look very well.'

'Did she say why she didn't come to the wedding?'

'No, all she said was that she has something to tell me.'

Bing pushed his hand through his hair. 'What do I tell your mum if she asks where you are?'

Marie thought of the little boy. 'Tell them one of the children was sick over me and I've gone home to change me dress. Mum will believe that as I sent him in for a brush and pan.'

Bing nodded slowly. 'I hope you know what you're doing.'

'She needs me, Bing.'

'Yes, I thought you'd say that.'

Marie bent to whisper she loved him and he began playing again. Pushing her way back through the crowds, she hurried to find Vesta.

Chapter 37

Vesta's eyes went very wide as she stepped into Marie's new home. She stood staring at the large space and comfortable furniture that surrounded a square hearth complete with a modern art deco-print fire screen. The picture rail went all the way round the walls, which smelled of fresh paint. A glass light hung from the ceiling by three chains and matched the pink-brown glazing of a lamp in the corner. A circular walnut cabinet with glazed doors stood to her left, with a cream dinner set arranged inside it, showing off its colourful red, orange and green flowers. On the triangular-shaped coffee table was a pretty ornament: a slim girl wearing a frock, who sat on a slab of marble, gracefully holding her floppy hat.

'Where did you get that?' Vesta asked as she walked over and touched the girl's head.

'It was our wedding present from Ivy and Johnny, along with a set of china.' Marie nodded to the glass case.

'I'm sorry I couldn't come on the 26th.'

'Why didn't you? I wrote to the Blue Flamingo to ask you.'

'Yes, I know.'

'So you got my letter and Mum's invitation?' Marie felt angry. At least Vesta could have written back.

'Can we sit down?'

'Help yourself.' Marie nodded to the couch.

Vesta sat on the edge. She was still fiddling with her bag. Her eyes were dull and lifeless. 'Marie, I'm so unhappy.' Her cheekbones stuck out and her skin looked pasty. Her fingers shook as she sat there, her thin shoulders and legs looking like sticks. 'I know I've only got myself to blame,' she continued. 'You must think I'm rotten not coming to the wedding. And I wanted to so much. On the day, I thought about you and wondered what it would be like to wear that bridesmaid's dress you told me about.'

'I bought it in case you came. It's still in the wardrobe.'

'Did you?' Vesta sighed. She looked distractedly around. 'You've got a home of your own and husband now. Are you happy?'

'Yes, very. But I wanted you at me wedding.'

'I would have come, if I could.'

'What does that mean?'

Vesta's lips shook as she tried to speak. 'I thought I'd found happiness with Teddy. I had stars in my eyes so bright that I didn't see what was really happening. Teddy made me feel like a princess. He spoiled me, bought all my clothes and took me to nice places to buy them. He gave me presents. I'd only have to say I wanted a new coat or dress, or some jewellery, and he bought it for me.'

'But clothes and jewellery aren't everything.'

'I know that now. I began to see what was happening when Teddy made me give up the Blue Flamingo. He said there were other people, famous ones, who were better to mix with and good for my career.' Her eyes grew cold. 'Do you remember I told you about the Christmas party?'

Marie nodded. 'Yes, where you met someone who said you could be an actress.'

Vesta laughed emptily. 'And I believed him.' She put up her hand to cover her mouth. 'I'm so ashamed.'

Marie had a bad feeling. 'Why?'

'I don't know how to tell you.'

'Just start at the beginning.' She waited as Vesta, through her tears, tried to continue.

'Teddy introduced me to Bill – William Dearlove – this director. Teddy said he was going to give me a part in his play, that I would fit in just right for what Bill wanted. The thing was, I didn't know what he really wanted, and I . . .' she put her hands over her face, 'I slept with him.'

Marie sat quite still. She could hardly believe what Vesta was saying. 'But you was with Teddy,' was all she could mumble.

'That's what I thought too. But I caught him kissing another girl.'

'What girl?'

'A very beautiful girl. She was all over him, and he her. It wasn't just a peck.'

Marie took a breath and nodded. 'Teddy is very attractive to women. That was obvious from the day we saw him at the Queen's.'

'I wish I'd never fallen for him.'

'We can't put back time.'

'If I'd never gone to that Christmas party, I'd never have met Bill. I didn't mean it with him. I can't even remember doing it, except waking up in the same bed as him. Even then, I didn't believe it had happened. I just had a terrible headache and couldn't think straight.'

'Because you'd had too much to drink?'

'Yes. It's the only thing that helps now.'

'But, Vesta, drinking isn't good for you.'

'It stops me thinking – feeling. And things have got so terrible with Teddy, I hate him even touching me, let alone—' She stopped, her choked sobs muffling her voice.

'Are you still seeing this Bill?'

'Teddy's still making me see him. If I don't do what Teddy says, he . . .' Vesta put her hand on her bruised cheek. 'He does this. That's why I couldn't be your bridesmaid. I looked so ugly.'

'You mean he hits you?'

Vesta nodded.

'You have to leave him.'

'I want to, but I'm scared. And, if he's of a mind, he will lock me in. Today I managed to get out, but only because I was nice to him and he didn't suspect what I planned to do.'

'Then me and Bing will come round and get you.'

'No. You mustn't.' Vesta's face was full of fear. 'It's not just Teddy, you see. He only does what the Scoresbys want. They pay him to get girls like me to fix up their rich clients. They're evil men and will kill anyone who stands in their way. Like Sid, the handyman that Dad replaced, and Irene and Joanie.'

'Then we must go to the police.'

'It's no use doing that. The Scoresbys have the police in their pay. And there's something else.' She stopped, looking down. 'I went to the Blue Flamingo with Teddy and found your letters in Wally and Leo's office, in a drawer.' She raised her eyes slowly. 'There was a gun there too. It was Teddy's.'

Marie felt as though she was seeing this at the pictures, not in real life. 'How do you know it was his?'

'He threatened me with it. I have to go along with what he wants, or else he'll—' Vesta began crying. 'There was a photograph there too.'

'Of who?'

'Me and . . . Bill. We were in bed together. Bill gave me a lot to drink and some kind of pill to take. I don't remember much after that. Oh, why did I do it? But he was kind to me and listened to all my troubles. I thought he was a friend, that I could trust him.'

Marie sat beside her, drawing her close.

'I was lonely,' Vesta mumbled. 'I thought you might

have written to the Blue Flamingo. I wanted to hear from you so badly. And Teddy found me in the office. He knew everything about the photograph. He said the Scoresbys used such pictures as insurance to get people to do as they want.'

Marie took a breath, trying not to show her fear and anger. Her lovely, beautiful, innocent sister! What had happened to her? What had become of the young girl who had fallen in love so trustingly?

'Teddy said I would never live down the shame if everyone was told I was a tart.'

'That's a terrible thing to say.'

'But he's right. And there's more. It's what I've come to tell you. And you are the only one who can help me. Will you?' Vesta's blue eyes lit up with hope.

'You know I'll help you if I can.'

'Promise?'

Marie frowned. 'You'd better tell me what it is first.'

'All right.' Vesta dropped her chin. 'I'm ... I'm expecting.'

Marie felt as though the world had gone silent around them. All she could hear was the throb of her heart. 'Are you sure?' she asked in a whisper.

'I've missed two periods. And I'm sick in the mornings.'

'Does Teddy know?'

Once more Vesta hung her head. 'He saw me being sick and guessed. He was furious and said it could be Bill's, or anybody's, for all he knew; that I was to go and see this woman he knew of, who helps girls like me.'

'What kind of woman?' Marie asked.

'She goes by the name of Nurse Jones.'

'Is she a nurse?'

Vesta shrugged. 'She looks like one.'

'Have you seen her, then?'

'Just once. To make arrangements.'

'You're not going through with it?' Marie gasped.

'What else can I do?' Vesta demanded. 'I've tried everything else. She told me to take a mixture of Epsom salts and ginger, but it just made me more sick. I sat in a hot bath and drank gin and the same happened again. I was very ill the next day but I still didn't lose the baby. Now she says she'll have to take it away.'

'You can't do that.'

'What choice do I have?'

'I told you, come and live with us.'

'I can't do that. Teddy would only come after me. And anyway, Bing wouldn't want me and a baby in his house. How could I look after it? I don't want a baby. I don't want something growing inside me, then looking at it when it was born and thinking I didn't even know who was the father.' She broke down, sobbing.

'Vesta, you could have the baby and then go away. Somewhere Teddy could never find you.'

'And what about the baby?'

'I don't know. We'd have to think about that.'

'I told you, I don't want a baby. But I couldn't give it away either. I'd rather kill meself.'

'Don't say that!'

'I mean it.'

'But will you go back to Teddy after?'

'No, I'm going to run away. I won't have a baby to worry about. I'll stand on me own two feet. As soon as the nurse has done it, I'll go back and pick up my things. Teddy's away so he won't know I've gone for a while.'

'But where will you go?'

'Could I have that money you made me save for a rainy day?'

Marie thought of the savings she'd put in the Post Office. It was meant to be for Ada but she couldn't refuse Vesta. 'Course you can. But where will you go?'

'To Liverpool.'

'Liverpool!' Marie repeated. 'But you don't even know where that is!'

'I do. They've got boats there that sail all over the world. I'm going to get as far away from London as I can.'

Marie shook her head. 'You've never been out of London.'

'I don't care. I have to get away. And the further the better. Can you get the afternoon off work next Friday?' Vesta wiped the tears from her cheeks.

Marie closed her eyes. She couldn't bear to hear Vesta talking this way. Would she really kill herself if she said no? Could she actually find her way to Liverpool, let alone go on a boat?

'Are you sure this is what you want?'

'It's the only way. I've thought about it long and hard. You promised you would help me.'

'I didn't know what it was you wanted when I promised.'

Vesta stood up, her thin body stiff and tense. 'In that case, there ain't much use me going on. I'll end it all.' She walked to the door.

Marie hurried after her. 'Stop.' She was terrified Vesta would do as she threatened. 'I'll help you.'

'You will?' Vesta stared at her, pushing back her lank hair. 'You'll come with me on Friday?'

'Yes.'

Vesta hugged her. 'What will you tell Bing?'

Marie knew Bing would stop her from helping Vesta. He would say her plan was crazy; that Vesta would never kill herself anyway. She looked into her twin's strangely bright eyes. 'Nothing, I suppose.'

'I'm sorry,' Vesta mumbled.

'So am I.' Marie felt Vesta's thin arms wrap around her. She knew Bing would be very angry if he found out. But if Vesta were to throw herself in the river, Marie would feel guilty for ever.

On Friday afternoon, they caught the bus to the Commercial Road. Marie watched the people on the street going about their business as though it was a perfectly normal Friday. To her, it seemed unreal. To get the afternoon off, she had told Mr Morton a relative had died. She was still praying that Vesta, at the last moment, would change her mind.

But when the bus came to a halt at the stop and they got off, Vesta was as determined as ever. 'It must be near here,' she said, taking a piece of paper from her pocket.

'Didn't you say you saw the nurse before?'

'Yes, but I went somewhere else.'

'Why is it different today?'

'She gave me this address and told me to come at two o'clock,' Vesta shrugged. 'Let's hurry up. These towels and bits of rag in me bag are heavy.'

Marie pushed her hair from her face. She was hot and confused. Why had Vesta been asked to bring towels and rags? Didn't nurses provide that sort of thing themselves?

'Are you coming?' Vesta said impatiently.

'Yes, but I still have me doubts.'

'Why? I told you, she's a nurse.'

After this, they walked on in silence. Marie wished there was something she could think of to make Vesta change her mind. But now, anything she said seemed to make her more determined than ever to do as she planned.

Finally they came to a stop. Vesta frowned up at the name of the street. 'Vanguard Lane. We've found it at last.'

The long, winding road was bordered by dilapidated terraced houses; some had their windows broken, some had boards nailed over the doors. Marie shuddered. 'It can't be here.'

'That's what it says on this.' She waved the piece of paper. 'Look, there's someone to ask.'

Vesta marched across the road to where an old lady, dressed in a grubby shawl, stood with a boy. They frowned suspiciously as Vesta showed them the paper. 'Is this place close by?' she asked.

'Who wants to know?' said the boy from under his cloth cap.

'Does Nurse Jones live here?' Vesta asked.

At this, the woman turned and disappeared quickly inside the building.

'What's it worth to you?' the boy demanded, wiping his dirty nose on his ragged sleeve.

Vesta fumbled in her bag and gave him sixpence.

'Top of the 'ouse,' said the boy, quickly pocketing the coin. 'Up them stairs.' He nodded to the doorway behind him.

Slowly, Vesta made her way in. Marie hesitated as the smell of lavatories filled the air.

'It's them lavs in the yard,' laughed the boy. 'Yer get used to after a while.'

Marie looked at Vesta. Surely this would change her mind? But Vesta was already going upstairs. Marie wanted to turn and run away from this dreadful place, but she didn't know how she could persuade Vesta to come with her.

Cobwebs hung from the ceiling and the stairs seemed endless as they climbed to the top.

'Nurse Jones?' Vesta called when they reached the only door on the half-landing. She pushed it open.

The attic was empty, except for one chair. Horsehair poked out from its worn arms and torn fabric. The window was so dirty that Marie could hardly see out of it. The bare boards of the floor were filthy. Many were missing, showing black spaces beneath.

'This can't be the place,' Marie said. 'No one lives here.'

'But it must be.'

'Even if this was the right place you couldn't—' Marie stopped as footsteps sounded on the staircase.

A tall woman appeared, her close-set dark eyes narrowing suspiciously when she saw them.

'Nurse Jones!' Vesta smiled. 'Thank goodness. We were just about—'

'Who's this?' interrupted the woman, glaring at Marie.

'Me twin sister, Marie.'

'I told you to come on your own.'

'Sorry,' Vesta apologized.

'Well, now you're here, let's get on with it. Come into the scullery.' She marched past them, clutching a black bag. Marie didn't like her at all. She was dressed in a belted navy-blue raincoat and her grey hair was pulled tightly back from her face in a bun. It was as though she was trying to look like a nurse.

Marie caught Vesta's arm. 'A proper nurse wouldn't use a place like this.'

'I don't care,' Vesta snapped, pulling away. 'She said she would do it and that's all that matters.' She looked into Marie's eyes. 'Remember, this is the only way and it will all be over soon. Then I'll be free of Teddy for ever.'

The scullery had a long wooden table that stood next to a brown-stained sink with a rusty tap. Besides this was a stove that looked as if it had never been cleaned. On the top was a battered kettle and large saucepan.

'Whilst I boil the water, take off your knickers and stockings,' said Nurse Jones as she removed her coat and rolled up her sleeves. 'Then lie on the table. Did you bring the towels and rags?'

Vesta nodded silently.

'But before you do that,' Nurse Jones said briskly, turning and holding out her hand, 'I should like my fifteen guineas.'

'But Teddy paid you,' said Vesta weakly.

'For advice, yes. I can't help it if that didn't work. I've had to rent this room for the day. Fifteen guineas is a small price to pay for what you want of me.'

'This place is rented?' Marie asked.

The woman smirked and said nothing. Marie was filled with fear. 'Let's go,' she begged Vesta, but she was already taking off her clothes.

'Marie, give her the money,' Vesta called from the table.

'But it's all we've got,' Marie protested. She had drawn twenty pounds, all their savings, from the Post Office.

Vesta looked up from the table where she was lying, her dress pulled up to her waist. 'Give it to her, please. I have to have this done.'

Marie felt ill as the woman placed the instruments on the filthy draining board. Wondering how Vesta could agree to this, Marie took the money from her bag, her hands trembling as she handed it over.

Even though Vesta had been given a potion to drink to numb the pain, she was in agony. The pail on the floor was full of bloody water, and the towels that Marie had folded under Vesta's buttocks were soaked with blood. Her legs were drawn up against her chest and spread wide. The instruments of torture had been inserted through Vesta's most tender parts and aimed upwards. Vesta had squeezed Marie's hand so tightly that her nails had dug into her skin. When Vesta had screamed, Nurse Jones had pushed a rag in her mouth. Marie had tried to take it out again, but was told not to interfere.

'If you don't want some busybody poking their nose in, you'd better keep her quiet,' warned Nurse Jones as she poked and pulled.

'She's in pain. Can't you give her something to help?' Marie begged as she held Vesta's trembling hands.

'It's nearly done now.' With a final twist of the long instrument, she swept the bloody mess coming from Vesta into the pail.

Marie held Vesta tight, burying her face in Vesta's sweat-soaked hair.

'One less mouth in the world to feed,' the woman sneered, as she wiped her hands on a rag.

Marie felt a rush of anger. 'How can you say that when you're supposed to be a nurse?'

'I perform a valuable service, my dear,' was the cold-hearted reply. 'Your sister will never have the bastard she conceived in her moment of lust and degradation.'

'It's not up to you to judge her,' cried Marie, as the dirty instruments were bundled in newspaper.

'Listen, you silly girl, I've done what was asked of me. Now get her washed and out of here or you'll have the landlord demanding more money for the rent.' The so-called nurse smiled through her thin lips. 'And don't turn your nose up at me, madam! This was purely a business arrangement. Your sister doesn't know me and I don't know her. If one word of what happened here is breathed to a soul – and that I was involved – I shall deny all knowledge of the event. And your sister will be revealed for the harlot she is.'

Marie's eyes filled with angry tears as the woman put on her coat, threw the newspaper-wrapped instruments into her bag and hurriedly left.

Marie held Vesta close. 'Oh, what have we done?'

Vesta mumbled, drawing her legs up and groaning softly. She was shivering, mumbling words that Marie couldn't understand.

For a moment, Marie felt numb, then in a rush of despair, she felt Vesta's pain as if it were her own. She stroked Vesta's damp hair and kissed her forehead. 'It's over now.'

'Is the baby gone?'

Marie nodded. 'I'm going to wash you, then take you home.'

'I have to get away from Teddy.'

'Yes, I know.' Using the last of the clean rags that were left, she washed and cleaned Vesta. Then folding a strip of it in two, she placed it inside her knickers.

'Come along into the other room.' She helped Vesta to the chair.

Vesta flopped down. Holding her stomach, she fell asleep.

Marie went back and fetched the pail. She couldn't look at the contents. She carried it downstairs and out into the yard. When she opened the makeshift wooden door of the lavatory, she retched. The smell was over-powering. Making herself go in, she tipped the contents of the pail into the lavatory bowl.

As she went back upstairs, the tears flowed. How could this be happening to them? Taking the pail to the scul-lery, she did her best to clean the table. When the last rag had been used, she rolled the soiled cloths and towels in some newspaper the woman had left.

'I should have stopped it, somehow,' she whispered to herself as she washed her hands under the rusty tap. But nothing would wash away the memory of the blood on Vesta and her stifled cries as her poor body was ripped apart.

Her twin was still sleeping, but it didn't seem to be a natural sleep. Her cheeks were a fiery red. Her skin was burning. Opening her purse, Marie took out a pound note. Seconds later she was flying down the stairs again. She saw the boy sitting outside on the pavement.

He jumped up. 'Keep away, missus. I don't want nuffink to do wiv yer!'

'I've got an errand for you. I'll give you this pound if you'll bring my husband here.' She held the note out. 'His name is Bing Brown and he's a crane driver in the docks.' She gave him the address.

The boy grabbed the money, looking slyly at her as she told him where to find Bing. 'Please ask him to come with the car. I'll give you another pound when you get back.'

He looked under his cap. 'Yer gonna call the law?'

'No. I just want to go home.'

'And yer got another quid?'

'Yes.'

Without a word more, the boy scooted off. Marie climbed back up the stairs with a heavy heart. Would he get Bing? Or would he run off, never to be seen again? It was a chance she had to take.

Vesta tossed and turned in the chair. Marie bathed her hot forehead. She whispered they would soon be home, not really knowing if it was true.

Chapter 38

Vesta was mumbling and hot. The skin around her eyes was puffy as she rolled her head from side to side. Was it the drug she had been given that was making her delirious? Every now and then, she would cry out and hold her stomach.

Marie didn't know how long they had been there. The smell from the lavatories was getting worse in the heat of the day. The building was full of the screams of babies and shouts of children playing in the tumbledown back yards. When would Bing come? What if the boy had run off?

'Marie?' Vesta whispered through her dry lips. 'Is my baby gone?'

'Yes.'

'I have to catch the train.'

'You can't do that now. We gave the woman all our money.'

'What's going to happen to me now?'

'I've sent for Bing. He'll help us.'

Tears rolled down Vesta's cheeks until at last she fell

asleep again. Marie was frightened that the landlord would appear. She knew what had been done today was against the law. Time ticked by slowly. If only Bing would come.

When there were steps on the staircase, she felt fear and hope. Fear that it would be the landlord, hope that it would be Bing. Her heart pounded a hole in her chest as the footsteps seemed to take for ever.

At last a figure appeared. It was Bing. His face fell when he saw them. Wiping the grease from his eyes, he stared at them. 'What's going on?'

'Bing, Vesta's ill.'

'I can see that.' He walked slowly over the rotten boards. 'What's wrong with her? Why are you here?'

Marie knew that she had to tell him the truth. 'Vesta was in the family way.'

'What?'

'Teddy made her see this woman who said she was a nurse and would get rid of it. But it all went wrong.'

'You mean it was done here?' He looked around in disbelief.

'Yes.'

'Christ Almighty!' Bing rolled his eyes. 'And you went along with all this?'

Marie was close to tears. 'I was worried Vesta might do something silly if I didn't help her.'

'She did something silly anyway. Do you know how much trouble this could get you both in?'

Marie dropped her head as he raked his fingers angrily through his hair.

Vesta began to moan and Bing hurried over. He kneeled beside her, his face concerned. 'She's in bad shape, Marie. Reckon she needs a doctor.' He rubbed his chin and frowned. 'I've got the car outside and we'll take her back to Ada.'

'Can't she come home with us?'

Bing shook his head slowly. 'For once, Marie, I ain't going along with what you want. Like it or not, she should be with Ada and Hector.' He took Vesta's hot hand and gave her a little shake. 'Vesta, it's me, Bing.'

Vesta opened her swollen eyes.

'I've come to get you out of here, gel, and take you home.'

'I don't want Mum to know,' Vesta whispered.

'It's either that or the hospital. And if I take you there, they're gonna know what's been done to you.'

Suddenly there was a noise behind them. 'Where's me quid?' called the boy from the half-landing.

Bing stood up and went out. He grabbed the boy's collar. 'You'll get your money, lad, but first I'd like to know who this place belongs to.'

'Dunno, it ain't none of me business.'

'You made it your business when you took my missus's pound. Now, who runs this dump?'

'An old geezer,' the boy snarled. 'Fings 'appen 'ere. Rotten fings. You'd better ask 'im if yer that nosy!'

'So this room is used for skulduggery, eh?'

'I ain't sayin' no more. Now, leave orf.'

But Bing pulled him close. 'Listen, you ain't seen me or these two ladies today. You wouldn't know us from Adam if you met us again and that visit you paid me in the docks and ride in me car never happened. Right?'

'If you say so, mister.'

Bing let him go. 'This is your pay, son, and be thankful for it.' He held out a few coins.

'That ain't a quid!' the boy exclaimed. 'She said she had another pound ter give me.'

'Take it or leave it,' growled Bing. 'Now 'oppit.'

Scowling, the boy grabbed the coins and ran off.

Bing looked at Marie, his face set hard. 'Let's get out of here. Make certain nothing's left behind.'

Bing wrapped his arms around Vesta and lifted her from the chair. Half carrying her, he helped her to the landing and began slowly to go down the stairs. Marie took the rags wrapped in newspaper. She looked round. There was nothing left to say what had happened; it was only in her mind that the vision remained of the pail and its terrible contents. Marie knew it was something that she would never forget, no matter how hard she tried. This terrible room, that woman who called herself Nurse Jones, the screams of the children on the hot, stinking day – all would stay in her mind for ever.

With Vesta curled on the back seat of the car, a blanket over her, Marie told Bing all that she knew. About the life her twin had led with Teddy, the wealthy man she had been forced to sleep with, the beatings she'd taken from Teddy and the day at the Blue Flamingo when Vesta had found the letters and photograph in the drawer.

'There was a gun too,' Marie added, 'and Teddy threatened to use it if she didn't do as he said.'

Bing's face was white under the dirt from the docks. His old clothes and boots still reeked of the oil and tar he worked amongst.

'She was planning to run away to Liverpool,' Marie added. 'to get a passage on a ship.'

Bing shook his head. 'It costs to do that.'

'We had twenty pounds in the Post Office. It was our pay from the club. Mum never wanted it, and I made Vesta save it for a rainy day.'

Bing turned briefly. 'Looks like the day came.'

'Yes, but that woman demanded it before she agreed to—' Marie stopped. She felt sick at the thought. 'Even if everything had gone all right, there wouldn't have been any left to go away with.'

'Why did you help her, Marie?'

'Because she said she'd kill herself if I didn't.'

He gave a long sigh. 'Vesta wouldn't have done that.' He glanced quickly over his shoulder. 'Not on purpose, anyway. As it is, I reckon she ain't gonna come out of this very easy.'

'Don't say that. She will get better, won't she?'

'Only the doctor will know.' He frowned at the road ahead and Marie fell silent. She listened to Vesta's soft

moans as she lay on the back seat and felt unable to believe
what had happened today.

When Ada opened the door she gasped at the sight of
Vesta's thin body as Bing held her against him. She put
her hand over her mouth.

'Mum, Vesta's not well, Marie told her.'

Hector appeared with a newspaper in his hands. He
dropped it when he saw Vesta and reached out to help
Bing carry her inside.

'Bring her to the bedroom,' Ada said, hurrying before
them.

Marie looked around their bedroom. It was just as it
always was: the big wardrobe and chest of drawers, their
records and gramophone on top of it. The big double
bed still had the same cover and Ada quickly pulled it
back. Bing and Hector lowered her.

'What was it, an accident or is she ill?' Ada asked, and
then she saw Vesta's bloody dress. Again her hand went
to her mouth. A little sob escaped.

'I'll tell you as we undress her,' Marie said.

'We'll wait in the front room,' said Bing, taking
Hector's arm.

When the men had gone and the door was closed,
Marie went to her mother. 'Mum, Vesta was going to
have a baby.'

Ada's face went ashen. 'Oh, my poor girl!'

'Teddy didn't want her to have it and made her go to a
woman who said she was a nurse and would take it away.'

For a moment Ada swayed. She steadied herself on the bedpost. 'You mean, she's lost the baby?'

'Yes.' Marie gently drew up Vesta's skirt and Ada saw her stained underwear.

'Oh, Vesta, what's been done to you?'

'I'm sorry, Mum,' whispered Vesta, her voice so soft they could hardly hear her. 'I didn't want you or Dad to find out.'

Ada clutched hold of Vesta's cold hand. 'I wish you had come to us. It don't matter what you've done, we love you and could have worked something out.'

Vesta sobs were smothered as Ada bent and held her close.

At last Ada stood up. Pressing her hand on Vesta's hot forehead, she turned to Marie. 'We must call Dr Tapper. He brought you two into the world and will know what to do.'

'Bing will fetch him.'

Ada took out her hanky and blew her nose. Pulling back her shoulders, she looked down at Vesta. 'Don't worry, you're home now, love. We'll soon have you right.' She began to unbutton Vesta's dress and Marie helped her, replacing Vesta's clothes and underwear with a nightdress and clean knickers. But, as she was still losing blood, these had to be padded out with rags. When all was done that could be done, Marie went out to Bing and gave him the address of the doctor.

'What's happened?' Hector asked after Bing had left.

'Vesta was going to have a baby.'

He drew in a shaky breath. 'A baby?'

'Yes, but she lost it.'

Hector sat down heavily. He rubbed his hands over his face. 'How can this have happened?' He looked bewildered. 'Was it Teddy's child?'

Marie couldn't tell him, as she didn't know. Before she could speak again, Hector shook his head gloomily.

'It's all my fault. All this has happened because of me.'

Marie put her arms around him. 'Dad, if Vesta hadn't gone with Teddy,' she reasoned, 'none of this would have happened.'

But Hector made no reply. His eyes were very far away. A haunted expression filled them.

Marie sat with Bing as Hector paced the room. Once again the minutes ticked slowly by as Dr Tapper examined Vesta.

When Ada and the doctor appeared, they jumped to their feet. Dr Tapper, dressed in black, with a grey beard and only a little white hair left on his head, lowered his bag to the table. Despite his age he was still called on in times of trouble.

'Vesta has an infection,' he told them. 'Pus has formed inside her womb and is leaking from her abdomen. This infection is caused by the monstrous procedure performed on her and she has suffered internal damage.'

'Will she be all right?' asked Marie anxiously.

'I'll do all I can to see that she is.' He looked sternly at them all. 'I hope you realize what was done was against the law.'

Marie saw Hector sink down to the couch. He buried his face in his hands.

'I'm sorry,' the doctor said more gently. 'But there is no easy way to say this. She won't be able to bear a child again.'

Ada sobbed quietly and Hector's eyes filled with tears.

'I've done all I can for today, but the wound will need to be kept clean, Ada, until the bleeding stops.'

'I'll see to that,' Ada nodded, wiping the tears from her cheeks.

'When the infection clears she'll start to improve. My professional opinion is that she should be in hospital. But of course . . . there are other things to be considered.' He pleated his grey eyebrows. 'The police should be informed.'

'No,' said Ada immediately. 'I don't want them coming round here to question me daughter.'

'Very well.' Dr Tapper put on his black hat. 'I'll call by again tomorrow.'

As Ada saw the doctor out, Marie looked at Bing. She knew that he had been right to bring Vesta back here. Vesta now had to regain her strength and recover from the infection. But to never be able to have children again! Even when she was well, Vesta would have to live with the consequences of the terrible thing that had been done to her.

*   *   *

In bed that night, Bing held Marie close. 'If only I hadn't let her do it,' she said sadly. 'When I threw away those rags with her blood on, I knew it had been very wrong to go there.'

'No use fretting now,' Bing whispered beside her. 'She said she was going to kill herself and you believed her.'

'I thought she might throw herself in the river.'

'Vesta was always one for dramatics.'

Marie put her arms round him tightly. But her mind kept playing over the events of the day. 'If only she'd decided to leave Teddy sooner.'

'Does your Mum know the whole story?'

'Yes, I told her.'

'What did she say?'

'Only that Vesta was innocent.'

'Yes, but she jumped into bed with another bloke too,' Bing was quick to remind her.

Marie closed her eyes at the thought. 'They gave her drink. She didn't know what she was doing.'

'There will always be an excuse for Vesta. But remember, she did what she did because she wanted to.'

'What will she do if she can't have children?'

'Come on now, stop worrying. At least the old doc won't report this to the law. Though I'd like to see that backstreet butcher get her comeuppance.'

'I don't want to think about it.'

Tenderly he kissed her. 'Vesta's in the best place now. Your mum and dad will look after her.'

'I would never have got her home without you.'

'I had the fright of me life when that kid turned up at the docks and said my missus was in trouble.'

Marie had felt sorry for the boy, living in a place like that. 'I thought he might have run off with my pound.'

'Let's hope he keeps his mouth shut.'

'You don't think he'll tell the police, do you?'

'No, that sort don't like the coppers, and, as usual, the landlord will get away scot-free.'

Marie heard the anger in his voice. It was dark and she could see only the outline of his face. There were deep hollows of black where his lovely eyes were. She snuggled close. 'I love you.' Men seemed to see things so clearly. Life to them was always a yes or a no. But for a woman there was always the in-between.

'And I love you. But now I want you to keep out of trouble. And no more telling fibs on Vesta's behalf.'

'I promise.'

He ran his hands over her body. She knew he wanted to make love to her, but instead he said softly, 'Go to sleep now. It's Saturday tomorrow and we're up early for work.'

But Marie didn't want to go to the factory. She wanted to be with Vesta instead. One more morning off work wouldn't harm. On Monday she could tell Mr Morton that she had stayed with her relatives. But that was yet another lie.

She had promised her husband there would be no more lies. And, as his wife, it was a promise she had to keep.

* * *

Every evening, after work, Marie went to see Vesta.
Things had changed at home. Ada had given up her job
to look after Vesta, and Hector was busking again.

'Your father has to bring in the money,' Ada said when
Marie called on Friday. 'Vesta has to be cared for.'

'Soon I'll be able to help out,' Marie told her. 'Mr
Morton is giving me a rise.'

But Ada shook her head. 'I won't hear of it, love. As
soon as we're on our feet again, I won't take a penny
from you.' Ada lowered her voice as she stood close to
Marie in the kitchen. 'Come and see if you can cheer up
your sister. She's down in the dumps.'

'Has the bleeding stopped yet?'

'Yes, but –' Ada lowered her voice. 'She's got no
control on her waterworks. Dr Tapper says it's the
infection.'

'Can't he give her something to help?'

'He's done what he can.'

When they walked into the bedroom, Marie's heart sank.
Vesta couldn't even sit up. Her lank hair hung over the
pillows and big shadows were under her eyes. 'I can't stop
wetting meself,' she complained when Marie asked how she
was. 'Mum has to keep washing my drawers.' She reached
under the sheet. 'And now I've got another wet pair.'

'Don't upset yourself, love,' Ada soothed. 'There's
plenty more on the airer.' Ada hurried out and Vesta
dropped her head to the pillow. 'I hate meself, Marie.
Look at me, I can't even wee in the pail on me own.
Mum has to help me.'

Marie held her hand. 'You'll feel better when the infection goes.'

'I don't want to live like this. I'd rather be dead.'

'You said that before and I believed you.'

'I meant it then.'

'But you don't mean it now. So stop trying to scare me.'

That brought a glimmer of a smile to Vesta's face. 'I know I'm a misery guts.'

'Yes, but you've got reason.'

'Was it Bing who got me out of that place?'

'Yes.'

Vesta pushed herself up and winced. 'I don't remember much after—' She broke off, looking away.

'You'll be better soon.'

'Marie, I'm scared. Teddy will find me again.'

'He wouldn't come round here.'

'That nurse might tell him what she did and he'd guess I'd come back to Mum and Dad. What if he turned up with that gun?'

Marie laughed, although her smile soon faded. The thought was ridiculous but Vesta looked frightened. 'He wouldn't, not in broad daylight. Not in Sphinx Street, with everyone about.'

'I'm not so sure.'

'Listen, don't worry about things that won't happen.'

Vesta managed a nod. 'I don't know what I'd have done without you. I know you think it was wrong what I did, but I wouldn't know how to look after a baby. And anyway . . .' She looked sad again. 'I didn't know who the father was. I'd always be thinking of what they did to me and the baby was the result. I might even have blamed it.' She gave a small sob and closed her eyes.

Just then Ada came in with a bowl of warm water. Over her arm was a pair of knickers and a fresh nightgown. Marie helped her to wash and clean Vesta. Her bones stuck out at all angles. She complained of the pain, causing her to draw up her legs again.

Ada covered her with the bedclothes. 'Would you like a bite to eat, love?'

'No, I just want to sleep and forget everything.'

Marie bent down and kissed her cheek. 'Don't worry,' she whispered, 'you'll soon feel like your old self again.'

In the kitchen, when the gas was lit and the kettle boiling, Marie sat with Ada at the table.

'Marie, Vesta is afraid Teddy might come round here,' Ada said worriedly.

'Yes, I know. But he wouldn't do that. He's too much of a coward.'

'If your father was home, I'd be happier.' Ada looked into Marie's eyes. 'Sometimes I catch myself thinking of the future and having my little girl back.' Ada raised her thin eyebrows, her eyes suddenly hopeful. 'I even dream of her finding a good man who will love her and protect her. But then . . .' Ada's face clouded and she looked sad again. 'But she can't have children. What man wants that?'

'There must be some.'

'After what happened to her?' Ada clutched her hands and entwined her thin, rough, red fingers. 'In any man's eyes she's damaged goods.'

'Don't say that.'

'But it's true, isn't it?'

Marie knew she was right, but Vesta could have died in that stinking hovel. She had survived the ordeal and now she had a future – perhaps not as it could have been, but still with the love of a family around her. 'One day she'll find someone to love.'

'I hope so. If only that Teddy hadn't given her all the luxuries of life that me and your father could never afford. Clothes, shoes, jewellery, going to posh places, they all impress Vesta. He was so clever. He gave her everything she loves and more. He bought her, like that other man did.' Ada shuddered, closing her eyes. 'I can't bear to think of what happened to her. Someone should punish them, but we can't tell the police.' She covered her mouth with her hands as tears shone in her eyes.

'Mum, let's take a day at a time.'

'Yes, Elsie said the same thing.'

'Does she know what happened?'

'With all the doctor's visits, I had to confide in her. There ain't much that me and Elsie don't share.' Ada looked down at her work-worn hands. 'Wippet and Nina know she's back home but I ain't told them much.' She gave a frown. 'Do you think it's a good idea to lock the front door?'

'Because of Teddy?'

'It ain't been locked in years. The key always hangs on the string. But I could ask Elsie to take that away and give Wippet and Nina their own.'

Marie hesitated. She knew her mother was very worried. Would Teddy really try to come round? 'It can't do any harm.'

'I'll go and speak to Elsie.'

Marie stood up. 'And I have a husband to feed.'

'Thank you for stopping by, love. You always put a smile on your sister's face.'

'See you tomorrow afternoon. As it's Saturday and me afternoon off, I'll do your shopping.'

But Ada only smiled. 'No, you have a home of your own now. In all this, have you forgotten you are Mrs Brown, not Marie Haskins any longer?'

As Marie walked home to Manchester Road she thought of the housework that awaited her: the light coat of dust everywhere, and the floors that needed washing and sweeping. She hadn't even changed the bedclothes. Bing hadn't complained that his dinners were late or even not cooked when he got home. He knew Vesta came first.

Marie smiled as she opened her front door and looked around. If she started now, she could have dinner ready by the time Bing came home. After that, she would attend to the housework.

Chapter 39

It was the following Friday when Marie found her sister sitting in a chair in the front room.

'It's wonderful to see you up,' Marie said as she slipped her key into her pocket. Every time she came now, she had to unlock the front door.

'Mum said she wanted to change the bed.' Vesta's voice was a whisper.

'Do you feel any better?' Marie sat down eagerly.

Vesta picked at the threads of her dressing gown. 'A bit.'

'Why don't you put some lipstick on?'

'What for? Who's gonna see me?'

'Nina and Wippet called in last week. Remember, they brought you some fruit? And Elsie gave you those flowers.' She nodded to the white chrysanthemums on the table.

'Yes, it was very kind of them.'

'Do you feel like putting on a blouse and skirt?'

'I haven't got any nice ones here.'

Marie smiled. 'There are some of our old clothes in the wardrobe. Mum kept them just as they were.'

'It's like a museum.'

'She's only doing her best.'

'I don't want to wear that old rubbish again.'

'It was good enough for us both once.'

'Yes, but then I didn't know what was good taste.'

Marie looked hard at her sister. 'Vesta, life won't be the same as when you were with Teddy. He might have spent lots of money on you, buying you things, but remember it was for a reason. You were just a clothes peg, and worse, *his* clothes peg.'

Vesta nodded. 'He knew my weakness was clothes.'

'And make-up, and shoes, and jewellery and—'

'All right, don't go on.'

Marie laughed and Vesta, after pouting, also laughed.

'It's nice to see you smile.'

'I haven't for a long time.'

Marie had an idea. 'I could bring some of my things round. I do have a few nice outfits. And we're still about the same size.'

'Would you?'

'Yes, it would be nice to talk about things like that again.' Marie twisted the two rings on her finger, recalling the hope she had had for Vesta turning up for her wedding. 'Your bridesmaid's dress is still in the bottom drawer of my wardrobe.'

'Did you really buy one for me?'

'Of course. I said I would.'

'But what would I want a bridesmaid's dress for now?'

'It can be altered,' Marie suggested quickly. 'When you start to go out again and begin a new life, it could be made very pretty.'

Vesta's eyes grew misty. 'I can't believe I'll have a new life. And as for the dress, it would always remind me that I'll never be a bride, or have a husband like you've got, or babies.' She got up and clutching her stomach, made her way back to the bedroom.

Marie knew she shouldn't have mentioned the dress. The next time the rag-and-bone man came round, she would get him to take it away. After all, Vesta was right. It would always be a reminder to them both and was no use to either of them now.

Another week went by and it was suddenly June. The Saturday afternoon was warm and dry, and Bing had suggested that, after their visit to Vesta, they could drive up West.

'It'll be a flying visit today,' Marie said. 'I'll give these clothes to Vesta and then we can go for our drive.' She had promised him that today they would do something nice on their own.

'Can't wait,' he grinned as he drove them to Sphinx Street. 'We'll go to Lyons for tea, then, take a walk along the Embankment.'

Marie was wearing her best floral dress for the occasion. She hoped she didn't look too bright and breezy; she still felt guilty for being happy when Vesta was sick. She was hoping the clothes in the bag might cheer her up.

When they climbed out of the car, the summer breeze lifted her newly washed hair and flapped at her frock. The air was filled with the promise of summer. It was just a week to go to their birthday. Marie hoped that in a week's time Vesta would feel like eating the cake that Marie planned to bake.

Bing slipped his arm around her waist as they went up the steps. She thought Vesta might be up today, as the doctor had told her she needed to exercise now the bleeding had stopped.

'I see you're still using the key to get in,' Bing said as Marie rummaged in her bag.

'Yes, just to be sure.'

'Don't reckon Teddy would chance setting the cat amongst the pigeons. What he made Vesta do was a crime. If Old Bill was told, he could be prosecuted and he knows it. And she ain't no use to him as an invalid, is she?'

'No, but Mum is happier this way.'

'Suppose it can't hurt,' Bing agreed as they went in.

Marie smiled at Nina, who was coming down the stairs. As usual, she wore a smart dark suit and high heels, but her face was hidden under a short grey veil that dropped from her pill-box hat. When she reached the bottom of the stairs, Wippet appeared on the half-landing above. 'Nina, don't go! Please listen to me.' He looked distraught, trying to hurry down the stairs on his short legs. In his haste, he tripped and fell, and Bing hurried to help him.

Nina turned and Marie gasped. Under the veil, Nina's face was bruised and battered. 'Oh, Nina, what's happened to you?'

'Nina!' Wippet struggled out of Bing's grasp. But by the time he got to the door, Nina had gone.

Wippet's body trembled. 'Oh, Nina, Nina, my love,' he whispered.

'Wippet, what happened? What's wrong?' Marie asked.

'Everything,' he groaned as he gazed up. 'Did you see what they did to her? They beat her up.'

'Who?' asked Bing in a bewildered voice.

'The man she called her uncle.'

'You mean he's not her uncle?' Marie asked.

'No. Nina wants people to believe he is. He met her when she was a cloakroom attendant and keeps her with his money. Whenever she tries to get away from him, he threatens to kill her.'

'So he's the one who did that?' Bing growled.

'Oh, no,' Wippet muttered bitterly. 'He's too much of a coward. He paid the Scoresbys to do his dirty work.'

Marie's mouth fell open. 'The Scoresbys? Are you sure?'

Wippet nodded. 'If only I could have protected her! But look at me. I'm useless.' Suddenly he put his hand on his chest and clutched the banister.

'Wippet, are you all right?' Bing asked as the little man tried to stand up.

'It's my heart,' Wippet gasped. 'I need my medicine. Will you help me back to my room?'

Just then, Elsie's door opened. 'What's going on?' Elsie blinked her eyes. 'I was just having forty winks. Oh my Gawd, what's wrong with Wippet?' She watched Bing lifting him up the stairs.

'He's got a bad heart,' Marie said sadly.

'I knew something was up,' Elsie breathed. 'I found him sitting on the stairs the other day, out of puff. What was all that commotion I heard?'

'It was Wippet chasing after Nina.'

'What's up with her?'

Marie quickly told Elsie what happened.

'I always thought there was more to the girl,' Elsie nodded, seeming unsurprised as Bing came down the stairs.

'Is he all right?' Marie and Elsie asked together.

'He ain't in the best of health,' Bing told them quietly.

'I guessed he was pining over Nina,' Elsie commiserated. 'That old sod who she called her uncle is just a dirty old man. And those Scoresbys – they are at the bottom of it all again.' She sighed. 'There ain't nothing that can be done about it either. While all these young girls fall into the trap of wanting the good life and thinking they can get it with sods like Teddy, then they'll go on doing what they do.' She looked at Marie. 'Sorry, love, don't mean to speak out of turn, but it's the truth.'

'If only there was something we could do,' Marie

nodded. But everyone knew that Teddy and the Scoresbys held a power in the East End that no one would challenge.

When Marie and Bing walked in to Ada's, Vesta was standing in the middle of the room. She was in her nightgown and barefoot, wearing her old resentful expression.

'Ah, now, here's your sister,' Ada said as she hung Vesta's dressing gown round her shoulders. 'I've been trying to persuade her to put on a dress from the wardrobe. But she don't like any of them.'

'I've got some nice things here.' Marie opened the bag. 'A couple of dresses that will be nice for the summer. And a little jacket for when you go out.'

'I don't know when that will be,' Vesta shrugged.

'It won't be long now.'

'The doctor says the infection is still there.'

'Yes,' said Ada, 'but he also said it's getting better.'

'Come into the bedroom and we can try some on,' Marie suggested, hoping it wouldn't be long before she could cheer Vesta up and get away.

Ada gave a big, bright smile. 'That's the ticket, girls. It's just like the old days, ain't it? The family's all together again. Now, Bing, Hector's just gone for a couple of ales, to have with our meal.'

'Mum, we don't want to put you to the trouble of cooking—' Marie began, intending to say this was just a short visit. But Ada waved her hand.

'It's no trouble, love. There's shepherd's pie in the oven and we've got sponge and custard for afters. Now run along, you two girls, and enjoy yourselves.'

Just then, Hector walked in, carrying a brown raffia shopping basket. The tops of four bottles stuck up and gave a little chink. 'Ah, everyone's here,' he grinned, giving Bing a slap on the shoulder and going to peck Marie on the cheek. 'This is wonderful, just like old times. All we need now is the grub, Ada.' He smiled, looking round him. 'I might even pour me and Bing a tipple now.'

Marie glanced quickly at Bing. He gave a quick roll of his eyes. Then as Hector took his arm and led him over to the dining table, Marie had a sinking feeling. Their plans for a romantic day looked set to be ruined.

In the bedroom, Marie put the bag on the bed and took out the two dresses and the jacket. She had also brought stockings, bra, slip and knickers, all of which were quite new.

Vesta sat down beside them. 'You weren't going to stay, were you?'

Marie blushed. 'Course we were.'

'You could never tell lies. Not like me.'

Marie looked into her sister's thin face. 'That's not a nice thing to say about yourself.'

Vesta pulled the dressing gown round her. 'I got very good at it when I left home.'

Marie sat on the bed beside her. It squeaked loudly. They turned to each other and smiled. 'The bed ain't changed, even if we have,' said Vesta, brushing her greasy hair from her eyes.

Marie laughed. 'Shall we put a record on?'

'I don't know.' Vesta glanced at the Victor phonograph, with its great brass horn and soft, velvety turntable. 'I've not played it since I came home. There are too many memories.'

'Let's share one together then.' Marie got up and lifted the top. She found the record she was looking for, and giving the handle a wind, she lifted the heavy arm. As the needle touched the record there were lots of jerks and bumps. The machine was very old now, but it still played. As she sat down on the bed again, a girl's voice began to sing 'In My Sweet Little Alice Blue Gown'.

After a while, the twins began to sing the words together. Words from their childhood. They still remembered them and when the music ended, Marie turned off the record.

She looked at Vesta, who wiped away a tear. 'That was meant to cheer us up.'

'I know. And it did.'

'A fine way of showing it.'

'It's just that I don't feel meself. And when I hear that, I think of who I was once. I won't ever be that person again.'

'No one is. We all grow up.'

'Yes, but you were sensible and grew up the right way. I even blamed you once for not following our dream. And look where it got me.' She put her hands on her stomach. There could be a baby in here and not an infection.'

Marie gave her a little shake. 'You have to stop this or you'll never get well.'

'Sometimes I don't want to. Sometimes I—'

'That's enough of that,' said Marie sternly. 'We've had all the dramatics. They don't work any more. Not even on me.' She stood upright.

Vesta stared up at her, looking astonished.

Marie couldn't keep a straight face. She burst into laughter. Suddenly they were laughing together. Marie felt so relieved. She had finally got through to Vesta.

'Now come on, try this dress and put on some make-up.'

'Yes, Mum.'

Marie helped her sister undress and put on the new underwear. She tried not to think about how thin and bent she looked. Instead, she kept talking about the shopping trips they were going to take when Vesta was well and, to her surprise, Vesta eagerly joined in.

'We never got to Lyons,' Bing sighed later that evening as he took off his jacket and threaded it over the back of the chair. They had just got back from Sphinx Street, where the meal had been shared by all, including Elsie, who had brought with her the usual bottle of port. 'I'll put the kettle on,' he told her, but Marie went to the fireside chair and sat down.

'Come and sit with me first.'

'Reckon it wasn't a bad day, after all.' He stretched out his long legs and grinned.

'Vesta looked pretty in that dress. And with a bit of make-up on, almost as good as new.'

'And your mum and dad and Elsie all perked up.'

Marie nodded. 'Do you think everything will be all right now?'

Bing looked into the empty grate. 'I think your sister's going to get well again, at least on the inside.' He glanced up at Marie. 'I don't know what's going on in her head, though.'

'She misses the things she got used to with Teddy.'

'Yes, but they came at a big cost.'

'She knows that now.'

'As for living back home again,' he continued, 'only time will tell. Your dad told me there have been a few ups and down between Vesta and your mum. That much ain't changed.'

'Mum is only trying to look after her.'

'Yes, and you'll do the same for our kids one day.'

Marie looked into his eyes. 'I hope so.'

'Any news on that front yet?' Bing asked, going a little red.

She knew he meant was she expecting. And she would have loved to have said yes, but she'd had her periods and was impatient herself. She shook her head.

He stood up and lifted her against him. 'Don't matter. Just gives me the excuse to try harder.' He laughed.

'I love you so much,' Marie whispered.

'I'd like that in writing, please.'

'Get the paper and pen then.'

She held his face between her hands. 'Do you really think we'll have kids?'

'Are you joking? We're going have a football team at least.'

'Vesta got pregnant quickly.'

'You've had a lot of things to worry about. That can't help.'

'I'm not worried any more.'

He kissed her passionately. 'No better time to give it another go than now.'

'You're a good kisser.'

'Is that why you wanted to marry me?'

'I don't know. But it didn't take me long to fall in love with you.'

'I told you, I'd always have kept trying.'

'If only Vesta can find someone like you.'

Bing's eyebrows rose. 'She could have had Charlie if she'd wanted.'

'Yes, but she never really liked him.'

'He gave up his girl for her. But it was Teddy she wanted.'

'I don't want to talk about any of that now.'

'Let's get cracking on that football team, then.' As their lips touched, she was glad they hadn't gone to Lyons. She wasn't going to feel guilty for having Bing as her husband. As he'd reminded her, Vesta had won Charlie's affections and it was Charlie who had suffered for it. Today Vesta had shown a glimmer of her old self, and Ada and Hector were happy once more. Now, all she had to think about was giving Bing his football team.

As they went to the bedroom and undressed, she knew she could never do what Vesta had done. Breaking people's hearts like Charlie and his girl's could only bring unhappiness. Next time Vesta fell in love it would have to be with the right man. And it would have to be for the right reasons. Not money and fame, but because she'd found someone who really loved her and would be her true friend and loyal lover all her life.

The banging noises woke Marie with a start. Bing's arm was still around her from their lovemaking as she sat up in bed. 'There's someone at the front door.'

'What time is it?' Bing threw off the bedclothes and switched on the light. He blinked at the mantel clock. 'A quarter to two!' he exclaimed, reaching for his trousers. 'Who the devil can that be?'

By the time Marie had slipped on her dressing gown, the banging had stopped. She hurried to the front door.

A small figure stood on the doorstep with Bing.

'Wippet!' Marie exclaimed as the small man tried to get his breath. 'What's wrong?'

'Teddy's turned up.' Wippet's eyes were big and round in their dark sockets. His small chest was rising sharply under his collarless shirt. 'I was woken by shouting, so I went downstairs. Elsie was very upset. She told me he tricked her into unlocking the door. Then he forced his way into your parents'.' Wippet put his hand on his chest, trying to catch his laboured breath. 'I couldn't do anything to help.'

'You did right to come here,' Bing said as he grabbed his jacket from the peg. 'Marie, get dressed. We'll take the car.'

She didn't see the dark streets and houses as Bing drove them towards Sphinx Street. From the happiness and hope they had all shared just a few hours ago, now they were all thrown back into fear.

Chapter 40

Bing nodded at the vehicle parked in the road. 'That's Teddy's motor,' he muttered, drawing the car to a halt. 'We're not too late.'

They all hurried into the hall; the door to Ada and Hector's rooms was ajar. Bing opened it. Teddy's back was to them. Marie saw Elsie and Hector sitting stiffly on the couch. They were wearing their dressing gowns and slippers. Neither of them moved. Fear shone from their eyes as they stared up at Teddy.

'What's going on?' Bing demanded and Teddy spun round. Marie saw his cruel mouth curl.

'I thought you might turn up,' he muttered. 'Always ready to poke your nose in where it's not wanted, Brown.'

'It's *you* that's not wanted,' Bing replied, glancing round. 'Where's Vesta?'

'I told her mother to help her pack.'

'No!' Marie stepped forward. 'She's ill. And doesn't want to go with you.'

Once again Teddy's lips drew back in a snarl. 'Ill? I don't think so. Her services have been paid for by a very wealthy client of the Scoresbys. Now she has to get back to work.'

'Both him and you can take a running jump,' Bing growled as he stepped forward. 'Get out or I'll call the police.'

This time Teddy laughed. 'The police? They would lock her away for what she's done.'

'It was you that made her do it,' Marie accused. 'She very nearly died.'

'She got in trouble.' Teddy shrugged, squaring his shoulders under his raincoat. 'It was nothing to do with me.'

'It was your baby she was having.'

'Prove it,' he challenged. 'It could have been anyone's.'

'The baby was yours,' said a small voice suddenly. Vesta and Ada came in from the bedroom. Their faces were white. 'I loved you, Teddy. But you betrayed me. I should have known at Christmas when I saw what you were really like. But I didn't want to accept the truth.'

'You silly cow. You were never anything to me. And you weren't exactly fighting off Dearlove when he took you to bed.'

Marie felt Vesta shudder beside her.

'Have you got your things?' Teddy snapped.

'Don't let him take her.' Ada rushed to Bing.

'She's leaving because if she don't go with him, he'll do Hector in,' Elsie explained. Her long, thin hair hung down over her black and gold robe and trembled as she spoke.

'I'd rather it be me,' Hector said, shuffling forward. 'I thought by working at the Duke's I'd be able to protect my family, but you made that impossible.'

Teddy tossed his head. 'What would I want with a stupid old man like you? You're lucky you're still around.' He turned to Vesta. 'Come here. We're leaving.'

'Stay where you are, Vesta.' Bing put up his hand. 'You're not going anywhere. It's him that's leaving.'

Marie saw Teddy's face darken. He went to Vesta and grabbed her. Bing caught him by his sleeve, ducking as Teddy threw a punch. He returned a blow of his own and blood spurted from Teddy's nose.

Teddy looked shocked as he put his fingers up to touch it. 'You'll be sorry for this,' he muttered, wincing in pain. 'By the time the Scoresbys get through with you, you'll wish you'd never been born.' He took hold of Vesta again. 'Now, for the last time, get out of my way.'

Marie wanted to pull her back, but Bing grabbed Teddy again. 'You don't scare me, you lowlife. You won't get the chance to ruin anyone's happiness again. I'm going to make sure of that.'

Teddy wiped the blood from his face. 'Stay away from me, Brown,' he muttered as he reached into his pocket. 'I came for my property and I'm taking it.' He drew out a gun. 'Try to stop me and you'll be the first to go.'

Marie held Vesta close. Would Teddy really shoot her husband? She was terrified.

'You've not got the balls, Teddy,' Bing challenged. 'And anyway, look around you, there are witnesses.'

'Witnesses?' Teddy laughed. 'They know better than to go against me and the Scoresbys. Hector will tell you what happens to people who get in the way, like old Sid and Irene and that tart Joanie.'

Bing stiffened his spine. 'You'll never get away with it.'

'Won't I? They'll fish you out of the river in a few weeks and no one will be any the wiser.'

'I'll see you hang first.' Bing lunged towards him.

Marie felt Vesta break away. Her scream echoed as she threw herself between Bing and Teddy. The gun went off with a loud retort and Marie saw her sink slowly to the ground. She lay there, limp and unmoving. Teddy stepped forward and stared down at her, his hand trembling as he clutched the gun. Slowly, as if unable to believe it was he who had pulled the trigger, he shook his head.

Ada's scream made him jerk. His eyes were suddenly wild as he looked around him.

Marie felt that what happened next was in slow motion. Everyone rushed to Vesta but it was Marie and Ada who were there first.

'Vesta? Vesta?' Ada sobbed as they cradled her in their arms. With tender fingers, she wiped away the blood from her face.

'Is she . . . is she . . .?' Hector groaned as he knelt beside them.

'Vesta, come back to us,' Marie breathed. She could see Vesta's eyelids flickering as though she were strug-gling to open them. 'Oh, Bing, what can we do?'

'I'll go for the doctor,' he said as he got up from his knees. But then Vesta's eyes opened. They were pale and unfocused.

'Dad, Mum?' Vesta tried to move her hand and Marie clasped it. Her fingers were very cold.

'You weren't to blame, any of you,' she whispered so softly that they all bent close again. 'It was only me. I'm sorry. I . . . didn't . . . listen.'

'Oh, love, you were just a baby, an innocent,' Ada said through her tears. 'It was that madman there—'

They all looked up, but Teddy had gone.

'I couldn't let him kill Bing.'

'Don't talk,' Marie whispered. 'Save your strength.'

'I love you all. Don't forget me.'

Ada let out a cry of pain. Marie's eyes filled with hot tears. She heard Bing's heavy footsteps as he ran from the room. But it was Vesta's last words that rang in her ears.

Wippet stood, once again powerless to help his friends. There was blood on Ada's hands. He heard the sobs and saw the tears of disbelief. He saw them all as he would always see them, no matter how long he lived – if he *was* to live – with grief carved in their features. Like his darling Nina, Vesta had had her life ruined by Teddy and the monsters he worked for. Wippet turned away from the scene and climbed the stairs.

His body felt weak and tired. He knew his span of years was almost over. The pain in his chest grew tighter. It clenched him in a vice so tight that it was all he could do to walk up three flights of stairs. In his small room he took the phial from the drawer and swallowed the laudanum. Seconds passed and, as the drug took its effect, slowly the agony eased. His heart had answered his dearest wish and it would not stop beating this moment. Wiping his sweating brow, he glanced at the window.

Still dark. Enough time to act before dawn.

Just as he'd always planned.

A soft chattering came from Kaiser's cage. Wippet gently took the little monkey in his arms and dressed him in a green felt waistcoat. Then, kissing his small head, he inhaled the monkey's familiar smell. The fairground returned: the sawdust, the heat and applause. They had played to many audiences in their time. People who waited with bated breath to see a man wrestle himself free from his chains, whilst trapped in a tank full of water. Or watch a little brown monkey with a white chin and owl-like eyes climb to the top of the tent and smoke a cigarette.

'Justice, my friend,' Wippet whispered as he stroked the warm, furry skull. 'Justice shall be had tonight. After all, what is there to live for without love, little treasure?'

Kaiser accepted the box of matches and pushed it into the pocket of his green waistcoat.

'Well done,' encouraged Wippet. 'You haven't forgotten. Now, take these, your special treats.'

Excitedly Kaiser turned the packet of Woodbines in his spindly fingers. 'Here, you may have one for the road, my trickster. And as many as you like when we reach our destination.'

Wippet waited as Kaiser performed his trick. When the cigarette was lit and the smell of tobacco enveloped them, Wippet gathered the tools of his former trade. Sliding the lock pick onto the bunch of keys on his leather belt, and a sheet of folded newspaper into his waistband, he nodded with satisfaction.

On the half-landing, he gazed at Nina's door. He smiled, recalling the day he had first seen her at the fairground. He had bobbed up to the surface of his tank, having successfully unlocked his chains. Gasping breath into his thirsty lungs, he had found love. True love. There had stood true beauty, applauding his feat of bravery. He had never stopped loving her since.

Wippet slid his stumpy fingers affectionately down the length of Kaiser's back. 'Our finest hour!' he whispered. 'Our most heroic adventure yet!'

Making no noise, he crept down the stairs and closed the front door behind them.

Chapter 41

Vesta lay asleep on the bed with Ada watching over her as Marie closed the bedroom door. She followed the doctor back to the front room.

'Well?' Hector asked as Dr Tapper appeared. 'Is she going to be all right?'

Dr Tapper nodded. 'The bullet grazed her skull, but will leave no permanent damage. I've given her something to make her rest and in the morning I'll call again.'

'Thank God,' Elsie sighed in a voice rough with tears, her face lined and aged under her long, wispy hair. 'What she's been through, God only knows.'

'This time it must be reported,' Dr Tapper answered. 'A few inches to the left, and the bullet would have killed her.'

'He wasn't aiming at her,' Bing pointed out. 'Vesta threw herself in front of the gun to protect me.'

'She done a very brave thing,' Elsie nodded.

'But we've got no proof.' Bing looked at the doctor. 'It's his word against ours. He could come up with any old nonsense. That it was Vesta who had the gun and he snatched it off her.' He shook his head slowly. 'Or deny he was here at all and get the Scoresbys to vouch for him.'

Elsie sat down on the chair with a sigh. 'So where does that leave us? It will all come out about Vesta and what she did, which was why we didn't call 'em before.'

'We can't put her through more pain,' Hector insisted wearily, pushing back his untidy dark hair.

'But someone's got to stop them,' cried Marie. 'Teddy could have killed Bing. And it was only by chance the bullet missed Vesta.'

'Already we've waited too long,' Dr Tapper protested. 'You saw it and are witnesses. He will be caught and tried.'

'No, he won't,' Hector said flatly. 'I worked at the club long enough to hear and see things that made me realize there is no justice in the evil world of those men. Teddy's as much a part of that evil as the Scoresbys. They are a law unto themselves.'

The doctor was silent.

'Hector's right,' Bing said with a sharp nod. 'They're a rotten package and the cause of what's happened to Vesta. We could get the law in on it, but it wouldn't do us any good.'

'If they started asking questions,' Marie agreed, 'we couldn't hide the truth. It would come out about the baby.'

'There must be another way to go about this,' Bing said angrily. 'I know some blokes in the docks—'

'Young man, if you're suggesting what I think you are,' Dr Tapper interrupted, 'you would be very unwise to take matters into your own hands.'

'No, Bing.' Marie went to him. 'Dr Tapper's right. You mustn't do that.'

'They've got to be stopped.'

'But you can't do it. I don't want you in trouble or put in prison.'

He put his arm around her. 'That wouldn't happen.'

'One thing's for sure,' Elsie said calmly, 'we've got to think about this carefully. Not do something we'll regret. It's bad enough as it is. But Vesta ain't dead. And nor is Bing. We've got to work out what's best for the family.'

Dr Tapper slid on his hat. 'You know my views on this. But I'm prepared to wait until tomorrow when I'll call to see Vesta. Meanwhile, I hope you will all decide to do the sensible thing.'

'That's the rub,' muttered Bing after he'd left. 'There ain't no sensible thing where Teddy and the Scoresbys are concerned.'

'The old boy has to say that, as a doctor could get in trouble for not reporting a crime,' Elsie muttered. 'You could have brought him back here to find a corpse.'

'Vesta took a bullet meant for me,' Bing agreed angrily. 'I should've sorted Teddy out long ago and would have if I'd known this was going to happen.'

'Let's all calm down,' Elsie said reasonably. 'We're angry and tired. Not to mention having been scared out of our wits in the middle of the night. I reckon we should try to get an hour or two's kip and then think what to do in the morning.'

'What if Teddy comes back?' Marie asked.

'He won't. He thought he'd killed her, didn't he? Then he ran off like the coward he is to get his story right with the Scoresbys.'

'As I said, let's all sleep on it,' Elsie advised again. 'You two can kip in my spare bedroom if you don't want to go home.'

Marie looked at Bing and he nodded. 'Thanks, Elsie.'

Just then Ada came into the front room. 'She's sleeping, but she's got a nasty wound on her head. An inch or two over and she wouldn't be here now.'

'Will it heal up?'

'Yes, given time.'

'Are you all right, Mum?'

'I can't believe it happened.' Ada shuddered. She looked very small and thin in her dressing gown.

'Come and sit beside me, love.' Hector patted the seat. She sank down, her shoulders slumped.

'Where did we go wrong, Hector?' Ada whispered. 'Have we let our girl down?'

'Not you, my dear.' He took her hand. 'I should have got a proper job years ago, after—' He stopped as Ada stiffened. Then, looking at Marie, he said, 'I'm to blame for all this.'

'No, Hector, be quiet,' Ada said sharply.

'It's time for them to know.'

'To know what, Dad?' Marie sat in the chair. She hoped that at last this secret that her parents had kept was going to be revealed.

'Your mother was having a baby when we first came to the island and lost it because of me.' He cleared his throat. 'A man I owed money to came to the pub where we were staying with Elsie. I wasn't there to face him and he demanded the money from your mother.'

As Hector spoke, Marie saw the images of her dreams. The visions in her nightmare; a woman protecting her unborn child and the big man towering above her. 'So it was Mum in my dream all along?' she faltered. 'It really happened?'

After a few moments, Ada nodded. 'You girls were with Elsie that night, in the room across the landing. The pub below was busy and no one saw him come up the stairs.'

'The brute!' Elsie grimaced. 'A loan shark who had allowed your dad to borrow money, then added his interest, making the debt impossible to pay back.'

'But why did we need money?' Marie asked, bewildered.

'I was living beyond my means and gambling,' Hector admitted. 'I thought I could pay the debt back on luck alone. What a fool I was!'

'You were a fool indeed, love,' nodded Elsie. 'But many wiser men have gone the same way and lived to learn a hard lesson.' She looked kindly at Marie. 'By the time I heard your mother's cries, it was too late. The animal had roughed her up, thinking she had money that might be hidden. She lost the baby that night in great distress. You must have followed me in and seen something before I managed to get you out of the room again.'

'So you see, I understand the pain Vesta must be suffering,' Ada murmured. 'But I couldn't tell her.'

'Why, Mum?' Marie asked. 'It might have helped.'

'Your mother didn't want you girls to think badly of me,' Hector said in a heavy voice. 'I didn't deserve her loyalty. Or her love.'

Everyone was silent, until Ada spoke again. 'I thought I could protect you girls from the badness in this world, although to you it must have seemed like nagging. I didn't want to spoil all your hopes for the stage and at first I didn't worry, as I thought they were just childish fancies. But when you got older I realized how talented and lovely you both were and that the dream could become real. I was torn. What was I to do? In my heart I believe everyone should be able to dream. Just like your dad, who is a good man and always thought the best of people.'

'For my own selfish reasons,' Hector admitted as he looked guiltily at Ada. 'I didn't want an ordinary job. No, that was beneath me! I was a performer. I wanted fame and fortune. And even after we lost our little boy, I couldn't stop myself from encouraging you girls to want the same.'

Marie went to kneel beside her mother. 'You should have told us.' She looked at Hector's crumpled face. 'We wouldn't have blamed you, Dad. Vesta and me would have done what we did anyway.'

Ada stroked her hand over Marie's head. 'Your father and I have had to learn that lesson the hard way.'

Once again the room was silent. Elsie sighed and, going to kiss Ada on the cheek, she whispered, 'Well, I'm too knackered to talk any more so I'm off to bed. I'll turn back the covers in me spare room for you two.' She went to the door. 'Just remember, we've got our girl back. No matter what's happened in the past, or today, we're all still together and in with a fighting chance to put everything straight. If we stick together, somehow we'll get through this.'

Ada managed a weak smile after she'd gone. 'Dr Tapper said Vesta only has a surface wound. I can change the dressing in the morning when she wakes up.' She looked at all their faces. 'But what are we going to do tomorrow?'

Marie hugged her. 'We'll think about that in the morning.'

'Let's get some sleep now, Ada.' Hector helped her to her feet.

As she and Bing left, Marie saw a pale light glowing through the glass of the front door. It wouldn't be many hours before morning. She watched Bing check the lock on the front door. She knew they wouldn't have much sleep. Teddy and the evil he had done was still haunting them.

Chapter 42

'We're safely in, Kaiser,' Wippet whispered delightedly as he returned the lock pick to its pouch. This clever tool, once used for his underwater escapes, had served him loyally again. But it was not water that surrounded him tonight, Wippet reflected with irony. It was the alcohol-laden air of the Blue Flamingo!

Sensing success, the monkey sprang lightly to the floor and curled his thin lips back in a smile. He chattered loudly and Wippet lifted a warning finger. 'Quiet, little acrobat, be patient. The fools have made our task easy. But we must still be careful.' With gentle hands, he returned the monkey back to his shoulder.

Taking care to step lightly across the thick carpet, Wippet glanced cautiously around. He thought the foyer of the club looked more like a bordello in coarse colours of bright red and blue. Pictures of cheap-looking women, their printed names unknown to him, hung from the walls. A staircase leading to the club's interior and edged by golden rope wound downwards.

'Tempting, but too dangerous to follow,' Wippet considered aloud. 'If we were to be seen, we couldn't outrun them.'

Kaiser made noises of agreement and Wippet turned to his left. He entered a door marked 'Management'. A long, gloomy passage stretched before him. In the cool darkness he smelled the scents of women, of powders and paints and performance. Even the damp and mould took on a mysterious appeal.

A short way on, and he stood still again. From deep in the club came the sound of voices. When he reached the end of the passage, he climbed another set of steps that led to the rear of the stage. The voices were louder here, challenging and aggressive. But there was one, all too familiar. The voice of a coward, begging for mercy. So, Teddy had returned to his masters – like a dog with his tail between his legs!

Warm satisfaction glowed inside Wippet as he considered his unsuspecting quarry. They could quarrel all they liked amongst themselves. Little did they know this would be the last time!

Wippet was about to reach for Kaiser when pain gripped him. Sweat beaded his brow and ran down his back. He waited for release, but instead the iron fingers tightened. He wiped his face with his sleeve and took the morphine from his pouch. How cruel it would be if he was to die here, in this dark passage, his task unaccomplished.

Through the agony, he clung to the drapes close by. He looked upward, through the suspended brackets to the stage backcloths. Each was rolled as tightly as a parcel. Above these, crisscrossing the roof like tram lines, were timber dry beams. Wood that for years had weathered the changes of time and design, defied builders and crafts-men, and survived to support the superstructure of a vast, commercial building.

'Climb high, my friend, as high as you can,' Wippet gasped. 'Find the warm spaces, light your matches and perform your tricks.' With an effort, he took the monkey in his arms and kissed his smooth, furry head. He gazed into the monkey's alert eyes. 'We have travelled a long and colourful road together. What more could we ask, than this? Our final adventure.'

In reply, Kaiser slipped his bony fingers to Wippet's trembling lips, tracing their outline as a lover might, in thrall to his mate. His enquiring touch was the last they would share and Wippet set his friend free for the final time.

The monkey sprang to the drapes and then to the backcloths. He chattered loudly in delight and excite-ment, swinging athletically into the beams above. A flash of green felt waistcoat and a long, spindly tail . . .

Wippet wiped his moist eyes. When he looked again, the animal had vanished.

A peace came over him. It was done. The voices became louder; Teddy's filled with fear, the others unfor-giving. What use had the Scoresbys for him now? Wippet thought bitterly. He had aimed a gun and pulled the trig-ger, but not on his masters' command.

'It's almost done,' Wippet groaned as he groped for the wall and fell against it. He stood, waiting, expecting the last violent stab of pain and preparing himself for the onslaught.

Digging his shaking fingers into the pouch, he brought out the second box of matches. Striking one, he threw it against the drapes. Then another and another. Soon all around him was shivering light. The tongues moved silently, greedily licking, absorbing the fabrics and the brittle, dry wood in every crook and cranny.

Chapter 43

Morning came with Sunday bells, but other sounds too. Marie jumped out of bed. They were in Elsie's spare bedroom. Everything came back; Wippet's knock at their door in the middle of the night and their hurried drive to Sphinx Street. Teddy trying to take Vesta and reaching in his pocket for the gun. Vesta stepping into the path of the bullet as he pulled the trigger . . .

'What's all the commotion?' Bing asked sleepily as he threw back the covers.

'I don't know, but the noise woke me up.' Hurriedly Marie put on her clothes and shoes.

'Is it coming from your mum's? It can't be Teddy again!' He grabbed his trousers from the chair. 'Or can it?'

When they were dressed, they rushed out and almost collided with Elsie.

'What's going on?' Bing demanded. 'It sounds like all hell's been let loose.'

'Don't know. I was still in the land of Nod five minutes ago,' Elsie muttered, tying the belt of her robe around her waist. The black silk and gold pattern caught the morning sun as she pulled the curtains and let in the light. 'Something's going on but I can't see what.'

'You stay there,' Bing ordered. 'I'll go and find out.'

But both Marie and Elsie spoke at the same time: 'We're coming with you!'

They hurried into the hall and across to Ada's. To everyone's surprise Ada stood alone in the front room. Dressed in her skirt and blouse, she was looking out of the window with a puzzled expression on her face.

'Are you all right, Mum?' Marie asked, rushing over to join her. 'We thought Teddy had come back.'

'No, thank God. That's the second fire engine this morning gone past at a rate of knots. Someone's place must be on fire.'

'Where's Dad?'

'He's gone to see what all the fuss is about.'

'Is Vesta all right?' Marie asked, and Ada nodded, a smile on her face.

'I've just taken her a cup of tea. She's got a very sore head and when we talked about last night, neither of us could believe it happened.'

'Neither can I. It was like a bad dream.'

Another fire engine's bell clanged in the distance. 'They're going up Manchester Road way, away from the docks,' Bing pointed out, 'towards Poplar.'

Marie left the little group and made her way to the bedroom. She crept in, wondering what she would find. Vesta sat, propped by the pillows, a bandage round her head. With tears in her eyes, Vesta opened her arms. They hugged and held each other tightly, too over-whelmed to speak.

'Oh, Marie, I'm still alive,' Vesta mumbled, not letting Marie go as she wiped away a stray tear.

'You might not have been if that bullet had gone over a bit.'

'Where did it go?'

'That's a funny question. No one thought to look for it. Into the wood or wall, I expect. One day we'll find it and think how lucky we are it went there and missed you.'

Vesta nodded, smiling through her tears. 'Mum said Teddy ran off and the doctor wanted to get in the police. I'm glad you didn't. I would have had all those questions to answer. They'd have found out about the baby. And you might have been in trouble too.'

'Yes, but Teddy will get away free.'

Vesta's face clouded. 'He was going to shoot Bing. But he shot me instead. I saw the look of surprise on his face. Perhaps he still thought something of me.'

'If he did, he wouldn't have run away.'

'What are we going to do now?' Vesta whispered. 'What if he comes looking for me again? I can't stay here. I'll have to go away. I'll just be trouble for everyone.'

'Did you tell Mum that?'

'No.' The noise drifted down the passage. 'What's going on?'

'There's a fire somewhere. We heard the fire engine bells and came rushing in from Elsie's. We all thought it was Teddy back again.'

Tears filled Vesta's eyes. 'You see, you'll never be free from him if I stay here. He told me I was bought and paid for; that I was his property and would soon be Bill's.' She put her hands over her face. 'I can't bear the thought of it.'

'Come along, don't upset yourself,' Marie whispered. 'You escaped death last night and are alive to tell the tale. We'll think of something today, I promise.'

Vesta hugged her again. 'Help me outside.'

'Are you sure you want to get up?'

'I ain't staying in bed. And I'm not keeping this thing on my head. It don't look very nice.'

Marie smiled. 'At least you're thinking about your looks again.' She helped her on with her dressing gown.

'I wonder what the noise is all about.'

When they got to the front room, everyone crowded round Vesta. Marie knew that they were all still in a state of shock. No one could believe what had happened last night.

Just then, the door flew open and Hector stood there. He had dressed hurriedly and the tail of his shirt was hanging out. Like Bing, he had a slight beard, and his moustache, usually so neat, was hanging down either side of his mouth. 'I can't believe it,' he blustered. 'I can't bring myself to hope . . .'

'What?' everyone cried at once.

'There's been a fire,' he spluttered.

'We know that,' said Elsie impatiently. 'Where?'

'It was so big, they had to use the emergency engines from the island they usually use for the docks.'

Everyone stared at him.

'Well, where the heck was it?' Elsie demanded again.

Hector looked at Vesta and Marie, his eyes wide. 'It's the Blue Flamingo and the Duke's. They burned to the ground in the early hours of this morning.'

It was later in the morning when the news was confirmed that the two clubs, the Blue Flamingo and the Duke's, and a number of warehouses had all gone up in flames. Marie and Vesta watched from the window as Hector went out to the street again to join the group of neighbours who were discussing the fire. Carts and horses stopped by and the drivers leaned down to give the latest news. But it was Bing who drove to Poplar at midday and returned in the afternoon with news that shocked everyone.

'It's true,' Bing told them as they gathered in the front room. 'There's just a big black skeleton of a building, bits of charred wood soaked in water and piles of ash where the clubs used to be. The bobbies are keeping people away so they don't traipse over the evidence.'

'What evidence?' Marie asked.

'Of what caused it and how the bodies inside met their end there.'

Vesta gave a little gasp. 'You mean someone's dead in there?'

Bing nodded. 'Maybe five or six, they reckon. And the rumour was, that one of them was small, very small, hardly bigger than a kid. And there was something else. A skull. And it wasn't no human skull, either.'

'An animal?' Ada breathed.

'Looks like it.'

'A cat or a dog?' Elsie asked, but it was Marie who said what they were thinking.

'Or a monkey.'

They all went quiet.

'Doors were all locked, but there weren't no keys in 'em,' Bing said after a while. 'Someone had it in for the Scoresbys and trapped them in there like rats. Has anyone been upstairs to Wippet's or Nina's?'

Elsie shook her head. 'Nina never came back after that day she left. But I'll go and see if Wippet's there.'

A few minutes later, Elsie returned. 'He ain't.' She caught her breath. 'Nor is Kaiser.'

'And Kaiser never goes out,' Vesta murmured. 'He just stays in his cage.'

'Well, he ain't there now,' Elsie sighed.

'Wasn't he with us last night when we came in?' Bing frowned.

Marie nodded. 'Everything happened so fast after that I don't remember seeing him again.'

'He must've been watching,' said Elsie. 'He must've seen it all and . . .' Her voice trailed away.

'It was Saturday,' Vesta whispered, sinking down to the couch. She held the bandage on her head. 'The brothers would have been there late into the night. Teddy would have gone there . . . he would have . . .'

Hector sat beside her. 'We don't know yet who perished.'

Marie looked at Bing. His face told her all she needed to know. The remains that were left must have been Teddy and the Scoresbys.

Vesta looked up with bleak eyes. 'I hated him, but I didn't wish him dead.'

'Afraid I can't agree,' said Elsie fiercely. 'If it is him that's gone, there ain't gonna be many who'll mourn him.'

Marie felt as Elsie did. She remembered all too clearly the day that Vesta had almost died. In that attic room, the so-called nurse whom Teddy had told Vesta to go to had almost ended Vesta's life. Teddy hadn't cared then. Instead he had just used Vesta, as he'd used other young women and sold them to others. She had no sympathy for him. Unlike her twin, she felt that, if it was he who had met such an end in the flames of the Blue Flamingo, then justice had been done.

Bing slid his arm around Marie. She knew that he, too, felt the same.

'*If* it was Wippet and Kaiser who set the place alight,' Elsie continued, 'they done a good job, in my opinion. If I'd known that one day Kaiser would use them fags he dropped all over the place to rid us of that bit of evil we was talking about, I would have bought him a packet or two meself.'

It was said lightly, but, as Marie looked at her mother and father, her twin sister and Bing, she saw the deep sadness in their eyes. They had all loved Wippet and Kaiser. The pair had not deserved to die, and yet perhaps it was the death Wippet had chosen. He and Kaiser were inseparable. For either one of them to be left alone would have been an agony. Wippet's heart had already been broken by what had happened to Nina. If he had tried to avenge her, then he'd succeeded.

Marie thought of him now and, beyond her sadness, she felt that he might be smiling his smile with his beloved friend chattering beside him. No one would mourn the Scoresbys or Teddy if they had perished. There would be other families who, like the Haskinses, would be set free.

And could live their lives in peace again.

Epilogue

Christmas Day 1937

'Say plum pud, lads!' Bing shouted, as Marie fought to keep both her sons safe in her arms. John was the most mischievous, at twenty-two months old, but his twin brother, Herbert, had his moments, and was now struggling to be free as Bing steadied his new camera.

'Smile for Daddy, boys, or we'll have to do it all over again.' Marie began to laugh as Herbert pursed his fat lips and blew bubbles in answer. It wasn't long before John was doing the same, until Bing grasped the moment and took the picture with a satisfied whoop of delight.

Marie lowered her sons to the floor, reflecting that they were outgrowing their summer sandals, now used as slippers. She had bought serviceable shoes for the winter but with the rate they were growing, they would soon be out of their sailor suits, bought in October. Not that her twins were impressed with their new white-and-blue outfits! When in his father's care this morning, as Marie had put on her new dress and coat and tried to arrange her hair whilst listening to the laughter erupting from the front room, John had managed to investigate the coal scuttle and the result had been a great source of amusement, especially to Bing, who applauded almost every action his sons made.

'Hurry up now,' Marie reminded her husband as she captured Herbert. 'It's already two o'clock, and if we're not quick, Mum will have served up the chicken before we get there.' She wrestled Herbert's coat on and sat him in the big perambulator kept in the passage. It was equipped with twin hoods and two pairs of reins that kept the misbehaving twins in check. It had been a gift from Elsie on their birth in February of 1936. Now, of course, it was nearing the end of its use. After she'd fastened Herbert in his seated position, it was left to Bing to secure the reins around John.

Marie watched her husband with pride. She was a full-time mother and wife now, her days at Ellisdon's long gone. Bing was a doting father and his sons were his pride and joy.

'Right, Mrs Brown, let's be off before these terrors escape,' Bing said, interrupting her thoughts. Slipping his new camera on the tray beneath the pram, he grinned. 'There's a party round at your gran and granddad's. Your Aunty Vesta is bringing her young man to meet us today, so behave yourselves, right?'

Marie smiled, too, at the cheeky grins the twins gave their father. Herbert had taken Hector's middle name, and John, Bing's dad's. Neither of the boys could sit still for long. They had inherited her blue eyes, but with their burnished golden locks that stood wilfully on end they were a mirror image of their father.

'Have we brought a change of clothes for these rascals?' Bing asked as he pushed the pram through the front door and out into the frosty winter's day.

Marie followed, nodding to the big space in the bottom of the pram. 'And our presents and a bottle of port too.'

'Everything but the kitchen sink,' grinned Bing as she fell into stride beside him. He bounced the pram several times, making the twins laugh. 'Look at 'em,' he said, 'you'd think butter wouldn't melt in their mouths.'

'It's hard to believe this is only their second Christmas,' Marie sighed. 'And it's two and a half years since the fire.'

'A lot's changed in that time.'

'Elsie was right. No one cared about Teddy or the Scoresbys. They died in debt for all their high living. The papers said that all the bodies found were buried in paupers' graves. Including the barman.'

'All except Wippet,' Bing reminded her.

'It was only right that everyone put together to give him and Kaiser a good send-off. It's nice to think he has a proper headstone over at Blackheath where he'd worked in the fair.'

'They reckon it was his fairground tricks that got him inside the Blue Flamingo and locked it tight as a drum,' Bing said reflectively. 'I know we've all talked this over before, but I think he'd been planning it.'

'But did he have to die too?'

'It was what Wippet would have wanted. He'd lost Nina and she was his life. When he saw that Teddy had shot Vesta, he must have decided he'd do the deed then.'

John turned round and blew a large raspberry. Herbert did the same. Bing and Marie burst into laughter. 'I hope you don't do that to Vesta's young man, Eric,' Marie teased. 'Grandma is hoping you'll be on your best behaviour.'

'They ain't got none, that's the trouble,' Bing chuckled. Then pausing he added, 'Do you think Vesta is really sweet on this Eric?'

Marie smiled. 'She talks about him all the time.'

'What does she say?'

'This and that.'

Bing rolled his eyes. 'Do you think they'll get hitched?'

'We'll have to give him the seal of approval first.' Marie looked up at her husband. 'But one thing I can tell you, she says he's not a charmer like Teddy.'

'That's all right then. And if he's a porter, he's got a good job. Sounds like a regular bloke.'

'Vesta says he is.'

'Do you think she learned her lesson?'

'She says so.'

'Does Eric know the full story?' Bing frowned.

'He knows she can't have a family. But he don't seem to mind about it. And he's very supportive of her dress-making business.'

'Well, I suppose that's a start.'

Herbert took hold of his brother's cap and pulled it down over his face. A big scream erupted and John tried to do the same.

'Now, now, you perishers, sit still.' Bing stopped the pram and took hold of his sons, seating them properly once again. They both sat quietly.

'You make a very good father,' Marie whispered as Bing returned beside her.

'And you make a very good wife.'

Suddenly there were screams again. They all looked up into the sky. Little specks of white were falling down and bouncing on the roofs.

'Bing, it's snowing!'

'You're right, it is.'

'Do you think it will settle? I hope so. The boys haven't seen it before. Just look at them.'

John and Herbert were gazing up, suddenly silent as little flakes settled on their faces.

Bing slid his arm around Marie's waist as they stopped in the silent street. It was Christmas Day, Marie thought, and her life was full of happiness.

Before she could speak Bing kissed her with warm and passionate lips. In that moment she knew that, whatever the future held in store, the Brown family of Manchester Road, East London, would make their very own mark on the world. The fire that had claimed Wippet's life had meant they could all start afresh and each had been given a second chance. Her mum and dad had their grandsons to cherish, and perhaps a new son-in-law next year. Vesta had turned her love of clothes into a new skill, and with it, found a man to love her. Marie herself and Bing had been blessed with a family and, despite their sons being rascals, they worshipped them.

Bing held her close, but the twins soon ended their moment. Crying out at the snow, they bounced up and down in the pram.

'Talk about getting your money's worth!' Bing laughed. 'I mean, if we can do that, we can do anything!' He cupped her chin in his fingers. 'What counts is, that we've got each other. To quote the old songs, it's love that makes this world go round. And we've got buckets full of the stuff.'

She was tempted to tell him that in six months' time those buckets could be overflowing. She had marked the days off the calendar carefully. It would be in June of next year that the new addition to their family would arrive.

But as Bing began to reorder his sons again, she smiled. She would save that special news till later. When they were at home this evening, locked in one another's arms, with the long night stretching before them.